Revolving Doors

Helen Macpherson

Yellow Rose Books
by Regal Crest

ISBN 978-1-61929-440-0

First Printing 2020

9 8 7 6 5 4 3 2 1

Original cover design by AcornGraphics

Published by:

Regal Crest Enterprises

Find us on the World Wide Web at
http://www.regalcrest.biz

Published in the United States of America

Acknowledgments

Yes, this story has been a long time coming. But sometimes life takes hostage of creativity for a little while, and there's not much you can do about it. A story is often a kernel of an idea. What makes it come to fruition are the coordinated efforts of author, publisher, editors, family, and friends. I'd like to thank Cathy for giving me yet another publishing opportunity, especially after such a long hiatus. Patty, it's been a ball having you as one of my editors. Our discussions have been informative and at the same time full of humour. Staci, many thanks for your incredible editing eye for detail. Sometimes authors can be so close to a story you can identify each whorl in the bark, but not the wood for the trees. To my readers Carol and Sandy, many thanks for your input and focus on what I sometimes missed. Finally, I'd like to thank my wife, Kate. During the times when I wanted to write but the words wouldn't come, she was always there for me. Her patience and love know no bounds.

Dedication

For Roger and Tilly — gone from our lives
but never, ever forgotten.

Chapter One

Present Day

RHIANNON SHARP REVERSED her sports car into a vacant spot within walking distance of the buildings that were to be her destination for the evening. She was surprised at the fortune of finding a park so close to the auditorium in what was such a built-up area of inner Sydney suburbia. She closed her eyes and centred herself, as the fading sounds of a somewhat prophetic if not haunting song by Sarah McLachlan filled the now quiet car. Its lyrics on remembrance perfectly captured the regret people often feel, not for what they achieved but rather for the opportunities they let slip from their grasp during their lifetime.

Nodding sagely, she pulled the keys from the ignition and stepped into the starlit night. She could barely make out the muted sounds of voices and laughter coming from the building in the distance. She braced herself. Was this what she wanted? Did she really want to be here? You could drive away now, and no one would be any the wiser. She could very easily do that. Stopping her was the knowledge to do so would potentially mean another twenty years of asking herself the same question. No. Tonight, one way or another, she would get an answer.

She bent down and reached across the passenger side of the car and pulled out a calf length black jacket which matched her slacks and complemented her burnished gold blouse. The glow of the streetlights against the tinted glass of the car's windows enabled her to check her reflection. She caught herself. Mirrored in the glass was an imposing three-story sandstone building. Memories long since relegated to the recesses of her mind came flooding back.

Bowral, Twenty-Three Years Ago

RHIANNON STARED VACANTLY around the dark, wood panelled room, her mind elsewhere. The measured voice of Mr. Swain, her family's lawyer, outlined the beneficiaries of her parents' estate. She cared little that the majority of their assets would remain in a trust for her until she reached twenty-one. How had things changed so quickly? She would give anything to have her mother and father beside her, just one more time.

Her parents were celebrating their twenty-fifth wedding anniversary in New Zealand when their car was sideswiped by a drunk driver on a scenic cliff drive. The impact was enough to push the car off the road, down a precipice and into the lake below. Neither survived the plunge into the icy waters of the glacial lake.

Rhiannon had been staying in Sydney with her mother's sister, Aunt Isabella Howard, when she received news of their death. She could still remember the sight of her aunt slumping against the hallway wall at the softly spoken words of the police officer standing in front of her. In an instant the tranquil southern highlands of New South Wales, her home for the past fifteen years, became a distant memory.

Her aunt's hand softly touched her knee. "Rhiannon, I can only imagine how difficult this is for you. Would you rather wait outside?"

"I need to be here." Rhiannon stared emotionlessly at Mr. Swain. "I want to be here."

Mr. Swain shuffled the papers in front of him and cleared his throat. "Ms. Howard, I understand you're aware of your sister and her husband's request for you to be named guardian for Rhiannon?"

"I am, and am more than willing to have her live with me in Sydney."

Rhiannon's head whipped around to Isabella. "But I don't want to live in Sydney. I want to live here. Why can't I still live at home?"

Mr. Swain rose. "How about I give you the room and you can discuss this with Miss Sharp." His hand turned the wooden handle. "Just let my secretary know when you wish to continue." He quietly closed the door behind him.

Isabella took Rhiannon's hands in her own. "You don't know how very sorry I am for the pain you're going through. Trust me when I say I very much understand you'd prefer to stay in Glenquarry. But at your age I can't let you live in a house by yourself. The state would never allow it."

Rhiannon lowered her head. No longer a child and not yet an adult, she fought to hide the tears brimming in her eyes. "Everyone I know is here." She took the handkerchief offered by Isabella and blew her nose. "My school is here."

"I understand. However, my surgical practice is on the north

side of Sydney. It's better I'm close to the hospitals I operate in."
She brushed the hair from Rhiannon's face. "I know you like your
current school. But there's a great all-girls school not far from me.
Given I'm on their board I'm sure they'll be able to offer you a
placement."

Rhiannon's eyes widened. "I don't want to go to a girl's
school. I've got nothing in common with girls."

"I think that's a little extreme Rhiannon. I understand you're
an introspective student. But you must have some girl friends in
your current school?"

"Some." She sniffled. "But I spend much more time with the
boys. They love to run around at lunch and play sport. The girls
only want to sit around and discuss boys. Being with them is
much better than sitting around with a group of stupid girls who
spend their lunch breaks gawking at boys and sharing gossip.
Please Aunt Isabella," she sobbed, "let me stay here."

Isabella pulled her into her arms. "Oh sweetie, please believe
me when I say I wish I could do that. I'd give anything to have
things back the way they were. But sadly, they're never going to
be the same."

Cowan Grammar Year Ten

AUNT ISABELLA USHERED Rhiannon into the lobby of the
administration building of Cowan Grammar and across to the
information desk.

"Can I help you?" asked the woman behind the counter.

"Good morning. I'm Ms. Howard and this is my niece, Rhiannon Sharp. We have an interview with the principal, Mrs. Remerson."

The woman consulted a page in front of her. "If you'll give
me a moment." She picked up a phone and punched in a number.
She smiled at Rhiannon and Isabella as she waited for the phone
to be answered.

"Good morning Mrs. Remerson. I have Ms. Howard and her
niece here to see you." She paused. "I'll let them know."

She put the phone's handset back into its cradle. "She'll be
with you in a minute."

Rhiannon's eyes scanned the entrance. Adorning the walls
were boards listing school captains and vice captains of yester-
year. Another listed the names of those awarded school colours
for their achievements in sport and academic subjects. It all

seemed so formal and not anything like her old school. The door opened and she turned, taking a step back in the process.

Advancing toward her and Aunt Isabella was a short, white haired woman. As she got closer Rhiannon was sure she could smell camphor which her mother had used when storing seasonal clothes. But her mother was always careful to wash it out of all her gear at the start of a new season. She'd never smelt it on a person before.

The old woman's rictus grin reminded Rhiannon of a jackal toying with its prey. She held out her hand and Rhiannon internally shuddered.

"Hello Miss Sharp, I'm Mrs. Remerson. Welcome to my school."

Rhiannon reluctantly took the hand offered her. It was cold and clammy and the flesh covering it felt too big for the bones and sinew it encased.

Mrs. Remerson motioned to the door she'd entered through. "Come with me please." She held up her hand when Aunt Isabella made to follow them. "It's fine Ms. Howard. I can take it from here. Vice Principal Jackson is waiting for Miss Sharp and me in my office."

Rhiannon's eyes widened. "I thought you were coming with me?"

Aunt Isabella reassuringly rubbed her arm. "It will be okay, trust me. I'll be here at three-thirty to pick you up. I promise." She smiled reassuringly at Rhiannon then glared at Mrs. Remerson before turning and leaving the school's administration building.

Rhiannon followed Mrs. Remerson into her office. The surrounding environment was sterile and emotionless, much like its owner. Standing in the space was a man she presumed was the vice principal.

"Hello Rhiannon." He held out his hand. "My name is Mr. Jackson."

Rhiannon took his hand. It was warm in a comforting sort of way. His accompanying smile reached his eyes, unlike Mrs. Remerson's.

"Sit down Miss Sharp," Mrs. Remerson said. "You should consider yourself very lucky. We rarely allow students to join us midterm. However, given your aunt is alumni and part of our board I decided to accommodate the request."

Mrs. Remerson's voice grated on. Rhiannon couldn't help but wonder how this was her school and why she was the only person able to allow Rhiannon to attend here. Although she very much wanted to ask just that, she held back. Now wasn't the time to make an enemy of someone who obviously had an over inflated opinion of her own self-importance.

"The school is named after Edith Cowan, the first Australian woman to serve as a member of parliament. It has a proud history and is an interdenominational school, although it hasn't always been the case."

The way she mentioned interdenominational made Rhiannon wonder whether she was trying to get a bad taste out of their mouth.

Mrs. Remerson checked her watch. "I have a meeting I must attend. Mr. Jackson will fill you in on the school's curriculum and requirements." She waved her hand, effectively dismissing them both.

She followed Mr. Jackson down the corridor and into surrounds which could not be any more removed from Mrs. Remerson's. Dominating its lightly painted walls were shelves of books. In one of the corners behind his desk stood a coffee machine and two jars, one full of cookies, the other candy. He motioned to a seat and closed the door.

Rather than sit behind his desk he sat opposite her. "I am so very sorry for your loss. I can only imagine what you're going through at the moment. If there's anything I can do to help your transition into Cowan Grammar any easier please let me know."

"Thank you, sir. I've never been at an all-girls school. This is new for me."

"It may take you a bit of adjustment." He reached out and snagged a piece of paper from his table. "But from what I've read one you're more than capable of mastering even given your most recent unfortunate circumstances."

Rhiannon frowned. "I don't understand."

"When I became aware of your arrival, I contacted your last principal so we could correctly ascertain your subject placement here. She sent me a report of your current grades and a summary of how you were regarded at the school."

Rhiannon's eyes watered at the mention of Reibey, her old school. She scrubbed her eyes, not wanting him to see how much not being there affected her. His deliberate oversolicitousness with the page he held told Rhiannon he had not missed her tears.

"Let's see, 'Miss Sharp is an introspective yet very intelligent and insightful student. She has consistently performed at the highest level in her academic endeavours. These are matched by her results on the sports field.'" He looked up. "What sport do you play?"

"I like anything. But I think she means softball, soccer and athletics."

He scanned down the page. "Here it is. Representation at state level for all three. I'm sure our physical education department will be very excited to hear about you." He perused the pages and his eyebrows arched. "It says here you're a challenging student, sometimes too much." He rose and motioned for her to follow. "We don't graduate wallflowers here Rhiannon, so you should be right at home."

Rhiannon followed him into the bowels of the school, all the while wondering whether she would ever feel at home in such a formal and single-gendered environment.

Present Day

THE SOUND OF squealing tires brought an abrupt halt to Rhiannon's reminiscing. She smiled ruefully. So much had happened since her time at this school. It wasn't that she disliked her final years. In fact, she found her time fun, if not somewhat constrained by the one-dimensional thinking by, thankfully, only a small number of her teachers. She could barely tolerate teachers who taught students as if they were nothing more than funnels one would pour water into with very little interest regarding the speed at which the water exited the funnel's smaller end. Thankfully, they weren't all tarred with the same brush. She was fortunate there were teachers who had genuinely challenged her mind and her own, yet-developing, ideals. Rhiannon hoped that tonight, along with the memorable ones, she would also run into some of the dead wood. It would be fun to engage them in a game of mental gymnastics, if for no other reason than to show them they had not succeeded in their "sausage factory" method of teaching; at least not with her. She straightened the collar of her blouse over her jacket and turned in the direction of the muted sounds of humanity.

Walking to the main entrance she casually glanced across the sports fields where she had found solace in the first few months at Cowan, while she'd struggled to fit into an unfamiliar group dynamic of schoolgirl cliques, carefully nurtured over four years. She had always possessed an envious ability to adopt a sport and master it with very little fuss. Her skill and height made her the pride of the physical education instructors who were always keen to ensure bodies excelled equally as well as minds. Looking at the back net of the softball diamond Rhiannon could almost hear the call of a strike and the words of her coach telling her to focus on the ball. It was easy for the coach to say. She wasn't facing a state level pitcher and a gorgeous one to boot.

By her young teenage years Rhiannon knew boys never interested her in the same way they did for most of her peers. Sure, they were fun to run and play with. She credited her remarkable speed and hand eye coordination with having to keep up with them at their own games. But it was as far as it went for her. When she had attended the coeducational Reibey, the boys would often play catch and kiss with the girls. When they did, she didn't merely pretend to run like the other girls. She ran flat out. The idea of a smelly and sweaty boy kissing her was the furthest thing from her mind. Now had it been catch and kiss with certain softball team members, the outcome may have been different.

Despite knowing her mind well before her recent sixteenth birthday and moving to an all-girls school, Rhiannon kept her own counsel. Sport provided her some degree of outlet and it was here she found others with whom she shared similar interests. Despite this, it was to some extent an unspoken secret between the few she had met. Notwithstanding the natural athleticism shared between these young women, Rhiannon felt no connection on an emotional level. Sure, they seemed to be interested enough in her. But the emotional attraction wasn't mutual.

She arrived at the foot of the auditorium stairs and took in the foyer in front of her. Through the glass doors and to the right of a desk stood a woman with a clipboard. Rhiannon watched the woman enthusiastically inspect what was obviously a list of names, in turn giving the woman opposite her a hug and a nametag to wear. Rhiannon shuddered. She had always hated labels. The thought of wearing a nametag for the evening made her skin crawl.

Electing not to have this be her first experience for the evening, she turned left and past the foyer. Her steps paralleled the building before she walked into what was during her tenure the upper quadrangle of her school. She took a seat at an all too familiar spot and smiled fondly. How much time had she spent here with her best friend Ginny? The upper quadrangle was their sanctuary. It was a senior's only area with junior students relegated to the lower quadrangle and sports ovals. The two of them would regularly take their morning tea and lunch at this very spot. The friendship they shared was one Rhiannon thought would last forever.

Cowan Grammar Year Ten

RHIANNON SAT UNDER a tree in the lower quadrangle, contemplating her next thought-provoking question for her some-what banal modern history teacher. The sounds of loud voices coming from behind the gym block interrupted her train of thought. Annoyed, she stood, smoothed her skirt, and headed in the direction of the dispute.

"I'm only going to ask you one more time four eyes. Did you tell Miss Stinson I'd been smoking in the lower quad toilets?"

Rhiannon turned the corner and silently observed the scene. Standing, her hands belligerently on hips, was a girl Rhiannon had accidentally bumped into in the corridor the previous day. The girl had rounded on her with such vehemence Rhiannon was sure had she not been taller of the two the girl would have flat-tened her on the spot. A few discreetly placed enquiries by Rhian-non to the school's quieter students uncovered she was Jackie Smethurst. She had an established reputation for victimising the meeker and smaller members of Cowan. Standing opposite Jackie was a schoolgirl, her brown hair loose about her face, effectively masking her features.

"How many times do I have to say it Jackie? I didn't tell Miss Stinson. If you'd stop and think for a moment, you'd realise how foolish you sound. How could I know how you occupy your day? It's not as if we share the same friends or anything."

The girl's tenacity impressed Rhiannon. If the situation were to escalate into something physical it was extremely unlikely the smaller one could hold her own against Jackie, let alone the feck-less group who followed the girl's tormenter.

The seemingly logical response was clearly not what Jackie wanted to hear, and she closed on the smaller student. Rhiannon walked around the group of girls standing behind Jackie to within the peripheral range of the two key parties. "I'd say her answer sounds inherently reasonable. Wouldn't you?"

Jackie wheeled. "Who the hell do you think you are, inter-rupting me?" Her eyes widened. "Oh wow," she sneered. "It's the poor little orphan girl. I let you off easy yesterday when you bar-relled into me in the corridor. If you know what's good for you, you'll go and crawl back under whatever hick rock it was you came from and let me get back to my own business."

Rhiannon refused to give Jackie the satisfaction of seeing the pain evoked by her callous words. "What, so you can go and beat to a pulp someone smaller than you? Gee that must be a heap of fun. I wonder why it hasn't caught on as a sport?"

Jackie strode toward Rhiannon, stopping mere inches from where she stood.

Despite her threatening stance, Rhiannon wasn't intimidated. "Didn't you hear what she said? She wouldn't be caught dead with the likes of you, let alone frequent toilets where you shorten your pathetic little life through smoking. She didn't dob you in. How many languages do you have to hear it in before it's absorbed by that Neanderthal brain of yours? Hang on, maybe not Neanderthal, as it would be offensive to that poor species."

Jackie's clenched fists remained at her side. While she might be willing to take on the smaller members of the school it was clear she wasn't stupid enough to raise her hand against Rhiannon. This was fortuitous, for Rhiannon was still fighting her own battle against the effect of Jackie's earlier hurtful words. The result was a barely contained anger which seemed to flow beneath an unusually composed surface. Just a hint of a response from Jackie would be sufficient for Rhiannon to lose any remaining ounce of her self-control.

Jackie stepped back and spat on the ground, narrowly missing Rhiannon's shoes. She turned and pointed at the girl who only moments ago had been the target of her vitriol. "Consider yourself lucky big, butch beanstalk here stepped in when she did. But remember she won't always be around." Jackie pushed her way through her gang and stormed off, her mob in tow.

Rhiannon walked to the girl who had been the subject of Jackie's taunting. She reached out and lightly touched her shoulder. "Are you all right?"

Obvious relief replaced the previously nervous countenance of the girl. "Yes, thank you."

Rhiannon shook her head. "I don't know how she manages to get away with it. Surely the teachers must know what's going on."

"She picks her targets very well. She's also backed up by her group of girls who have nothing better to do with their life than be sycophants to her." The girl lightly grasped Rhiannon's forearm. "I'm sorry for what she said. I can only imagine how hard it must have been for you to lose your parents."

"I suppose it's something I have to live with." Rhiannon

inhaled deeply, reining in emotions which these days always seemed close to the surface. "How did you know about my mother and father?"

"A little while ago I overheard Mr. Jackson speaking to one of the teachers about a student who was joining the school midterm. He said she'd been left an orphan due to the death of her parents."

"I'm sorry. I haven't introduced myself."

"You don't need to. You're Rhiannon Sharp. I've seen you around." She extended her hand. "I'm Virginia Shulman."

"Shulman. It's a Jewish name isn't it?"

"Yes. My grandparents came out here from Switzerland. They fled there to escape persecution in Germany around the start of World War II. While a lot of my family still live in Switzerland, my grandparents decided to come to Australia."

"Is that why Jackie was teasing you?"

Virginia shrugged. "I suppose it's some of it. It helps to have thick skin."

Rhiannon pursed her lips. "You shouldn't have to. It's hard to be different though, sometimes standing alone from others."

"Isn't that what you do? I've seen you in Geology and Modern History. You're the only one who speaks to the teachers like you do. You do keep them on their toes though." They shared a laugh. "But you don't seem to hang out with any one group of girls."

"I don't feel I need to. Besides, it's always hard to make friends at a new school. I've made some friends, mostly on the sports field."

Rhiannon watched Jackie and her gang search for another playground victim. She turned back to Virginia. "Has she ever done this to you before?"

"A couple of times but no more. I keep an eye out and make myself scarce if I see her seeking out potential targets," Virginia replied.

"You don't have to worry anymore. And nor does anyone else."

Cowan Grammar Year Eleven: Final Term

RHIANNON FLOPPED DOWN next to Ginny in their usual spot in the senior's quadrangle. A light rain began to fall, and she wiped her face. "Where is everyone?"

"Afraid of a little water I suppose," Ginny replied. "And as for why the quad is vacant, if you recall we're a little early getting out our Modern History class."

"How was I to know Mrs. Barwell would take a dislike to us making sandwiches during her lesson?"

Ginny lightly slapped Rhiannon's stomach. "I have *no* idea why. Maybe it had something to do with the fact they were tomato and onion and we were sitting right in front of her. Or maybe it was because this was the last day of term and she'd about had enough of you and your unrelenting inquisition."

Rhiannon touched her chest, her face a picture of innocence. "Who, me? Besides, it was only twenty minutes before the end of a double lesson."

"You're going to have to be careful next year. As vice-captain I doubt you'll get away with what you did this year." Ginny jumped at the sound of nearby thunder. "That was close."

The rain which had only been feather light moments ago had quickly progressed into a fully-fledged summer shower. "Luckily, I'll have you to keep me on the straight and narrow." Rhiannon grabbed Ginny's hand.

Ginny awkwardly grabbed her glasses with her free hand and stashed them in her pocket. "What are you doing?"

Rhiannon snagged her now-free other hand. "Come on, let's dance. You told me you always wanted to recreate the dance scene from the fifties musical you liked."

"You lunatic," Ginny protested. "He had an umbrella."

Rhiannon continued to tug gently at Ginny's hands. "Come on. For me?"

"Oh, what the heck." Ginny stood, releasing one of Rhiannon's hands. "It's the last day of year eleven. Here goes nothing."

Together they tap danced across the space, singing at the top of their voices, jumping in puddles, and swinging from light posts as they went.

"Miss Sharp, Miss Shulman what *are* you doing! Get out of the storm before you catch yourself a cold."

Rhiannon and Ginny's heads simultaneously whipped around to the open window at the top of the quadrangle and Mrs. Remerson's angry face. Before she could say anything more the two bolted to the nearest exit and safely beyond Mrs. Remerson's prying eyes.

Rhiannon flopped down on the lounge in the Senior study and wiped her face of the remnants of water from the shower. "Gee it's quiet in here."

Ginny sat next to her, using paper towel from the dispenser above the sink to wipe her glasses. "They're still in class remember."

"Ah, yes." Rhiannon couldn't hide the cheeky grin which spread across her face. "I remember now."

Ginny leant back next to Rhiannon and put her glasses on, spending time to meticulously adjust them like she always did. Rhiannon loved the way Ginny was so particular with everything. It was one of many things she liked about her.

Ginny threw the now damp paper towel on the table. "We are in so much trouble."

"Because of the dancing?"

Ginny lightly punched Rhiannon. "Because of the dancing, not to mention the sandwiches in Modern History." She nonchalantly flung her arm around Rhiannon and rested her head on her shoulders. "You are crazy, but we do make a great team."

Despite the dampness of their clothes, Rhiannon could feel a sense of warmth between them, a warmth which was rapidly growing into a heat. Ginny snuggled closer. Has she any idea what she's doing to me, Rhiannon thought.

Rhiannon turned her body and leant over to Ginny, their faces close enough for her to see her own reflection in Ginny's glasses. She studied Ginny's face for any evidence of the effect of their closeness. It was there in Ginny's flushed features, her pupils slightly dilated.

Rhiannon swallowed nervously. "I wish you were going to be here over Christmas break."

"Me too," Ginny replied softly. "At least last Christmas we could spend time together. But all the family is off to Switzerland for the whole six weeks."

"I'm not much better. Aunt Isabella has signed us up for a series of hikes on the South Island of New Zealand. She says it gives her a real chance to have a break. Which I suppose is true. We'll be out of phone reception for most of the time." She reached up and wiped a damp curl from Ginny's forehead, allowing her hand to rest against Ginny's face. "I know it will be fun. But I'd rather be with you."

Ginny opened her mouth just as the bell rung. The sounds of the outside school world began to hum through the closed door of the study. Ginny got to her feet.

Rhiannon stood and found herself pulled into Ginny's arms. The fact the hug seemed to linger much more than normal wasn't lost on Rhiannon.

"I'd rather be with you too." Ginny slowly pulled out of their embrace in time for Rhiannon to hear the door open and see a group of girls walk through it. "See you at our bench in the upper quad first day of year twelve?"

Rhiannon smiled. "Wild horses couldn't keep me away."

From across the room through an ever-increasing mass of bodies Rhiannon watched Ginny stuff her bag with the prescribed year twelve reading material for the Christmas break. She lifted her hand in response to her goodbye wave and Ginny headed out the door.

Rhiannon released a breath she didn't realise she'd been holding. I do like you but have you any idea how much? What would you do if I told you? She ran her fingers through her raven locks, promising herself to find the right moment to discuss it with Ginny next year.

Cowan Grammar Year Twelve

RHIANNON ENTERED THE upper quad on the first day of the new school year eagerly looking for Ginny in their usual spot. She wasn't there. More pointedly, the other seniors stared at her and turned away. She noticed one of her friends from Ancient History class and headed in her direction.

"Miss Sharp."

Rhiannon turned at Mr. Jackson's voice. He gestured her to him.

"Yes sir?"

"Miss Sharp would you come with me please?"

The crowd silently parted for them and she followed him across the quadrangle and into his office.

"Please take a seat," he said, closing the door.

Rhiannon frowned. She was at odds to understand why she was here. Was it the lunch prank she and Ginny had played on their Modern History teacher at the end of last term? If that was the case, why wasn't Ginny in here with her?

"Sir, I apologise if we upset Mrs. Barwell with our onion and tomato sandwich making in her class before break. Be assured, as vice-captain I won't be doing such things this year."

Rather than sit behind his desk Mr. Jackson eased himself into the seat next to hers. He stroked his beard apprehensively and brought his eyes to hers. "I'm afraid I have some bad news for you."

Rhiannon felt a sense of unease bubble up inside of her. "The sandwiches were mine, not Virginia's. If one of us deserves punishment it most certainly should be me."

Mr. Jackson held up his hand. "It's not the sandwiches Miss Sharp. It's Miss Shulman. There was an incident over the term break. I'm not sure if you're aware or not but Miss Shulman and her family went to Switzerland for the Christmas holidays."

"I am. We spoke about it last year. One of her cousins is celebrating her bat mitzvah and the family were heading over for the event."

Mr. Jackson's eyes peered deeply into hers, the silence in the office palpable. "Did Miss Shulman mention the family's skiing holiday?"

Rhiannon nodded.

"Miss Shulman was skiing when she lost control and skied into a tree. She seemed fine at first and continued skiing for the rest of the afternoon. However, later in the evening when her mother went to get her for dinner, she found her unconscious and unresponsive. They rushed her to hospital."

She searched his face. "I don't understand."

Mr. Jackson's expression spoke volumes.

A sense of foreboding settled over Rhiannon and she knew she had to get out of the room. She thrust her chair back and wheeled to leave, as if doing so would stem the words she intuitively knew were coming. Mr. Jackson gripped her forearm, halting her flight.

"She arrived at the hospital unresponsive. An MRI and subsequent tests showed she had a clot on her brain which she must have gotten as a result of the collision earlier in the day. She never regained consciousness. Her parents tried to reach your aunt to let you know."

Rhiannon slumped against the wall, losing the fight to stem her tears. "We were hiking in New Zealand. There was no reception. We only arrived home late yesterday evening."

"I'm terribly sorry." Mr. Jackson pulled his phone from his jacket. "I'll call your aunt. I don't think this is the best place for you today."

Present Day

RHIANNON BOWED HER head. "Oh Ginny," she whispered.

The first weeks of term one of year twelve had almost been too much to bear. How different could those last few weeks with Ginny have been if only she'd had the courage to tell her how she really felt? How would Ginny have responded? Sadly, Rhiannon would never know.

Rhiannon instinctively shielded her eyes from the glow of a guard's torch.

"Excuse me, but can I help you?"

She slightly turned her head, trying to avoid the bright light. "I'm fine thanks. I'm here for the reunion and I thought I'd take the time to look around before facing the noisy masses."

The guard lowered his torch. "I know what you mean. I went to one of these things a couple of years ago and went home with the biggest headache. All anyone wanted to do was talk at you as loudly as was humanly possible. If that wasn't enough, most of the people there were more interested in seeing who had the best job and who was earning the most. It turned me off going to one of them ever again."

"I think I know what you mean. I'm beginning to wonder whether this was such a good idea after all."

He motioned to the hall. "If you haven't been in there yet I'm sure you could easily slip away. I doubt anyone would notice."

Rhiannon knew it was exactly what one part of her wanted to do. What did she expect to achieve by attending tonight? An answer. She stood and shrugged. "I could. But unfinished business and all. Hopefully, it won't take too long."

"And hopefully it won't be too painful for you," the guard added as Rhiannon strode in the direction of the auditorium.

She took the stairs two at a time, adopted her game face and opened the door. She watched the excited nametag lady she had seen earlier send another woman down the entrance corridor and into the school proper. She turned and faced her.

"Hi and welcome to the Cowan Grammar reunion." The woman's sickly-sweet words were almost sufficient motivation to cause Rhiannon to turn and run but she held her ground.

She peered around her surrounds, attempting to avoid the eager face of nametag lady. A map affixed to the wall displayed the several rooms set aside for the reunion. She mentally sighed. This makes things a bit more difficult but not insurmountable, she thought. She returned her gaze to the woman closing in on her.

"Thanks, I'm class of '82 and was wondering—"

"Are you? Wow, I'm class of '83. Now if you give me a minute, I bet I can work out who you are."

Slightly embarrassed yet aware people had to get their excitement somewhere, Rhiannon patiently waited as the woman, Margaret Peters, assuming the nametag was her own, picked up the 1982 Yearbook. The woman examined the photo in the book and gasped.

"You're Rhiannon Sharp! I'm surprised I don't remember you. I still recall the day you stood up to Smethurst when she was going to thump Virginia Shulman."

Rhiannon caught her breath. It had been a long time since she'd heard Ginny's name spoken.

"It was such a shame she died when she did. You were good friends, weren't you?" Margaret continued, seemingly oblivious to the effect her words were having on Rhiannon.

Rhiannon closed her eyes and composed herself. She armed herself with her most no nonsense, business-like stare and returned her attention to Margaret. "We were. Now if you don't mind, I'd like to go and mingle. I'm keen to see if I can catch up with anyone." She grabbed a map of the reunion's layout and headed for the door behind the table.

Margaret scampered after her. "Wait, you can't go yet! You haven't got your nametag."

Rhiannon rolled her eyes. She turned and decided to try another approach to escape Margaret's extreme attentiveness. She closed the distance between the two. "Yes," she said, in a voice she normally used for quieter, more intimate settings. "But I think it would be much more exciting if people were forced to try and put a name to my face. Don't you?"

Margaret blushed. She nervously studied her clipboard and returned her focus to Rhiannon. She shyly dipped her head, the ghost of a smile on her face. A blast of cold air heralded the arrival of another group of alumni into the foyer.

Rhiannon motioned with her head. "Don't you think you should go and see to those ladies? After all you can't have too many people wandering the school without their nametags, can you?"

Margaret glanced over her shoulder at the group and returned her gaze to Rhiannon. "Um, I don't think so," she stuttered. "They should have their identification. Have a good evening." She scurried to the newly arrived group.

Rhiannon walked down the corridor and around the corner, out of sight of the foyer. She stopped and leant up against the wall. Relieved at escaping without the encumbrance of yet another label, she perused the map in her hands, realising the closest area dedicated to the reunion was the teachers' lunch-room. Serving as the food area, it was just down the hall from where she was. Appropriate, Rhiannon thought.

She had only been in there one other time, the event being the annual captain and vice-captain morning tea with the principal and school subject masters. Given she held one of those appoint-ments, she knew she had to attend. But it didn't stop her from hating the idea. The whole event was very stilted and false. Fortu-nately, she took solace in the twinkling eyes of the English mas-ter, Ms. Matheson, who for the last two years of her schooling had been her English teacher. She had readily identified Rhiannon's challenging mind and gone out of her way to work Rhiannon to her fullest mental capacity. Rhiannon rose to the challenge, post-ing grades never made before in the school's history.

She glimpsed again at the map and at the library, the second main space dedicated to the reunion. She grinned crookedly at the irony. The quietest location in the school had been set up to include a dance floor. The final main reunion space was the audi-torium which had apparently been set aside as a quiet area. It held the pictorial testament to the history of the school and Rhi-annon's schooling years. The teacher's study, not to mention food, was as good a place as any to start. She placed the map in her jacket pocket, eased off the wall and moved to the semi-open door.

Small groups filled the room, all talking and happily consum-ing the finger food, which liberally adorned the tables placed up against most of the walls. Rhiannon headed to the drinks table and picked up a glass of champagne. She moved to one side and took up an unobtrusive position along a part of the wall not filled by tables and food. The vantage point enabled her to surrepti-tiously view the small groups of ex-students as she tried to locate her goal for the evening. This wasn't the most social way for her to achieve her aim. But she couldn't think of anything worse than engaging in meaningless small talk to accomplish why she was here.

"Still avoiding crowds and pretentious chit-chat I see Miss Sharp."

Rhiannon almost dropped her glass. Preoccupied in skim-ming the many faces in her surroundings, she'd failed to sense the close presence of another person. Usually this was a skill she had capably mastered, specifically for social functions where she preferred to keep her distance. Or at least to know when someone was breaching her personal space.

"Some things never change, do they?"

She turned and faced the woman opposite her and sorted through her mental filing system, trying to put a voice to a name. While the face possessed a few more traces of a life well lived, the strawberry blonde hair and hazel eyes were unmistakable.

"My God, Ms. Matheson, how are you?" Rhiannon's eyes moved over the body of her old English master, unashamed at her appreciation of a woman she had always felt was particularly beautiful, on the outside and in.

"You know it's been quite a while since someone called me Ms. Matheson." She smiled. "I think the time for formality is long gone now Rhiannon. Please call me Elly."

Rhiannon laughed lightly. "It's funny how we fall back on established ground isn't it? After all these years it's still difficult to break away from the teacher student relationship."

"Not too hard, I hope. Although it's great to see you again I trust you're not here to take me to task over your past English marks?"

Rhiannon was sufficiently world wise to not miss Elly's open appraisal of her. "If there was one thing you always were, it was honest. When I scored low nineties on my work it was because I deserved it. Nothing more, nothing less."

Elly tilted her head. "Still hard on yourself I see. I was hoping some of your perfectionism would have rubbed off of you by now. After all, you've grown into quite a handsome, influential and established woman in your own right."

Rhiannon lifted her champagne glass to her lips as she considered Elly's words and actions. She sipped the cool liquid and held it in her mouth then swallowed, secretly touched by Elly's piercing gaze.

"You know, my memory's not entirely crystal clear about my school days." She discreetly scanned their immediate space, ensuring no one else was close enough to overhear their conversation. "But I'm fairly sure I wouldn't have forgotten if you'd looked at me then like you are now."

Elly's eyes sparkled. "Still as forthright as you were back then. As you're well aware, there was a significant difference between what we were at Cowan and what we are today. I'd have never allowed you to see any such thing given your age. For me to pursue anything between us would have been irresponsible on a number of moral and ethical levels, not to mention illegal, on my behalf."

Elly's candid response surprised her. Rather than pursue the line of discussion, she opted for safer ground. "Sorry. I couldn't help myself. Do you want to sit down? With my height, standing in this crowd makes me a little too conspicuous to prying eyes. It's not something I particularly want."

She motioned to a corner where two seats had become vacant. "What about over there?"

"That's fine," Elly replied and walked to the corner, Rhiannon closely following her.

Elly eased herself into the chair and placed her drink on the table between the chairs. "What a strange thing to say. A reunion's an unusual place to try and hide if you don't want to be seen."

"I know. But there are a few people I'm hoping to catch up with tonight. My work sees me spend most of my time outside Australia and it's been a long time since I've been back home. As a result, it's been years since I last saw anyone from here. In fact, with some, the last time I spoke with them was the last day of school. I was hoping maybe they had also decided to come tonight."

Elly toyed with the straw in her gin and tonic. "Is there anyone I can help you with? Admittedly I haven't been here too long, but I have seen a couple of familiar faces."

Rhiannon almost said her name and caught herself. For reasons she couldn't quite fathom, she felt the need to find her on her own and not necessarily with the help of anyone else regardless of how striking they were.

"It's okay, I'll have a squiz around later. If they're here I'll find them and if not, so be it. What have you been doing over the past twenty years?" Rhiannon asked, seeking to deflect any further interest regarding her goal for the evening.

"I stayed in teaching until I finished my doctorate. For the last ten years I've been doing speech therapy and working with deaf children."

"That's a bit of a change in direction," Rhiannon said and took a sip of her champagne.

"It is but it's an extremely rewarding job, not that teaching wasn't. It's just when I was in mainstream education, the likes of you and your consistently inquiring mind were few and far between. I began to fear I was beginning to take the easy way out when it came to teaching and was turning into the type of teacher I despised. And it scared the crap out of me. I can happily say I completely adore what I'm doing now."

"Good on you for finding something you enjoy. There aren't too many people who can say they love what they do for a living."

Elly dipped her glass in mock salute. "Thank you. On a more personal note I can also live my life openly and without the fear of knee-jerk reactions of homophobic parents." She reached across and tapped Rhiannon's knee. "Enough of me. What about you? In the past few years you seem to be popping up everywhere important. Last time I saw you was at a women's dinner in Sydney where you were the keynote speaker. It was the Packer dinner if I remember correctly. At school you always came across as a student resolute in her beliefs. But I don't think I ever saw you as outspoken as you were that night, when you spoke on child abuse."

Rhiannon sobered. "I remember. I'd just finished doing a week of volunteer work on a children's help line. I was so angry, listening to calls from physically and sexually abused children. It took all my willpower to respond to them and not react to what they were telling me. I think what disgusted me the most was the age of some of the kids."

Elly reached out and lightly grasped her thigh. "I completely understand. How does someone do that to another human being, let alone a child?"

Elly's touch quelled the anger threatening to resurface at the memory. "I don't know. Christ, it's not as if there aren't enough places where people can go and find sex or find a ring to belt the crap out of someone. Why they focus their rage and lust on children is beyond me. And it certainly wasn't hard to be as frank as I was." Rhiannon shook her head to try and dispel the memory. "You were there? Why didn't you come and say hello?"

Elly quirked her brow. "If I recall correctly you seemed to have your hands full with quite the entourage of attractive, attentive women. I would have had to have used a fair degree of elbow grease to get even remotely close. Aside from that, I was there with my partner and she began to feel a bit under the weather. After everything I'd told her about you, we had every intention of saying hello. But we had to leave rather quickly. I'm not sure who was more disappointed. Not to worry. All's well that ends well. I'm glad you came tonight. It's been great catching up with you."

A comfortable silence descended between them as Rhiannon studied Elly. She smiled fondly, remembering back to her final day at school. "Do you have any idea of the impact you had on me?" Seeing Elly's panicked reaction, she laid a comforting hand on her forearm.

"Sorry, that didn't quite come out the way I meant it to. I was thinking about the last day. Everything was so strained. There was so much I wanted to speak with you about. But no matter how hard I tried the right words wouldn't come." Rhiannon exhaled loudly through her nose. "It's ironic a student who could waffle crap with the best of them should clam up when I most needed to speak. But you seemed to know just what to say."

Elly slightly tilted her head to one side. "What do you mean?"

"At the luncheon we were sitting next to each other on the table at the front of the auditorium with the school captain, the rest of the subject masters, principal and vice-principal and the place was filled with girls yelling over each other to be heard."

Elly narrowed her eyes, as if attempting to dredge up a memory from the past. "That's right, we were. You were unusually quiet throughout the luncheon, as if something was weighing heavily on your mind. Despite the best attempts of a number of people at the table to engage you in conversation you wouldn't be drawn. To me you looked lost."

Rhiannon recalled the moment, as if it was yesterday. "You turned to me and told me a story. Do you remember it?"

"As a matter of fact, I do. I told you the story about my first English master who never put any of his teaching degrees and awards on the wall. One day the Principal visited his office and asked him where they were. He said he never hung them because in the scheme of things they didn't matter. The Principal calmly answered him, saying they did if you made a difference. At that moment in time I was trying to give to you something I'd used as a guide for many years and that was to make a difference."

Rhiannon's eyes softened. "I've never forgotten what you said. It's been a mantra for me over the last twenty years. Whenever I find myself wondering about my latest direction or the value of my actions, I think back to those words."

Rhiannon crossed her legs and smoothed the crease of her slacks as she sought a way to get an answer to something which had plagued her since that last day. "You said you'd meet us at the club that afternoon for a farewell drink."

Elly nodded warily.

"Why didn't you turn up?"

The expression on Elly's face almost made any answer she could give redundant.

"Rhiannon, you were and remain my most favourite student.

You pushed me beyond the boundaries, at times forcing me to challenge my own position on issues. Remember the day in class when we argued over the hidden meaning of a poem?"

Rhiannon stroked her lip, in turn resurrecting memories from long ago. "It was a Judith Wright poem, wasn't it? I think it was the first poem of hers which we discussed midway through the first term of year eleven."

"I'd spent the better part of ten minutes patiently trying to convince you, without vocalising the words, I knew the poem better than you, and my patience was waning."

Rhiannon chuckled. "Christ, I must have been a pain to teach."

"You weren't. You were merely attempting to understand why one opinion could matter more than someone else's. Here I was insisting on the poem's meaning being quite clear. Except you didn't see it the same way. You came back at me with the idea I could bite into a chocolate bar and taste chocolate and you could do the same and taste strawberry and we would both be right. Our tastes were our own, based on our perspectives. Given they were our own they couldn't be wrong."

Rhiannon took as sip from her glass. "As I said, a pain."

"I think it was at that moment I knew my feelings for you weren't exactly pure, if you know what I mean. Despite this, I was still a teacher and you my student. On the last day I wanted so much to come and have a drink with you. But I was afraid. Seeing how cast adrift your feelings were, I was extremely conscious of how easy it would be for me to take advantage of your compromised emotions." Elly pursed her lips. "Knowing that made me steer clear of the club."

Rhiannon rubbed the front of her neck, her eyes distant. "I was so lost that day. I was about to leave behind people who meant a lot to me. You were one of them. People make promises about keeping in touch, but it doesn't work out that way. I knew there was a good chance I wouldn't see you again. And as for me being led astray," she raised a brow, "you must have sensed the feeling wasn't all one sided?"

"I'd be lying if I said I didn't. However, besides the obvious teacher/student issue there were a raft of other issues to consider, not the least of which my age. Eight years was a large difference between two people back then." Elly lifted her glass to her lips and drank as they both pondered her comment.

"Mind you, it's funny how the age gap, although chronological, seems to reduce the older you get, isn't it?"

"Yes, it is," Rhiannon replied.

"But setting age and reciprocal interest aside for a moment," Elly smiled enigmatically, "there were other people closer to your age who had eyes for you that day."

"There were. And they left too," Rhiannon said quietly, fingering the stem of her champagne glass. "You know if I was prone to complexes, I'd say there seems to be a trend in my life of people leaving me or standing me up."

Elly playfully swatted her arm. "If that's the case, it doesn't seem to have adversely affected you." She cast a cursory glance at her watch. "Heavens, I didn't realise it was this late. I know this sounds like I'm walking out on you, but I've got to get home. My partner, Jen, works at Lander's Hospital. She's on the night shift, and we only pay our babysitter for a set time. Not surprisingly, we have a little girl who is none too happy when she wakes up in the middle of the night and finds the house empty. Neither might I add is her biological mother."

"Is that you?"

"No. Jen is. I tried, but unfortunately I couldn't carry the pregnancy full term." Elly picked up her bag and reached into its depths, searching for something. Her hand came out holding a card. "This is my number. Let's try and make it a little less time between when we see each other again. I'd very much like for you to meet Jen. I'm sure the two of you could keep each other amused for hours on end."

Rhiannon stood, drew a card from her jacket pocket and handed it to Elly. "Thanks for the offer. I'd love to meet her. If everything goes to plan my current contract will keep me in the country for at least the next twelve months. It should be ample time to catch up." Without giving it any great deal of thought, she unabashedly pulled Elly into her arms. "I'm very happy for you," she whispered. "She must be a very special woman."

Breaking the closeness of the hug Elly touched the tip of Rhiannon's nose. "Oh, she is. And I hope you find who you're looking for tonight. Take care." Elly eased herself from Rhiannon's arms and was out the door before Rhiannon could say anything else.

She reached down to the table and drained the dregs of her now warm champagne. Placing it on a tray of empty glasses, she moved out of the room. She glanced to the right and followed the tendrils of eighties music wafting from the interior of the library.

Chapter Two

RHIANNON STEPPED THROUGH the door and into a space which when she'd first arrived at Cowan had been her sanctuary from the many sights and sounds which had assaulted her fragile senses. She'd spent hours on end in the library, ensconced in the unusually comforting presence of books.

Unlike her high school years, tonight a muted lighting bathed the multitude of shelves and computers. The song playing, while slightly loud, was at least one she remembered. There was too much music today she had little time for. At least the twenty-one-year-old track warbling through the speakers was one she enjoyed and could at least understand the lyrics. Songs which shouted at you didn't interest her in the least.

She stopped inside the door, allowing herself to adjust to the softer lighting. She cast her eyes around her surroundings, hoping to find the person she was seeking but to no avail. Instead she found herself searching her mind to try and place the smiling visage of the short woman rapidly closing in on her.

"The things you see when you least expect it. G'day Tack. How the hell are you? Somebody mentioned they'd seen you harassing some woman at the reception area. It's good to see some things don't change."

Rhiannon smiled at the moniker no one had called her since school. "Tack" was a reference to her last name of Sharp and the creative Australian habit of using a sobriquet, sometimes with only the most obscure links to the actual name of the person. Hers came from "Sharp as a tack." She held out her hand to the Rubenesque woman in front of her. "Robin Beresford, nobody's called me that in years. I'm surprised you can remember it after all this time."

Robin gripped the hand in her own. "You know me, always the font of useless information. It seems to get into my mind and sits there in an ever-increasing filing cabinet of superfluous minutiae. Mind you, in my current job it helps to have a great memory."

Rhiannon inwardly smiled at Robin's none too subtle cue. It was obvious she was keen to tell her about her employment. "What is it you're currently doing?"

"After I left school, I spent some time in Teacher's College. It didn't take me long to realise if I ever had to actually deal with teaching children, I may just have to murder them. Thankfully for all concerned my epiphany came shortly after my first practical teaching tenure. I was let loose on a class of ten-year old students." Robin shuddered. "They were bloody horrible. Runny noses and bereft of any focus whatsoever."

"What else did you expect from kids that age?"

"I don't know. Silence, obedience perhaps. You know, sit there and do what you're told."

Rhiannon chuckled. "They're not dogs, Robin."

"Anyway, one practical teaching experience was enough for me. I withdrew from there and applied to study law and, lo and behold, you see in front of you a barrister no less."

"You know it kind of suits you. I can always remember you during those Inter-School debating sessions. You possessed an uncanny talent in being able to take an argument and stretch it to suit your means. Of course, you also used your skills exceptionally well to suit your needs, especially when talking a teacher out of giving you detention."

Robin tucked her chin to her chest and huffed. "Pot, this is kettle, over! I might have been good at talking my way out of things, but *you* left me for dead. When you weren't standing up to bullies or helping the other students, you were tying some teachers in knots. I reckon the only reason they didn't kick you out was half the time they didn't know you were calling them fools until you were long gone from the classroom." The two women shared a laugh. "What are you doing now?"

"I've begun a stint of consulting with a Human Resources group in town. They're keen to use my global experience to improve the face and focus of their company. I'm on a twelve-month tenure and I have to say it's nice to be back in Australia. Travelling's fine but there's nothing like getting home to where your roots are." Rhiannon furtively scanned the room again.

"You seem to have been doing quite a lot of travelling. I think the last time I saw you was on some American current affairs show, discussing your latest book. Your allusion to organisational culture being more representational of an iceberg was very insightful. You had me in stitches though, with the way you fielded some of the interviewer's vapid questions. It was clear he hadn't done his research on you or the book." Robin grasped Rhiannon's hand and drew her in the direction of the refreshment table.

"They do say better to remain silent and maybe he should

have." Rhiannon picked up a plate and filled it with a selection of raw vegetables and hot canapes while Robin secured herself a drink. Rhiannon walked to a group of chairs that afforded her an unimpeded view of the area. She sat down and Robin took a seat beside her.

She sighed inwardly. It wasn't she didn't welcome Robin's presence. It was just Rhiannon's preference was to be left to her own devices so she could try and seek out whom she came for. She forced a smile at Robin.

"Aside from consultancy, being a world-renowned writer and global traveller, what else have you been up to?" Robin playfully nudged Rhiannon in the ribs. "Has anyone else occupied you on these travels?"

Rhiannon popped a small quiche in her mouth. She was beginning to remember why she hadn't attended any of these reunions until now. People weren't happy until they'd squeezed every last intimate detail out of you.

She wasn't in the closet when it came to her personal life. But she wasn't necessarily out either. The people who needed to know did and those who didn't, well, they didn't. And you, Robin are one of those who doesn't need to know, she thought. Especially if your ability to gossip is as finely honed as it was when we were at school.

Despite her response being mercifully delayed through a mouthful of food, Robin was still waiting expectantly for an answer. She swallowed the morsel. "Not really."

"You're joking right? As gorgeous as you are, it's a wonder you're not beating them off with a stick!"

"Looks aren't everything you know," she offered lamely, trying to avoid further discussion.

"It's easy for you to say. I remember those school dances with Pembroke Boys college. They couldn't keep their eyes off you. But a black hair, blue eyed combination, not to mention your height was all the incentive most of those pimply faced adolescents needed. And what's more, the years clearly haven't been unkind to you. Appearances mightn't be the be all and end all. But they sure give you a foot in the door."

Can we stop talking about me please? "I suppose you're right. There hasn't been anyone on a regular basis for a long time now. Travelling around the place isn't a sound foundation for a relationship. What about you?"

Robin positively glowed and Rhiannon groaned silently. She hoped she wasn't about to be subjected to an unending stream of family photographs. If that happened, it was entirely possible she'd be here all night, when there were certainly other places she wanted to be.

"You probably don't remember Jim Steinman, but he and I were an item during my senior years at school. He was my first husband." Robin made a face. "And I think I only married him to satisfy my mother. She seemed to think if I waited too long her chances at being a grandmother would be severely impeded. Not surprisingly, the marriage didn't last long past the first year and we separated with more than a moderate degree of antipathy between us." Robin's face mirrored her words, as she seemed to recall a time not at all comfortable for her.

"I don't see Jim anymore and I haven't a clue what he's doing with himself." Robin paused, a faraway look in her eyes. "After him there wasn't anyone else for quite some time. And although it was nice not to have to tailor your life around someone else's, it was very lonely."

While Rhiannon hadn't been without companionship, it was the permanence which normally went with such company her life lacked. "You're not telling me anything I don't know. Try living out of a suitcase and finding a partner who understands your rather unorthodox working hours."

Robin blinked, as if returning to the present. "I know what you mean. A couple of years ago I finally met a man and we seemed to click. We do have our differences, yet these seem to complement the two of us. We got married, for the second time for each of us I might add, late last year. I've been happy ever since. He's also a barrister and you wouldn't believe how I met him."

Regardless of whether she wanted to or not, Rhiannon knew she was destined to hear about their meeting anyway. She substituted her thoughts with a more diplomatic response. "How did you?"

"Each year my practice requires its barristers to undertake a month of pro bono work. I normally work with the local magistrate, providing legal aid to people who can't afford such. On this particular day I assisted a woman whose house was broken into by a robber who had subsequently been attacked by the home-owner's dog. She was worried the defence was using the dog attack to overshadow the larger offence of the break-in. She was heartbroken at the possibility that the result would be she would lose her dog and the robber would get off scot-free. You've probably worked out by now the defence was Daniel, my husband-to-be. But you'll never guess who the robber was."

"I haven't a clue. But I can see you're dying to tell me. Who was it?"

"It was bloody Jackie Smethurst! You remember her?"

"She's not someone you readily forget."

Robin shook her head. "I couldn't believe my luck. Having been on the receiving end of her verbal and physical abuse at school, I was more than happy to do my job. Anyway, it turned out she was a repeat offender. The judge was unsympathetic that the owner's dog bit her while breaking into the said owner's property. The dog got off, she went to jail, and Daniel and I went for drinks later. And the rest, as they say, is history." She laughed. "Isn't it amazing what goes around comes around? After Jackie being such a bitch to so many of us at school, to find herself in a position when one of her victims finally got the last say. That's the sort of story which would make a great movie."

"It would. Life certainly does turn full circle sometimes. Maybe in prison she learnt there's more to life than bullying people and taking the easy way to prosperity." She peeked at her watch, suddenly seeking a way to diplomatically extract herself from the conversation. "I better keep going. I've got an early morning conference and I've not yet seen everything." She stood and offered her hand to Robin. "It was great to catch up with you again. But if I'm going to make any sense in the morning I'm going to have to push on."

"Likewise," Robin said, taking the proffered hand. "Make sure you don't go without seeing the auditorium. Someone's gone to a great deal of trouble to create a visual history of our school years. The range of research and photos is amazing. Mind you, given the shape some people are now I expect there are a few who'd probably be more comfortable *not* seeing what's on the walls." She walked with Rhiannon to the door. "Of course, you're not one of them. I expect if I don't see you again, I'll at least *hear* about you Rhiannon. I look forward to your next book, whatever it may be."

"Thanks." Rhiannon beat a hasty exit before she could be accosted by anyone else. She rounded the corner leading to the auditorium, conscious of the raucous sounds coming down the corridor from the teacher's common area. The escalation in noise made it sound more akin to Parliamentary question time than any kind of meaningful discussion. She hurried down the corridor to the auditorium. Unlike the library and common area, Rhiannon was relieved to see this part of the reunion lacked the crowds filling the other areas.

The entrance to the soundproof auditorium was closed. Yet the light from the darkened windows and under the doors was sufficient evidence it was still open for people to walk through and recall school memories, for some with more fondness than others.

Rhiannon noiselessly opened the door and found herself irrepressibly cast back twenty years in time. Her regression had very little to do with the multitude of photos adorning almost every spare area of the back wall. What triggered the recall was the sound emanating from the piano in the front far right corner of the room. The soft lighting made the figure at the piano hard to define. The music coming from the instrument ensured the player could never be mistaken for anyone else.

Cowan Grammar Year Twelve

RHIANNON WAS DEVASTED by Ginny's death. The memorial service held by the school did little to assuage her pain. Despite comforting words offered to her by students and teachers alike, she felt hollow inside. In the period immediately following the service she concealed her loss through continuing to keep an eye out for students subjected to Jackie's bullying. This at least afforded her a tenuous link with Ginny and how they had first met.

A month after the memorial service she found herself again in the office of the vice principal.

Mr. Jackson consulted a page. He stood and walked around his desk, carrying the page with him. "How are you Miss Sharp?" He took a seat.

She tried to gauge whether his query was anything more than a polite conversation starter. His earnest features were testimony it was not. "It's hard, sir." She looked down at her hands. "It's so very hard."

"First your parents and now Virginia. It's no wonder you're finding things difficult. One such loss would be enough to break many people." He placed the paper on the coffee table between them. "I'm very worried about you Rhiannon, as are your teachers," he said, choosing his words carefully. "I understand you're very quiet in class."

Rhiannon nodded.

"I'm told, I might add, it is a relief for some of your teachers.

But for the majority of the others, they're very much missing your thought-provoking interjections."

She shrugged non-commitally. It wouldn't be hard to guess who the teachers were who were relieved she was silent, not that she cared either way at the moment.

"Have you given any further thought regarding seeking professional support?"

She crossed her legs, creating a further barrier between the two of them. "I haven't but thank you for mentioning it after the memorial service. I just can't come to grips with the idea of speaking about Ginny to an absolute stranger."

He covertly glanced at the paper in front of him. "I expect what I'm about to say is the furthest thing on your mind. But it would be remiss of me not to discuss the matter with you. Your teachers have seen a noticeable drop in your grades since you commenced year twelve. This is one of the most important years of your life," he said compassionately. "And I'll always be here to speak whenever you wish. I know it's hard for you to hear this, but you must find a way to move on."

Rhiannon bowed her head. On a cerebral level she knew everything he was saying was true. Emotionally though it was another matter. "I know. It's just I can't seem to get motivated."

Mr. Jackson leant back in his chair. "Your physical education teacher mentioned you'd given up team sports. Are you doing anything to keep physically active?"

"I've put more focus into running and have taken up triathlons." At least these provided her the opportunity for minimal interaction while still retaining her physical fitness. In reality, it was more about escaping the pain she felt. She would often run until she couldn't run any more.

"Ms. Jenkins mentioned as much. Is it helping?"

"It gives me the freedom to think. Cycling to school also allows me to manage an early run and still get to lessons on time. It's better than doing nothing."

"It is indeed." Mr. Jackson stroked the top of his lip between his thumb and forefinger. "I understand you've been having some problems with your pushbike."

Rhiannon struggled to tamp down the anger threatening to bubble to the surface. Someone had been letting down her tires. She was sure it was Jackie or one of her minions. She'd run into Jackie two days after Ginny's memorial service only to have her scoff at Ginny's or, as she called her, 'four eyes' death. Had it not been for Ms. Matheson's timely intervention, Rhiannon was sure she would have flattened Jackie right in the middle of the corridor. She collected herself and returned her focus to Mr. Jackson's expectant face.

"I have. I also lost a wheel last week." She knew Jackie wouldn't be so stupid to confront her again, not after what had nearly happened in the hallway. This was merely her way of breaking her down. But Rhiannon hid her feelings deep, swearing to herself she wouldn't give Jackie the satisfaction of seeing how much it was affecting her.

"Any idea who might be doing this?" Mr. Jackson queried.

"It's nothing I can't handle."

"It's not what I asked. But I can see I'm not going to get an answer from you." Mr. Jackson rose from his seat and reached for the phone. "You've certainly got more important things you need to focus on than mysteriously flat tyres and missing wheels."

He punched a number into the phone's keypad. "Andrew, it's Stephen Jackson here. Could you please arrange to have Miss Sharp stow her bicycle under the stage in your maintenance shed? I understand it's a little unusual. But in this case, I would appreciate it if you could make an exception. Thank you. I'll send her down to get a key from you. Bye." He returned his focus to Rhiannon. "That was Mr. Fogarty, our maintenance manager. He'll have a key waiting for you."

"Thank you, sir, but it will be okay."

Mr. Jackson held up his hand. "It will be now. For your own sake, I do need you to focus on your studies rather than be bothered by such goings on." He opened his door, effectively ending any further discussion. "My door will always be open if you need to talk."

THE WARM ORANGE light of dawn bathed the upper quad as Rhiannon wheeled her bike through the gates and to the maintenance door. It had been a damp ride this morning, but she didn't care. She dug into her jacket pocket, pulled out a key she'd received the day prior and unlocked the door. To one side at the rear of the space was the spot cleared by Mr. Fogarty for her to stow her bike.

Locking the wheel stand into place, Rhiannon looked up. The muted sounds of a piano wafted down from the auditorium above. She didn't realise anyone else was here at such an early hour of the morning. Despite not taking music during her schooling years she was reasonably sure the piece was classical. And whoever was playing it was very good.

She locked the door of the maintenance shed and walked up the stairs to the door at the rear of the hall.

Rhiannon unobtrusively slipped inside and took a seat in the back row. Relieved the girl playing the piano had not heard her, she sat, mesmerised by the sounds pouring forth. She reached down and snagged a towel from her bag, using it to wipe the excess water and perspiration from her body while she listened to the glorious sounds coming from the instrument. The composition was so haunting, as if whoever had created such music had suffered a terrible loss. Unable to translate into words, the composer instead sought solace in music, hoping, in some small yet significant way to convey what they were suffering and project the pain away from themselves.

The ability of the piece to encapsulate the depth of her own loss astounded Rhiannon. She sat back and released a ragged breath. Like the music, she was doing exactly the same thing in pursuing solitary sports and keeping people at arm's length, convinced she'd suffered too much to ever let anyone so close again. The haunting melody encased her in a cocoon of sorrow. She leant forward, placed her head in her hands and silently wept.

The person at the piano continued on, too absorbed in the music to be aware of her solo audience. Rhiannon wasn't sure how long she'd sat there sobbing. Drained and yet strangely calm for the first time since the memorial service, she wiped her eyes, grabbed her sports bag from the chair she'd placed it on and noiselessly made her way out of the auditorium.

From that day on it became part of Rhiannon's morning ritual. She arrived early at school yet not early enough to arrive before the pianist. In the few times she did she would wait in the maintenance shed for the sounds above to begin, only then stealthily entering the hall and sitting in her usual spot in the back row. She would listen for at least half an hour before leaving to shower and change for the coming day.

While the arrangements the pianist played could never replace the loss she felt over Ginny, they helped her to realise she must reconcile this part of her life and move on. To remain in mourning for her and the unrequited love Rhiannon felt for her was an insult to the vivacity of Ginny and the all-too-short life she had lived.

RHIANNON GENTLY CLOSED the auditorium door and tip

toed to her seat. She went to place her bag next to her when the music came to a halt, filling the surrounds with an awkward silence.

"You know if you wish to sit and listen, I wouldn't mind if you moved a little closer. I won't bite."

Rhiannon froze, her bag hovering over the chair beside her. *How long has she known I was here?* "It's fine, I can hear it okay from where I am." She placed her bag down. "Besides, I'd hate to disturb you in the middle of playing. You're very good, you know."

The student stopped rearranging her sheet music and rose from her chair. Walking toward Rhiannon was a slight-figured girl, the crest on her blazer indicating she was also a senior. Pulled back in a ponytail was a mass of gossamer fine light brown hair interspersed with hints of honey. This complemented a fine-boned face which had the most amazing eyes. Their incredible shade of verdant green reminded Rhiannon of the lush forests she'd visited with Isabella, in New Zealand.

She paused in front of Rhiannon and held out her hand. "I'm Angela Drayton and you are?"

She closed her slightly open mouth and studied the offered hand, the fingers long and delicate yet obviously possessing the strength needed to convey the intensity of the music in the manner she did. She wiped her sweaty hand on her lycra shorts and carefully took Angela's. "Rhiannon Sharp. I don't think I've ever seen you until I began listening to you in here. I'm sure I would have remembered."

Angela smiled. "You know I could say the same thing. Of course, it's not that your reputation doesn't precede you."

Rhiannon's eyes widened.

Angela held up her hands placatingly. "I didn't mean to shock you. What I meant to say was your reputation for standing up for those regularly bullied by some of our more dull, good for nothing classmates is well known. As for us ever meeting, I don't think we have. May I sit down?"

Rhiannon shifted her bag, allowing space for Angela to sit beside her.

"I suppose it's because we don't exactly have the same senior curriculum. Mine is very music oriented. Yours is more focussed on..." Angela eyes flitted over Rhiannon's perspiration-clad clothes. "Outdoors pursuits."

"I also study Gaelic," Rhiannon blurted, wondering why she all at once felt the need to qualify her academic pursuits.

"I didn't mean to be rude. I wasn't aware you took Gaelic as a subject."

"Why should I be offended when what you've said is essentially true? Other than the one language, my studies are primarily historical rather than musically focussed. My junior years capably confirmed my lack of musical talent. Thankfully for teacher *and* student, after finishing my mandatory four years of the subject I was happy to move on to something more suited to my strengths."

Angela rested her elbow on the chair. "You've been listening to me for about a month, haven't you?"

"I hope I didn't disturb you," Rhiannon replied, frustrated Angela had been aware of her presence even from the beginning.

Angela waved dismissively. "It doesn't bother me. It's just I suppose I was used to having the school to myself at this time of the morning."

Rhiannon tilted her head. "You never acknowledged I was in the hall. You played as if there wasn't any interruption whatsoever."

"You were terribly good at entering and leaving very quietly. In the past I've had cleaners interrupt me and they would put a herd of rampaging elephants to shame."

"How did you know I was here?"

"I'm not sure but I knew it on the first morning. It was almost as if I could sense another presence in the hall. I assumed you were more comfortable to sit and listen than to make conversation, which suited me fine. My training requires me to practice day and night if I'm to be accepted into the Australasian Conservatorium of Music at the end of the year."

"You sound good enough to be there already. Not that I'm any judge of course." Rhiannon studied Angela's face. "You play with such emotion. It's as if you're an extension of the piano."

Angela blushed. "I'm not used to hearing such praise. But you're right though. I do sometimes get carried away."

"Where do you go, I mean in your mind, when you play?"

Angela glanced at the piano. "I find myself trying to picture the composer's frame of mind when they originally wrote the music. What were they doing? Where were they at the time of writing? Why did they write like they did? Were they rewarded for their efforts? Had they been chastised, rebuffed by a suitor, perhaps suffered a loss? Focussing on the motive behind the music allows me to put myself in their shoes per se and play with a depth sometimes not immediately obvious through merely notes on a page."

Rhiannon scanned the auditorium, reflecting on Angela's words and her own recent loss. A featherlight touch to her arm brought her back to the present.

"Is that why you sometimes cry when you listen to me play?"

Rhiannon shifted uncomfortably, disconcerted to think Angela was aware of the grief she had tried so desperately to hide. Exposing the root of her pain wasn't an option with this almost stranger beside her. But for reasons she couldn't quite fathom she was decidedly reluctant to lie. She met Angela's eyes. "You could say that," she said, her voice hoarse.

"I know we don't know each other terribly well. But if you want to talk, I'm told I'm a good listener. I promise whatever we discuss won't go any further." She shook her head ruefully. "It's not as if I have anyone to share anything with should you happen to tell me anyway. My studies keep me fairly absorbed, leaving little time for the trivialities of adolescent friendships."

Rhiannon blinked. Angela's straightforwardness held no hint of pretension or bitterness. I suppose it's who she is, and she's driven to succeed. But at what cost, she thought.

"You must be very serious about your career. Is it so important to you, even over friendship?"

"My music is the centre of my life," Angela replied, self-assuredly. "I've trained for so many years for the one thing, which is to train with very the best at the Conservatorium. I've been chasing this dream for as long as I can remember. I suppose friends just fell by the wayside." She smiled. "Not to worry though. There'll be time once I'm there to form friendships."

Rhiannon lowered her head, not allowing Angela to see the shadow of pain which flickered across her features. She composed herself and raised her eyes. "Life is full of missed opportunities Angela. Your music is obviously important to you. The depth of skill and emotion when you play is obvious testimony. But don't wait too long for something you think will be there when you expect it to be. Don't hold people at arm's length for too long or you may find when you finally lower your arm there isn't anyone there. Trust me." Rhiannon offered Angela a forlorn smile. "I know." She rose and soundlessly left the auditorium.

RHIANNON RAPPED HER knuckles on the table in front of her. "Okay, quiet down in the back there. As you all know our last day of school tomorrow is the one day of the year when we can get away with just about anything."

Kim Hunt, the school captain, waved her hand. "As long as it doesn't cross the boundaries into bad taste, character assassination or irreversible damage."

"Thanks for reminding everyone Kim. As your appointed leader of the muck up day proceedings, I don't need to tell you we have plenty to do. But at this rate we'll get nothing done tonight." Rhiannon cast her eyes over the faces before her. "Susan is everything good to go for the bubbles in the school fountain? They need to be done first thing tomorrow morning in time for Mrs. Remerson's arrival."

"I'm all over it Tack, like a seagull on a chip." The seniors shared a laugh.

Rhiannon ticked one of the tasks off the clipboard she held in her hands. "You all know what we're about to do has to be done very carefully. The cleaners are still around the school as is the head cleaner, Mrs. Davis. You need to get your gear to each of the teacher's studies without being detected." Rhiannon consulted the sheet she held.

"Robin, you're in the English study with the balloons. That's going to take a lot of hot air." Rhiannon smiled. "But I'm sure you can manage. Can I have fifteen volunteers to help Robin?"

Willing hands shot into the air. "Great. I'll need another fifteen in the math office. It's the other one which we'll fill with balloons. We'll also need thirty girls to carry the boxes for the science and teacher's common area. These are the furthest away, so I suggest you put out early warning posts along the corridor."

Rhiannon checked more items off the list. "That just leaves the social science and music study. Have we got the paper for those?"

"Over here Tack," came a call from the rear of the group.

Rhiannon acknowledged her thanks. "Angela, are you okay to cover down on the music study?"

"I am. I know it's only small, but I could use another pair of hands."

"No worries," Rhiannon replied. "I'll come and give you a hand once I've checked to make sure everything's underway. The rest of you work on the social science offices. You know where to find me if you need me."

Rhiannon looked at the expectant faces in front of her. "Let's try and have this all done by seven o'clock. And for heaven's sake keep the noise inside the rooms down to a dull roar please. The last thing I want is for Mrs. Davis to find out."

RHIANNON GAVE THE pre-arranged two quick and two long raps to the door of the music study. She surreptitiously checked the corridor and entered.

Angela closed the door behind her. "Secret knocks and warning posts. It sounds more like a military operation than muck up day."

Rhiannon put her hands on her hips and smiled. "Would you expect anything less?"

Angela grabbed another sheet of newspaper off the table and proceeded to scrunch it into a ball. "I suppose not. I've no doubt all the team sport you play gives you an insight into strategy. If it was left to me, we'd all still be in the senior breakout area." She threw the ball into the mounting pile on the floor.

Rhiannon joined Angela's newspaper efforts. "And if it was left to me to play the piano tomorrow, we'd all be running screaming from the auditorium. It's a skill you possess which I'll never have. Have you decided what you're going to play?"

"I have. And before you ask it's a secret. It's something I've been working on."

"You wrote it yourself?"

"I did, and I only recently finished it. I hope you like it," Angela replied softly and reached for another piece of newspaper.

Rhiannon waited for her to turn. "If you wrote it, I'm sure I will. Will I get to listen to it during your rehearsal tomorrow morning?"

"You won't. The hall's already set up for the luncheon. You won't be able to hear it until I play the piece after the speeches tomorrow."

"It doesn't matter, I'll look forward to it all the same."

They worked silently beside each other, systematically bunching up newspaper which had been collected for months before throwing it onto the ever-increasing pile on the floor.

Angela reached for another paper from the pile in the corner. She turned and tripped, barely managing to check her forward momentum.

Rhiannon reached out to her and stopped when Angela righted herself. "Are you okay?"

"I'm fine. It's these smooth soled shoes and all this paper. They make for a slippery combination."

Rhiannon cast her eyes around the waist high mound of paper which after two hours of non-stop work capably covered the floor. She lifted her foot and tapped her shoe. "It wouldn't be a problem if you wore joggers. Always good for grip."

"And not in keeping with the uniform code." Angela threw a wad of newspaper in her direction. "I don't know how you get away with it."

"As I've said to you on many occasions..." Rhiannon whipped her head to the door and held up her hand at the voice in the hallway, just outside the room. "It's the head cleaner," she whispered.

Angela froze. "She's coming in here isn't she?"

Rhiannon put her finger to her lips and carefully waded to the entrance. She put her ear against the door, listening for the footfall of the cleaner to pass. Satisfied she was far enough down the corridor, Rhiannon stepped out and very carefully closed the door behind her.

"Mrs. Davis, can I help you?" she asked, holding her ink-stained hands behind her.

Mrs. Davis jumped and turned. "Miss Sharp isn't it? Where did you come from? Never mind. I believe you're the leader of these muck up day activities."

"Yes Miss, I am."

"Then I must say I'm most concerned at some of the goings on currently happening in this school. The shift for my cleaners is about to end and I hear there are some inappropriate shenanigans occurring in this building."

Rhiannon couldn't help but wonder when shenanigans weren't inappropriate. Rather than highlight this, she instead forced her face into an image of innocence. "What sort of actions do you mean Miss? Could you be more specific? I've been very careful in ensuring whatever we do doesn't leave any lasting harm to people or property."

Mrs. Davis scrutinised Rhiannon's face. "I know you've had your fun with some of the teachers of this school. But you've always been very courteous to me and my cleaners. Regardless, I've heard you and the students are filling the teachers' studies with all sorts of material. Papers, balloons, boxes and other such matter."

"You're joking! I can't believe this is happening. Let me assure you Mrs. Davis nothing permanent is being done to the school. I've allocated my tasks and I believe they're being fol-lowed to the letter." Rhiannon knew she hadn't entirely told the truth. However, she hadn't exactly lied either. The students *were* doing exactly what she'd tasked them to do.

The incredulous look on Mrs. Davis' face revealed she was far from being convinced.

"I'll tell you what I'll do. I'll call my teams together and reconfirm the tasks I've given them. If there is any irreparable damage, then I'll ensure it is cleared up right away."

"I don't know. It's getting late." Mrs. Davis said, a hint of uncertainty in her voice.

Rhiannon moved to the door of the music study. "If it's not enough, I'm willing to go through every study with you." She grasped the door handle. "Commencing with this one. We can check just to be sure. I know your day is about finished and this may take a bit of unpaid time. However, if that's what has to be done then so be it."

Hesitation shadowed Mrs. Davis' features. She quickly cast a glance at her watch. "My staff and I are already fifteen minutes over shift and that's time Mrs. Remerson will not compensate my team or me for. I am going to have to trust your judgement Miss Sharp. But all the same, I'd appreciate it if you would contact your teams and confirm nothing permanent is being done."

"Yes, miss."

"I also want you to ensure there will not be additional work for my cleaners at the end of tomorrow. Should this not be the case you will leave me no recourse than to speak with the principal." Mrs. Davis turned and stomped down the stairs.

Rhiannon breathed a sigh of relief. She opened the door of the music study, which was strangely vacant. She closed the door and scanned the cramped quarters. "Angela," she whispered. "Where are you?"

There was a slight rustle of papers and Angela surfaced in the far corner. She was obviously seated, with only her head clearing the mass of newspaper concealing the rest of her body. "I can't believe you did that! What would you have done if she'd called your bluff? When I heard the door handle rattle it was all I could do to dive for the furthest corner and hope she didn't start removing the paper piece by scrunched up piece."

Rhiannon laughed and walked to where Angela sat. "It was only me. But had she asked me to open the door, I expect there would have been some fast explaining to do. I was hoping when you heard the handle turning, you'd have the presence of mind to hide," she kicked the bundle, "in all of this. That way the only thing Mrs. Davis would have seen was a space full of paper. She'd have been outraged. I'd have been suitably shocked. I'd have told her I'd look into it right away. All things said and done, you concealed yourself pretty well." She held out her hand to Angela. "Let me help you up. I'm sure you've got newspaper ink all over you."

Angela was almost upright when she began to fall. Without sufficient purchase on the paper-covered floor, she careered toward Rhiannon, her arms outstretched in front of her in an attempt to break her fall.

With ease borne out of years of physical activity, Rhiannon effortlessly caught Angela's forearms, grasping them firmly while in the same action pulling Angela to her.

Rhiannon looked down and softened her grip on Angela's arms. She had acted instinctually, needing to stop her from falling face first into the paper. Drawing Angela to her had seemed a logical course of action. But the feelings now coursing through her were far from logical. How long had she felt this way? Was it only because Angela was so close to her?

She returned her gaze to Angela and waited silently as Angela's eyes searched her face, as if seeking something.

"I was sure I was going to fall. Thank you," Angela said, her voice barely above a whisper.

Rhiannon trailed her hands down to Angela's and slightly grasped them. "I would never let you fall." She mentally kicked herself at how her words sounded. "I mean, I was afraid you'd hurt your hands if you fell."

Angela swallowed deeply, her eyes never leaving Rhiannon's. "Of course. That makes inherent sense. What between the paper and my playing and all, what would have happened, it could have been disastrous. Oh crap, the way I'm carrying on you'd think I'd hit my head."

"It's probably the shock. Your body's reacting without thinking."

In concert the two glimpsed down to where Angela's thumb lightly stroked Rhiannon's hand.

Rhiannon's breathing hitched at the energy evoked through their connection. While there had been unintended touches between them throughout the year, this was different. An unusual warmth began to form in the pit of her stomach.

Despite the blush suffusing her features, Angela made no attempt to remove her hand. Silence enveloped them and, for a short moment in time, it felt as if they were the only people in the world.

Rhiannon was at a loss. While Angela stroked her hand, her thoughts returned to twelve months ago when she and Ginny had gone their separate ways for the Christmas holidays. There was so much she had wanted to say then and yet she'd held back. Did she want to run the risk of doing that again, not saying what she really meant? Was she willing to take a chance?

She gathered her courage and smiled sadly at Angela. "You know, I'm going to miss you when we leave here."

Angela's features were inscrutable, as if she was fighting something she wasn't quite sure of. "I..." The sound of a turning door handle caused Angela to release her intimate grip, as if realising they shouldn't have been that close.

Both turned when Robin stepped through the door. "Hey, Tack, nice job. You too Angela."

"Thanks," Angela replied.

"I'm glad I found you though. It seems Mrs. Davis is on the warpath and some of the girls have taken refuge in our breakout area."

Rhiannon silently cursed. What was Angela going to say? She closed her eyes and rubbed the back of her neck and returned her full focus to Robin. "I know. She came by here earlier. I assured her everything was okay, so you can let the girls know they can carry on. If we don't get a move on, we're going to be here all night," she finished frustratedly, less about the halt to work than the interruption to her conversation with Angela.

"I tried to get them to get on with it but they were a little reluctant," Robin said uncertainly. "Besides being as ugly as a bucket full of farts when she's angry, Mrs. Davis isn't terribly nice with people she finds making a mess in *her* school."

Rhiannon glanced down at Angela's light touch on her arm. "Maybe you should go and speak with them. Don't worry, I'll finish up here and you can get the others back to work."

Rhiannon clenched her jaw. This was definitely not her preferred option and yet it was obviously what had to be done. She scrutinised Angela's face. *What I very much want to do is continue the conversation we were having before we were rudely interrupted,* she thought, vainly hoping Angela could somehow read her mind.

"Tack?"

Rhiannon composed herself and returned her focus to Robin's expectant face. "Okay, let's go and get these people going again. Knowing most of them, it was probably more an excuse to take a coffee break."

She waded through the paper to the door. Passing through it, her gaze strayed to the corner where Angela now stood. Her back was to her while she continued the task at hand, making it impossible for Rhiannon to further gauge Angela's reaction to the words she'd spoken earlier. She closed the door and resolutely strode down the hall to the senior study.

AS THE DOOR closed Angela turned. She let out a shaky breath, attempting to reconcile what had just happened. There had been glancing touches between them during the course of the year. But it was nothing like this. What they just shared was so...encompassing. And I had to start babbling as if I was a woman possessed, she thought. She rolled her eyes. If that wasn't enough why did she stroke Rhiannon's hand? She'd never done that with anyone before. What must have Rhiannon thought? Would she still want to be friends?

Angela whipped a piece of newspaper from the pile, crushed it vigorously and threw it to the far side of the room. While there were some students from music class she sat with at times, Rhiannon was different. She was the only real friend Angela had. And when Rhiannon said she was going to miss her Angela felt something she'd never felt in her life. But what exactly did Rhiannon mean? Given Rhiannon's popularity, Angela was certain there were many people Rhiannon was going to miss as they were going to miss her.

She rubbed the side of her head. And what was she going to say? Sorry, I don't know what's wrong with me. Sorry I'm stroking your hand but for reasons I can't quite explain it feels the right thing to do. Angela craned her neck and closed her eyes; grateful Robin's interruption had stopped her from making a complete fool of herself. Maybe it was for the best. After all, it was her studies she needed to focus on. There would be plenty of time for everything else. Despite her silent affirmation, she couldn't help but wonder who she was trying to convince, if anyone. She slowly picked up another piece of newspaper and scrunched it into a ball and distractedly let it slip from her hands onto the pile in front of her.

RHIANNON SWUNG OPEN the study door, the noise harshly reverberating against the wall it collided with, causing the group inside to jump to their feet. Rhiannon inwardly chuckled at the sight of more than one senior with coffee running down the front of their blazer.

"Robin tells me you're afraid of Mrs. Davis?"

The cacophony created by a multitude of voices speaking all at once caused Rhiannon to hold up her hand. "One at a time please."

"She's been patrolling the corridors and she scares the willies out of me," one senior protested.

"It's okay. I ran into her and we spoke. She's gone home now. Can you, if you've finished where you're working..." Rhiannon scowled at the number of girls who were looking anywhere else but in her direction. "Is *anyone* finished?"

"Blowing up those balloons is very hard," Robin wailed. "We needed a rest. That's when Susan came in and said Mrs. Davis was walking up and down the corridors, muttering like a mad woman as she went."

"I understand and can't blame you for taking a break. But there's nothing to worry about, so can we all please get back to work? After all, we've got the chicken and champagne supper to go to." She watched eyes light up around the room. "But *only* when we've finished what we're doing here. How about I come and see where you're all up to?"

Rhiannon spent the next thirty minutes taking a quick tour of each of the studies. She was generally happy with the progress and was sure another hour should see most of the work complete.

She made her way back to where Angela had been working, her unruffled outward demeanour at odds with her raging internal emotions. She opened the door.

"Damn it." The lights were out, the space empty except for the accumulation of newspaper now completely covering the desks. She hurried to the senior study. Her eyes tracked to where Angela normally stored her backpack, its absence confirming what Rhiannon feared. She had left for the evening.

Rhiannon walked the corridors and wondered whether Angela's departure was because of the conversation they had begun just before she'd been called away. She'd chosen her words carefully, attempting to not disclose what her true feelings were. But what was Angela going to say?

She stopped and leant up against a wall, eyes closed in frustration. Tomorrow was the last day of school and the likelihood of her speaking privately with Angela was borderline at best. She cow-kicked the wall with the back of her heel. There wouldn't be a piano rehearsal either. She had to somehow find time in what promised to be an already full day, to speak with her. Rhiannon pushed herself off the wall and continued down the corridor to do a final check on the 'sabotage' before at last calling it a day.

Chapter Three

THE FINAL DAY of Rhiannon's schooling years flew by and it wasn't long before she found herself at the graduation luncheon. Her eyes tracked the room seeking out Angela. She smiled. Of course, she's with her music teachers. Where else would she be?

Oblivious to Rhiannon's appraisal, Angela spoke animatedly, her hands fluidly demonstrating something, a rare smile lighting up her features.

Why hadn't she recognised her feelings for Angela earlier? Or had she known about them all along and refused to act on them? A hand on her shoulder brought her out of her introspection.

"Rhiannon it's almost time for the vice captain's address. I was wondering if I could first have a word with you."

"Of course, Ms. Matheson." She followed the English master, grateful of the chance to speak with her one final time before the day's activities drew to a close.

HER VICE-CAPTAIN'S ADDRESS was short yet heartfelt, thanking the staff for their efforts and wishing the graduating class the best in their endeavours. From her vantage point on the stage she could effortlessly scan the crowd, her eyes resting sometimes a little too long on Angela. She sat near to the piano, in readiness for her performance.

"And good luck everyone." The audience clapped enthusiastically as Rhiannon gathered her speech and headed off the stage.

"Thank you, Miss Sharp," Mrs. Remerson said. "Now ladies, after what must seem forever for some of you, at last the day has arrived."

Rhiannon blocked out the words of a woman she had very little time for. Walking back to her seat she glanced casually across to where Angela had taken her place at the piano. Rhiannon placed her notes on the table.

Ms. Matheson pulled out the chair for her. "Are you going to sit down?"

"No," Rhiannon whispered. "I think I'll get a bit closer to the piano. I hear she's very good."

Ms. Matheson smiled enigmatically and pushed the chair back into place. "I'm sure she is." She made a shooing motion with her hand. "Off you go. I'll catch up with you before the end of the function."

Rhiannon stealthily weaved her way through the group, hopeful a seat close to Angela would give her the opportunity to speak with her once she'd finished her composition. She chose a seat immediately behind but slightly off to one side, thus affording her an unimpeded view of Angela.

While Mrs. Remerson droned on, Rhiannon watched Angela flex her hands and centre herself. She'd seen her do this the very few times when of a morning she'd arrived before Angela started her practice.

"What lies in front of you as you leave Cowan Grammar today may seem insurmountable but surmount it you must." In emphasising her point, Mrs. Remerson's hand slapped the lectern.

Rhiannon blinked and returned her focus to Mrs. Remerson's address, clapping when required, despite her interest firmly being elsewhere.

Finally, Mrs. Remerson's address came to an end. A hush settled over the gathering and the opening chords of Angela's concerto began. It was not as sombre as some she'd heard Angela play. Yet nor was it light and frivolous either. The music seemed to call on the listener to remember, like one might do when reminiscing days long past.

Angela played with the same focus Rhiannon had come to know, her fingers sweeping over the keys, barely touching them. Although she'd heard her play many times before, this was different. She knew the arrangement was meant for everyone there. Yet Rhiannon felt as if the music solely focussed on her. It was as if it were telling her something. It bespoke of wonder and joy, friendship and wanting and something much deeper she couldn't quite put her finger on. She silently cursed Angela's missed opportunity to play it during her regular rehearsal on that last morning. At least she would have been able to ask her about the piece. She would have loved to understand just what Angela was trying to convey and why it made her feel the way it did.

She hit the last key and there was a stunned silence followed by wild applause throughout the hall. Angela shyly acknowledged the group and turned her back to collect her music.

Conversations in the auditorium recommenced, the room again filling with hubbub.

Rhiannon rose from her chair and stood, slightly to the left of the upright piano. "Angela that was beautiful."

"Thank you. It means a lot to me coming from you."

Angela's candour briefly surprised Rhiannon and she struggled to form a coherent sentence. "It's lucky few people know you can play so well. Or you might have had more than me listening to you."

"I was happy it was only you," Angela replied.

Gazing into each other's eyes the crowd and noise surrounding them ceased to exist. They were again alone like they had been during many a morning practice. Angela's face was reminiscent of what Rhiannon had seen last night. Her eyes were piercingly intense, as if she was searching for something in Rhiannon's own. An excited squeal from the masses behind them broke the moment. "Do you want a hand with your music?"

"No!" Angela clasped the sheet possessively to her chest. She closed her eyes then opened them, letting out a deep breath. "Thank you," she said, this time her voice more measured.

"Angela, can we —"

Angela held up her hand. She picked up her bag and turned to Rhiannon. "I've got to go."

"But..." Before Rhiannon could get any further Angela was gone, manoeuvring her way through the luncheon tables and to the rear of the auditorium. Temporarily stunned and then shocked into action, Rhiannon went to follow her.

Mrs. Remerson stepped in front of her, effectively halting her progress. "Miss Sharp, a moment please."

"Yes Miss," Rhiannon managed, still watching Angela.

"You've come such a long way since joining us. That was a nice speech you made. Why, it reminds me of one I heard when I first began to teach."

Rhiannon nodded absently, barely aware or in fact interested in what Mrs. Remerson had to say. Instead, she watched Angela leave the hall.

Chapter Four

NOW TWENTY YEARS later, Rhiannon again stood in the auditorium listening to music from someone she hadn't heard play in this space since the day of the Year 12 luncheon. The final chords of the classical piece died in the surrounds of the sound-proof hall. Angela tilted her head as if listening for something, then she lowered it.

"Hello Rhiannon," she said, not turning away from the piano.

Rhiannon walked between the rows of chairs to where Angela sat. "It always amazed me how you seemed to know I was there." Rhiannon came to a halt beside Angela. "I could have been anyone just now. Why were you so sure it was me?"

When Angela finally looked at her Rhiannon couldn't help but feel they were again back at school on their last day. Angela's piercing green eyes studied her own, as if searching for something.

Rhiannon silently took in the same face she hadn't seen this close in such a long time. The years had been kind to Angela, her delicate features much the same yet with a greater degree of maturity and assuredness about them. The teenage fullness was gone, replaced with soft yet defined lines, her high cheekbones elegantly framing her eyes. Rhiannon spared a glance at Angela's lips. Lightly dusted with a subtle colour, they gave her an air of confidence and yet introverted sensuality at the same time. The cream silk shirt and black slacks did little to hide the lithe figure they contained. The long, delicate fingers interlaced in Angela's lap were just like Rhiannon remembered. They belied no hint of nervousness, if in fact there was any.

Angela blinked, as if breaking the spell. "I always knew. I can't explain why. It was a feeling I seemed to get when you were in the hall." A slight blush suffused her cheeks. "Maybe it's how you walked. I have to say though, for a jock you were surprisingly light on your feet," she finished, charting the conversation onto safer, more inconsequential ground.

Rhiannon raised her brows. "I believe you're mistaking me for my noisier male counterparts. Besides, on a soccer field it's better to be able to sneak up on an opponent and steal the ball from them than give them the time to get away from you because you're too loud in your approach. And these days, on and off the field, I've found it to be a very effective strategy."

"You seem to have made a name for yourself in business circles. If what I've read about you is correct, you've a hand in a number of things. High profile mediation and negotiation and human resource management. And also, notwithstanding, in your spare time — if there is such a thing — writing."

Angela's awareness of her career filled Rhiannon with a warmth she hadn't felt in a while. "It keeps me busy," she deflected nonchalantly.

"That's one word for it. How do you find the hours in the day?"

For Rhiannon being busy was her sanity valve, keeping her occupied so she didn't have to think of other things. "Hey don't you talk! If the media is any indicator it seems you've been working just about non-stop since you left school. And I see you've achieved your goal. Australasian Conservatorium of Music alumni and concert pianist no less, feted by the world's best composers and symphony orchestras. That couldn't have left you much time either."

A shadow crossed Angela's features. She studied her hands and smiled ruefully. "It's the price of fame I expect. At least when I come home, I'm not as easily recognised as when we're overseas. When we're touring Lachie and I never get a moment to ourselves." She scanned the auditorium. "What's the time?"

Rhiannon creased her forehead. "Lachie? Who's Lachie?" she blurted.

Angela returned her gaze to Rhiannon's face. She frowned slightly, seemingly surprised by abruptness of Rhiannon's query. "He's my son. Do you have the time? Playing for a living means I've gotten used to never wearing a watch. Suffice to say it normally results in me being late for rehearsals if not missing them in their entirety." Not waiting for an answer, Angela's hands followed her eyes to Rhiannon's right wrist. She gently grasped Rhiannon's hand to better read the time.

Angela's touch was enough to send Rhiannon back to the moment they had shared in the music study the day before they graduated. So engrossed was she by the memories it evoked, she was oblivious to everything else, most notably Angela's sudden sense of urgency.

Angela released her hand and the spell was broken. She

closed the key lid, stood, and again returned her focus to Rhiannon. "I've got to go."

Angela's words shook her from her pensive state. "What do you mean you've got to go? I've only just found you." She could have kicked herself at the faux pas, wondering how Angela must have interpreted her words. "I mean we haven't even had a chance to catch up."

"I know. But the time has crept up on me. I told the babysitter I'd be home by ten at the latest. At this rate I'll barely have time to catch a taxi and be back there before the clock strikes the hour." Angela pulled herself into her jacket. She reached behind her neck and released her shoulder length hair free of the confines of the garment.

This isn't happening again. I haven't waited twenty years to have you leave even before I have the chance to finally speak to you about those last days at school, Rhiannon thought. She took a calming breath and tamped down an overwhelming desire to bombard Angela with questions.

"I might have a solution for you. I've seen about as much as I want to see here. If it's okay by you I could drive you home, before I head back to my hotel."

A shadow of doubt clouded Angela's features. "Are you sure you're leaving?"

"Absolutely, and besides, I've got a morning teleconference." Rhiannon motioned around the hall. "This was my last stop and then I was headed to my car."

"I don't want to take you out of your way."

"Trust me. You wouldn't be." It was only at that moment Rhiannon realised she didn't have a clue where Angela lived. She smiled inwardly. She could live three hours away and she'd still be happy to drive her there if it meant spending the time with her.

Angela folded her arms. "Where are you staying?"

"The Gables."

Angela dipped her head, in acknowledgement. "Only the best boutique hotel on this side of town. Is it as nice as they say?"

"It is," Rhiannon replied. It was the most expensive establishment on this side of Sydney, with commanding views of the harbour, especially from her room on the upper floor. "But it's only temporary. I'm waiting for the tenants who are currently in my house to finish their lease before I can move in." Angela headed for the rear door of the auditorium and Rhiannon followed, resolute she wouldn't lose sight of her like she'd done twenty years ago.

"At least for the next twelve months Sydney will be my home base." She reached out a hand and lightly stopped Angela's progress toward the exit. "So, can I take you home? Believe me, I wouldn't offer if I didn't want to."

"Thank you. Given how close your hotel is to where I live, it would be very foolish of me to refuse. And it's not much out of your way. Do you know Persimmon Street?"

"I do," Rhiannon replied.

"It's where we live. I believe The Gables is only a few blocks south of there."

"It's settled then. Let me show you to my car and I'll have you home in time to pay your babysitter." Both women silently made their way out of the school grounds, preoccupied with their own introspection.

THE SILENCE OF the sports car afforded Angela the privacy she needed to order her thoughts. She stared out the window, the lights of Sydney passing them by, all the while remembering how she felt when the auditorium door had opened.

Despite managing to catch up with a few of her teachers in the teacher's common area, it was self-evident she would gravitate to the one place she'd spent most of her schooling years. When she walked through the doors of the auditorium the piano had been too much of a temptation for her. Sitting down in front of the upright took her back years. She didn't know how long she'd sat at the instrument, often only vaguely aware of the people who regularly entered and exited the hall without interrupting her. That was until her final visitor.

As she had finished the closing ritard of what was to be her last piece for the evening, the door opened. Concentrating on the music yet casting her senses further, a smile rose unbidden to her face. An innate feeling deep inside her told her Rhiannon was in the hall. It was a strange sensation, a comforting reassuring presence and sense of calm that Rhiannon always evoked in her, unknowingly or otherwise.

Yet when she touched Rhiannon an entirely different feeling replaced that calm. What had been an innocent grasping of Rhiannon's hand transformed into something else. The strength and energy emanating from Rhiannon surprised her. In the recesses of her mind she was back in a space full of newspaper, falling, being caught and feeling a similar sensation. It was all she could do to force herself to release Rhiannon. And despite her protestations regarding Rhiannon's offer of a lift home, she was quietly pleased.

She shifted her focus from the city passing them by to the inside of the car and the reflection off her passenger window, which enabled Angela to clandestinely view Rhiannon's face. Bathed in the soft glow of the interior dashboard lights, her profile was silhouetted as she confidently shifted gears and negotiated the night traffic. Her assuredness was one of the many things Angela remembered about her. And from what she'd seen earlier in the hall, it was obvious Rhiannon kept herself in shape despite the intervening years. Her body still conveyed the same quiet strength which had set Rhiannon apart at school.

"Nice view?" A smile graced Rhiannon's face.

Angela bit her lip, wondering if she'd been caught. She turned to Rhiannon.

"Uh yes...I love the lights of the city," she replied lamely, grateful for the dark interior of the sportscar which masked her obvious embarrassment. "You said you were going to be here in Sydney for twelve months?"

Rhiannon nodded, her attention divided between Angela's inquiry and negotiating a roundabout.

"You mentioned something about a lease. I didn't know you owned a house in this area."

"I don't. It's my aunt's. After retirement she lived in the last Federation Style house in Durack Street, Balmoral."

"The design was popular around the turn of last century, wasn't it?"

"Yes, it was. Her home was in the Federation Queen Anne Style. She hung on grimly to it while all the others in the street were torn down and replaced with more modern options. She passed away a couple of years ago without ever having married. Her only other sibling, my mother, was killed years ago, in New Zealand."

"I remember you telling me about your parents."

Rhiannon nodded. "Aunt Isabella left her estate to me in her will. This included a lifetime of art and collectibles and a number of houses. I kept a few items which were very dear to me and auctioned most of the rest, giving the proceeds to charities I knew she supported. Given how much I travel, I didn't want the unnecessary burden of a property portfolio. Consequently, I'm now out of the property market except for the Durack street property and my parents' home in the New South Wales southern highlands."

"Who looks after the home in the southern highlands?"

"I have a manager, and she and her partner live on the property. They've been there for a long time now. They ensure its upkeep while at the same time having a place to live for as long as they wish."

"You must like it a lot if you kept it when you sold just about all the others."

"I do. It's a great place to get away from everything and find myself again. Of course, I haven't been able to get there as often as I'd like to."

"Just turn at this next light," Angela said.

Rhiannon indicated and rounded the corner. "Aunt Isabella's home, while not my favourite, gives me the ability to live in Sydney without being forced to pay the exorbitant costs associated with having to rent or buy a home here. So, my somewhat opulent current abode is only temporary. And for that I'm grateful."

"I know what you mean. Hotels, regardless of how nice they are, can be quite uncomfortable after a while. At the start of each tour they're a bit of a novelty to me. But when we're near the end, it becomes almost too much for Lachie and me to bear. Mind you, it does make coming home special. See the fence over there? Turn in there and we're here."

FOR RHIANNON, THE drive was over all too soon. There was still so much she wanted to say to Angela. She negotiated the wooded driveway and brought the car to a halt within walking distance of the front steps. A silence descended the vehicle, neither of them moving, the two of them searching to find something to say. Rhiannon twisted in her seat and faced Angela.

"It's been great seeing you again. But I feel as if we've barely had the chance to catch up. I'd like to do that if you want to. Would you mind having brunch with me tomorrow?" She held her breath, waiting for Angela's reply.

"Lunch would be better. It will give me the morning with Lachie before his grandmother picks him up for the first week of the school holidays. We sometimes get very little time together. It's nice to spend a morning with him. Mind you, knowing he's going out to grandma's place I'm not likely to get any sense out of him at all."

Relieved, Rhiannon exhaled. "Now that you mention it lunch would probably suit me also. It will allow me to get my teleconferencing over and done with, hopefully freeing me of clients who tend to try and contact me on a weekend."

"Does that happen often?"

"More than I care for but it's to be expected given I have clients all over the world. All the same my free time, which includes tomorrow, is sacred. Despite how much the deal is worth. How does one o'clock sound? I'll meet you in the lobby and we can go from there. And if you don't want to go too far the hotel does have quite a good restaurant and a very lovely view of Sydney Harbour."

"I've heard great things about The Gables restaurant. Strangely though, despite living close by I've never had the opportunity to eat there."

"Now you do. I'll arrange a reservation for the two of us when I get back." She reached into her pocket and pulled out her mobile. "Call me if your plans change and I'll do the same. What's your number? I'll text you so you have mine."

Angela quickly rattled off her cell number and watched Rhiannon's number appear equally rapidly on her mobile. "I'll need to remember to check it tomorrow. I don't usually carry it around on me." Angela grasped the handle and pulled the door open. "I'll see you at one o'clock tomorrow."

"I can't wait."

Angela eased herself out of the vehicle and into the cool night air. Heading up the path to her house, the motion sensor lighting picked up her presence.

Rhiannon watched Angela's retreating figure, her movements measured and yet assured, not too dissimilar to how she played the piano.

Angela reached the stairs, turned, waved, and continued her journey.

Rhiannon returned the wave and waited until the front door closed before starting the car and reversing down the driveway.

THE JOURNEY THROUGH the quiet suburban streets was a quick one and it wasn't long before Rhiannon pulled up at the front of the hotel. One of the hotel's valets opened her door and she alighted from the vehicle.

"Good evening ma'am. Are you a guest of the hotel?"

"I am. Rhiannon Sharp." She waited while he consulted his pad.

"Thank you, Ms. Sharp. Will you be needing the car again this evening?"

She handed the keys across to him. "No thanks. Could you please park it for me?" It was obvious this was his job. But her experience of hotels told her it was likely he wasn't regularly asked as politely as he'd just been to park a car. She suspected he often merely had keys thrown in his general direction.

He tipped two fingers in salute. "Certainly, ma'am."

She acknowledged his words and walked through the door opened by another hotel staff member, and into the foyer. Strolling to the elevators the quiet sounds of a piano playing in the bar checked her progress. Drawn by the music she headed into the predominantly empty surrounds.

The barman put down the glass he was polishing. "Good evening ma'am, can I get you anything?"

Rhiannon pointed to the bottle on the left of the top shelf. "May I have that single malt please?"

"Certainly." The barman pulled the bottle down and poured a generous nip into a heavy crystal glass. He reached for a smaller glass, filled it with water and placed it on a small silver tray, with an eye dropper. "Do you want me to open a tab for you ma'am?" He placed the drink and tray in front of Rhiannon.

"This one will be enough." Rhiannon used the dropper to place a measured amount of water into her glass. "If you could place it on suite 1205, Rhiannon Sharp."

He pressed the screen of the cash register in front of him. "Consider it done."

She picked up her glass and moved to the privacy of one of the intimately lit corners of the bar. She sat down, took a sip of her drink, and replayed the night's events.

It had been great to catch up with Elly. And it had been a very pleasant surprise to discover after all these years she was a lesbian. Rhiannon had often wondered. Finding out for sure certainly explained a lot of the tension she had often felt between the two of them. She couldn't help but wonder what might have happened had Elly turned up at the club that afternoon.

Memories of Ginny which had resurfaced during the evening still caused her great pain. She shook her head and took another sip of her drink. And yet out of such a tragic loss had come her friendship with Angela.

Their burgeoning friendship had been unexpected, given they seemed to move in different circles. Yet despite this, it grew. But it had only been in the last days of school Rhiannon began to realise what she felt for Angela went very much beyond that of school mates.

Tonight, when she'd heard the piano playing in the auditorium her heart had just about leapt from her throat. She had prayed she might run into Angela again. But in actuality she didn't hold out much hope she would. And although it was great to catch up with her, there were still so much left unsaid between them.

Rhiannon stroked her upper lip. She was fairly sure she'd caught Angela scrutinising her in the window's reflection during the drive home. But what did Angela's actions mean? Were they those of a friend merely interested in seeing how she looked after all these years? Or was it something else? After all, given Angela now had a child she must be married and most likely very happily so.

Was she too late yet again? Rhiannon stood and drained the last of her drink. She headed out of the bar and to the relative loneliness of her room.

Chapter Five

ANGELA THREW HER arms up in exasperation at the plethora of clothes covering her bed. How hard could it be? It was only a lunch for heaven's sake, not the Opera House Gala. The ringing of the doorbell interrupted her attempt to retrieve another blouse from the walk-in wardrobe to add to the mess. Her eyes tracked to the alarm clock by her bed. "Oh crap. Is that the time?"

She headed down the hall and opened the front door. "Hi Mum," she said and pulled her mother into a hug.

"Hi sweetie. How are you?"

A blond-headed ball of energy, careering into her mother's leg, cut Angela's answer short.

"I'm ready Gramma. Can we go?"

Maureen Drayton knelt down and pulled Lachie into a hug. "Good morning little man. It's nice to see you too."

Lachie took in Angela's nonplussed face and returned his gaze to the woman in front of him. "Good morning Grandma. How was your drive?"

Maureen ruffled his hair. "It was fine sweet pea. How about you get your gear together and we'll be on our way after I have a quick catch up with your mother."

Lachie quickly disengaged himself and sped down the hall.

Angela sighed. "I haven't a clue where he gets all his energy from."

"You were much like him when you were young, if not a *little* bit more controlled." Maureen stepped back and scrutinised Angela's face. "Are you okay? You seem a little flustered."

Angela touched her cheeks, feeling the warmth there. "I'm fine, a little tired and busy, that's all. Do you want a cup of tea?" she asked over her shoulder and walked through to the kitchen.

Maureen followed her. "I'm fine. I had one before I left home. But I wouldn't mind a cool drink. You had your reunion last night, didn't you?"

Angela reached into the cupboard and attempted to retrieve two glasses. "Yes, I did."

"How was it? Did you catch up with anyone interesting?"

Angela juggled the glasses she was holding, barely managing to safely place them on the bench. "It was fine, much like reunions are I suppose." She pulled a jug of water from the fridge. "I caught up with a friend I hadn't seen in years."

Maureen sat down at the breakfast bench. "Who was that dear?"

"It was a girl called Rhiannon." Angela filled the two glasses. "You probably don't remember her."

Maureen crinkled her eyes. "I vaguely remember someone called Rhiannon but not much more. Did you catch up on old times?"

"We did to some extent. But we didn't have much time. I'm meeting her for lunch today." Angela surreptitiously cast a glance to the clock on kitchen wall.

Maureen followed Angela's gaze. "You're not late, are you?"

"Of course not. I *can* keep time when I need to, Mother." She paused at Maureen's knowing look. "Maybe not always but I can for important things."

Maureen drank her water and placed the glass on the bench. "When are you meeting her?"

"I've still got about fifty minutes until I have to be there."

"Surely you're not wearing that." Maureen rose from her seat. "Do you want me to help you pick out what to wear?"

"No," Angela blurted, grateful of the distance between the kitchen and her bedroom and the mess created through her indecision in settling on an outfit. "I mean it's fine. I'm sure I'll find some old thing to wear."

Lachie dragged a bag into the kitchen. "I'm ready. And I've cleaned my room Mum. But why has yours got clothes everywhere?"

Angela closed her eyes. Out of the mouths of babes. She opened them and looked at the twinkle in her mother's eyes.

Maureen stood. "It's because she's tidying up her walk-in robe." She picked up Lachie's bag. "Come on. We better be on our way."

Angela followed them to the door and kissed her mother's cheek. "Thanks Mum. I know he always loves staying with you."

Maureen returned the kiss. "I suspect it's the kids next door he enjoys, rather than me. We'll see you next Sunday, around midday?"

"That you will." Angela knelt down and pulled Lachie into a hug. "Now you be good for Grandma and do what she tells you. And don't spend all your time with the Saunders children, okay?"

"Yes Mum," Lachie replied and gave Angela a kiss.

Angela waved as her mum's car reversed down the driveway. She watched them round the bend, then turned, stepped inside, and closed the door before heading back to the mess which was her room.

Time constraints finally caused her to settle on a light summer dress, complemented by a pair of flat soled sandals. She pulled her hair into a neat ponytail, grabbed her keys, and headed out the door to lunch.

RHIANNON PULLED ON a light aquamarine linen blouse which had taken her far too long to choose. Buttoning up the blouse, she cast her eye around her suite. It was a mess, created by her selection and almost automatic dismissal of various items of clothing. She hadn't spent this much time in choosing an outfit in she didn't know how long. In truth she'd spent most of her time trying to second guess what Angela might wear while also not wanting to appear to have gone to so much trouble. And yet it was exactly what she had done.

She ran her fingers through her hair and checked her reflection. "Get a grip Rhiannon. This is simply a lunch, not a prelude to a seduction." She checked her watch, grabbed her card key, and headed down to the foyer, albeit early, to await Angela's arrival.

She chose a seat in a quiet area of the foyer which while unobtrusive, allowed her an unimpeded view of the hotel entrance. She scanned her surroundings. The foyer wasn't overly large. Collections of plush leather chairs strategically positioned throughout the space, afforded their occupants a modicum of privacy during their discussions. The light lemon walls and cream carpet were an effective counterpoint to the area's darker-toned furniture.

Rhiannon reached forward and picked up one of the magazines dotted on the coffee table in front of her. She flicked through the periodical's contents, innately sensing someone was heading her way. Somehow, she knew it wasn't Angela.

She indifferently glanced up and quickly returned her focus to the journal. Her rudimentary gaze identified an immaculately dressed male, in his early forties if she had guessed correctly. With his tanned features, some might regard him handsome. Rhiannon didn't think so.

She hoped her lack of interest in her intruder would be a sufficient hint for him to not disturb her. Despite her best attempts to ignore him, it was obvious he would not be swayed.

"Excuse me, I hope you don't mind, but you're Rhiannon

Sharp, aren't you?" Without asking, the man sat down in the seat beside her.

Appearing as if her attention had been diverted from a life and death task, rather than recipes she was currently perusing, she regarded the man beside her.

"Yes. I didn't catch your name," she said, knowing she could live her whole life and not regret not knowing his name.

The interruption extended his hand. "Malcolm Pearson. I work for Global Consulting Solutions. I happened to catch your presentation last year in the States called The Yet Untapped Resource of an Organisation–People. It was quite an interesting and challenging talk."

Gripping the other man's hand in her own, she observed his eyes cringe at the strength she conveyed in the handshake. She had never liked an insipid handshake, whether given by a man or a woman. "Thank you. I'm glad you enjoyed it. However, if you don't mind—"

Before she could say anything further, Malcom cut across her words, something which was a pet peeve of hers, professionally and personally. "Seeing we're staying in the same hotel; I was wondering if I could interest you in lunch? I'd be very interested to hear more of your views regarding the organisational empowerment of individuals."

She attempted to appear as if she was considering his offer when, in fact she was grimacing inside. It wouldn't be too bad if his interest in the subject was genuine. His roving eyes were more than ample evidence professional discourse wasn't his sole intent.

"Thank you for the offer. But I'm meeting someone for lunch and other than that I'm fairly busy."

He held out his hands in a gesture of largess. "There isn't anyone here yet. Let me tell you how my company has embraced organisational empowerment."

She so did not want to hear about his company. Rhiannon smiled politely while trying to shut out the drone of Malcom's voice. It was a skill she'd developed over many years for situations similar to the one she currently found herself in. The man stumbled on blindly, oblivious to the body language she was projecting.

She cast a glance to the foyer's entrance. Angela had come through the doors and was looking her way, her face masking an emotion Rhiannon couldn't quite fathom. Impatience perhaps? No, that wasn't quite it.

Angela moved across the foyer, stopping short of the coffee table in front of Rhiannon. "Excuse me. Am I interrupting something?"

Malcom turned and regarded Angela with annoyance.

Rhiannon rose. "This is my lunch appointment. I'm glad you enjoyed the initial seminar. There's another coming up in a couple of months in Melbourne. If you're down there, maybe you can catch that one also. This one will focus on teaching leaders how to maximise the benefits of emotional intelligence and body language to aid in achieving optimal business outcomes."

Without further thought Rhiannon completely disregarded Malcom in favour of Angela. She cast her eyes appreciatively over her. "Hi. That colour looks great on you," she said and gestured to the entrance to the restaurant.

"It's nothing. Just something I had lying around at home." Angela cast a dismissive glance over her shoulder at the businessman, still seated and stunned at Rhiannon's sudden departure. "I'm sorry if you knew him. You seemed to be discussing something about business."

"Don't be sorry and thanks for butting in when you did. I wasn't speaking with him. He was speaking *at* me. He just plopped himself down and started to ramble." Rhiannon clicked her tongue in disgust. "Of course, that was after checking me out first."

Angela sighed deeply. "Why is it many men believe unaccompanied women sit in foyers waiting to be saved from the monotony of life?"

"I know what you mean. I travel solo a lot and..." Reaching the restaurant entrance, Rhiannon halted. "Good afternoon, I have a reservation for two under Sharp."

The maître d' checked the list in front of him. "Welcome Ms. Sharp. If you would follow me, please?" He wove around the tables, finally stopping at one beside a window. "I trust this will be acceptable?"

The table had commanding views of the harbour, liberally dotted with boats and yachts, all taking advantage of the cloudless, sun-soaked day.

Rhiannon turned to Angela, who wordlessly concurred. "This is fine."

He respectively pulled out a chair for them both and spread a fine linen napkin on each lap. "My name is Michael." He took the three folders from under his arm and placed one each in front of Rhiannon and Angela and one on the table between them. "Your waitress today is Jessica and she'll be over shortly to take your orders. But if there is anything I can do, please don't hesitate to ask." He executed a half bow and quietly withdrew.

"What were you saying a moment ago?" Angela asked, as she settled into her seat.

"I was going to say I can't begin to tell you how sick and tired I am of businessmen in hotels with time on their hands thinking they're God's gift to women."

"Are you surprised men come up to you like they do? I'm sure they find you very attractive. After all, you're a beautiful woman. And with your baby blues I'm sure you get all sorts of offers." Angela's eyes nervously skittered away from Rhiannon's. She picked up the menu, suddenly inordinately preoccupied with its contents.

"Good afternoon, my name is Jessica. Would you prefer sparkling or still water?"

Rhiannon looked at Angela. "Do you have a preference?"

"I'm fine either way."

"Sparkling will be fine."

Jessica pulled a pad from her apron. "Let me tell you about our specials today."

Jessica recited the list while Rhiannon mulled on Angela's candid words, trying hard not to read inferences which weren't necessarily there. She kept her focus on the server and nodded politely, even though she wasn't really listening. Out of the corner of her eye she could see Angela looking at her, similarly to how she had done on their trip home yesterday evening. An awkward silence heralded the end of Jessica's listing of the specials.

"Could we have a few more minutes to decide," Angela asked.

Jessica replaced the pad in her apron. "Certainly. I'll go and get your water and give you some time to peruse the menu."

"I don't know if it's much to your taste," Rhiannon said, watching the server walk away, "but the seafood here is excellent. The chef always makes a point of buying direct from the fish markets every morning, so you know it's always fresh. I must admit though, while you can't go past fresh prawns or oysters, I'm a bit of a sucker for mud crab."

"I love seafood of just about any kind, with the exception of sea urchin." Angela shuddered. "I have never been able to come to grips with eating something that colour." She placed her menu on the table. "It sounds like you eat here often. Is this where you normally stay when you're in town? Funny how we haven't run into each other before now, with me living not too far away from here."

If she'd known where Angela lived, she didn't doubt they would have been having lunch a lot earlier than today. "I don't often find myself in Sydney but it's where I stay when I'm here."

"I'd have thought most of your business would be on the other side of the harbour."

"It is. And it is a bit of an inconvenience staying here. However, I find this a lot quieter and more personal than some of the boutique hotels in the city centre."

"I agree. When you're in the limelight privacy can be very important to you."

"Absolutely. I also keep my business life as far away from my private life as I can."

Jessica returned and unobtrusively filled their water glasses before again leaving them alone.

Angela opened her mouth and almost as quickly closed it. She reached for her water and took a sip, then placed the glass back down. "I don't mean to pry but do you mind if I ask you something personal?"

Rhiannon swallowed; her mouth inexplicably dry. She wondered just what it was of a personal nature Angela wanted to know. "I don't mind." She lifted her eyebrow in challenge. "If you allow me the right of nonreply."

"Of course." Angela fiddled with her cutlery, as if searching for the right words to frame her next comment. She raised her eyes to Rhiannon's. "Is that why you publish your poetry under the name of Virginia Shulman?"

Rhiannon's eyes widened. How had Angela managed to make the connection? On top of that her poetry, while capable of being read by either gender, was primarily written from a woman's perspective about women. Very few of the mainstream critics of her works had ever caught on to the subtle nuances interwoven in her poetry. But members of the gay community weren't so blind. Was Angela trying to tell her something?

"How did you know?"

"I performed in a charity event in London early last year and happened to have some time off. I went to one of those book come coffee shop places. You know the ones?"

"I do," Rhiannon replied. "I often spend a lot of time in them."

"I was casting my eyes over the latest releases section of the store when I spotted a notice board promoting a book by Virginia

Shulman and the name rang a bell. It was then I remembered your friend who had passed away just before her final school year. We spoke about Ginny once."

"I remember." As she battled to regain her composure, a soft hand covered her own.

"Are you okay? I didn't mean to dredge up old memories."

"It's fine. After not hearing Ginny's name spoken in such a long time, I've heard it twice in as many days." Rhiannon tilted her head. "You were saying?"

Angela withdrew her hand. "I found it strange to see her same name on the other side of the world and I opened the book jacket to see if there was a biography on the author. Imagine my surprise when I found a picture of you. Why do you publish under her name?"

"It's a long story. Suffice to say, to succeed in the business world a certain image is necessary. That image doesn't involve writing poetry. On a more personal level I wanted there to be a clear separation between my professional writing and my poetry. Don't get me wrong, I'm proud of both. However, my poetry represents a side of me I don't wish some people in the business sector to be able to readily identify with me. Did you buy the book?"

Angela reached across and playfully slapped Rhiannon's arm. "Are you kidding? Of course, I did. I was terribly excited to think I knew someone who was so talented. Some of the poems in there are quite profound. It's almost like you've experienced some of those emotions yourself."

Rhiannon considered the works contained in her latest book. "Some of them I have. I take a lot of inspiration, both good and bad, from my life and those close to me. Nature also plays a big part."

"Some of the poems are, I don't know..." Angela shrugged and gazed at Rhiannon. "Right, if you know what I mean. I think my favourite is the one where you use the analogy of the poker player to discuss whether or not one should show their emotions and risk loss or fold their hand and gain nothing as a consequence. That's quite cleverly done."

Rhiannon blushed at Angela's comments. It wasn't as if she hadn't heard such sentiments in her life. Yet they carried a greater weight coming from her. "Thank you, your feedback means a lot to me." Seeing Angela's features redden slightly, she headed for safer ground. "Enough of this talking, how about lunch?"

Before she could lift her hand to signal their waitress,

Angela's delicate hand had lightly grasped her wrist. She creased her brows, looking first at her wrist and at its captor, trying hard to dismiss the warm sensation the action caused.

"I'll understand if you've got commitments. But I'd be very grateful if I could get your signature in my copy of your book. I've never had one signed by an author. Would it be asking too much for you to drop around tonight? I could fix us a small supper, and if you're interested there's a new release on cable we could watch."

Rhiannon's mouth curved in a smile. "Turnabout's fair play. I'd be happy to sign your book. But I would like to see you play, if it's not asking too much. I didn't get much of a chance last night."

Angela released Rhiannon's arm. "I suppose it's only fair. I'll have to go easy during my rehearsal this afternoon, so I have some energy left for you."

Rhiannon baulked and she cleared her throat. Angela's guileless features didn't conceal any double meaning to her words. She navigated the conversation to safer ground.

"Before we start talking supper at your place, how about we get lunch out of the way first? Do you want to go halves in a seafood platter? It's their house specialty and it's very good. It may make for a late supper though if that isn't too inconvenient for you."

"Not at all and a platter sounds great. Lachie's not a great lover of seafood and I'm afraid a platter for one isn't quite the same."

Rhiannon signalled Jessica to the table and ordered for them both.

"Do you want some wine with your lunch?" Jessica asked, jotting their order down.

Rhiannon consulted the wine list and chose a Hunter Valley Semillon. "One of these would be fine please."

"A perfect choice ma'am, and an award winning one I might add. I'll get it for you." Jessica took the wine menu from Rhiannon and headed across to the restaurant's bar area.

"I'm terribly sorry. I ordered the wine without even thinking. If you want something else, I'm sure I can get her attention."

"It's fine. I'll probably only have a glass anyway or this afternoon's rehearsal will be a complete waste of time."

Rhiannon cast her eyes over the harbour view, struggling to find a way to ask her next question. She returned her gaze to the woman opposite her. "If I'm overstepping the mark here please let me know. But I figured with you having a son there would somehow be a father in the picture. Yet you haven't mentioned him."

A flash of hurt flitted across Angela's face and Rhiannon mentally kicked herself. "My apologies. It's none of my business, let's talk about something else."

Angela slightly raised her hand off the table and shook her head. "It's okay. It's a reasonable assumption for you to make and in part of the case not incorrect. Shortly after I began my first international tour, I performed with the Gerhusen Symphony orchestra."

Rhiannon furrowed her brow. "I think I've heard of them. Aren't they the orchestra made up of musicians who are hand-picked from around the world?"

"That's right. They're one of two such orchestras structured that way. Patrick was the principal violinist and obsessed about his work, much like I was. We shared the fruits and the failings of such dedication, given both of us had never left the time aside to seek any real company outside our career. Besides, we found we had a lot in common and it seemed only natural for us to become friends. One night after a little too much celebrating, we found ourselves in bed and one thing naturally led to the other. When Patrick found out I was pregnant he was set on doing..." Angela used her fingers to emphasise the point. "The responsible thing. We married in a quiet ceremony to ensure Lachie had a father and a mother. It was a comfortable arrangement, despite me having to give up touring for six months after the birth of our child. Patrick elected to do the same, and in retrospect it was a good thing." Angela paused; her eyes distant.

A prolonged silence settled around them, so much so that Rhiannon wondered whether Angela had finished her story. The sound of a harbour ferry horn broke Angela's introspection.

"The two of us continued to practice during our sabbatical. However, Patrick began to experience difficulty in getting his fingers to respond to the messages he was sending them. This coupled with ever increasing headaches drove me to force him to see a specialist. It wasn't long after he was diagnosed with an inoperable brain tumour. Fortunately, he got to spend at least some time with his son. Had it not been for the birth he would have continued to work right up until his illness became debilitating. As it was, the outcome was rapid after the diagnosis and I found myself having lost a husband and gained an eight-month-old bundle of love to raise by myself. He's seven now, and very much an independent spirit, like his father."

Rhiannon looked down at her own hands tightly clasped in her lap, her mind recalling her own loss with Ginny. "I'm terribly sorry Angela. I didn't mean to bring up what must have been painful memories. Sometimes I wonder if my mouth engages well before my brain does."

Angela smiled wanly. "It's okay. It's cathartic to talk. As time has passed it's not as painful to speak about it as it used to be. And besides, the fame of Lachie's father has meant there are plenty of photos and documentaries made about him for his son to see when he's of the right age."

The arrival of a wine waiter enabled them sufficient pause to reorder their collective thoughts. Rhiannon tasted the wine and declared it suitable.

Angela tasted the wine. "It's very nice." She placed the glass down. "Did you ever marry?"

Rhiannon scrutinised Angela's comment, attempting to gauge any underlying reason for her words and found none. "No. There hasn't seemed to have been enough time. And I suppose I've never met the right person. I've been in a couple of relationships but nothing lasting or serious enough to warrant marriage."

Rhiannon inwardly cringed at her duplicity. She hadn't entirely lied yet she hadn't told the truth either. If she'd found a woman she loved and cared enough for she would have married her. That said, she was fairly certain Angela was asking about conventional life partners and not same sex. She justified her deceit in that she still wanted to have supper with Angela, which might not happen if she knew about her sexuality.

Jessica arrived, with another waiter in tow. "Excuse me. If you don't mind, I'll get you both set up for your platter."

Rhiannon picked up her glass and Angela leant back in her chair, affording the two servers better accessibility to the table. "I can't wait to hear more about these relationships."

Rhiannon barely managed to stop herself from spitting out the sip of wine she'd just taken. "Tonight perhaps," she deflected, as their late lunch began to arrive at their table.

Chapter Six

ANGELA WALKED THROUGH the front door of her home and tossed her bag on the blackheart sassafras hallway table. She wandered through to the kitchen, grabbed a water from the fridge and made her way to her music room. While she couldn't quite work out why, she felt strangely light-headed and refreshed, despite having consumed only one glass of wine with what had turned out to be an excellent lunch.

Running through her warmup routine as she'd done so many times before, she had every good intention of getting in at least three solid hours of rehearsal prior to the appearance of her guest for the evening. Yet despite her best efforts, her focus was elsewhere. Her mind drifted back to her school days when she would play undisturbed and yet comforted by Rhiannon's presence.

In an effort to settle her thoughts, she rose and walked to a small table off to the side of the piano, which held a smattering of her music selection which she frequently practiced. She picked them up and flipped through the contents, finally pulling out the piece she had executed on the last day of school. She looked at the title and smiled a crooked grin. There was really no need to have it in front of her when she knew the three short movements by heart. Maybe it was merely the comfort of seeing the title and the memories it evoked in her. She shook her head, filing away such thoughts for closer examination at a later time.

The music filled her surrounds as she again became one with the instrument. At times, her hands flew across the keys, yet at others much more slowly in concert with the score. In her mind she pictured Rhiannon behind her, listening like she had done many years ago. Reaching the final coda her fingers stilled, coming to rest on the keys.

She sat in the silence, her mind replaying the events of the afternoon. When she'd walked through the front hotel entrance, her eyes had tracked instinctively to where Rhiannon sat. Her face, while beautiful, held a measure of enforced patience. It was only then Angela noticed the annoying man, who dared to lean so far forward into Rhiannon's personal space. For a moment she'd thought his presence heralded a third party for their lunch, something she resented but couldn't quite understand why. Thankfully, it wasn't the case. She was glad to have Rhiannon to herself for the afternoon. It was like old times.

She enjoyed herself immensely, as the two of them seamlessly fell into the same conversational niche they had so long ago. They told stories and shared thoughts, and before too long time had gotten away from them. Despite how comfortable their conversation had been, Angela sensed there was something about Rhiannon which she couldn't quite put her finger on. Rhiannon had been herself, but there were moments when she seemed to be holding something back. Yet despite this, at the same time she seemed to want to desperately share whatever it was with Angela.

Initially Angela thought it was her poetry. When she'd mentioned her work, the surprise on Rhiannon's face was unmistakable, almost as if she'd been caught doing something wrong. But what was it? Was there more to her explanation regarding separation of her professional and creative work? Was she ashamed at having someone make the connection? Angela shook her head. Rhiannon needn't worry. Her poetry was so expressive, effortlessly capturing the essence of specific moments or actions in time.

Angela's fingers absently traced the title of the music in front of her. She blushed recalling the infrequent touches they'd shared during lunch. While fleeting, the frisson created when Angela brushed Rhiannon's hand was palpable, creating a warmth within her. It was an unfamiliar sensation, yet she welcomed it all the same.

And then their goodbyes at the front of the hotel had Angela perplexed. Rhiannon had stepped toward her, as if to give her a hug. At the last moment she checked herself, instead opting for a gentle rub of Angela's upper arm. In that moment Angela had been strangely disappointed by her actions. Angela knew she wasn't a tactile person. But she couldn't help but admit she would have welcomed the greater contact between them.

She closed her eyes and massaged the back of her neck. What did it all mean? The chiming of the carriage clock on the small shelf brought her back to the present. Was that the time? She had a mountain of things to do in anticipation of Rhiannon's arrival. And her wool gathering was getting her nowhere.

She rose, collected the musical piece, and carefully placed it on the top of the pile on the small side table and left the room.

FROM ACTIONS BRED out of years of deadlines, Rhiannon

rang Angela's doorbell right on the pre-arranged time of seven o'clock. Although Angela had waved off the need for her to bring anything, Rhiannon made it a habit never to arrive empty-handed. On her way she'd stopped at a local liquor store and was relieved to find a respectable range of cellared vintages, at an equally decent price.

As she waited, she again nervously smoothed down the front of the white linen blouse she wore, the wine in its paper bag clutched tightly in her other hand.

Angela opened the door, her eyes quickly skimming over Rhiannon. "You look great. I'm glad you could make it. Come on in."

"I'm happy to have been invited." Rhiannon held out the bottle to Angela. She subtly appraised Angela, dressed in turquoise blouse and informal black slacks, liking what she saw. "I hope you don't mind but I couldn't come without bringing something."

"You obviously found the cellars off Kingston road." Angela took the bottle from the proffered hand and motioned Rhiannon inside. "You know you didn't have to bother, but thanks all the same."

"It was no trouble. I have to say I was pleasantly surprised. It's not often you find a cellar selling not only fine wines but also a fair share of vintage labels to boot. Although, I expect around here there'd be ample people willing to part with money to secure a good red or white." She waited in the hallway for Angela to close the door.

"I enjoy both but have very little knowledge when it comes to a good or bad wine. When it comes to choosing one, I'm a bit of a label girl. If it's nice I buy it." She pulled the wine from its wrapper. "And what lovely artwork there is on this one."

Rhiannon followed Angela down the hallway and into the lounge room. "I'm glad you think so. I wasn't sure what we were having, so I figured a Tamar Valley Pinot Noir would cover just about anything."

"Make yourself comfortable while I put this in the kitchen. I'll give you the grand tour in a minute. In the meantime, can I get you a drink?"

"Do you have any scotch by chance?" Rhiannon called at Angela's retreating figure.

"I've got a single malt if you're interested. It's a favourite of mine," Angela replied, her voice filtering through the doorway.

"That will be fine, with a dash of water if I could." While

Angela busied herself with the drinks, Rhiannon studied her surroundings. She still hadn't seen the full exterior of the house in daylight, assuming it would mirror the clean, contemporary lines of its interior. The home was very large and modern, initially giving the impression of restraint. Yet the furnishings and individual touches of its owner belied a warmth not immediately obvious. Rhiannon couldn't help but think the design, in some small way, reminded her of Angela.

A soft tan leather sofa, replete with a chaise lounge on one of its ends, dominated the centre of the space. In front of this was a light burl wooden coffee table — huon pine if she wasn't mistaken. A sideboard of similar wood and a rather impressive entertainment system dominated one wall. Another table was solely dedicated to Angela's work, with awards and photographs from orchestras she had performed with throughout the world.

Rhiannon turned from the obvious evidence of Angela's success to a much more personal space in the room. A sofa table sat against another wall, littered with photographs of, given the resemblance, Angela's family. She walked across and perused the collection, including a wedding photo with who could have only been Patrick.

She glanced at the myriad of baby and infant photos, her eyes coming to rest on a more recent shot of Angela and her son. She picked it up and studied it closely. The shot was clearly taken in an unguarded moment, capturing to perfection the adoration on Angela's face for the young boy beside her.

"That's my little man Lachie. All blond hair and blue eyes. He's a good child, if at times a little too driven for a child his age."

Rhiannon had been so pre-occupied with viewing the photo she almost dropped it at Angela's sudden proximity.

She gave the photo to Angela and accepted a crystal tumbler in its place. "I wonder where he gets *that* trait from?"

Angela smiled crookedly. "His mother is obviously a bad influence. Far too often he sees me sitting in front of a piano practicing for hours on end."

"You know, I once remember a senior telling me she'd have ample time for friends later and that her music would inevitably come first. Now here you are with a young son." She sampled the peaty, yet smooth Islay malt.

Angela lovingly wiped an invisible speck of dust from the photo's frame. "What he needs is someone who can get him out of the house and show him there's more to life than merely music."

She returned the frame to its place on the table.

Angela's words surprised her. Was she after another husband, possibly a father figure for Lachie? Rather than put her foot
in her mouth, like she had done during the course of their lunch,
Rhiannon redirected the conversation.

Her fingers toyed with the top of the crystal tumbler. "I
assume you've changed your mind on the focus on work first,
find friends later approach."

Angela her tilted her glass in a mock toast. "I suppose I had
that coming to me. But as a mother you see life from a completely
different perspective and things no longer revolve around your
own wants and needs. I don't regret my hours of training or the
doors it's opened for me. But I wouldn't wish such a lifestyle for
my son. There are enough pressures in the entertainment world
without him being forced to grow up in the shadow of his famous
father."

"Not to mention his equally famous mother." Rhiannon
added. "Don't be so quick to dismiss your own fame. I'm sure
he's proud of what you've achieved and what, I expect, you'll
continue to achieve."

Angela turned, but not quite quick enough to conceal the redness suffusing her features. "How about I give you a tour now?"

"Lead on," Rhiannon replied. "I'm right behind you."

RHIANNON FOLLOWED ANGELA up the stairs leading
from the games area below. "You have a lovely home. I've no
doubt you could play hide and seek inside it and not find people
for days."

Angela chuckled. "It is a bit too much sometimes. We bought
it shortly after I married Patrick. It was the only one on the market which would accommodate space for the two of us to
rehearse, without getting in each other's way."

"Were you intending to settle in Sydney after Lachie's birth?"

"It was one of the options we'd discussed. This place gave us
the ability to continue to practice, without having to leave the
house, while we made up our minds." Angela opened a door and
motioned Rhiannon through it. "This is my music room."

Rhiannon cast her eyes over the surrounds. They were not
overly expansive yet by no means were they confined. Central to
the space was the unmistakeable lines of a Grand piano, its glossy
dark reflection absorbing the discreet lighting of the room. The
surrounding grey coloured walls seemed to have a porous finish.

Curious, she reached out and touched one of them. "I've heard of foam floor tiles in a gym but what's this?"

"It's called acoustic absorption foam." Angela closed the door.

"Does it act as sound-proofing inside here?"

"That's another foam. While this gives a reasonable degree of soundproofing, its main function is to help stop sound from continually bouncing off surfaces when I'm practicing in such a small space. It covers all the walls. As a result, this is one of only two rooms in the house without windows."

"I'm assuming Patrick's was the other?"

"Correct."

To the left of the piano was a music system.

"What's the sound system for?" Rhiannon queried.

"It often helps when I'm rehearsing a piece, to have the ability to blend my playing with other orchestral instruments. I don't do it often, but it seemed a worthwhile addition when I initially designed this space."

Angela moved to a climate panel next to the door. "You might feel a bit colder in here than the rest of the house. To ensure the piano is kept in optimum condition, the thermostat is at a constant twenty-one degrees Celsius, and a humidity of around thirty-five to forty-five per cent. Do you need a throw, or are you warm enough?"

"I'm fine thanks."

Angela motioned to a leather recliner to the right and with full view of the piano. "Please take a seat. Feel free to put your drink on the table beside you. You should have enough space, if you shift the sheet music a little."

She made herself comfortable behind the instrument and splayed her hands and wiggled her fingers, as Rhiannon had seen her do before in preparation for playing. "To coin a well-worn cliché, do you have any requests?"

Rhiannon smiled. "Let's get something straight. I've come to hear you play because what you can do with a piano is incredible. But it doesn't mean I've come any closer to being able to tell one artist or piece from the other. I focus more on how the music makes me feel, so surprise me."

"Still the savage beast hey, capably soothed by music." Angela flexed her wrists and ran her hands up each of her forearms, lightly gripping them as she went.

Rhiannon pouted. "I'll give you savage beast."

After one final stretch of her hands, Angela lightly positioned her fingers on the piano keys. "Let's see what I can play for you. I'm still reasonably warm from my rehearsal earlier this afternoon. In which case, why don't I begin with Chopin's 'Heroic Polonaise,' followed by the third movement of Beethoven's 'Appassionata —"

"*Gesundheit.*" Rhiannon almost laughed at Angela's perplexed visage. "Sorry, I thought you sneezed."

"It's the name of a piece, you goose. I might follow that with the fourth, fifth and seventh movements from Chopin's 'Etude Opus Ten,' and end with something modern. A Nyman piece perhaps?"

"One of the pieces from the film, which was set in New Zealand, produced by Jane Campion?" Rhiannon waggled her index finger at Angela's astonishment. "Ha! Not so savage after all." She settled back into the chair. "Play on maestro."

For about the next half hour Rhiannon sat entranced by the sounds radiating from the Grand piano, conveyed through the skilful hands of the artist seated in front of it. It wasn't merely the music which entranced Rhiannon. It was, in reality, the first time she had actually seen the depth and intensity of emotions of Angela when she played. Her face, like clouds on a windy day, shifted from concentration to rapture, from happiness to the depths of sorrow then yet again cresting to passion, her fingers moving over the piano at an almost incomprehensible speed.

Angela's performance unsettled her, yet in a delightfully sensual way. She was so beautiful. It was a good thing she had never seen her from this angle during her rehearsals at school. God only knows what might have happened.

Completely mesmerised by the performance, Rhiannon imagined a multitude of scenarios with Angela, none of which seemed even remotely possible in the cold light of day. So absorbed was she in her thoughts and the miasma of the music weaving itself around her, she failed to realise Angela had even finished.

ANGELA LIGHTLY RESTED her fingers on the piano's keys, signalling the end of the informal recital. Although she was intimately familiar with her own musical abilities, it was a long time since she'd played with such emotional intent. Quietly pleased, she turned to Rhiannon, keen to see her reaction to the performance.

For a fleeting moment, and in the silence of the room, Rhiannon's face was unguarded. It was as if a door opened, exposing

Angela to a hauntingly familiar image. She explored her memories, trying to recollect when she'd seen it before. It was in the music study, the second last day of school, when Rhiannon held her, after stopping her from falling. Angela's eyes widened as she attempted to marshal the thoughts racing through her mind at breakneck speed. She examined her feelings, trying to reconcile how she felt.

Rhiannon blinked and shook her head. "It's hard to find words to adequately express what I've just heard. Astonishing and remarkable, sublime all come to mind. I'd give anything for the talent you have. To be able to play with such vigour. It's a wonder you're ever allowed to rest."

Angela rose from the piano, pausing as she reached for a towel to dab away the immediate effects of her performance. "You have your own talent Rhiannon, even if you're a little reluctant to admit you do. What you do with words is every bit the same as what I do with music. We both make our own medium come to life, allowing other people an insight into that which lays beyond the reality of everyday life."

A silence descended between the two, each seeming to search for something to say. Angela turned back to the piano and closed the key lid and returned her gaze to Rhiannon.

"Listen, I want to freshen up a bit before we have some supper. I always feel a bit like a dishrag after a rehearsal."

Rhiannon's gaze travelled the length of Angela's body. "You look fine to me...I mean, I understand. It can't be all that comfortable being wet."

Angela walked to the door and opened it. "I'll only be a minute. If you want to go through into the kitchen, I'll meet you there and we'll have supper. In fact, why don't you open the pinot you brought? There are glasses already on the benchtop. Help yourself." Her last comments echoed down the hallway as Angela walked to her room.

RHIANNON RUBBED HER face vigorously and released a pent-up breath. She bent to retrieve the whisky glass from where she'd placed it, her eyes at once drawn to the top piece of sheet music on the table. She frowned and picked it up.

The author of the piece was Angela, its title in Gaelic. At the bottom corner of the page was a date. "She must have finished writing this the week we left school," Rhiannon muttered.

"'*Dìreach dhi.*'" she narrowed her eyes, searching through her mental Gaelic database which she'd sparingly used since finishing her Gaelic exam at the end of year twelve. "*Dìreach*—it means *just* if I remember." She worked to correctly form the phrase created by the connection of the two words. Her eyes widened. "'Just for her.' But who was her? Is it me?" She opened the cover, disappointed there was nothing on the inside jacket to indicate who 'her' was. Rhiannon carefully placed the composition on the pile and, deep in thought at her discovery, headed to the kitchen.

ANGELA DISTRACTEDLY DROPPED the towel in the laundry basket in her bedroom and walked across to the ensuite, her thoughts in turmoil. She turned on the hand basin taps and sluiced her face with cold water. Replaying the scene in the music room moments ago, her damp hands gripped the sides of the washbowl.

Engrossed in her performance, her immediate surroundings had faded into the background and she'd been only peripherally aware of Rhiannon's presence. That was right up until the moment when she'd finished and turned to her. The undisguised look on Rhiannon's face surprised her. The fluttering in her belly, elicited by Rhiannon's gaze, was one she hadn't felt in a long time. Rather than pursue the matter, she'd fled, using the excuse of changing to marshal her thoughts.

She pushed herself off the basin and wiped her hands. In the privacy of her bedroom, she unbuttoned her damp blouse and dropped it into the washing basket. How did she really feel about what just happened? She opened a drawer and removed a wool, short-sleeved blouse. She pulled it over her head and checked herself in the mirror.

"Come on Angela," she whispered. "It's like you felt in the music study, the second last day of school."

She loosely tucked her blouse into her pants. But what did it mean for her? Did Rhiannon's feelings run deeper than merely friendship, or was she completely misinterpreting Rhiannon's response? And what should I do about what I saw, she thought.

Angela dragged her fingers through her hair. She closed her eyes and used a calming technique to sufficiently collect herself to enable her to face Rhiannon without, hopefully, making a complete fool of herself.

RHIANNON TASTED THE pinot and was impressed. She

handed a glass of wine to Angela. "I'm glad it's not only the label on the bottle which is a work of art. So is this pinot."

Angela moved across the kitchen and took the proffered glass. She swirled the contents around and took a sip, her eyes never leaving Rhiannon. "Lovely."

What just happened here? It was as if the conversation shifted gears. Or was she reading too much into what Angela's words? In an effort to mask her confusion, she slightly moved away from Angela's proximity.

"I don't know about you but I'm a little hungry. Now wasn't part of the deal you were going to feed me?" Rhiannon asked, using humour to try and redirect the obvious tension between them to safer ground.

Angela placed her glass on the counter. "Some host I am. Of course, that was part of the *deal,* as you aptly put it. If you can tear yourself away from this liquid ambrosia, we'll have our supper ready in no time."

Angela retrieved a selection of small plates from the butler's pantry and fridge and placed them on the kitchen island. "Given our rather substantial late lunch, I figured a charcuterie board would be more than ample food." She removed the covers and picked one of the plates up. "The night is still warm. I thought we'd eat outside on the back patio." She motioned to the other plates. "Could you bring those two out for me please?"

Working together, they made short work of the food transfer and in very little time were sitting down to supper. The conversation was light, almost as if neither party wanted to transgress too deeply into the evening's events to date.

Angela snagged a crusty roll and broke a piece from it. She grabbed a dab of butter and spread it across the piece. "Last night you mentioned you were here for twelve months. What happens after you've finished?"

"I don't know. It's been a while since I've stayed in one place for as long as this current tenure." Rhiannon spread a measure of pate onto a biscuit. "In my younger years there was such a novelty to seeing so much of the world."

"And you seem to have seen quite a lot, if your biography is any indication. France, London, Paris, Los Angeles, Wellington, and the South Pole of all places. What did you do when you worked in Antarctica?"

Angela's breadth of knowledge regarding her life secretly pleased Rhiannon. "I was employed by the Antarctic Treaty Secretariat to oversee a mediation between a couple of the sovereign states, who have overlapping regional claims. They were keen to use someone completely removed from the secretariat itself. I merely happened to be in the right place at the right time when the offer came up."

"Did you get to travel to Antarctica?"

"I did, but only for a short while. Seeing the territory gave me a clearer understanding of exactly what was in dispute." Rhiannon reached across and picked up a piece of cheese. "How did you find out about what I'd done?" She popped the morsel in her mouth.

"I was in London a few years ago and saw you being interviewed by the BBC. The interviewer led off with an overview of your curriculum vitae." Angela's eyes twinkled mischievously. "Who would have guessed a sportswoman could go so far?"

"It's a good thing I know you're joking, or I might have to remind you who's the stronger of us."

Rhiannon laughed as Angela held up her hands in mock surrender.

"Was that when you were playing with the Royal Philharmonic?"

"Yes. Why do you ask?"

"I had some time off and caught one of the performances you gave. It was quite brilliant."

Angela dipped her head. "Thank you. Why didn't you come and say hello?"

Rhiannon shrugged. "I tried to. I managed to wrangle a backdoor pass. But just when I came through the door and got within hailing distance of you, you were on your way out another door and I missed the opportunity to catch up."

"That's a shame. One of the biggest problems I have when playing overseas was always feeling as if I was in a sea of strangers and yet sometimes alone. It would have been nice to see a friendly face." Angela held up one finger, her eyes distant, as if recalling something. "It's like the poem you wrote on loneliness. I always felt I was, as you said, a being on the fringes of so-called humanity, never breaking through." She twitched her lips. "Listen to me, wallowing in the realms of the morose. Speaking of your poetry, now it's time for *you* to honour your side of the bargain." She rose from her chair and moved inside.

Rhiannon took advantage of Angela's temporary absence to consider the night's events. She rubbed her brow, perplexed at the mixed messages Angela seemed to be giving. Angela was happy to see her. Of that she had no doubt. Despite this, Rhiannon was at odds on what to read into Angela's remarks when she found her examining the photos in the lounge. Was she hoping to settle down again, find a father figure for Lachie? If that's the case, what should she make of Angela's expression when she returned from changing, not to mention her words when she tasted the wine?

Rhiannon raised her arms above her head and stretched exasperatedly, feeling the joints in her shoulders pop as a result of her action. She returned her hands to the table in front of her. It was patently obvious she'd been out of the courtship game for far too long. She hadn't a clue whether what she was picking up on were feelings of friendship, or something much deeper. She rolled her head, to try and ease the stress in her neck and almost missed Angela's return.

Angela placed the book on the table between them and sat down. A look of concern graced her features. "I'm not keeping you up, am I? I didn't think to ask when you arrived back in Australia which, by the looks of you, wasn't terribly long ago." Angela made to pull the book from where she'd placed it. "I didn't mean to press you about the poetry. If you want to call it a night, I'll understand."

Rhiannon placed her hand on the book, her fingers lightly grazing Angela's. "It's all right. I get a little bit stiff travelling for such long hours in a plane. I've booked in for a full body workout with the hotel masseuse tomorrow. She should help me to get back to my old self without too much trouble."

Angela's fingers retreated from the book and Rhiannon picked it up, gently turning it over in her hands. The well-worn cover was far from pristine, as if carried a great way by its owner. The book's spine lay claim to repeated opening. Yet it was obvious the wear wasn't one of neglect but moreso one associated with continual use.

"Did you buy this second hand?" she joked. "It looks as if it's been around the block a few times." Rhiannon raised her head, her next words dying on her lips at the wistful look on Angela's face. Rhiannon could feel an unmistakeable redness in her cheeks. However, she could no more break contact with Angela's eyes than she could cease to breathe.

"I bought it new last year, and ever since I've carried it with me wherever I went. It's served as a great salvation for me, capturing in words what I was never able to say. You've got quite a talent you know."

They gazed into each other's eyes, the silence of the evening settling over them. For a fleeting moment Rhiannon felt the years fall away. They were again in the auditorium on the last day of school, her feelings the same, yet not quite so disordered as back then.

Angela shivered and broke the silent tableau. She rubbed her arms and rose from her chair. "You know it's a little chilly out here. I'll be back in a moment." She walked inside.

Rhiannon's eyes tracked Angela's sudden departure, still very much aware of the lingering silences between them. She was humbled and yet enlightened this book, *her* book of poetry, had been Angela's constant companion. Despite wanting to tell her just that, Rhiannon struggled for a way to utter the words, without scaring her with a profession which had the potential to ruin the evening. If she was being honest with herself, she was slightly relieved when Angela made the excuse to go inside.

Rhiannon stood and walked across to the waist high rail surrounding the verandah. She scanned the dark waters of Sydney Harbour, to the glittering lights of the city beyond, attempting to reconcile the conflicting feelings and thoughts spinning through her mind. Her preoccupation barely registered Angela's return. A soft touch on her shoulder caused her to turn, to where Angela stood, shadowed by the patio's soft lighting.

"Are you warm enough?"

Rhiannon nodded. Oh, if only Angela knew.

"I'm sure I could find something which might fit you. Or do you want to go inside?"

"I'm fine out here if you are. Tell me," Rhiannon motioned to the book on the table, "did you have any favourites?"

Angela's eyes tracked to where the book lay and her eyes creased slightly, as if sorting through the book's table of contents. "You know, each of them held something for me, so much that at first I thought they were meant for me. But then I showed your book to my manager."

"What did he say?"

"My manager is a she. She said she could see the same thing, albeit anchored to her life's experiences. You seem to possess an uncanny ability for capturing thoughts and emotions and being able to crystallise them into words, like you're speaking directly to one person. Sorry, I expect it's a long way of saying I find it hard to pick a favourite because I love them all. But if I had to single out one which resonates with me above the others, I'd have to say it would be the one I mentioned this afternoon. The analogy about the poker player and love."

Rhiannon smiled sadly. It was one of her earlier pieces and was about a woman she was falling in love with, yet the love wasn't reciprocated. There had been a strong friendship between her and Hayley. Despite this, Rhiannon had feared crossing the boundary into something deeper, especially when Hayley admitted to her the burgeoning feelings she had for another woman. Their friendship had remained strong. Despite Hayley's interest for the other woman petering out, Rhiannon never broached the topic of how she felt with her, instead electing to play it safe. She couldn't help but wonder what might have been if she'd made her emotions clear. The sound of knuckles knocking on the balcony's balustrade brought her back to the present.

"Hello, earth to Rhiannon. Are you still receiving me? Over?"

"Sorry. I drifted away there for a moment. I know it must seem a bit odd. But even today, sometimes merely the mention of a poem I wrote, no matter how old, elicits a response in me."

Angela smiled. "I can empathise. There are pieces of music which I hold very dear. They're more often than not my own compositions and they make me feel the same way. Some of them are so strong I often don't need to play them to feel the emotion of sound and feelings they evoke through just thinking about them."

Rhiannon cast her mind back to the sheet music she'd seen in the piano room. Was "*Dìreach dhi*" one of those?

"I remember the poem you're talking about though. It's a bittersweet favourite of mine and one I wrote quite a few years ago. It meant a lot to me at the time when I was writing it."

"In what way?" Angela asked and immediately held up her hand. "I didn't mean to be so direct. There isn't any need for you to explain, if you don't want to."

Even in the soft grey lighting which surrounded them, Rhiannon could readily see the mortification in Angela's face. "It's okay. When I write my poetry, I always do it from a personal perspective and I always have someone in mind. I wrote that one about ten years ago, but it still remains at the forefront of my thoughts. As for what you and your manager gleaned from my poems, you're right. I suppose there's something in my poems for everyone. If they look closely enough."

An awkward silence lingered between them. Angela's fingers drew a soft line along the balcony's balustrade. "Have you written anything lately?" she asked, her voice so soft Rhiannon barely heard her.

"I have, but it's a work in progress." The silence hung between the two, the invitation awaiting its acceptance.

The connection which existed since their re-acquaintance seemed to rapidly shift, the air between them charged with energy. As Rhiannon struggled to make sense of the change, Angela moved closer.

Rhiannon was mesmerised by the look of wanting on Angela's face. How had they arrived at this point so fast?

Angela reached across and softly touched Rhiannon's wrist and released it. "Will you share it with me?"

"I will, as long as you don't laugh," Rhiannon replied, trying to diffuse the rapidly building tension between them.

"I'd never do that, regardless of what your poem might be about. I'm honoured you would share something you're still working on with me."

Rhiannon closed her eyes and bent her head, marshalling words which had only recently come to her.

Where did you come from?
Walking into my dreams like that.
You–one who is so far away,
but a welcome visitor all the same.
Picking up from where we never really managed to start.
A visitor known only to me.

You come into my dreams
with your warm smile and sparkling, verdant eyes,
giving me relief from my everyday life.
Offering no more than a gentle hand in friendship,
and warm thoughts when I most need them.

We seem to spend a lot of time
coming and going in each other's lives.
Like people in a revolving door
you are always on the way out,
and I on the way in.
Like parallel lines we run beside each other.
When will those lines ever cross?

The time you spend inside my mind
can never be too long.
Such thoughts could only be surpassed
by your actual presence.
But, alas, with the day's early morning rays you dissolve,
leaving me with nothing but memories and dreams.

With the hope, someday, those dreams will come true.

Rhiannon lifted her head from its previous contemplative position, to find herself captured by Angela's eyes. She smiled shyly, afraid to ask and yet at the same time desperately craving Angela's opinion.

"What do you think?"

Angela studied Rhiannon's face. "Rhiannon, that was truly touching. You may say I have a gift. But it takes me ages to transfer into sound what seems to take you so little time to put into words."

Try as she might, she couldn't disguise the effect of Angela's words. For a moment the music to the careful dance they had moved to all night ceased.

Angela gazed at Rhiannon, as if weighing up the risks involved in posing a question she was obviously dying to ask. She took a deep breath. "Who was this one about?"

Despite their muted surroundings, Rhiannon could see the nervous uncertainty in Angela's face. It was as if she was desperate for a reply to what she'd asked and yet in equal measure somewhat fearful of the answer.

Momentarily taken aback with how best to respond, Rhiannon arrived at her only real option. "I could give you a trite response right now and we could both step back. But I don't know that I want to do that. So instead let me be up front with you. Which is probably for the best—I was never very good at being untruthful." She studied the wooden deck and again raised her eyes to Angela's. "It was about you. The poem was about you and me and the way I see—I've always seen the two of us."

Before she could utter another word, Angela moved away, her face now masked by the balcony's lighting, her focus preoccupied with the garden and beyond.

Rhiannon grimaced, unsure of how to proceed. Was Angela embarrassed or disgusted by what she'd said? She struggled with what to do next, before her thoughts returned to the key reason why she had attended last night's reunion in the first place. What she'd waited to ask for so long was still bereft of a response. She moved toward her, yet not close enough to invade Angela's personal space.

"The last day of school, after your recital. Why did you leave?"

AS IF CAUGHT in a vortex, Angela's mind flooded with early memories of Rhiannon. Like it was yesterday, she recalled the first time she'd been aware of Rhiannon's presence, when she ran through her piano drills in the auditorium. To the discipline she'd shown, with part of her focus on the piano and the rest on the rear of the room, when she'd heard Rhiannon's quiet weeping. To initial introductions and a friendship which grew without pretence or pressure. To the music study when, for a fleeting moment Rhiannon had held her, feeling for the first time in her life as if she were finally home. To the confusion of those feelings and the need to find the space to try and make sense of what they essentially meant.

Feelings which for so long Angela had concealed behind emotional floodgates couldn't be held in any longer. She turned and closed the distance between them, aware nothing other than candour would suffice, despite the impact it may have on their newly resurrected friendship.

"I was confused. We seemed to share such similar interests but at the same time had little in common. You, for the most part, were a sports fanatic. I was completely focussed on becoming the best pianist there ever was, at the expense of everything around me. I remember telling you how important my potential career was, on the first day we spoke." Angela shook her head disgustedly, recalling the supercilious words she'd uttered. "God, I must have sounded like a right pillock."

"You weren't being silly at all. Just self-assured. Angela—"

She held up her hand and turned slightly away from Rhiannon. "Please, I need to say this. How I presented myself to others couldn't be further from reality. I felt like I was a boat, untethered and adrift in an ocean of doubt about many things in my life. Then, during muck up day preparations, when I tripped and you caught me, you anchored me. For the first time in my life I felt I belonged. Suddenly nothing mattered. Not my grades, my parents or, most of all, my aspirations as a musician. Only the feelings you evoked in me meant anything. And while you grounded me, at the same time you scared the hell out of me. I was so close to my dream and in the simple act of trying to catch me you brought to the forefront a frightening perspective I don't think I was ready to accept. I could see how you felt, and I was afraid. Afraid of what might happen to my dream, yet most of all afraid of what I felt for you."

"The day of graduation, I watched while you moved about the hall, patiently talking with people who stopped you, but all the while intent on reaching your final destination, regardless of how many roadblocks you encountered. Have you *any* idea how difficult it was for me to flawlessly play that piece, knowing you were seated so close?"

"I didn't, but I really didn't want to be anywhere else but near you when you played," Rhiannon replied softly.

"When I turned and saw the look in your eyes, I knew I had to get out of the hall. If I hadn't…well…I wasn't quite sure what would have happened next. But I know it most likely wouldn't have been conducive to the school's morals and high code of conduct. So, I left, before you could say anything."

"I'd have given anything to be able to finish our conversation, but you were gone." Rhiannon tapped her finger against the railing. "How long had you felt that way for me?"

Angela's arms hugged her body. "Longer than I realised or was willing to admit to. Do you remember when you went to pick up my music sheet, at the end of my recital?"

Rhiannon nodded. "You were very protective of it, as if you were afraid of anyone seeing it. Why?"

"It had taken me the better part of the month to compose that piece of music and I wanted you to be the first to hear it."

"But the hall was already set up for the farewell luncheon and you weren't allowed to rehearse."

"I didn't know that was the case until late on the afternoon of our second last day. Until then, I'd been hoping to get the chance on the last morning of school to play it solo, for you. I thought, in some way, the music would help to convey what I felt about you. The title of it was '*Dìreach dhi.*'"

"I saw the piece tonight, on the table in your piano room." Rhiannon carefully licked her lips. "It means 'just for her.' Doesn't it?"

"It does, or at least I hope it does." Angela laughed softly. "You should have seen the look on your Gaelic teacher's face when I asked him to provide me with a translation. I had to tell him it was a piece for my mother, and I wanted to surprise her. In fact, the person it was for, and who I wanted to surprise, was you. But I didn't want anyone around when I played it for the first time. And for reasons I can't readily explain, after I'd played it at the luncheon, I didn't want you to see the piece because I knew you'd easily make the translation."

"I wouldn't have said anything. At least not there."

Angela again turned to face Rhiannon. "You must have known how I felt. Why didn't you follow me?" she whispered.

Rhiannon smiled ruefully. "You've no idea how much I tried. Initially you shocked me with your sudden departure. By the time I managed to pull myself together to follow you, you were already halfway across the hall when the principal accosted me. When I finally talked myself free, I ran to the senior's breakout area. But it was empty. Figuring you'd already left, I returned to the hall. I'd made a promise to go with some of the girls to the club later, after the function finished. Once exams began, our schedules were different and there wasn't any way we were likely to cross paths. And when the exams were over, we both went our separate ways, carving out our respective professional lives. Years later, when I heard of your initial successes, I was so very pleased you'd achieved your dream. All the same, I never stopped wondering whether you'd finally stopped holding people at arm's length long enough to let others in."

Angela found herself reminiscing on how long she'd not allowed others too close to her, running away from anything emotional which could have thwarted her professional dream. If it hadn't been for the persistence of Patrick, she'd be still holding people at a distance, ensuring a safe yet barren place for her to live out her life.

Seconds seemed to lapse into minutes as Angela mentally replayed her last twenty years. Rhiannon's movement away from her, to a more detached distance, broke her contemplation.

The defeat reflected in Rhiannon's face spurred her into action. She moved forward and covered her hand over the larger one tensely clenching the balcony railing. Her eyes searched Rhiannon's shadowed face. "It's not the case now. As you see, I'm not holding anyone at arm's length and I'm certainly not running anywhere." She held her breath, awaiting a response to her somewhat bold actions. Rhiannon's hand turned, their fingers entwined. Angela released a sigh of relief.

RHIANNON STUDIED THE delicate, yet strong hand encased in her own. "You know, I've been doing some pretty good running of my own over the years. In the past I've received more invitations to attend school reunions than I care to count. But this is the first one I've bothered to go to."

Angela's thumb tenderly stroked Rhiannon's fingers. "Why this one?"

"I suppose it was because I've also had enough of holding people at arm's length. I wanted some answers of my own. Last night, when I couldn't find you, I began to think my return had been, for the most part, a waste of time. Then, when I entered the auditorium, I knew it had all been worth it. For many years I'd wondered why you left the auditorium the way you did. It was something which had plagued me for so long. If I was ever to get any closure, I needed an answer."

Angela silently studied Rhiannon's hand, securely entwined with her own. "Did you get the closure you were looking for?" she uttered, seemingly fearful of the answer.

Rhiannon reached out and carefully tilted Angela's face until it was almost level with her own. She cupped Angela's cheek and stroked it gently, revelling in its texture. "I suppose you could see it that way. But I'm hoping you'll see it as more of an opening."

Without breaking contact, Rhiannon closed the distance between the two, careful of any hint Angela wasn't comfortable with the inevitability of where the moment was heading. She slowly lowered her head and ever so delicately brushed her lips against Angela's. What started as the softest of touches soon built as arms encased bodies and years of memories flooded back, with questions asked and answers given. The soft interplay of tongues was met with an acceptance and welcoming of a dance which seemed natural and yet had waited so long.

Secure in the silence of their surrounds and the embrace of each other's arms, neither was aware of how long the moment lasted.

Angela tentatively placed her fingers against the side of Rhiannon's face. "Will you stay?" The request hung in the air, its possible responses multi-faceted.

"As long as you want me to. As long as you want me to."

Chapter Seven

IN THE VERY early light of morning, the only sound interrupting the native calls of the parrots in the trees was Rhiannon's footfall, as she navigated a course from her hotel.

Her morning run was a regular routine, regardless of where she stayed, or what the weather was doing. On top of it being part of her fitness regime, today it also seemed the only way she was going to get some much-needed energy back into her body after what had been, in effect, twenty-four hours without sleep.

She hadn't slept since leaving Angela's place earlier that morning, so she was not surprised to find herself struggling to again come to grips with the winding, hilly streets of Middle Harbour. Her last "home" in the States had been relatively flat compared to this, presenting minimal challenge to her running. These streets couldn't be more different.

Rhiannon stopped to stretch her calves in anticipation of tackling what was reputed to be Sydney's steepest street. With a twenty-five percent gradient dominating over half its incline, it rivalled some of those she had tackled in San Francisco. Since her schooling days the street had become an annual charity run, known as the Awaba Angst.

She could have avoided the street altogether. But where was the fun in that? She lifted her face to the ghost gum trees lining the bottom of the hill. Liberally dotted with a riot of kookaburras, they all seemed to be laughing at the fact she was even going to make the attempt. She blocked the noise out of her mind, stretched her quads and thought back to the previous evening.

Rhiannon's arms encircled Angela as they half-sat, half-reclined on the chaise lounge of Angela's sofa. "Are you sure you're comfortable?"

Angela snuggled back deeper into Rhiannon's embrace. "Shouldn't *I* be asking you that? We've been in this position for hours. I'm pretty sure I got the better part of the bargain here, using you as a pillow."

Rhiannon nuzzled the top of Angela's head. "You can use me for a pillow anytime. Are you okay with this?"

"I'm more than okay. Plus, I couldn't think of any better way to reminisce on what we've both done since leaving school."

Angela's fingers traced a lazy path up and down Rhiannon's forearm. "I do have a something to ask you though."

Rhiannon chuckled. "Ask away."

"You never did tell me why you took Gaelic at school. I mean, it seemed such a strange choice, given your other subjects."

"I did it for my mother. She was from Scotland. My father met her at a Celtic music festival she was singing at, and they just hit it off."

Angela slightly turned, to see Rhiannon's face. "You never told me your mother could sing."

"It never came up in conversation. She had a divine voice, and when she sang in Gaelic, it took my breath away. It's such a very lyrical language and a dying one at that. It was sheer luck both my old school and Cowan offered it as a subject. It enabled me to continue my studies." She toyed with Angela's soft brown hair. "And allowed me to put it to good use."

Angela lightly tapped one of the legs she was snuggled between. "You never mentioned before now that your mother was a singer. I've never heard you sing."

"And you most likely never will. I couldn't carry a tune in the shower, let alone anywhere more public."

Angela went to laugh but instead coughed, the tremors carrying a not too unwelcome vibration against Rhiannon's chest.

"Are you okay?" Rhiannon reached over to the side table and snagged one of the lime and sodas resting there. She placed the drink in Angela's waiting hand. "This might help."

Angela took a sip and handed the glass back to Rhiannon. "Thanks."

Rhiannon took the glass and returned it to its original place, smiling at the casual interaction between them. She brought her hand back to Angela's waist and clasped her other, effectively hugging a semi-reclining Angela.

Angela toyed with her thumb, something Rhiannon immediately recognised as a habit she'd displayed as a student, when she was nervous or trying to work out how to ask something. She bent her head and softly kissed Angela's ear. "What are you thinking about?"

"Um...I just wondered...I mean I was wondering how you knew you preferred women."

Rhiannon leant back against the chaise, easing Angela back with her. "I always knew something wasn't quite right but couldn't work out what."

"What do you mean?"

"In junior high all the other girls could talk about was which boy was the cutest. I couldn't have cared how they looked. But there were a couple of the girls who made me feel strange whenever I was near or saw them. But at the time I didn't know why."

Angela placed her hands over Rhiannon's. "Did you have anyone you could talk to?"

"Not anyone I felt I could trust, and I did feel like I could tell my mum. Besides, I didn't have any tangible idea of what was going on with me."

"How did you work it out?"

"One weekend, when I was about fourteen, I stayed at my Aunt Isabella's so we could go to a soccer game between the Matildas and the Football Ferns. That's the New Zealand women's soccer team. Aunt Isabella lived in a big house and one of her friends was staying with us, so we could all go to the soccer together."

Angela turned to see Rhiannon's face. "I'm assuming the other person was a woman."

Rhiannon nodded. "She was a fellow surgeon and friend of my aunt. I was always a late riser when I was young, not normally getting out of bed on the weekends until well after nine. But this morning we were seeing my favourite team and I was very keen for us to be on our way. I was up at the crack of dawn and had headed to the kitchen to get some breakfast."

Angela snickered. "I think I know where this is going."

"There they were, in each other's arms and at that moment everything clicked for me. It was sort of funny though, because Aunt Isabella's friend just about had a heart attack. I'm an athlete but I'd never seen someone move so fast."

"Was your aunt afraid she'd been caught?"

"I think so, but I didn't care. I was finally happy I wasn't the only one who felt like I did about girls. It also gave me the chance to talk with someone about what was going on."

Angela settled herself back into Rhiannon's arms. "It must have been a bit of a relief when you lived with her."

"It was, for both of us. It turned out Aunt Isabella dated men and women, but her last partner of fifteen years was a woman." Rhiannon paused, still hearing the sound of Isabella's voice when she told her Judith was gone.

"Are you all right?"

Rhiannon eased her head onto the back of the sofa. "I'm fine. I was remembering when Aunt Isabella rang and told me Judith had passed away. She was devastated."

Angela made to disentangle herself from Rhiannon. "We don't have to talk about this if you don't want."

Rhiannon was surprised at the pain the remembrance brought her, even after so many years. "It's okay. It was very sad." She hugged Angela to her, and Angela settled back down. "But I prefer to remember the fun times they had."

"How did they meet?"

"Judith was a theatre nurse, in the same hospital my aunt worked at. They often worked in the same operation suite. And when they did, they apparently always clashed, over the most trivial of things. It came to a head one day, and my aunt demanded Judith meet her in her office."

"She was calling her on the carpet?"

"She was. Anyway, the meeting was not too different to how they reacted with each other in the theatre. They finally got to a point where they were toe to toe and shouting at each other when Judith just out and kissed Aunt Isabella."

Angela put her hand to her mouth. "Oh my God. What did your aunt do?"

"She kissed her back, finally realising what existed between them wasn't professional, it was emotional. They were together from that day on."

"And I suppose the rest of the theatre staff were happy for the peace and quiet?"

Rhiannon chuckled. "Very much so."

Silence descended and Angela again began to toy with her thumb. Rhiannon nudged her. "Another question perhaps?"

Angela turned in Rhiannon's arms. "You know the day in the music study."

Rhiannon sensuously raised her brow. "Yes," she said, drawing out the word.

"When you held me. The feeling between us seemed so strong. So much so I thought you were going to kiss me."

Rhiannon closed her eyes, recalling vividly the moment they'd shared. She opened her eyes. "It's because I almost did. I was very tempted."

"Why didn't you?"

"For starters, although I sensed there was something going on below the surface between us, I couldn't be sure how you'd react. I mean, after our first few months of discussions and random meetings in the senior's study, it didn't take me long to work out what I was feeling extended beyond merely friendship. But showing you how I felt by kissing you was a damned big and potentially dangerous step. Especially when I wasn't sure if you felt the same way."

Angela toyed with Rhiannon's fingers. "What if I'd welcomed it?"

"I expect we would have had a lot of explaining to do about why we had newspaper ink stains in places where they shouldn't be." Rhiannon laughed at the blush gracing Angela's face. "Not to mention, I don't think we would have ever finished our muck up day task in the time I'd told everyone else to finish in. Speaking of which..." Rhiannon glanced at her watch and her eyes widened. "Is that the time?"

"Hmm?" Angela snuggled back down into the comfort of Rhiannon's chest.

"It's two in the morning."

Angela sat up. "Is it? Where did the time go?"

"I haven't a clue." Rhiannon eased Angela from her recumbent position and stood. She reached down, grasped Angela's hand, and pulled her into her arms.

"I'm going to have to run. I've an international business call due in my suite in two and a half hours and there's still a few things I need to check on before I take it." She moved an errant strand of hair from Angela's face. "Given what's happened over the past few hours, I know where I'd prefer to stay."

Angela's fingers stroked Rhiannon's neck, coming to rest on the top button of Rhiannon's blouse. "I expect you'll have to learn to organise yourself a little better. Won't you?"

Angela pulled Rhiannon into a hug then escorted her to the door. "What does your day hold after the conference call?"

Rhiannon picked up her car keys from the hallway table where she'd left them earlier in the evening. "This call isn't supposed to go much longer than about forty-five minutes. I'm expected at the firm I'm working for at about nine-thirty."

"That leaves you little time for sleep."

"It won't be the first time I've pulled an all nighter."

"Who are you working for again?" Angela worked the locks on the front door and switched on the motion lights to illuminate the garden path. "I don't think you told me their name."

"I'm currently contracted to a consulting company called Peak Personnel Solutions. It's owned by a dear friend of mine and his..." Rhiannon caught herself, strangely unsure of how Angela might respond to hearing Luke was gay, "partner. Their focus is on maximising the human resource aspects of the companies they consult with. They're a relatively new organisation with some fairly good credentials, even for a young group operating in the business they're in. Apparently one of the reasons they brought me on board was to entice some of the big guns of business, while at the same time allowing them to develop from my experience."

"If that's why they hired you, you must be very highly regarded in your field."

"I am," Rhiannon replied, attempting not to sound too sure of herself. "It seems to have already paid off. Luke called me just before the reunion to offer me a stint analysing and providing solutions for some personnel issues with a company in the Sydney CBD. The project is less complex than what I'm used to undertaking but I'm sure it will be interesting all the same." Rhiannon searched her memory for the name of the company she'd fleetingly perused in the briefing portfolio sent to her by Luke. "I think Luke said their name was Gardely and Balen. But I'm not one hundred percent sure."

Angela drew her brows together in thought. "You know, the name rings a bell, but I don't know why. Are they involved in any major projects at the moment?"

Rhiannon shrugged. "I'm not terribly sure what their current projects are. Most of the ones listed in the portfolio and HR documents they gave me are over six months old now. And I don't know if any of them are still extant. I expect I'll have a better idea of what they're involved in when I meet with them later this morning. Having said that, I'm sure they'll have disclosure clauses about what I can mention to people outside their company. It seems to be the way business is done these days."

Angela put a hand on her hip and clicked the fingers of her other hand. "Damn, now what am I going to do? I suppose I'll lose my industrial espionage pin if I can't pump you for information."

Pulling Angela to her, Rhiannon chuckled. "And here I was, thinking you were interested in me, when you were only ever after what I hold in that thick skull of mine."

Angela's hand encircled the back of Rhiannon's neck and she looked into her eyes. "I'd have to say my interest definitely lies in the whole package and not merely a part of it." She gradually pulled Rhiannon's head down to her waiting lips.

The two stood locked, arms entwined around each other. The kiss, which had started off as something relatively innocent, rapidly progressed toward a decidedly more passionate outcome.

Rhiannon broke the embrace and stepped away. "I think I better go, otherwise there's going to be some rather annoyed people in New York when I don't take their call." Rhiannon reached out and brushed Angela's face. "Can I call you tonight?"

Angela tilted her head into the contact and smiled. "I'd be disappointed if you didn't. I think there's still much more for us to talk about." Before she could qualify her comment, a yawn broke forth and she attempted conceal it with her hand. "But you're right. I think we both need to get a little rest."

Rhiannon gently grasped Angela's hand and gallantly raised it to her lips. "Till tomorrow," she said and made her way down the steps and to her car.

A particularly raucous squawk from the trees above brought Rhiannon back to the present. "That's enough from you," she muttered. Realising any further reminiscing was merely delaying the inevitable, she shook her legs and arms and resolutely made her way up the hill.

ANGELA STRETCHED LANGUIDLY. Having woken at the outrageously late hour of ten in the morning, she lay in bed and mentally mapped the day before her. Firstly, there were some very much needed rehearsals she had to do. Despite her current short touring sabbatical, it was still necessary for her to rehearse at least once a day, twice if she could manage. "Of course," she snickered. "That didn't quite go to plan yesterday, did it?"

Stretching her arms above her head, she recalled the last twenty-four hours and its amazing turn of events. Or maybe not so much a turn of events, as a circle coming its full course.

She pressed the button by her bed and watched the curtain to the back-yard window silently raise, letting in the morning sun. Rolling onto her side, she scanned the outside. "A call to the gardener might be in order too. The back yard is starting to take on jungle-sized proportions." She didn't mind a bit of overgrowth. It had the tendency to attract the native birds dominating this part of Sydney. Unfortunately, it also attracted other unwelcome visitors such as spiders and other creepy crawlies. It was only last week she'd wandered out to find Lachie's full attention captured by a red back spider while it calmly went about the business of weaving its web.

"Lachie!" Angela sat bolt upright in bed, her mental meandering abruptly halted. Her eyes widened as her thoughts went to what had passed between her and Rhiannon and what it might mean for her son. She checked herself. What *was* the current situation between Rhiannon and her? What did she want it to be? Certainly, she'd welcomed the warmth and comfort Rhiannon had given her. They were feelings she'd willingly reciprocated last night. But, in the cold light of day she couldn't help but wonder just exactly where they were both heading.

For too long it had been only her and Lachie. How would he react to such a dramatic change in circumstances, if indeed there was one to react to? The more Angela thought about it, the greater her confusion became. She was in no doubt she had feelings for Rhiannon. But where did that fit into her life? Before she could over analyse the matter any further, the shrill sound of the phone echoed around the room.

She picked it up and answered vaguely, her thoughts well and truly elsewhere.

"Hello, Angela are you there?"

The clipped tones of her close friend and head of the Save the Con group, Phillipa Power, snapped her from her pensive state. "Sorry Phillipa, I was away with the birds. How are you?"

Phillipa chuckled. "More to the point, how are you? You sound a million miles away."

"I had a bit of a late night." Before she could say anymore, Phillipa cut in.

"Really," she said, a strong emphasis placed on the word. "And who was it that you were out to all hours with, hmm?"

A stain of red suffused her features, and Angela was grateful for the degree of visual anonymity the phone call afforded her. "It's not what you think. I had a friend over for dinner, that's all."

"Okay." The unmistakeably eager tone of Phillipa's voice filtered down the line. "And what's his name?"

Angela slightly shook her head and sighed. "It wasn't a man if you must know, it was just an old school friend of mine I met at the reunion I went to the other night. She's a businesswoman now and only recently arrived back in Sydney after being abroad. We were catching up on things." Which I don't intend to share with you at this stage, Angela uttered under her voice.

"Oh." The disappointment in Phillipa's voice was obvious. "You know there are a wealth of men out there I know who'd love to take you out to dinner, if you'd only leave that house of yours. You're too young to sit there and do nothing at all."

"Phillipa, that's not the case and you know it. I have Lachie and my music and more than enough other things to occupy my time."

"But none of them can keep you warm at night."

Angela mulled over the events of the previous evening. Breaking herself out of such thoughts, she endeavoured to redirect the focus of their conversation. "I'm sure you didn't ring to lecture me on various aspects of my love life or lack thereof. Why did you call?"

"Sorry, I got side-tracked there for a minute. I wanted to see whether you're free on Tuesday evening. We're having a small function at the Con to raise money for the legal fees needed to fight the proposed changes they're thinking of making to the Con's buildings. It's horrendous the designs some of these companies are coming up with."

Angela listened absently while her friend launched into her normal tirade about the shocking state of affairs regarding suggested architectural improvements to the Con, or the Australasian Conservatorium of Music as it was more formally known.

Under the auspices of upgrading the existing buildings, some of which were well over one hundred years old, the state government had tendered for architectural improvements to the structure. Sadly, some of the submitted options paid scant attention to the Conservatorium's historical style. The final three tenderer's designs were austerely modern. They had the potential to take a building which was a stunning example of the romantic and picturesque gothic architecture of early Sydney and turn it into something akin to a bordello. Alumni of the Conservatorium had formed a fighting fund against any significant changes to the building's architectural style.

"What do you think?"

"I think the evening's a great idea." Angela replied, hoping to conceal the fact she'd missed the majority of what her friend had rattled on about.

"Of course, you think the evening's a good idea, but what about your contribution?"

Angela studied the phone in surprise, realising she'd obviously missed a key element of Phillipa's call. "My contribution, what contribution?"

"You haven't been listening have you?" Phillipa said, exasperated. "I was asking whether you would mind doing a little recital for the group. We figured we could charge a minor entry fee which could go into our slush fund for saving the Con."

Angela's silence was sufficient indication of what she thought of the idea.

"Come on Angela. I know it's been over a year since you performed in public. But it would very much help the cause. It wouldn't have to be too much, only a couple of pieces."

Angela scowled. The last thing she wanted to do was to give a performance without adequate preparation. But it wasn't the first time she'd weaselled her way out of such a request. To do so again wasn't in keeping with helping a cause she was supposed to be supporting.

"A couple of small pieces, but that's *it* Phillipa. I don't want to spend the whole evening tied to a piano, regardless of how much people might enjoy my playing."

"Great! We'll slot you in for say eight o'clock and following your recital will be the auction. I do appreciate your help with this one. It will make for a wonderful evening."

"I'm sure it will," Angela replied, despite feeling the opposite.

"Oh, I forgot to mention, you can bring someone if you want."

Angela's lips thinned at Phillipa's obvious attempt at match-making.

"Don't get me wrong, I'm not saying you should bring a date or anything so terrible as that. What about your school friend? If she's only recently returned, it mightn't be a bad idea to see if she's interested."

Angela smothered a laugh, wondering how Phillipa would react if she was actually aware of the nature of just where Rhiannon's interests lie. "I'll ask her and get back to you. But I can't make any promises. She's only just begun work with a new company and she's doing consulting. Not to mention, I'm not wedded to the idea of you recruiting anyone I might bring along to the evening. It's sounds too much to me like you're taking advantage of my friends."

"Never! And I'm shocked to think you'd consider the only reason I'm asking you to bring her or anyone for that matter is to get them interested in the cause."

Angela's laughter halted any further protestations from Phillipa. "Stop trying to sound offended. I know you better than that. I'll get back to you regarding numbers. Just make sure everything's ready for the recital. In fact, if you could I'd appreciate being able to drop by on Tuesday afternoon for a short rehearsal. And seeing how I'm giving up my time, the least you could do is ensure my favourite piano is waiting for me." Aside from the one at home, Angela had always harboured a preference for the Sumato, one of the grand pianos on extended loan to the Conservatorium.

The phone's earpiece filled with Phillipa's long-suffering sigh. "You don't make things easy, do you? You do realise this will mean moving and retuning it before tomorrow?"

"Of course, I do. But you *do* want me to play, don't you?"

"Yes," Phillipa growled in jest. "I'll make sure it's ready. When do you want to rehearse?"

"What about two o'clock tomorrow? It should give them enough time to get it into position."

"I'll check with the staff and if it's likely to be a problem I'll get back to you. If you don't hear from me assume the time is fine. I'll see you and your friend tomorrow night."

"I'll let you know about Rhiannon. And no pork barrelling either or I'll refuse to play."

Saying her goodbyes, Angela rung off. She scrolled through her contacts and made herself comfortable on the bed, pulling up the three-season doona while she waited for the connection to go through.

"Good morning, Rhiannon Sharp."

Rhiannon's business-like tones echoed down the line, momentarily catching Angela off guard. It was the first time she'd heard her speak that way and she couldn't help but smile at the mental image it generated of a steely-eyed woman in her business suit, mixing it in an environment dominated by men.

"Hello Rhiannon Sharp, can I help you?" The second time the words were uttered with a degree of impatience.

Remembering some people did work relatively normal hours, Angela answered without further delay. "It's Angela. If I've called at a bad time I can call back."

"No, not at all. I should have looked at my caller ID." Rhiannon's voice softened. "I simply wondered what was going on when there wasn't any answer from your end. How are you?"

Angela smiled at the relative laziness of her morning so far. "I expect probably a little better than you, seeing how you're at work and I'm still in bed."

"Being in bed does seems a much better option."

Angela gasped.

"I mean, don't take it the wrong way," Rhiannon managed to stammer. "I didn't mean that you and me...well...you know...oh hell!"

Picturing Rhiannon's face, Angela laughed tenderly. "I know what you mean. You just threw me for a second. Have you learnt anything about your consultancy you can share with me? Something I could sell to the opposition perhaps," she finished in jest.

"Now I know you're making fun of me. But don't you worry, there'll be time enough for me to pay you back. In short, the group I'm working with are finding it hard to retain their skilled workers, which isn't uncommon to what's being experienced by most organisations today. They want me to review the matter and suggest some ideas for how to resolve the situation."

"What seems to be the problem?"

"I'm not entirely sure yet. I'm only beginning to get my head around the outcomes of my very preliminary analysis. They seem to pay their people a decent wage. But I'm not sure they realise financial reward isn't the sole motivator for working in a company. The thing which never ceases to amaze me is none of the solutions I'll end up suggesting are rocket science and yet they seem blind to what internal problems exist."

"I know what you mean. But sometimes you don't know what the situation is until it's explained to you by someone further removed from the problem. Anyway, what I was calling about is whether you were doing anything on Tuesday night."

Angela listened to the sounds of movement from the other end of the line.

"Hang on, let me have a look in my organiser. Tuesday — it's clear from what I can see here. What did you have in mind?"

"An old friend of mine from the Con is organising a function to support her latest favourite cause and she's asked me if I'd perform a small recital. She said I could bring someone along and I wondered if you were busy." Angela unconsciously held her breath, waiting for Rhiannon's reply.

"That's the Conservatorium I'm assuming?"

"Sorry. I get used to using its abbreviated name, forgetting it's not always known as such by everyone."

"There's no need to apologise. I'd love to come along. Let me get a pen so I can jot down the details. What time is it due to start and what's the dress?"

"It's after five attire and the recital is at eight o'clock. I suspect the evening will most likely start about seven thirty. I'd like to be there by about seven, to limber up my fingers before I play. I was thinking we could save fuel and go together. But if it's too early, I can meet you there if you want." Angela's voice trailed away, realising she was making decisions for Rhiannon without even asking her.

"That's fine by me. I'll leave the office early enough to change. If you want, I can pick you up at say, about six thirty? It will give us plenty of time to fight the bridge traffic if need be."

Angela nodded out of habit; despite the fact she knew she couldn't be seen. "Sounds like a plan. Now I expect if I'm to sound anything akin to a concert pianist tomorrow evening, I best get some rehearsing under my belt."

"If last night was any indication," Rhiannon's voice lowered to a more intimate, sensuous level, "then I expect you've got nothing to worry about, except perhaps some of your more ardent fans throwing themselves at your feet."

Angela blushed. "That was different. I was playing for an audience whose opinion means a great deal to me. I have to honestly say I haven't played so well in a long time."

"I'm flattered to think that was the case."

"You always had that effect on me. Whenever you listened to my rehearsals, I always focussed on playing as well as I possibly could. Funny isn't it that after all these years I'm only now realising that."

"Yes, but better late than never. Hang on a minute."

There was a muffled exchange of words between Rhiannon and another party before she came back on the line. "I'm going to have to go. It seems I've been summoned to the executive floor. Can I still call you tonight?"

"Of course. I'm expecting a call from Lachie around seven but any time after would be fine. I better get my act into gear. If I don't the day will have gotten away from me and I'll be still lounging in bed." Angela rose and headed to her wardrobe to lay out her clothes for the day ahead.

"As fun as it sounds, you're right. I'll call you later this evening and you can tell me how your rehearsals have been going. I'll talk to you soon."

RHIANNON FOLLOWED THE executive assistant sent to summon her out the elevator and onto the executive floor of the company. Cream carpet and warm wood was the overriding theme, with paintings of contemporary Australian artists adorning the walls. She examined one of the artworks—originals, from the Heidelberg School if she wasn't mistaken. Aunt Isabella would have been impressed.

"If you'd follow me please."

She walked down a corridor and found herself ushered into a conference space, two walls of which were almost floor to ceiling glass, with commanding views of the Opera House and across to Neutral Bay. She pulled her eyes away from a view which always left her spellbound, to the man walking toward her, hand extended.

"Ms. Sharp, it's nice to finally meet you. I'm sorry I wasn't here when you first arrived. I'm Thomas Gardely."

She took the proffered hand. "Please call me Rhiannon."

"Only if you'll call me Thomas. We are delighted to have you on board. Let me introduce you to my senior management team."

Rhiannon graciously shook the hand of each of the men, consciously filing away faces and names should she need to dredge them up at a later date. Despite her polite outward countenance, she couldn't help but be frustrated by the lack of any women or diversity representation on their team.

"Please take a seat." Thomas motioned one of the executive assistants forward. "Libby, I'll have a coffee, black please. Rhiannon, do you want anything?"

Rhiannon eyed the water on the table. "Thank you, Libby. I'll be fine with the water."

The remainder of the group took their respective seats, eyes eagerly seeking out their CEO.

"Roger has already provided you with a copy of our prospectus?" Thomas dismissively motioned his thanks at the coffee placed at his right side.

"He has, as well as some HR material, which enabled me to begin my analysis. I'm impressed at the broad reach of your organisation. I have to say I was surprised your prospectus didn't list any of your current projects." The shifting of seated bodies around the table and the furtive glances shared between the majority of its occupants were not lost on Rhiannon.

"We do have an expansive portfolio," Thomas replied. "And we are very circumspect regarding disseminating such knowledge more widely than it needs to be. This allows us to retain our competitive edge in the market."

Rhiannon sipped her water and weighed the non-verbal undercurrent clearly flowing through the room. "I understand. I once led a team delivering an Australian Army contract and they were very clear on intellectual property and conflict of interest. I doubt I'll need to be explicitly aware of each of your projects. I see my focus as primarily on the human resources aspects of your company."

Thomas reached into the folder he held and pulled out a one-page document. "I'm glad you're familiar with non-disclosure. I have similar requirements here." He handed the document across to her. "This is our standard proprietary information agreement.

Could you please review it? If you don't have any concerns can you sign it and hand it off to your executive assistant by, say, tomorrow morning?"

Rhiannon took the document. Even the Australian Army hadn't required her to sign such a declaration. They had taken her at her word. She took a deep breath and cast a rudimentary eye over the paper in her hands. "It seems fine to me. But if you don't mind, I'll take it back to my office and have a closer look at it." She put the paper down in front of her. "To be clear though, my integrity and my word is my bond." She met the faces of each of the executives. "I would never discuss anything I do while contracted to a company without first gaining their written consent."

More than one set of eyes avoided her steely blue stare.

"That's exactly what I've heard about you. Now, let's begin, shall we?" Thomas motioned for the presentation to start.

RHIANNON MADE HER way back to her allocated office, all the while mulling on the meeting and Thomas Gardely's insistence on not discussing her work with anyone. She walked into her office and closed the door behind her.

She dropped the paper on her table and took a seat. She'd never been in the habit of discussing her work outside of normal hours. That had more to do with the fact that, despite her previous relationships, her work was not something she normally wanted to share with her girlfriends. Would it be any different with Angela? There was still so much they needed to talk about.

She swivelled her chair to the view outside and stared out her window, wondering just where their relationship was heading. In the cold, rational light of day she thought on the events of the night before. Was it the magic of the evening, a passing experiment, or was Angela interested in something more? Rhiannon was very eager to give their rekindled friendship every opportunity of developing further. But was that what Angela wanted?

The buzzing of her mobile interrupted her train of thought. She reached back to her table and picked up her phone. "Rhiannon Sharp," she answered distractedly, her mind still dominated by thoughts of Angela.

"Are you always this vague on the phone Ms. Sharp, or only with certain people?"

Rhiannon immediately recognised Elly's measured tones. "You should know us right brained types. Always away with the birds on one concept or another." The two shared a laugh. "How are you and more to the point, how can I help you?"

"I'm fine. I was telling Jen I'd caught up with you at the reunion and how you'd gotten back into town after being away for a while. She thought it might be a wonderful idea if we got together for dinner. Are you free tomorrow night?"

"A catch up sounds great. But I've got a date for tomorrow evening." Rhiannon closed her eyes, strangely embarrassed at how her words must have sounded.

Elly chuckled. "I've heard of fast workers but that *is* quick. I didn't think you'd been back in the country long enough to find someone who piqued your interest. Or did you happen to find who it was you were searching for on Saturday night?"

Rhiannon opened her eyes and rocked back in her chair. "I did. But I don't know if I should call tomorrow night's occasion strictly a date. I've been invited to a function at the Conservatorium. I thought it would be nice to get back into the social side of things." Not to mention be with the company I'm going with, she added silently.

"Why don't you ask Angela if she wants to come along to dinner?"

Surprised, Rhiannon brought her chair to its previous upright position. "How did you know?"

"Remember on Saturday evening I mentioned there were other people who only had eyes for you on the last day of school?"

"Yes."

"I was referring to her. If ever I couldn't find you in the room, all I had to do was find Angela and follow the path of her eyes. I wondered at the time if the two of you were more than merely friends."

Rhiannon ran her fingers through her hair. "We were great friends and she supported me through what could have been a very difficult final year. I often used to sit in the hall when she rehearsed of a morning. It relaxed me quite a lot."

"When did you realise what you felt might be more than friendship?"

"I sensed something early on, not long after we first met. But it was only on the evening before the final day of school when I realised it was possible her feelings also ran deeper than just friendship. Then it was the final day, and everything was incredibly difficult." Rhiannon paused, lost in thought.

"Rhiannon," Elly's concerned tones carried down the line. "Are you okay?"

"I'm fine, just thinking too deeply I suppose. Angela was at the reunion, in her usual place in the hall. I briefly caught up with her. But she had to leave. I drove her home and we met for lunch the next day and followed up with dinner. Suffice to say, we finally got around to talking about what we should have spoken about twenty years ago."

"It sounds promising or...isn't it?" she finished, her tone uncertain.

It comforted Rhiannon to be able to discuss what was happening between the two of them with someone else. There weren't too many people she could do that with. "It is. But it's still early. There seems to be something between us. But I'm still not entirely sure if this is what she genuinely wants. It seems to be relatively new to her."

"Do you think she might be uncomfortable coming to dinner at our place?"

"I don't know. While she's not said anything in the short time since we've reconnected, I suspect she's never gone out with a woman. But I'd be surprised if she hasn't rubbed shoulders with gay artists in the world of music."

"Do you think there's more to her concerns than merely a relationship with you?"

Although she hadn't mentioned anything, it would be naïve for Rhiannon to believe Angela wouldn't be conscious of any potential reaction her son might have to her new friendship.

"On top of the relative newness of what's happening between us, she lost her husband to terminal illness in the first year after their son was born. She's a single mother, with a seven-year-old to bring up. I'd be foolish to think this wouldn't influence her choices, more broadly. Maybe a dinner might be just the thing to help her to work through any reservations she might have regarding the two of us. I'll see if she's interested and get back to you."

"If you can't make it tomorrow, does another night work? We're home all this week."

"Could we make it Wednesday? I'd love to catch up with you and meet Jen, even if I end up going stag," Rhiannon replied, strangely disappointed at the prospect of attending the dinner alone.

"Wednesday's fine. Make sure you let me know how many I'm cooking for and if there's anything the two of you don't eat. I better let you go. Could you let me know by say, Wednesday morning at the latest?"

"Not a problem." Rhiannon jotted down the directions to Elly and Jen's home on the notepad in front of her. She finished the call, making a note to ask Angela whether she wanted to go to dinner when she called her later that evening. But how was she going to explain their dinner partners?

AFTER WHAT SEEMED an endless day spent in business attire, Rhiannon was relieved to be able to finally relax in shorts and T-shirt. She made herself comfortable on the lounge in her suite, scrolled through the recent callers on her phone and tapped on Angela's number. While she patiently waited, she couldn't help but wonder what Angela was up to. If she had to guess, she'd be rehearsing, especially given her recital the following night.

"Hi Rhiannon," Angela said breathlessly. "Apologies about the delay. I don't always carry my phone around with me. It was lucky I had the piano room door open otherwise I'd have never heard it ringing in the kitchen."

Rhiannon grinned at having correctly deduced what Angela was doing. "That's okay. I'd have left a message."

"How was your day?"

"It wasn't too bad, just the standard corporate grin and grip, followed by registrations and security pass issues. The office is pretty nice though. It's got great views of the harbour." Rhiannon paused, suddenly feeling as if the conversation was somehow all one sided. "Angela, are you there?"

"What, oh sorry, I'm listening. It's just I'm a little preoccupied with tomorrow night. It's been a while since I've played in public."

Rhiannon couldn't help but smile. It was as she'd remembered when Angela would rehearse in the school hall, her focus consumed by the instrument before her. "That's okay, we can talk about my day some other time. But if you've got a minute could I ask you if you had anything planned for Wednesday night?"

"I'm free. With Lachie and my rehearsals, I really don't get out that much."

"In that case a friend has invited me to her place for dinner. She said I could bring someone, and I was wondering whether you would like to join me?"

Rhiannon again waited, at odds to determine the root of Angela's prolonged silence. "It will just be the four of us," she added, hoping that would make the evening more amenable to Angela.

"That sounds fine," Angela said her voice tentative. "Can we discuss it further tomorrow when you pick me up?"

Rhiannon sensed the change in Angela's tone, but was it borne out of preoccupation or uncertainty? She pulled herself into a seated position on the lounge.

"Sure; no worries. I'll let you get back to your rehearsal."

"Thanks. I don't mean to sound so vague, it's just—"

"Don't worry about it. We'll have plenty of time to talk about it tomorrow."

Chapter Eight

ANGELA ENTERED THE recital hall where she was due to perform that night. It was one of two auditoriums designed for such a purpose—its twin situated at the opposite end of the building. The room, understated in its architecture, was predominantly taken up by seating and a large stage, with sufficient space to accommodate two grand pianos. The soft violet carpeting was a little dated against the light wood walls, and yet the surrounds held warm memories for her. When she'd attended the Con, she'd spent endless hours practicing and playing in this space.

She timed her arrival perfectly. The piano technician on the stage was just closing his tool case. He stood and turned, a smile gracing his features.

"Miss Drayton, it's nice to see you again."

Angela walked onto the wooden stage. "Mr. Christian, what a surprise." She gazed fondly at him, recalling all the times he'd readied pianos for her, both here and in the Opera House. "I thought you'd retired years ago."

Mr. Christian wiped a minuscule speck of dust from the Sumato. "I did for a while but there was nothing for me to do. I have another specialist who works with me and she normally supervises the moving and retuning of pianos. But when I heard it was you here tonight, I told her I would personally see to this. It's lovely to have you playing again."

"I'm not back full time. This is more a favour for a friend."

"Either way, I'm very excited at the prospect of hearing you tonight. Your music is always such a pleasure to listen to."

Angela dipped her head at the compliment. "Thank you. I'm glad you can make the recital." She glanced at the piano. "However, if there's to be one, I better get on with a rehearsal."

Mr. Christian picked up his tool case. "It's all ready for you. I might see you again tonight?"

Angela nodded as he left the stage, already preoccupied with the Sumato grand piano in front of her. She spent the first part of her rehearsal warming up and testing the instrument. Although she had previously played the Sumato, she always liked to reacquaint herself before she commenced any more comprehensive compositions.

Satisfied, she shifted from her warmup to the pieces she

would play, her mind visualising the audience for the evening. She knew she would be among friends, and they would graciously pardon any rustiness caused by her sojourn from performing on a more regular basis. They would just be happy for her to be entertaining them. Despite this, she knew she would settle for nothing less than a perfect performance, if not for her friends, but more importantly for Rhiannon. She shook her head, forcing thoughts of her from her mind, in favour of the clarity she needed for her rehearsal. In the end, the practice lasted the greater part of the afternoon, barely leaving her time get home, shower, and change in anticipation of Rhiannon's arrival.

RHIANNON PRESSED ANGELA'S front doorbell and stepped back. She'd finished the brainstorming with Gardely and Balen's HR team that afternoon, with scant time to return to the hotel, shower, apply a light dusting of makeup and change.

While she waited, she moved in front of one of the glass panels paralleling the door. The ambient motion sensor light of the porch afforded sufficient opportunity for her to scrutinise the platinum slacks and deep burgundy silk blouse she wore. Given she was still waiting for the majority of her clothing and effects to arrive from overseas, she hoped this, and the accompanying full-length platinum buttonless jacket, would pass muster for the Conservatorium. Hearing the lock release, she stepped back as the door opened.

Angela had dressed similarly to what Rhiannon had previously seen her wear when she performed in London. She wore a midnight black, fitted bodice and full skirt dress, her arms bare so as to not hinder her ability to play. In the modest v neck of the dress in the hollow of her throat sat a flaming harlequin opal in a modern gold setting, its multi-faceted colours reminding Rhiannon of a stellar constellation. Rhiannon's eyes slowly travelled up her body to Angela's green eyes and was struck dumb by the piercing, wanting gaze she saw there. She cleared her throat, trying to rein in her own less than pure thoughts.

Oblivious, Angela reached out and fingered her jacket. "You look beautiful. The colour suits you," Angela said warmly.

"No more than you do," Rhiannon replied, relieved at last to be capable of forming a coherent sentence. "I've only seen you in that outfit once before and you took my breath away on that occasion as well."

Angela motioned for Rhiannon to follow her. "Do you want

to come in? I've got to get my wrap and purse."

Angela slightly turned, revealing her mostly bare back to Rhiannon's eyes. She swallowed, forcing herself to tamp down the tendrils of desire filling her being. "I think it might be best for both of us if I wait here and you grab your wrap."

Angela glimpsed quizzically at her.

"I'm afraid if I come in, we may not end up anywhere near where we're supposed to be."

Angela slightly lowered her head and smiled shyly; her eyes still focussed on Rhiannon's. She turned and went back into the lounge.

Rhiannon rubbed the junction of her neck and shoulder, attempting to release the exquisite tension trapped there. How was she ever going to make it through this evening, especially if Angela kept looking at her the way she just did?

DRIVING ACROSS THE Harbour bridge, it was hard for Rhiannon not to appreciate the beauty of Sydney Harbour at night. The multi-coloured neon lights of the business district cast an intermittent rainbow over the inky black water, resulting in a shimmering kaleidoscope of colour off the dark waves. On Bennelong Point stood the Sydney Opera House. Warm subtle lighting bathed the building, making it come alive. The white sails of the building created an illusion the sails, although concrete and covered in thousands of white tiles, were in fact in motion. Meanwhile on the water, the Sydney ferries continued to ply their trade, carrying passengers across the vast body of water, to the multitude of inlets dotted along its northern shores.

Rhiannon negotiated a path around a bus. "Despite how many times I travel across the bridge at night I never tire of the view."

"I know what you mean. I love those festivals they have, when they light up the Opera House in all the different colours and designs." Angela settled back into her seat. "It makes the building come alive."

Rhiannon nervously wetted her lips. "I was wondering whether you'd given any further thought to our dinner invitation tomorrow night. It will only be us and the two women who live there together."

Through the corner of her eye Rhiannon saw the subtle change in Angela's body language when she mentioned Elly and Jen's relationship. Angela shifted in her seat, her face turned toward the passenger window, as if trying to avoid giving Rhiannon an answer.

"Are you sure you're all right with the idea of coming to dinner? I'd understand if you didn't want to. The last thing I want you to feel is uncomfortable. In fact, why don't we talk about this later? I should have realised now wasn't a good time." Rhiannon silently groaned. *She's about to give a recital and you're talking about dinner. Maybe you can talk with her at the end of the evening you bean head, instead of the beginning.*

ANGELA KNEW SHE had, in principle, agreed to go to dinner when Rhiannon raised it with her yesterday. But her mind was preoccupied during their call. When Rhiannon had mentioned dinner, she hadn't given much thought to the makeup of the other couple. Now she wasn't entirely sure how she felt about the invitation. But hadn't she asked Rhiannon out to tonight's function? But that was different. It wasn't solely the two of them and another female couple she hadn't yet met. Tonight was a public event with people she knew. She was strangely grateful for such a setting, in amongst so many others. It offered a degree of anonymity for the two of them and what they had only, most recently, begun to share. An introvert at heart, she found the idea of sitting down to dinner with two other people a little daunting.

Realising she'd considered her reply for far too long, she struggled to translate her thoughts into an answer which wouldn't offend. "It's okay. I'm just not too good around people I haven't met. It's strange I know, considering I can sit in front of a packed concert hall and play and think nothing of it. But they're a reasonable distance away, if that makes any sense."

Rhiannon eased her grip on the steering wheel. "There's the possibility you'll at least know one of the women tomorrow night. Do you remember Elly Matheson, the English master at our school?"

"I do."

"I caught up with her at the reunion and she suggested she'd like to catch up with me when I got a chance. She rang yesterday and asked whether I was free for dinner sometime this week. She said I could bring someone along if I wanted and I thought of you."

"You mean she's..." Angela faltered, trying to find the right words to frame the relationship. "I mean...she's seeing a woman?"

"Yes, Elly's gay." Rhiannon replied offhandedly. "And given they have a little girl, I suspect they've been together for some time." Rhiannon merged onto the off ramp for the Conservatorium. "Why don't you give it some thought? If you're not comfortable with coming, that's fine."

Embarrassed at how accommodating Rhiannon was trying to be, Angela made up her mind. "I'd love to go with you. It will be interesting to catch up with Elly after all these years. I didn't see her at the reunion on Saturday. But then again, I wasn't looking for her either."

Rhiannon focussed on turning across the busy street and into the Conservatorium driveway. "I'm always amazed and more than a little bit relieved we managed to hold onto this building in its original state, given it was finished in 1821."

Angela cast her eyes over the white walled gothic architecture, its crenelated false ramparts nestled comfortably in the surrounding grounds. "It's seen its uses over the years. It's hard to think it was initially built for the sole purpose of stables for the horses of Governor Macquarie." She motioned to a partially concealed driveway to the left of the building. "Go down that way. It leads to parking out the back. There's not a lot of spaces but we're still early, so we might be lucky."

Rhiannon negotiated the narrow lane way and found a space to the rear of the area. She reached into the back and snagged Angela's wrap and moved around to open the sportscar's passenger door.

Angela took Rhiannon's hand and stepped out into the evening air. She looked down as Rhiannon continued to hold her hand, softly grazing her fingers with her own. At the release of her hand Angela couldn't help but feel a sudden loss. This was soon replaced by a sense of warmth, when Rhiannon stepped behind her and settled her wrap around her shoulders. For an infinitesimal moment Rhiannon's hands encircled her.

"Angela, is that you?"

At the sound of Phillipa's voice, Angela broke the connection but not before she shared a regretful smile with Rhiannon.

"Hello Phillipa."

Phillipa pulled Angela into a hug and air kiss and just as quickly released her. "How are you? I didn't realise you'd be here this early. But what else should I expect, getting in one more rehearsal are you?" She turned to Rhiannon, not waiting for Angela's response. "And you must be?"

Phillipa's eyes flitted between Angela and Rhiannon, expec-

tantly waiting for Angela to make introductions. Angela struggled with just how to do that. It was clear to her that she and
Rhiannon were more than friends. But should she say so? She
genuinely had no clue how Phillipa would react to the truth of the
situation.

"This is just an old school friend of mine, Rhiannon Sharp. As
I mentioned to you yesterday, she's in town on business after not
being in the country for a while."

Rhiannon extended her hand. "Hello Phillipa. Thank you for
allowing me to come tonight. I've often admired the amazing
architecture of the Conservatorium, but I've never actually been
inside."

Angela was privately relieved at Rhiannon's ability to effortlessly shift into small talk. And if that wasn't enough, Rhiannon
had, unknowingly, hit upon Phillipa's greatest love. Angela
rolled her eyes. She wouldn't be surprised, if by the end of the
evening, Phillipa had converted Rhiannon to her cause.

The three walked to the building's entrance. "Is that so? Why
don't I show you around while Angela goes through her final
preparations?"

Rhiannon held the door open, allowing Angela and Phillipa
to enter the foyer of the heritage building. "That's sounds fine.
You don't mind do you Angela?"

"Not at all. Phillipa could you? I need to get myself in order,
so I don't make a complete fool out of myself."

Angela failed to completely conceal the relief gracing her features. Given Rhiannon's covert gaze and subsequent contemplative expression, she was certain Rhiannon hadn't missed it either.
What Angela couldn't reconcile was whether her actions were
solely driven by the need to rehearse, or more about removing
herself from Phillipa's inquisitive stare?

Phillipa chuckled. "I doubt there's any chance of *that* happening if what I've heard about this afternoon's rehearsal is any
yardstick of your performance tonight." She linked Rhiannon's
arm in her own. "I'll give Rhiannon a tour and we'll meet you in
the cafe at seven-thirty, where we've set up a small supper prior
to your recital. Please do make it there, rather than waiting by
your piano like you often do. There are a number of your friends
here tonight, who are very keen to see you again."

Rhiannon glimpsed over her shoulder at Angela, as Phillipa
gently pulled her into the depths of the building, in turn leaving
Angela alone with her thoughts.

Angela walked down the hallway to the recital hall. Despite

the warmth of the building, she pulled her wrap tightly around her, as if in protection. Everything seemed to be happening too fast. First Rhiannon's dinner invite, and now the idea of mingling in a group of people with Rhiannon so close by. She was excited at the prospect of being escorted by someone who, despite the many years they'd spent apart, knew her better than most of her friends. Conversely, she was reticent. How would her friends view their friendship?

She wasn't a stranger to gay musicians. She'd been in orchestras all over the world with artists whose partners were the same sex. But given all her close friends were either married or in varying degrees of heterosexual relationships, she'd never given the matter any great deal of thought. How would those same friends react to the discovery that while she'd found someone again, it was a woman?

She walked through the entrance into the recital hall and closed the door behind her. At least for a while she was alone, free of any potential distractions the evening might hold.

"Come on Drayton. Shake out of it and focus on the now." She moved to the piano, sat down, closed her eyes and slowed her breathing. She emptied her mind of any distractions till, finally, all she could see in her mind's eye were the notes of the pieces, her fingers mentally running over the keyboard in front of her. Arriving at a state of serenity, she began her final rehearsal.

RHIANNON USED THE pretence of straightening her jacket to discreetly disengage her arm from Phillipa's grip. "Were you a student here, Phillipa?"

"Oh gosh no. I love to listen to artists perform. But I don't have a musical bone in my body. I leave the magic of music to people like Angela. You were schoolfriends I hear," Phillipa said as they turned the corridor leading to the far end of the building.

"We were. But I was only at the same school as Angela for just over the last two and a half years," Rhiannon replied cautiously, her internal radar effortlessly picking up on Phillipa's overly zealous interest.

"That's funny. She's never mentioned you until yesterday. Did you take music when you were at school?"

"I didn't. And she's probably not mentioned me because we went our separate ways at the end of school," Rhiannon deflected. "We were good friends while we were there though. But it's been a long while since we last ran into each other." They walked through into a small area which, given the cabinets around the walls, was the historical part of the Conservatorium. "Wow, this is interesting."

Rhiannon's comments were sufficient to distract Phillipa, who promptly launched into what was undoubtedly some sort of sales pitch but for what, Rhiannon was unsure. She was very familiar with the tactic, primarily when attending charity functions. She made a mental note to ask Angela what it was that Phillipa was trying to draw her into.

In the meantime, she was grateful for Phillipa's informative ramblings, as it gave her time to think on the evening's events. She hadn't missed Angela's initial reticence and slight discomfort when she'd introduced her to Phillipa, and then the look on Angela's face when Phillipa offered a tour of the building. She had seemed relieved, but why? Was it because of her? Was she uncomfortable being seen with her?

Phillipa lightly grasped Rhiannon's forearm. "And if you think that's amazing, come and see what they uncovered in the grounds in front of the Con, when they undertook an archaeological dig here last year."

Rhiannon nodded as she and Phillipa crossed the room to the other side of the exhibit. It had been over two years since Rhiannon had been involved in a serious relationship. She'd always been discrete when in public with another woman. Her caution was easily aided by the fact most times people saw what they wanted to see; their view often overly influenced by stereotypes. A good-looking, tall, immaculately dressed, svelte woman with long dark hair and brooding blue eyes was not exactly their poster child stereotype of a lesbian. The result was most times when she escorted another woman to a function hardly anyone batted an eyelid. All the same, she never tried to hide who she was. On the few occasions someone made inquiries, she told them to either mind their own business or had been painfully forthright, depending on the situation.

She somehow got the feeling tonight was not the night for candour. Despite the energy she felt between the two of them, she was sure Angela still struggled to form a comfortable frame of reference for her feelings.

"Let me take you through to our main recital hall. It has the most amazing acoustics."

"What makes it have such a clarity of sound?" she queried politely, allowing Phillipa to continue on a topic obviously dear to her, while she returned to her own contemplation. She was painfully aware of the effect Angela had on her. What wasn't clear to Rhiannon was how obvious this was to everyone else. She would need to be circumspect around Angela tonight, and not put her into a position she clearly wasn't ready for.

RHIANNON ADOPTED AN inconspicuous position next to one of the tables in the small café, while across the room Phillipa busied herself with a group of what were obviously reporters, if the camera one held was anything to go by. She chose a canape from the plate offered her and cast her eye around her surrounds.

The crowd wasn't overly large, not much more than fifty. By her estimation she was one of the younger guests there tonight. She popped the canape in her mouth and checked her watch. It was well past seven-thirty and Angela had still yet to make an appearance. Two men halting in front of her cut short her review.

One man stuck out his hand. "Good evening, I'm Brett Dean and this is Stuart Murray."

Rhiannon returned the shake. "Hi, Rhiannon Sharp."

"Is this your first time in the Conservatorium, Ms. Sharp?"

"Please call me Rhiannon," she replied. "It is, Mr. Dean. It's an amazing building."

"Brett and Stuart is fine. These events can be pretentious enough without having to add to them by referring to each other by surnames. What brings you here tonight? Are you part of Phillipa's heritage team, or whatever that thing of hers is called? I saw you with her earlier."

"I'm not, but she did give me a lovely tour when I first arrived." The light from the camera accompanying a reporter unexpectedly cast a beam across the three of them and she shielded her eyes. "I'm a guest of Angela Drayton."

"Are you a fellow artist?" Stuart took a beer from the platter of one of the servers circulating through the group.

"I'm a businesswoman. My speciality is in HR, negotiation and conflict resolution."

"Rhiannon Sharp." Brett rubbed the back of his head, eyes creased in thought. He scrutinised Rhiannon. "I remember now. You mediated a deal for the Antarctic secretariat. My wife and I were working for the Australian Antarctic Division at the time." He turned to Stuart. "Her work was a stroke of genius."

"How do you know Angela?" Stuart asked.

"We were in the same school for our senior years." Rhiannon again checked the room for Angela.

"What was she like at school? Did she play the piano back then?" Brett queried.

Rhiannon returned her gaze to the men in front of her. "I don't tell tales out of school as a rule." She wasn't quite sure how, but at that exact moment she knew Angela had entered the cafe.

She looked across the expanse to the fight or flight figure that was Angela. While to others she might have seemed poised, her back was too stiff, her hands gripped in front of her, creating a barrier between her and others. Angela's eyes finally came to rest on Rhiannon. She smiled and her body relaxed.

Rhiannon returned the smile and responded to Brett and Stuart, her eyes never leaving Angela's face. "But I can tell you she was the consummate professional. It's a pleasure to meet you both. If you would excuse me."

She moved across to meet Angela as she headed in her direction. The same television reporter and team who had been near her earlier temporarily halted Angela's progress.

Rhiannon made a detour for a server and removed a glass of water and serviette from a silver salver, precariously balanced by the waiter holding it. She walked around the reporters to Angela's side.

"Excuse me." She handed the water to Angela. "You looked like you needed this."

"Thank you." Angela took a long sip of the drink.

"Not a problem."

"My rehearsal may have been a little longer than was necessary." Angela wiped the residual water from her upper lip. "Excuse me for a minute," she said before focussing on the news crew in front of her.

Rhiannon stepped behind Angela, far enough aside to not interfere with her interview but close enough to still be a comforting presence.

For the next few minutes Angela politely answered the reporters, interspersing her response with sips from the glass she was holding. They thanked her and moved on, having finally secured their sound bite.

Angela opened her mouth to speak and Phillipa was at her side, tapping her watch. "I'm glad you could tear yourself away from the piano, even if you *are* late."

"Better late than never." Angela glimpsed around for somewhere to put her now empty glass.

"Let me." Rhiannon removed the glass from Angela's hands. She walked over to a server not far from where they stood and placed the glass on the tray before returning to Angela's side.

Phillipa playfully tapped Angela's arm. "I'm only teasing you. I'm glad you could come and play tonight. You have such a talent. It's a shame you don't perform as regularly anymore."

"Talent comes in many forms." Angela tilted her head to Rhiannon. "Rhiannon is an artist. She writes the most expressive poetry."

Rhiannon fought to contain her blush, without success. "Thank you," she managed.

"I thought Angela said you were a businesswoman. You're also a poet?" Phillipa raised her brows and pursed her lips. "What a dichotomy."

The shutter of a camera halted Rhiannon's response. The three looked toward the noise. A reporter muttered a soft thank you and walked to the next group of people.

"A dichotomy maybe. But people are the sum of a number of parts. Their lives shouldn't be solely judged on one part alone," Rhiannon replied.

"You're right. They shouldn't. What's your poetry about?"

Before Rhiannon could reply, a minor disturbance on the other side of the room distracted Phillipa. In doing so, she thankfully missed the fleeting glance shared between Angela and Rhiannon.

"You'll have to excuse me," Phillipa said. "Those damned reporters are bothering the governor, and I expressly asked them to leave her alone. I'll be back." Phillipa had barely finished her sentence and she was gone, leaving them alone.

"Are you okay?" It took every ounce of Rhiannon's willpower to not reach out and reassuringly stroke Angela's arm. "You looked a little out of it when you first came in here."

"I'm a bit overwhelmed, that's all. Phillipa's a good friend, but I'm very grateful you're here. You help to calm these nerves of mine."

A television camera panned over the two of them and Rhiannon checked her response. They both smiled woodenly, Rhiannon inwardly willing the man to move away, which he finally did. "Damned media. It makes me feel as if we're all goldfish in a bowl sometimes. You must tire of it, don't you?"

Angela shrugged. "It's a necessary evil of being in the spotlight. But I don't care for it though. Surely there are better stories for them to cover."

"That's the governor assuaged," Phillipa said, returning to the two of them.

Angela slightly distanced herself from her on Phillipa's return. Rhiannon noted Angela's action, but filed it away for further contemplation at a more appropriate time.

"And it's about time for your recital." Phillipa unobtrusively motioned across the space to a young man, who raised a bell and rang it twice.

The boy's actions reminded Rhiannon of an opera she'd attended overseas, where the lights dimmed to advise the patrons the opera was about to commence. Their proximity to the recital hall entrance guaranteed that Rhiannon would snare a front seat, affording her a perfect view of Angela.

With the hall finally filled, Angela looked out across the audience. Her eyes momentarily rested on Rhiannon's before she returned her focus to the instrument in front of her and began to play.

RHIANNON AND ANGELA stayed long enough after the recital's end to mingle with the assembled group and ever-present media. Rather than stay for the auction, they graciously made their excuses and left. Each was silent on the return journey, as if examining their own thoughts of the evening.

Rhiannon brought the car to a halt. She didn't make any attempt to open Angela's door, fearful her actions would imply she would welcome an invitation inside, when she wasn't sure it was what Angela wanted.

Angela released the seat belt and turned to her. "Would you like to come in?" she said, her voice unsure.

"Do you want me to come in?" Rhiannon asked carefully.

Angela nodded and alighted from the car. She walked up the steps to the front of the house and opened the door, Rhiannon closely following. She put her wrap and purse on the small table and continued down the hall.

Rhiannon closed the door behind her and followed Angela into the lounge. She halted short of where Angela stood, her back to Rhiannon.

Angela turned. "Could I ask a favour?"

"Anything."

"Could you hold me for a moment?"

In two strides Rhiannon closed the space between them and encased Angela in her arms. As she soothingly stroked Angela's back, the tautness in Angela's body seemed to melt away and she snuggled further into Rhiannon's shoulder. For a moment both took comfort in the quietude created through their connection.

Rhiannon slightly eased away from Angela. She drew her fingers lightly through Angela's hair before her hand came to rest on Angela's cheek.

Questioning, Angela raised her face, as Rhiannon slowly lowered her lips to Angela's. Angela's hand rested lightly on Rhiannon's neck as she melted into the kiss.

Rhiannon's kiss was chaste, in no way seeking to ignite intense desire through their connection. Instead she hoped to convey she was there for her should she need her. She broke the kiss and coaxed Angela out of their embrace. Her hand trailed down Angela's forearm and clasped her hand. "Why don't we sit down?" she said as she led Angela to the sofa.

Angela seated herself, never breaking the contact between the two. "What happened tonight? I mean I was happy with my performance. But the whole evening seemed to be incredibly awkward except when it was only you and me. I've never felt like that before."

Rhiannon looked down at the fingers entwined in her own and returned her eyes to Angela's. "I think the ideal has caught up with the reality. Maybe I was expecting things to be different to what they are."

Angela frowned. "I don't understand what you mean."

"I'm not helping much am I?" Rhiannon strove to find the right words. "What I'm trying to say is this is new ground for both of us. In the past I've obviously taken some things for granted, not the least of which is how I act in public when I'm out with another woman. I've never started this sort of friendship with a woman who, you know, has never previously dated a woman. I'm assuming going out with a woman is new ground for you."

"It is...and it isn't. Once before I married Patrick, a woman asked me out. She was a violinist in the orchestra I was with. I wasn't naïve. I knew for all intents and purposes the invite was a date. We went out for a drink but nothing more. I don't know what I was expecting. It was pleasant in a platonic sort of way. But there wasn't any emotional connection whatsoever." Angela stroked Rhiannon's hand. "Not like what we seem to have. And besides, when I was with her, I spent the whole evening wondering whether anyone from the orchestra was going to see us."

"Was it you were worried about someone from the orchestra seeing you out on a date? Or was it the fact the date was a woman?"

"Yes...no...oh I don't know."

"It's difficult when you're trying to sort out not only your own feelings but also how your friends will react." Rhiannon slowly pulled Angela's hand to her lips and placed a gentle kiss on her knuckles. "What you need to know is I'd be unhappy if you felt you were being forced into something you didn't want to be part of. I can take things at your pace or, indeed, step back if it's what you'd prefer."

"I don't want you to step back at all. It's just the depth of what I feel for you is new to me. I loved Patrick dearly. But how you make me feel is profoundly different. You have to believe me when I say there's only one thing grounding me at the moment and that's you." She covered their entwined hands with her other hand. "I don't know where this is going. But I know, this evening when we were together, I found myself wishing the rest of the world would go away. But that can't be the case and I've just got to work through it, if you'll allow me to do so that is," Angela finished, the timbre of her voice unsure.

Rhiannon pulled Angela into an embrace. "Take your time to work out where you stand. I'll wait. At the end of the day if all we have is friendship then I'm going to have to accept that." She kissed the top of Angela's head. "Although I'd be lying if I said I didn't want it to be more."

"I do too. Which is why tomorrow night scares me, but I want to go at the same time if that makes any sense. I don't want to have to think twice about what's going on around me when I look at you. Because trust me, if I look at you even remotely close to how you look at me, we'd be crazy to think that sooner or later someone won't realise what's going between us." Closing the distance between them, Angela captured Rhiannon's lips with her own.

Rhiannon returned the kiss. As Angela's tongue touched her lips, shyly seeking entry, Rhiannon responded, igniting the intimate contact between them. Angela's fingers traced a lazy path across Rhiannon's stomach, her fingers trailing up Rhiannon's side, ever so slightly coming into contact with the side of Rhiannon's breast before finally coming to rest on her shoulder.

Rhiannon's hand played across Angela's delightfully naked back. Despite her comments regarding pacing their relationship, Rhiannon knew she was rapidly approaching a point where it would be hard to control her actions, despite Angela's apparent willingness to escalate matters.

Rhiannon broke their kiss and released a shuddering breath.

She rose from the lounge, reached down for Angela's hand, and pulled her up. Holding her at arm's length, she could clearly see the undisguised hunger radiating in Angela's eyes.

"As much as I want to stay, I think I'd better go before, well..." A shy grin graced Rhiannon's features. "You know. I think you need time to think about what's happening between us, before you rush into anything."

Rhiannon walked to the front door and halted, Angela's hand still in her own. "I'll pick you up at about seven tomorrow. But if you change your mind it's okay. Just give me a call and let me know. I won't mind. I'd prefer you be comfortable than you go somewhere out of some mistaken sense of obligation."

Angela brought her free hand up to Rhiannon's face and caressed it lightly. "I do want to go. And seven will be fine. I'll call Lachie a little early tomorrow, that's all."

Rather than return to the passion they had shared in the lounge moments ago, Rhiannon kissed Angela on the cheek. "I'll see you then."

Chapter Nine

WEDNESDAY ENDED UP being quite a productive day for Angela. She managed to get a solid block of practice in the morning and finish some much-needed tidying around the house in the early afternoon, without the presence of the hurricane commonly known as Lachie. He was a good boy and would normally pick up after himself. Of course, that was unless he was too preoccupied on completing whatever he'd set his mind to. When that happened, he'd drive toward it with scant regard for anything which might get in his way. The result was normally a trail Angela would find, usually with her son at the end of the mess. It used to frustrate her when he would attack a plan in that fashion. But she soon realised his actions were not far from being a mirror of her own single-mindedness.

The shrill ring of the phone afforded her a temporary respite from the task of ridding the fridge of sauces and jams well past their use by date. She pulled the cleaning gloves from her hands and picked up the mobile. Her mother's number danced across the screen.

"Hi Mum."

"Angela darling, how are you?"

"I'm fine. But why are you calling this early? Is everything all right?" A note of alarm entered her voice as a myriad of scenarios involving possible injuries to Lachie raced through her mind.

"Everything's fine. I rang you to let you know Lachie won't be here this evening. He's camping in the Saunders' backyard with their three sons."

The Saunders were her mother's next-door neighbours. She breathed a sigh of relief. "Thanks for letting me know. I was going to call earlier tonight anyway. I'm going out to dinner and I didn't want to miss him. Obviously *camping* has a higher priority over speaking with his mother," she uttered with mock indignation.

Maureen chuckled. "The apple doesn't fall far from the tree with him, does it? You were not that different when you were his age. There were always more important things for you to do than to sit still for any great amount of time. In fact, on more than one occasion you neglected to tell me where you were going at all." Both women laughed in reminiscence. "You seem to be getting out a bit lately."

"What do you mean?"

"I had one of those breakfast programs on in the background this morning and they mentioned there had been a function at the Conservatorium featuring a recital by you. There was a voice over and some great footage of you at the piano and during the reception. How did it go and who was that with you?"

Angela's mind went from calm to overdrive. She rarely watched the television and didn't have a clue the media had telecast anything about the evening's recital. Sure, they were there. But the television and print media always attended such functions, taking what amounted to reams of footage which they usually never aired. She pinched her forehead between her thumb and fingers. If they'd televised the evening's events there would naturally be footage of her and Rhiannon together.

Realising her mother was still waiting for an answer, she attempted to redirect the conversation. "Why does the media feel the need to waste everyone's time with such reporting?"

"Hey calm down. In fact, I didn't see it at first. I was busy getting Lachie ready for his camping trip. He was having breakfast in the kitchen when, all of a sudden, he was shouting at the TV, with a full mouth of cereal I might add. After wiping the bench clean of the results of his outburst, I only managed to catch part of the report. To be honest, I was surprised to hear you were playing in public again."

"It was only a small function to assist the coffers of the Save the Con committee and the additional legal aid they require."

"I know most of the Sydney social set. But I couldn't place the person standing beside you in a couple of the screen shots. She seemed very engaged with what you had to say."

Angela dragged her fingers through her hair. "It just frustrates me so much. You'd think there'd be something more worthwhile for them to report. I haven't been in the public eye for over twelve months. I don't know why they'd be interested in me now."

"Sometimes you amaze me Angela. Of course, they're interested in what you're doing. You're an internationally renowned concert pianist. In fact, you're probably lucky they've left you alone for this long. I half expected you'd have the media and your manager figuratively breaking down your door by now with offers to perform again somewhere in the world. Speaking of which, was the person you were with chasing you for a performance?"

Angela nearly dropped the phone. Despite the nature of her mother's inquiry, it was the innocuous double entendre which flooded Angela's mind. Rhiannon had indeed chased her, and she'd finally allowed herself to be caught. But certainly not for any musical performance.

She thought back to the conversation they'd shared last night and Rhiannon's sometimes unguarded admiration of her. Had this been caught on film? If it had then what should she tell her mum?

She cursed silently, wishing she'd seen the piece so as to better gauge whether the camera had captured their emotional interaction. "She's not an agent, she's just the old school friend I met at the reunion I went to the other night—Rhiannon Sharp."

"The one you went to lunch with the other day?"

"Yes," Angela replied, silently praying for a respite from any further questioning from her mother.

"Hmm, now you've mentioned her last name, it is familiar. She's an author, isn't she? I was in the local bookstore last week. I remember seeing something written by her in the business section. The book had something to do with people and how they're the link to a successful organisation. I must admit it struck a chord that it had taken someone so long to point out the blatantly obvious to the rest of the world. All the same, from what I read it was well written and showed a depth of subject commitment beyond merely book sales."

Angela released a breath, relieved at the redirection. "She's a businesswoman of some note and has recently begun a new job in town. When we were at school, she'd often listen to me rehearse of a morning and we'd chat after I'd finished. It was nice back then to have someone to talk to who had interests outside of music."

"I hope she enjoyed herself. Who are you going to dinner with tonight?"

Angela wondered just how much she should tell her mum. Telling her she was going out with Rhiannon again would no doubt generate further comment. Maybe a creative interpretation of her dinner partners might be in order. "It's a group of friends that's all, most of whom I don't think you'd know. While I love Lachie dearly, sometimes it's nice to go to an adult dinner party every now and then."

"I know what you mean. Kids are wonderful. But it's pleasant to have grown up company every once in a while." The sound of a doorbell echoed in the background. "I've got to go love, someone's at the front door. Let me know how your evening goes."

"Before you go, is Sunday still okay for me to pick Lachie up?" Angela asked hurriedly.

"You know I'm more than happy to drop him off if it suits you better," Maureen replied.

"It's okay, I'll come to you. A drive in the country will do me good. Say about two in the afternoon?"

"Okay." The doorbell rang again. "I better go. Whoever's at the door is incredibly insistent." Maureen said her goodbyes and ended the connection.

Angela hung up, struggling to come to grips with her evasion during their call. She'd always shared a strong and entirely open relationship with her mother. She had greatly helped her during the early stages with Patrick's untimely death. They'd always been able to talk about anything. But how would she explain Rhiannon? And if she couldn't explain Rhiannon to her mum, who could she explain her to?

She returned to her task of cleaning out the fridge, all the while trying to rationalise what was developing between her and Rhiannon, and what it meant to her current life. She was all too aware she'd inevitably have to face the situation soon. It was just the *how* she struggled to come to grips with.

ANGELA GLANCED OUT the at the residences lining the streets of Balmain. Most of the mid-1800's residences had been lovingly restored by their owners, and for that she was glad. Sydney had so much development, often at the cost of the city's history. She peeked across the car, to a yawning Rhiannon.

"Sorry. I think the jet lag and early mornings are finally catching up with me," Rhiannon said, merging lanes.

Angela rested her hand on Rhiannon's thigh. "I don't think you actually mentioned when you got back into Australia."

"It was only a few days before the reunion. I made sure I was in time for that and also to meet with the new firm I'm working with. I couldn't leave any earlier because I still had some loose ends I needed to tie up in Boston."

"Is that where you lived, before here I mean?"

"It was, although the company I was with had offices in a number of major US cities. In fact, I've got another call I need to make very early tomorrow morning, to finish tying up the last few loose ends of my previous job."

Angela tucked a strand of hair behind her ear. "How do you balance your work with the hours of your current job? You must be just about dead on your feet."

"I negotiated my current contract similarly to how I normally do. It means I bill based on hours worked, rather than a conventional day. It gives me greater flexibility to still do the things I need to do."

Rhiannon indicated and pulled her car into a parking spot on the other side of the road, opposite a warm, honey sandstone home, its architecture reminiscent of an 1850's workers cottage. On either side of the front door were a set of windows, complemented by louvered storm shutters which were now more for decoration than utility. A small front verandah, at any time a necessary inclusion to combat the heat of Sydney, finished what was obviously a meticulous and historically sensitive restoration.

As Angela disengaged her seatbelt, Rhiannon quickly grabbed the small package from the back seat, then strode around to the passenger side of the car and opened the door for her.

She took Rhiannon's hand, smiling at the chivalrous act. "I can open the door myself you know."

"I know you can, but I like to open it for you. Does it bother you?" Rhiannon asked, a note of uncertainty in her voice.

"Not at all," she replied, while they waited for a break in traffic to cross the road. "In fact, I appreciate the gesture." She glanced casually at Rhiannon's moleskins and chambray blouse. "I don't think I told you when you picked me up, but you look lovely."

Rhiannon's eyes slowly tracked up Angela's body, her look more than signalling her appreciation of the tan dockers and yellow blouse she wore. Angela struggled to contain the sensual heat building inside her. How did Rhiannon do that without saying anything at all?

"I'm not lovely, not this old warhorse." An overzealous car weaved down its lane and Rhiannon pulled Angela back from where they were standing. "But you're gorgeous."

Angela took Rhiannon's hand and they hurried across the road. "I think you're selling yourself a bit short champ."

Their conversation was momentarily halted while Rhiannon pressed the front doorbell. After the shortest of intervals, Elly opened it.

Rhiannon held out her hand. "I picked these up at Stirling chocolatiers today. I thought they might be a nice addition to after dinner coffee."

Shaking her head, Elly took them from Rhiannon's hands before pulling her into a hug. "You really didn't need to. But given they're from Stirling's, I'm extremely happy you did."

As Rhiannon hugged Elly, Angela closely scrutinised Elly's face, for any hint of surprise at Rhiannon's dinner partner. She saw none.

Instead of pulling her into a hug like she had with Rhiannon, Elly held out her hand. "Hello Angela. It's lovely to see you again. Before we go too much further, I have a rather tragic confession to make." She paused at Angela's confused countenance. "I am an unashamed fan of yours and absolutely love listening to you play." She held up her hand placatingly. "But don't worry. There are no pianos in our house, so there's no chance of me making you sing for your supper."

Angela smiled shyly. "Thank you. It's always nice to find someone enjoys my music."

Elly stepped back and looked at Rhiannon, incredulity mirrored on both their faces. Simultaneously they turned to Angela.

"Angela, you can't be serious," Rhiannon protested. "How could anyone *not* love your music? I'm sure there are plenty of people around the world who love the way you play." She reached for Angela's hand. "I know I certainly do," she finished, her voice lowering in register.

Elly cleared her throat, her eyes briefly glancing down at the intertwined hands. "I don't mean to be rude but if we don't get inside Jen will wonder where I've gotten to with the two of you." She stepped aside and ushered them in, closing the door behind them.

The exterior of the house carried through to the walls of the lounge. But it wasn't purely the design which made Angela smile. Even if Rhiannon hadn't already said as much, it was obvious a child lived here, the childproofing of the space bearing testimony to such a presence. Strategically placed on the highest of shelves was anything remotely sharp or fragile and out of reach from, by her estimation, a child of walking age. A soft laugh escaped her mouth and she turned to Elly. "How old is your daughter?"

Angela and Elly shared an unspoken understanding of the blatant giveaway the room presented. "Olivia's three and is going through an extremely tactile phase at the moment." Elly moved across to the mantelpiece positioned over a fireplace which dominated the surrounds. She picked up a photograph and returned to Angela and Rhiannon. "It's past her bedtime, but here's a picture of her."

Angela took the picture and gazed down at the family composition which greeted her. Encased between Elly and a slightly
smaller, dark-haired woman with delicate Asian features was a
little girl, dressed for a fancy-dress party in a mini swan outfit, a
cheeky grin splitting her features. Olivia was a mirror image of
her maternal mother, with porcelain skin and deep brown eyes
and tufts of hair escaping from the costume she was wearing.
"What a pretty girl."

"Don't be fooled by the small body or those deceptively innocent features." The group turned at the sound of the voice.
"Olivia can be a terror when she sets her mind to it." Walking
toward them could only be the daughter's mother.

"I'm Jen and you must be Rhiannon."

Rhiannon barely acknowledged the introduction before Jen
gripped her hand and pumped it vigorously.

"You're exactly like Elly said you'd be."

"Thank you," Rhiannon replied and glanced at Elly. "I
think."

Elly winked.

Jen turned her gaze to Angela. Angela watched, in almost
chameleon fashion, her demeanor change. "And you must be
Angela," she said reverently. She held out her two hands and
lightly clasped Angela's with her own. "I'm sure you hear this all
the time, but I'm honoured to meet someone so talented as you.
You play with a depth of emotion I've not often heard."

Angela silently acknowledged Jen's comments, feeling as if
all at once she was at peace. She struggled to understand where
this feeling was coming from. It wasn't Jen's touch or indeed her
compliments. It was Jen's eyes. Dark as they were, they sparkled
in welcome while at the same time radiating a serenity and har-
mony, drawing their recipient in. Making them feel comfortable
in her presence. She recalled on the way over, Rhiannon mentioning Jen was a nurse. Angela had no doubt the compassion and
peacefulness she projected would capably serve her in her profession.

"That's no mean compliment Angela. Jen's father once was a
concert pianist," Elly said.

"Can I ask who your father is?"

"His stage name was Sumato Akimasa." Jen used the Japa-
nese custom of citing his last name first.

Angela's eyes lit up. "I remember him. We have a grand
piano of his at the Con which I dearly love to play any time I get
the chance. His recitals are renowned for their power and perfec-

tion. And his ability to seemingly become an extension of his instrument was truly amazing. Mind you, the one thing which always struck me was despite how passionately he played, he never seemed to look exhausted after a performance. I feel like a limp dishrag when I'm finished performing."

"You're right. He never did perspire a lot. It's a genetic trait and not a very good one if I do say so. In fact, his inability to properly sweat would often cause his system to almost overheat, similar to a runner's if they don't get enough fluid into their system when they're running. I remember one time—"

Elly quickly reached across and placed her fingers on Jen's lips, effectively halting any further discourse. "Medical stories are off the table tonight please. If I have to sit through one more procedure over dinner there may be blood and it definitely won't be mine."

Jen circled her arm around Elly's waist and chuckled. "Okay, I promise."

Angela watched their interaction, wondering if she and Rhiannon looked like that. For a fleeting moment, her mind wandered to the morning's discussion with her mother and what she may have seen on the morning's TV show. Her sudden silence wasn't missed by Jen, who all too nonchalantly disengaged her arm from around Elly.

"I've tossed the salad and prepared the cheese platter. The pre-dinner nibbles only need to be put together." Jen made shooing motions with her hands. "Elly, why don't you and Rhiannon go and plate them up and leave me to show Angela around? You can't get into too much trouble with that can you?"

"I'm sure Rhiannon and I will manage to keep all our fingers intact." Elly tugged a slightly protesting Rhiannon through the door. "You go and have your mothers' meeting."

AS THE KITCHEN door closed behind them, Rhiannon continued to cast her eyes in the direction of where they'd recently left Angela and Jen.

"Skilled as you are, you can't see through walls. You do know that, right?" Elly tugged her across to where an assortment of food dominated a white marble kitchen island.

She pulled her hand free of Elly's grip. "Of course, I do. But maybe I should go with them."

Elly washed and dried her hands and reached into a cupboard, pulling out an assortment of plates. "If I recall you're a leader in the fields of negotiation and mediation, aren't you?"

Rhiannon fought to contain her impatience. "Yes. But what's that got to do with anything?"

Elly fanned the plates on the island and began to apportion food between them. She motioned to the food. "Help me with this, won't you? Isn't part of doing either of those jobs about being good at reading non-verbal cues and body language?"

Rhiannon washed her hands and again joined Elly at the island. "Of course, it is." She separated slices of prosciutto and placed them on one of the plates.

"In which case I thought you'd have picked up on the fact Jen wanted to speak with Angela."

Rhiannon dropped the smoked beef she'd been holding. "I don't think Angela's ready for that."

Elly's gentle grip on her forearm halted her attempt to go after Angela. "Hey, calm down. I know you've only just met Jen. But do you think for a minute she would say anything which would make Angela uncomfortable?"

Rhiannon hung her head, suddenly embarrassed at her visceral reaction to protect Angela. "I don't," she said quietly.

"Jen is incredibly intuitive, which is a good thing in this relationship. Because sometimes I'm about as thick as two short planks when it comes to discerning what others are thinking. And she obviously picked up on something about Angela. Don't worry, it won't be the Spanish inquisition."

"Sorry. I didn't mean to react the way I did."

Jen reached into a drawer and pulled out a set of multi-coloured cheese knives. "Don't worry about it. I also think time with Jen might allow Angela to ask any questions of her own, without you hovering around like a worry wart."

Rhiannon picked up the beef she had previously dropped. "I know. It's just everything between us is still in its early stages at the moment."

"How is everything between the two of you?"

Rhiannon shrugged. "It's going okay...I think. Last night's recital seemed to go well. But I think she's still very skittish about how she should react in public." Rhiannon rolled the beef slices and placed them next to the prosciutto. "I mean, it's not like we were in each other's pockets or anything at the recital. It's all very new to her, even if how we feel for each other isn't."

Elly pulled a wad of paper napkins from the cupboard and placed them on the tray. "I gather you're not used to having to maintain such a distance in public."

"No. I mean I've never ever been overly demonstrative when I'm out anywhere. But I've never hid the fact I was gay either. With Angela though it's different, given this is the first time she's gone out with a woman."

"Ah." Jen nodded. "She's trying to work out how to make everything fit in to the life she already has. You'll have to tread carefully. But I suspect you already know that."

"I do, and I know we still have a long way to go." Rhiannon finished arranging slices of calabrese on the meat platter and moved to Elly's side. "I do appreciate being able to talk with you about this. My aunt was always a good listener. But since she passed there's not been anyone I could speak with."

"I'm sorry to hear about your aunt." Elly pulled Rhiannon into her arms and hugged her. "I'll be here for you. You can always speak to me if you need to."

ANGELA ATTEMPTED TO adopt an air of insouciance, with only fleeting success. She glanced to where Rhiannon had gone and felt strangely empty with her forced departure.

Jen turned back to Angela. "Why don't I show you around? I need to check on Liv anyway, to make sure she's actually gone to bed rather than play with her toys, as she is wont to do."

Angela relaxed, recalling the handful Lachie was at that age. "I know what you mean. I remember putting Lachie down for a sleep one afternoon in the bedroom of a friend. They had wardrobes along one side of the walls, with mirrors for doors. He was absolutely fascinated by them. I left him for about half an hour and decided to check he was where I'd left him on the bed. He was in the middle of the bed all right, and completely preoccupied with examining himself in the mirror. I'll never forget when he caught sight of me. He went from vertical to horizontal in matter of seconds." The two shared a laugh.

They paused outside the entry to Olivia's bedroom and Jen silently opened the door. A warm glow bathed the surrounds, courtesy of the iconic koala night lamp sitting on the chest of drawers decorated with eucalyptus leaves, yellow wattle, and gumnuts, accompanied by small woodland nymphs who swung from a smattering of the leaves. Asleep in the middle of a small bed and protected by a safety rail was Olivia, clutching a stuffed bilby to her chest.

Just like Lachie at that age, Angela thought. Jen walked over and drew the blanket back over the sleeping form. She quickly

checked the baby monitor and they departed unnoticed, Jen closing the door behind them.

"She's a real cutie." Angela walked behind Jen to the back of
the home.

"She is, but boy has she got a temper when she wants to.
Some days it takes every ounce of our patience not to send her to
her room and leave her there until she's eighteen. But we love her
dearly."

Angela didn't miss Jen's emphasis on the plural possessives
of *our* and *we*.

"Let's go through to the back garden. I don't think it will be
too cold out there. Besides, we're far enough away from the other
two to ensure we're not roped into helping with their tasks."

Jen turned on the patio light and fiddled with the outdoor
area overhead heater. "Make yourself comfortable."

Angela sat down on an outdoor chair and perused her surroundings. Solid cream walls enclosed a small garden offset by
sprigs of jasmine, it's heady scent noticeable in the night air. In
one corner of the yard in a bed with light brick edging, was a pur-
ple crepe myrtle, the first of its early spring blooms just starting
to appear. Taking in her surrounds, Angela mulled over the best
way to diplomatically pose the myriad of questions going
through her mind.

"There, that should help ward off the night chill." Jen took a
seat beside her.

Angela half turned to Jen. "How did you and Elly meet?"

"It was comedy and fate in equal measure. We attended a
women's camping long weekend in the Blue Mountains, where
we were scheduled to do a short hike along the Six-Foot track
with some friends. The two people who were respectively supposed to be coming with us couldn't make it. Consequently, we
were thrown together in the same tent for the weekend. We didn't
get on terribly well at first, finding it difficult to agree on any
form of common ground. But as the weekend progressed, we realised there was something between us worthwhile pursuing. And
pursue it we did. That was about ten years ago now and we're
still going strong. Sure, we've had our ups and downs. In the
beginning, not everything ran smoothly, and there are still some
speed bumps."

"Such as..." Angela flinched. "Sorry, I don't mean to pry."

Jen waved dismissively. "It's okay. My parents are still coming to grips with us being married. We continue to have our
moments with them. For all her bluff and bravado, Elly is the

peacemaker in this relationship. She'll avoid any potential conflict with my family for the sake of our happiness. I suppose it's like everything. It takes time but the end result is certainly worth it."

"Is everything okay with your work and friends? I mean, if you don't mind me asking."

"It's fine. Where Elly works now, they don't have any issue with her lifestyle. As for my job, there are quite a few gay people in the medical profession, and I think it makes it easier. We have gay and straight friends who all accept our relationship."

Angela looked down at her hands, trying to reconcile how her friends and mother would react to her very recent change in circumstances. Jen's hand covered her own.

"From the way you and Rhiannon interact with each other, I'm assuming you are together?"

Angela exhaled. "We...I...I think we are, but it's only a very recent reconnection."

The intensity of Jen's gaze made Angela feel as if Jen were searching her soul. "There's an emotional strength I sense between the two of you. It's multi-layered, and one sometimes people go their whole life without experiencing. That said, I'd be lying if I said everything is beer and skittles when you start a new relationship. For some people it is. But for others not so much." Jen squeezed Angela's hand. "The key is to reconcile what is most important for you and Rhiannon and make that your compass." She lifted her head when the door to the outdoor entertaining area opened.

"There you are," Elly said. "Jen love, can you take one of these plates?"

Jen eased out of her chair to help her partner.

What if I don't know what's important, Angela thought. She glimpsed up as Rhiannon placed a platter of nibbles on the glass table, her eyebrow raised at her. Angela smiled reassuringly and slightly shook her head.

"I'll go and get the wine." Rhiannon stepped through the door entrance and back to the kitchen.

Elly somewhat theatrically flopped down into one of the patio chairs. "What did you think of Olivia?"

"She's delightful."

Jen moved from her previous seat to one next to Elly. Sitting down, she casually rested her hand on Elly's thigh.

"I don't think I said it when we first arrived, but you have a beautiful home."

"Thank you. Jen was gifted it when her parents retired to the New South Wales Southern Highlands," Elly replied.

"Where abouts in the Southern Highlands?" Rhiannon placed a tray of glasses and a bottle of wine on the table. "Shall I do the honours?"

Jen motioned to the bottle and glasses. "Go right ahead. They bought a home at Bundanoon."

Rhiannon poured a generous amount of wine into the three glasses and smaller level into her own. She handed the glasses to the other three. "I know where it is. It's a charming part of the highlands. It's not so commercialised as some of the other towns around there, that's for sure. And it's not too far from where my house is."

Angela snagged a strawberry from one of the plates. "I remember you mentioning you had a home down that way but not where it was."

"It's just outside the town of Glenquarry." Rhiannon looked at Jen and Elly. "It was my parents' home. I have a couple of friends who live on the property and manage it for me when I'm not around. Which is most of the time."

"It must be nice to have a home away from the hustle and bustle of the city. I'd love to visit it sometime," Angela said.

"I'm sure that can be arranged." Rhiannon tipped her glass to Angela. "I'll put a good word in with the owner."

Elly grabbed her glass from the table. "Enough of that. After all our effort I believe I deserve a drink, and so do you Rhiannon. Before we do though, a toast."

Angela raised her glass and, with Rhiannon's, met Jen's and Elly's across the middle of the table.

"Here's to renewed friendships," Elly said. "May they like fine wine, only get better with age."

RHIANNON MANOEUVRED THE sportscar around the streets of northern Sydney, all the while turning over in her mind the events of the evening. When they'd first arrived, and given Angela's seeming discomfort, she'd been concerned the dinner wouldn't be a long one at all. She soundlessly thanked the powers to be for Jen and her serene approach to things. She had taken Angela under her wing. And the longer she and Angela stayed the more relaxed Angela became, to the extent she actually seemed to be enjoying herself.

The only hiccup was during the main meal when Elly alluded

to seeing the two of them on the morning's current affairs program. Angela had offhandedly mentioned how her mother had contacted her, stating she'd seen them as well. She joked lightheartedly, suggesting she was surprised her mum, after being used to years of her having a media presence, still felt the need to ring her every time she saw her on TV. Rhiannon had surreptitiously viewed the interaction, Angela's light-hearted, almost blasé replies very much incongruent with her tense body language.

Rhiannon suspected Jen had also picked up on Angela's contrived response and carefully concealed demeanour. Angela had barely finished when Jen had closed the line of conversation, suggesting the two of them made a great couple, before she segued to a more innocuous topic.

Rhiannon followed Angela through the front door of her home and to the lounge, taking a seat while Angela prepared a nightcap for them. "You seemed to enjoy yourself tonight."

"I did." Angela poured a measure of Muscat into two long-stemmed dessert glasses.

"What's this about a news article? I didn't turn on the television this morning." Rhiannon asked flippantly. "Did we look good?"

Angela took a seat beside her and offered Rhiannon one of the two wines. She half turned to Rhiannon, resting her knee on the seat between them. "What do you think? You could have turned up in a sack and you'd have still outshone everyone else who was there."

Rhiannon lifted the glass to her mouth, only to have it immediately filled with luscious warmth. The wine's flavours were an exercise in regressive memories of Christmases long since gone. The wine's spicy chocolate, toffee and raisin flavours coated her mouth and slid down her throat.

She tipped the glass in compliment. "This is very nice."

"It's from the Rutherglen in Victoria." Angela nosed the wine. "I don't know what it is about this, but I always want to smile when I smell it."

"I know what you mean. It's almost Pavlovian, the way it makes you feel." Rhiannon took another sip before broaching what she'd been dying to ask for the greater part of the evening. "About the news clip," she met Angela's cautious eyes, "did your mother say anything?"

"She thought you were some sort of industry person at first, chasing me for a performance somewhere or other. I told her you were just an old school friend and she seemed to be satisfied with the answer."

Rhiannon shifted imperceptibly. She leant forward, placed her Muscat on the coffee table and turned to Angela. "Is that what we are? Just old school friends?" she asked quietly.

Angela closed her eyes and scrunched her face. She shifted her Muscat from her left to right hand and placed it besides Rhiannon's. "Not at all. It's just...I don't know. I didn't think telling my mother about the nature of our friendship was something to be discussed over the phone, if at all."

Rhiannon couldn't disguise the distress she felt at those words. Angela reached for her hand, entwining her fingers with Rhiannon's.

"We seem to hit on the important conversations at the most inconvenient of times. You need to get some sleep if you're to function tomorrow and yet we do need to talk about a lot of issues between the two of us."

Rhiannon glanced away, trying to contain her own emotions.

Angela lightly clasped Rhiannon's face and turned it toward her. "You must know what I feel for you I haven't felt for anyone in such a long while. But this," she touched her own chest then rested her palm on Rhiannon's, "is all new for me. When I'm with you time seems to fly by. Despite the short time we've been together again, when you're away from me the hours drag on endlessly. And yet I'm still struggling to find a way to explain to others what it is I feel for you. But, be assured you're much more than just a school friend." Angela finished, snaking her hand to the back of Rhiannon's head, bringing it to her own waiting lips.

As their kiss deepened Angela pulled Rhiannon to her, entwining her in her arms. Angela's hands matched the sensuous dance of their tongues, mapping themselves against the shifting musculature of Rhiannon's back.

The hesitant then sure teasing touch of Angela's tongue elevated Rhiannon's emotions to another plane. She moaned at the greater contact, drawing Angela even closer. Separated by the light fabric of her blouse, Rhiannon was intimately aware of Angela's aroused state as, she suspected, Angela was of hers. She entangled her hands in Angela's hair and trailed a path of kisses to the hollow point in Angela's throat.

Rhiannon found herself drawn down onto the lounge. In an effort not to crush Angela, she eased herself onto her side, her free hand reaching up to ever so gently palm Angela's breast. Angela arched up into her hand, attempting to increase the exquisite contact there. Deepening their kiss, her hand moved down to the bottom of Angela's blouse, in search of skin. She teased her fingers under the blouse and splayed her hand against Angela's taut stomach, her fingers softly brushing the bare flesh.

Angela cried incoherently at Rhiannon's ministrations. She reached to Rhiannon's waist, her hands feverishly working Rhiannon's belt free.

Till that moment Rhiannon had barely managed to suppress the flood of desire threatening to burst forth. Allowing Angela to go any further would break down any remnant of self-discipline she possessed. Reluctantly she broke free from Angela's lips. She rested her forehead against Angela's and fought to regulate her now-roughened breathing. Rhiannon slightly eased off Angela and looked into her glazed eyes.

"It seems conversations aren't the only things we have bad timing for. I really do have to get back to the hotel and get some sleep."

"You could stay," Angela said, the intent of the invitation obvious.

"I'd dearly love to, but I've got my early morning call and there's work, including a needs analysis which is going to take some time." At Angela's disappointed frown, Rhiannon reached down and brushed an errant hair from her face and drew Angela up from her semi-sated state on the lounge. "Believe me when I say there's nothing I want more than to stay and continue what we've started. But I don't want to rush this moment between us. I want to make love to you Angela and stay with you."

Angela released a ragged breath. "Oh God, have you any idea how you make me feel when you say that?" She pulled her into a hug and nuzzled Rhiannon's neck.

"And I certainly don't want it to be hurried, like some tawdry, fumbling encounter." Rhiannon chastely kissed the top of Angela's head, as she fought to control the surge of pleasure again created by Angela's close contact.

"How about a compromise?" Rhiannon eased out of Angela's embrace. "If I'm to have the initial needs analysis done on time, I'm going to have to work some late hours between now and Saturday morning, when I'm due to present my findings."

She halted at Angela's crestfallen features. "I present the report at nine and should be finished before midday. How does a picnic for the two of us sound?"

"When you work the hours I do, it's easy to forget there are other jobs with more structured hours. A picnic sounds like a great idea. Do you want me to prepare anything?"

Rhiannon shook her head. "Don't worry about it. The hotel has a range of picnic baskets I can order. I was thinking we could go down to Clifton Gardens reserve. It's a bit out of the way, and there shouldn't be too much of a crowd. If you meet me at the hotel, we could walk down the hill to the park. There's a small beach there. If it's hot enough, we could always go for a swim."

Angela and Rhiannon stood. Hands entwined, they walked to the front door. "I appreciate that, especially the not having to do anything part. It's the sort of picnic I like." She opened the door for Rhiannon. "I guess I'll see you on Saturday?"

"I wouldn't miss it. How about we meet in the foyer, say around 12.30pm?"

"Okay."

Rhiannon brought their hands up to her mouth and kissed the back of Angela's hand. "Till then."

ANGELA WAVED AS Rhiannon's car reversed down her driveway. She closed the door and leant back against it, taking stock of the evening. Despite initial misgivings, she was surprised at the speed at which the night progressed. It seemed they had only just arrived when it was time for them to leave.

Recalling the interaction between Elly and Jen, Angela smiled. She certainly wasn't a stranger to gay musicians during the course of her working life. But she'd never witnessed what home life was for same sex partners. Before they arrived for dinner, she'd wondered if she would be altogether comfortable in what she had perceived to be an improbable setting. Over their meal, as the reality of what she was privy to dawned on her, Angela was profoundly embarrassed by her own prejudices. The love and friendship Elly and Jen shared was no different than that of heterosexual relationships.

She pushed herself off the door, wondering if she and Rhiannon would ever share such a life together. She sighed, as the nature of the transient careers of the two of them hit home, and what it most likely meant for their future. That said, it made whatever she and Rhiannon shared now even more important. She cast her mind back to Jen's prophetic words to her that evening, regarding reconciling the important things in her life and making those her compass. She knew Rhiannon was very much that compass.

She walked through the entrance to her bedroom and stared

at the lonely bed dominating the space. All of a sudden Saturday couldn't come soon enough.

Chapter Ten

RHIANNON CLICKED THE laser pointer to the screen and her final presentation slide appeared. "As you can see, my initial analysis of your situation reveals you have a highly experienced, motivated and intelligent group of people working for you. There isn't any doubt the financial incentives you give them are more than generous. But it's not going to stop the skills exodus you're currently experiencing. Monetary stability is understandably an intrinsic human need. However, it is not the sole determinant for people remaining with an organisation. At least eighty per cent of the people I spoke with felt they were working in a company which didn't recognise their integral worth."

One of the vice presidents thrust up his hand, a scowl on his face. "How can you say that when you've only just finished telling us we reward them very well financially?" He whipped closed the presentation folder in front of him. "It doesn't make sense."

"But it's not how your people see it. You're seeing this issue solely from your perspective."

She cast her eye around the room, realising the majority of the audience was also struggling to come to grips with her message. "Let me try this from another angle. How many of you have ever received a present from someone, either recently or when you were younger and all you got was money? Can you remember how you felt?" She quickly arranged her notes, giving the group time to consider her statement.

"I'm pretty sure you were all very happy to get the money. But in some sense, it was almost as if giving the money was a convenience. The giver didn't have to invest any physical or emotional rigour about what to buy. That, in fact, was left to the recipient." She could see the penny drop in the faces of at least half her group.

"It's also how the greater majority of your people perceive it. Humans need more tangible recognition of their worth. This shouldn't be solely through remuneration. It should include acknowledgement of their efforts at team morning teas, attendance on courses and promotion. These are tactile and emotional aspects of recognition which serve to motivate people. Sure, keep rewarding your team financially. But also reward them emotionally. Studies have shown this is the key to retaining your personnel. Putting meat on the bones of your organisation through flexible approaches to recognition will result in a more harmonious work environment. And if you think you're getting great ideas from your people now, studies show teams in such working environments exponentially improve their outputs. I'd be more than happy to come up with some ideas for you to consider if you're interested." She allowed the group to talk among themselves while she packed up her presentation.

Thomas Gardely cleared his throat and rose from his seat. "I'm very impressed with your findings, Rhiannon, and would be more than happy to hear any proposals you might have for the company. Let me be the first to start embracing your suggestions. I propose, in recognition of your efforts, you take Monday off. You can start your plan of action on Tuesday with my senior staff on a more specific to work area basis. As for the rest of the day, I've no doubt you have plans which don't revolve around being stuck in an office for the next eight hours."

Rhiannon thanked Thomas, gathered her things, and left the boardroom. Already her mind was abuzz with how she and Angela might spend their time together.

ANGELA COULD ALREADY feel the twinge of strained muscles in the tops of her legs. "You could have told me our picnic involved a preliminary two kilometre forced march. I'm wondering whether I should have opted for something sturdier than sandals."

"What are you complaining about?" Rhiannon huffed. "You're only carrying your towel. I'm lugging our lunch and wine to boot!"

Angela glanced down the tree lined street, occasionally catching glimpses of the harbour beyond. "That might be the case. But something tells me you're more than used to this sort of physical activity. The closest I get to it these days is the walk I made down to the hotel this morning." She swatted an ever-present fly away from her face. "Are you sure it wouldn't have been just as easy to get the hotel limousine to drop us down at the beach?"

"What and miss such a marvellous walk? Besides, there's a method to my madness." Rhiannon shifted the hamper from one hand to the other. "I think we're going to need to work up an appetite. Otherwise we'll need to call for the limo for our journey home."

Angela was incredulous. She grabbed Rhiannon's free arm, effectively halting their progress. "You mean we're going back up that hill, on foot?"

"We have to walk off lunch, don't we? And walking back up on foot is quicker than on your hands." Rhiannon stepped clear of Angela's mock swipe. "If you insist, I'll call for the car to take us back up the hill. I'm sure I packed my mobile somewhere in the hamper."

"Thank heavens," Angela replied, relieved. "Next thing I know you'll have me running." She shuddered at the thought.

Rhiannon smirked. "That's next week's plan. You know, I've been around the world and seen some waterways, but Sydney Harbour has to be one of the loveliest sights there is, especially on days like today."

As they got closer to their destination, the trees gave way to an uninterrupted view of the waters of the harbour, liberally dotted with pleasure boats and yachts bobbing around on its deep blue-green surface.

Rhiannon pointed to one of the large green and yellow ferries making its way from one side of the harbour to the other. "It's the Manly to Circular Quay ferry, by the looks of it. When we were still at school, I sometimes used to miss a day and come and ride the ferries. That was before they were all enclosed like that one."

"I remember the old ones," Angela acknowledged. "They always seemed a bit rickety to me."

"Quite the opposite in fact. They were solid, and not being enclosed meant you could still feel the sea spray on your face. I used to love catching the Manly ferry on rainy and windy days. The feel of the boat heaving through the swell when it passed across Sydney Heads always meant the journey was a precarious one. In fact, every once in a while, the waters coming in through the heads were sufficiently rough for them to cancel the ferry altogether. But on the days when they didn't, the ride was amazing and yet terrifying at the same time. I used to wonder whether it matched my life—feeling in control but only by the most tenuous of threads," Rhiannon finished almost inaudibly, as if for a moment her mind had returned to an earlier time in her life.

Angela reflected on Rhiannon's words, recalling days when Rhiannon had missed her morning rehearsal. While there weren't too many of them, she wondered if these days had coincided with bad weather days. "I often wondered where you got to when you weren't in the hall. You always seemed a little distant for a few days after your absences."

Rhiannon shrugged noncommittally, seemingly lost in her own thoughts.

Angela cut short any further conversation on the matter, at least for the moment. She sensed there was more to Rhiannon's disclosure and yet realised the subject was one better explored when they were not walking down a hill.

Angela's hand grasped Rhiannon's arm. "If you want to talk about it, I'm more than willing to listen."

Rhiannon turned her head and smiled at Angela. "Thank you, I might take you up on the offer. Maybe after we've had a bite to eat."

The beach they finally arrived at was one of the many small inlets dotting the harbour foreshore. Densely wooded headlands at either end of the beach jutted into the harbour, providing a sanctuary from rougher seas. The water gently lapped the golden sand, infrequently interspersed by larger waves created by the wake of marine traffic. Angela watched a man dive into the waters of the inlet from a small yacht moored in the deeper waters to the front of the beach.

At one end a jetty enclosed a harbour pool, patrolled by life-guards. A grassed area, with a smattering of picnic tables completed the tableau.

Rhiannon pointed to a group of Port Jackson figs dotting the opposite far end of the beach. "What about there?"

"That's a good idea," Angela replied and motioned with her hand. "That way we're not in the way of the cricket game that's setting up over there. And besides, I'd prefer not to have a ball land in my lunch."

They settled on a spot sufficiently distant from the beach cricket match which was now in full swing.

"It's not too busy here either." Rhiannon removed the picnic basket from the hamper and absently dropped it just short of the ground, her eyes casting occasional glimpses at the cricket game.

Angela's eyes tracked to where Rhiannon's attention was focussed and couldn't help but internally laugh at her restlessness. It was obvious age hadn't quelled Rhiannon's competitive spirit. She was clearly champing at the bit to join in the fun. When the beach cricket ball rolled to within a few metres of their picnic blanket Angela knew the battle was lost.

With pleading eyes Rhiannon picked up the ball and turned to Angela.

"Go," was all Angela could manage and Rhiannon was half-way down the sand, leaving her to set up the rest of their repast.

IN BETWEEN PLACING the multitude of food containers and plates on the blanket she took time to take in the scene in front of her. Angela voyeuristically viewed Rhiannon, her toned body chasing the ball along the sand to retrieve it, before pivoting and throwing it back in the direction of the stumps. Rhiannon's shorts were delightfully modest, affording Angela a tantalising view of legs whose muscles moved with lithe testimony to Rhiannon's ongoing fitness regime.

Angela turned to the picnic basket to retrieve two glasses.

"Boyd you bloody goose. Why did you have to hit it so hard? Now who's going to get the darned ball?"

She turned back in time to see the ball they'd been playing with continue its graceful descent across the water, before setting some thirty metres from the shore. Without thought Rhiannon was into the surf and swimming out to the ever-retreating ball.

Angela stood up and cupped her hands. "Hey, marine girl. How about you finish up for now and come and have some lunch?"

At the sound of Angela's voice, Rhiannon looked over at her target and reluctantly turned away. She swam with easy strokes to the shore. Reaching the shallows, she rose out of the water and moved toward Angela.

Angela silently thanked the powers to be the other group had also broken for lunch and were far too preoccupied to see the vision moving with sure strides through the shallow water. Rhiannon's white cotton blouse had lost its opaqueness. Angela alternated between relief and frustration at the bikini top now clearly obvious through the see-through blouse. Thankfully, the soaked top did little to hide the tanned flat stomach of the other woman who, preoccupied with wringing some of the seawater out of her hair, was impervious to the effect she was having on Angela. How the hell was she ever going to make it through the rest of the afternoon? She offered a towel to Rhiannon.

"Thanks." She took the towel and briskly rubbed herself.

I'll do that, Angela's mind shouted. She turned away, under the guise of grabbing the bottle of wine, unexpectedly fearful of the longing she struggled to conceal.

Rhiannon lay the towel over one of the lower limbs of the tree they were sitting under and flopped her damp body down on the blanket beside her. "That was great fun! Why didn't you join us?"

Again composed; Angela passed a glass of wine to Rhiannon. "I could have I suppose. But who would have gotten lunch ready?" She chuckled at Rhiannon's apologetic features. "Don't worry about it. I saw more than enough from here and managed to set up lunch at the same time. Now let's eat before the flies and the ants conspire to carry this away."

A REPAST OF seafood, salad, and a couple of glasses of wine relaxed the two. Although Rhiannon had restricted herself to only a couple of glasses, she was reluctant to go for a swim, having seen too many people get into trouble by mixing alcohol with water. Angela, after listening to one of the tales Rhiannon shared regarding such an incident, opted to do the same. Notwithstanding, their afternoon discussion had been one which was long overdue.

As they shared their interests the conversation again found its way to Rhiannon's poetry. Angela listened, transfixed by Rhiannon's explanation of the story behind some of the poems contained within her books.

Angela shook her head as she cleared the remains of their picnic from between them, returning the empty cartons, plates, and utensils to the hamper. "I'm surprised by the depth of the poetry you seemed to write when you were in your senior years."

Rhiannon frowned. "What do you mean?"

Angela closed the hamper and semi reclined on the blanket, her weight balanced on her elbows. "I'm amazed you could write as profoundly as you did at such a young age. I mean the one about the sparrow is a great example."

"I was inspired by events and many people. Ginny was very much one of those." She sipped her wine and threw the remainder of her low-salt nuts to the seagulls dotted along the beach. She had enjoyed her afternoon with Angela, in particular the ease with which they seemed to be able to speak on any topic at all. All the same, she was surprised at how willing she was to share with Angela the source of a number of her poems — Ginny. She very rarely spoke about her. At school when Rhiannon had sparingly spoken to Angela about Ginny, she always held something back, reluctant to fully share her pain with anyone. Yet now it seemed cathartic to again speak her name.

She put her glass to one side and reclined on the blanket next to Angela. She placed her hands behind her head and gazed up at the sky. "I haven't spoken about Ginny this way with anyone, not in a very long time."

The touch of Angela's hand on her thigh broke Rhiannon's focus. She turned her head to see Angela had rolled onto her side, her eyes examining her intently.

"You mentioned a lot of your poetry was inspired by Ginny."

Rhiannon nodded, somehow sensing where Angela was headed.

"Were you and her friends? I mean...you know...in the sense you and I are friends?"

Rhiannon eased herself onto her elbows and cast her eyes over the now-shaded waters of the harbour. She returned Angela's gaze. "I'm pretty sure I was in love with her, although nothing ever came of it. Till then I'd never felt so deeply for another person. There were times I sensed she felt the same way. I mean, it was as if both of us knew there was something different about our friendship. It was just we were reluctant to cross that line. And to do so was such a big step. The last Christmas break we had away from each other gave me sufficient time to reflect and I'd decided to tell her how I felt when we returned from holidays. Unfortunately, it was too late."

Try as she might, Rhiannon couldn't hide the ache of her reminiscence. Angela reached for her hand and stroked it reassuringly. "I'm sorry I asked you about Ginny. It's obviously still painful for you to talk about her."

Rhiannon gazed at their entwined hands. "It is, even now. At the same time, it feels liberating to be able to say Ginny's name and have someone finally understand what she meant to me."

Rhiannon rolled onto her side, her hand still clasped in Angela's. "I don't think you realise the strength and friendship you gave me in our final year. Without you I don't know what I'd have done. Even if I couldn't share what I felt for Ginny with you back then, being able to talk to you and listen to you play was the balm I needed. Your friendship meant a lot to me. It still does." Rhiannon plucked an errant leaf from Angela's hair. "I want our friendship to be much more if you'll allow me."

"So do I." Angela smiled wanly. "It's just there seems to be so much else to be considered. When we're together, nothing else matters and I feel I could stay with you for as long as you'd have me. Then the rest of the world comes barging in and I don't know how to deal with it." She tilted her head to one side and rubbed her shoulder. "Lachie, my son, I haven't a clue how he might react to a relationship between us and that's only the start. I know what I want and it's to be with you. Yet at the same time there are so many competing pressures."

Rhiannon was strangely heartened by Angela's words. She may not have realised it but for the first time she'd referred to their friendship as a relationship. Unknowingly or not, it was a significant step. Despite this, she understood Angela's reticence.

"How you're feeling is to be expected. I mean, for the greater part of my life I knew I wanted to be with a woman. After this long, you're only now discovering an interest, at least in me. It's understandable for you to feel like you're being pulled in opposing directions. I sensed you felt that way at the recital and while we were at dinner the other night. And we haven't even begun to discuss your son up until now."

Angela released her hand from Rhiannon's. "He means the world to me. He's my life."

"I've never raised a child, so I can only begin to imagine what he means to you. But I want you to know I'd never come between you two. However, do you think you're putting up walls, without giving our relationship a chance?" She reached across the blanket and again encased her fingers with Angela's.

"My Aunt Isabella used to say there's only one way to eat an elephant and it's one bite at a time. If you tackle a problem and see it as the size of an elephant it will always seem insurmountable. Why don't we take this one bite at a time and see how we go? After all, I've waited twenty years to tell you how I feel. Do you doubt my patience?"

Angela sighed in relief. "How is it you can make issues seem so easy?"

"Problems can be big or small, whatever you want them to be. It's all in the perspective of how you see them which helps to make them resolvable." Rhiannon reached over and picked up her glass of wine. She drank and offered its contents to Angela.

Angela took a sip, seemingly deep in thought. She handed the glass back.

"You know, I have to pick up my son tomorrow. If you weren't doing anything, do you want to come for the drive? I'd like you to meet my mum and for her to meet you. I wasn't entirely up front with her the other day when we spoke on the phone and that doesn't sit well with me. I'd prefer she knew about the two of us."

Rhiannon sat up and faced Angela. "Meeting your mum." She swallowed nervously. "Are you sure it's what you want? I'm more than happy to come on the drive with you. But don't feel like I'm forcing you to do something until you're ready."

"Don't tell me you have a thing against mothers-in-law?" Angela dodged Rhiannon's mock shove. "She's nice you know and doesn't bite at all. At least not too deeply."

Angela yelped as Rhiannon leapt across the blanket. She pinned Angela down, her thighs alternating between Angela's legs.

Rhiannon ran her fingers along Angela's ribs, searching for a ticklish spot. Finding one, she began her assault. "I'm not frightened of mothers-in-law." She swatted the hand impeding her from her target. "And believe me I can bite back if necessary." She grabbed both of Angela's hands and trapped them above the Angela's head.

Rhiannon studied the face perilously close to her own, aware of her leg which, through her actions, now snugly rested near the junction of Angela's thighs. "Finally, be thankful we're in a public place or I don't think I could stop myself from kissing you right now."

Mere centimetres separated the two and a slow sensual smile began to grace Angela's face. "What makes you so sure that would stop me?"

Angela reached up and captured Rhiannon's lips with a lingering kiss which promised so much. The sound of thunder reverberated across the harbour, causing both of them to reluctantly release their connection.

"Wow," Rhiannon said. "I never knew your kisses could do *that*." She laughed at Angela's blush. Before she could utter much more the first splashes of rain hit her back.

Rhiannon reluctantly rolled off Angela and reached for her bag. "If we don't want to get soaked, we better pack up and make for cover. I'll call the hotel for the limo."

Rhiannon pulled her mobile from the side pocket of the hamper while Angela packed the remains of their picnic.

"Darn it! I knew there was something I was supposed to do last night." Disgusted, Rhiannon shoved the mobile back into where it had been only moments ago. "I forgot to recharge the phone. Do you have your cell on you?"

"I don't. I barely remember to carry the thing and often forget where I've put it in the house." Angela picked up the basket containing the remains of their meal and moved closer to the trunk of the tree under which they'd shared their lunch. "I suppose we'll have to take cover from the storm here then."

Rhiannon put her hands on her hips. "You don't do picnics

very much do you?" Seeing Angela's confusion, she continued. "Trees are the worst places to wait out a thunderstorm. They tend to attract lightning." She barely masked a giggle when Angela jumped away from the tree as if it were a snake.

"What do you suggest? We can't stand here and get wet."

Rhiannon smiled wickedly.

"You can't be serious! We can't walk back to my place. We'll get soaked. And besides, it's all up hill!"

Rhiannon chuckled and took the picnic basket and towels from Angela's hands. "No more soaked than if we stay here. It's not too far." Angela's facial response was sufficient evidence she didn't fancy Rhiannon's proposal.

"How about we go to the hotel and wait out the storm there? There're towels in my room and you can dry yourself off while the rain passes. Come on. We're only getting wet standing around here."

A bolt of lightning and the sound of thunder much closer to where they stood cut short any further vacillation on Angela's behalf. "Okay," she grumbled. "Let's get going, or we might get chargrilled as well as wet."

RHIANNON GRATEFULLY ACCEPTED two towels from the doorman and offered one to Angela. "I feel like I've taken a shower with my clothes on."

Angela rubbed her head and proceeded to blot down her body. "You can talk! I feel like I missed the spin cycle on my washing machine." In deference to the carpeted lobby, she removed her sandals and wiped her feet.

Rhiannon towelled her hair and shivered. "That should do, at least until we get upstairs." She took the towel from Angela and returned them to doorman. "Thank you. By the way, could you please have a pot of coffee and pastries sent up to 1205? It's in the name of Rhiannon Sharp."

He tipped his cap and accepted the towels. "Certainly, ma'am."

"Thanks," Rhiannon replied. They walked through the foyer to the waiting elevators, relieved they were bereft of people. It ensured a swift journey to Rhiannon's floor.

Rhiannon ushered Angela through her door and closed it behind her.

The suite was the epitome of understated elegance. A large cream rug, on which sat a light tan sofa and matching chairs, dominated the floor in the lounge. Separating sofa and chairs was a white marble coffee table and to one side of the space was a workstation.

Angela glanced around. "This is very nice. Is this where you normally stay when you're here?" She pointed to the far wall. "Does the fireplace work?"

"It's a gas fireplace, only made to represent wood. I think its function is aesthetic and more about setting the mood. The thermostat is the temperature heavy lifter in here," Rhiannon called over her shoulder as she walked through to the bedroom.

She opened the wardrobe and pulled out two plush bathrobes. Returning to the main room, she handed one across to Angela and motioned with her head. "The bathroom's through there. Why don't you take a shower and put this on? I'll try and find something of mine which might fit you until we can get you home."

Angela's eyes tracked down Rhiannon's figure. "I'm sure a pair of your shorts will capably do as my pants." She giggled. "Has anyone told you you're quite tall?"

Rhiannon grabbed Angela's shoulders and tenderly propelled her in the direction of the bathroom. "Can we have this conversation later? I'd like to have a shower once you're finished and sometime before I die from hypothermia."

While Angela took a shower, Rhiannon adjusted the thermostat of the lounge and bedroom, bringing them to slightly above their current cool setting.

She walked across to the heavy drapes in the lounge and pulled them open. The remaining privacy curtain afforded a world class view of the harbour, while at the same time preventing anyone from seeing into the space. At the sound of a chime Rhiannon turned. "That was quick." She headed across to the suite door and opened it.

"You ordered afternoon tea ma'am?"

"I did. Thanks for being so prompt." She stepped aside, allowing the waiter to wheel in a small cart. "If you could put it on the coffee table, please." Rhiannon signed the bill the waiter had given her, including a tip for such speedy service.

She'd barely closed the door when a robe encased Angela entered the room, her towel drying her fine brown hair. Rhiannon attempted to adopt an air of nonchalance, while all the while her mind filled with images of what Angela's robe covered.

Angela seemed oblivious to the effect she was having on her. "Ooh coffee and cake, just what I need." She put the towel over her shoulders and made a beeline for the coffee pot.

Angela bent over, her back to Rhiannon. The bathrobe did little to conceal the soft curve of Angela's backside.

Rhiannon shook her head, in an effort to break her train of thought. "Give me your towel and I'll put it back in the bathroom."

She deliberately avoided Angela's touch, fearful doing so would shatter any remaining vestiges of her fragile self-control. "I'll only be a minute." She turned and headed for the relative safety of the bathroom.

Leaning against the now-closed bathroom door, she released a pent-up breath, painfully aware her reaction had little to do with the wet clothes she was wearing. She peeled herself out of her clothes and entered the shower. She turned it on, allowing the water to at least for a moment block out the wave of desire which all but consumed her.

ANGELA PLACED HER empty coffee cup on the table and took up a place in front of the lounge's double windows. From here she could see the harbour and the storm lashing it. It never ceased to amaze her how quickly it could change from serene cool blue-green waters to one of grey whitecaps, lit up by lightning which similar to fireworks strobed the harbour and surrounding shores.

As the sounds of Rhiannon's shower cut off in the background, she replayed the afternoon's events. The picnic served to reveal yet another facet of their developing friendship. Indelibly printed on her mind was Rhiannon when she exited the water. Her blithe ignorance of the effect her clinging, wet T-shirt had on Angela only exacerbated matters. Her own self-discipline developed through years of piano playing was the only thing that stopped her from tearing Rhiannon's shirt from her body despite them being in such a public place. And when they kissed, the powerful warmth created by Rhiannon's leg between her thighs ran the gamut of a slow burn, to a low-grade surge of electricity to her whole system.

Her entire being hummed with anticipation of where they were inevitably heading. Excepting Patrick, her intimacy with men were few and far between. And yet none of them seemed to come even remotely close to the reaction Rhiannon evoked in her, by her sheer touch.

Angela jumped at Rhiannon's sudden presence.

"It's great isn't it," Rhiannon said. "It's one of the reasons I love staying here. On days such as this I could sit here for hours and do nothing but watch how nature places us mere mortals back into perspective in the bigger scheme of things."

Angela's focus alternated between the show in front of her and Rhiannon's reflection in the glass. "If I remember correctly you wrote a poem about the ocean, didn't you?" She turned to face Rhiannon. "Is this where you got your inspiration?"

"The harbour yes. But not this window. Years ago, I was stuck in a seminar at Middle Head in Mosman which had been dragging on for a couple of days. The only good thing was the seminar rooms were literally at the top of a headland with uninterrupted views right out through the heads of Sydney Harbour. On this particular day, the seas were so rough that you could see the waves hitting the cliffs of North Head, and the white spray breaking over the top of it. I don't think I learnt a lot that day, although it did give me inspiration for the poem. I know it sounds strange, but I do enjoy these types of days, especially when I'm out of the rain rather than stuck in it."

Angela gazed deeply into Rhiannon's cerulean eyes. "While there might be better places to be right now, I can't think of one."

Stepping forward she wrapped her arms around Rhiannon's waist and lay her head against her chest. Despite the contact they had shared since rekindling their friendship a little over a week ago, this was different. Rhiannon's arms encircled her, heightening Angela's senses to almost a point of pain. Through the terry towelling of the robe, Rhiannon's heart was redolent of a presto composition, the reverberation creating a fast, steady beat in Angela's ears. Despite the storm raging outside, in her life she couldn't recall when she'd ever felt this safe.

As Rhiannon stroked her locks, Angela buried her face deeper into the soft towelling of the robe. Her face came to rest on Rhiannon's naked chest, the scent of aloe vera on Rhiannon's skin filled her nose. Without thinking, she pressed her lips against the soft skin and Rhiannon's heart seemed to begin to beat even faster.

"Angela."

She gazed up as Rhiannon's hand cupped the side of her face before lowering her lips to meet her own. Rhiannon's gently teasing tongue belied the control Angela could feel thrumming in Rhiannon's body. She broke free from the kiss and ran her fingers down the lapels of Rhiannon's bathrobe, to the sash holding the materiel closed. She looked up, silently seeking permission. A barely imperceptible nod was all she needed, and she tugged at the ties.

The belt fell to the floor and Angela's eyes followed the path her hands were taking, as they moved inside Rhiannon's robe. She carefully opened it and eased it back off Rhiannon's shoulders, watching it slide down Rhiannon's body, to the floor.

The room was silent except for the storm raging outside and the heightened breathing of the two of them. Angela fought to stay the hands aching to touch the perfection in front of her. Rhiannon's body contained a strength borne out of years of physical activity. Yet her power was tempered with a softness, giving the illusion of strength and comfort at the same time.

She released a shuddering breath and hesitantly reached out, the need to touch Rhiannon winning the battle over her ever-dwindling restraint. The back of her fingers lightly caressed the side of Rhiannon's breast.

"So very lovely, so soft."

Rhiannon's face reflected her own want, and Angela faltered. "I...I'm not sure what to do."

RHIANNON DREW ANGELA to her. The coarseness of the cloth against Rhiannon's naked skin did nothing to assuage the need racing through her body, yet she was mindful of startling Angela with the depth of her need. She exhaled and kissed the top of Angela's head. "You know what to do. Think about what pleases you as a woman. I'm sure it wouldn't be too dissimilar to what pleases me."

Angela broke their embrace and reached for Rhiannon's hands, bringing them down to the tie of her own robe. "Show me."

Rhiannon ever so carefully loosened the ties of Angela's gown, then opened it and gradually peeled it away. It pooled on the floor, in turn exposing the beauty contained within. Her eyes lingered on Angela, her fingers itching to trace the perfection before her. "You are so incredibly beautiful," she uttered breathlessly.

She pulled Angela into her arms, marvelling at how seamlessly they moulded together, like pieces in a puzzle in a delicious meeting of skin against skin. Rhiannon's fingers played in the small of Angela's back. "You don't know how long I've wanted to hold you like this."

Angela lightly brushed Rhiannon's shoulder with her lips. "I wasn't aware being with you could feel this way. No music can ever describe, right at this moment, what I feel for you."

Rhiannon delicately disengaged herself from the embrace and took Angela's hand. She led her into the bedroom and halted. She studied Angela's face. "Are you sure this is what you want? I would never—"

Angela placed her hand over Rhiannon's protesting lips. "I have never been surer in my life. This is exactly where I want to be."

Rhiannon took Angela's hands in her own and walked around to the side of the bed, all the while searching Angela's face for any hint of indecision. What greeted her instead was unbridled hunger. Without breaking contact, she eased Angela onto the bed, lightly covering her body with her own.

She kissed Angela deeply, hoping to convey with her actions the depth of emotion she felt for her. Angela's tongue sensuously danced with hers, her hands, first shyly then with greater purpose mapping a pattern across her waist before reaching up and tentatively cupping Rhiannon's breasts. Angela's thumbs grazed her nipples and Rhiannon shuddered uncontrollably.

Rhiannon's lips blazed a path of light kisses on Angela's skin. She nipped the edge of Angela's jaw, delighted when Angela angled her chin, affording her greater access to the pulse point on her neck. Angela's breathing quickened as Rhiannon came to rest, her head between Angela's breasts. She looked up, eyes questioning.

"Yes, God yes," Angela uttered through half-lidded eyes.

Rhiannon lowered her mouth to Angela's left breast and lightly kissed the warm curvature there. Her tongue teased her areola, evoking a guttural response from Angela as the surrounding skin pebbled with the pleasurable contact. She slightly lifted her head and took Angela's nipple in her mouth, running her tongue across the aroused flesh.

With a measured, delightful intent, Rhiannon placed a succession of kisses from one breast to the other. Angela turned and slightly shifted her breast toward Rhiannon's lips, impatient to again feel her touch. Her fingers entwined themselves in Rhiannon's hair and she pressed Rhiannon to her breast. Rhiannon closed her lips around Angela's nipple, feeling her sigh in response.

Rhiannon lavished attention on Angela, her hand trailing down her stomach, finally coming to rest in the juncture of Angela's hip. She lazily ran her fingers along the delicate crease of Angela's thigh, every so often encroaching onto the extremities of Angela's hair.

As Angela's legs opened, Rhiannon ran her fingers through Angela's crisp curls. She halted, almost imperceptibly, then moved her hand farther down, revelling in Angela's damp heat.

Angela's moan was almost enough for Rhiannon to climax. By a sheer force of will she didn't know she possessed, she tamped down her own ardour.

"Rhiannon, please." Angela shifted her body, seeking a greater release from Rhiannon's ministrations.

Rhiannon's lips broke contact with Angela's nipple. She kissed Angela's stomach, her head coming to rest just below Angela's navel. Angela's scent triggered a primal response in her, one which she was fast losing the battle to contain.

Shifting, she settled between Angela's thighs, her tongue lovingly caressing her centre. Angela's body tensed. Yet it was clear her response wasn't one borne out of fear. Rhiannon couldn't help but wonder if anyone had ever touched her this way. Angela bowed her hips, offering more of herself to Rhiannon's demanding touch.

Seeking greater contact, Rhiannon reached up and entwined their hands, all the while applying an unrelenting sensuous pressure to Angela. She dipped down and tasted her, intimately aware of Angela's rapidly building tension. Moving up, her teeth lightly swept over her clit, causing Angela to cry out. Angela's hand held Rhiannon's in a vice-like grip, her hips moving in concert with Rhiannon's efforts. Then, for an infinitesimal moment Angela was breathless, her body perfectly still, as if suspended in time.

"Rhiannon," Angela screamed as she moved unrestrained, against her mouth. Rhiannon put her other hand across Angela's waist, holding her in place while she convulsed on a wave of passion. Finally spent, Angela carefully released the grip she had on Rhiannon's hand.

Rhiannon rested her cheek below Angela's waist, and trailed a path of featherlight kisses across her stomach. She raised her head. "Are you okay?"

Angela's smile mirrored her satiated state. "Okay doesn't even come close to describing how I'm feeling right now. I never knew it could feel this way between us." She reached down and tugged Rhiannon's hand. "Come here."

Never losing contact, Rhiannon made her way up Angela's body. She settled herself above her, one leg either side of

Angela's. Bending down, she captured Angela's lips with her own.

Without breaking the kiss, Angela's hands gripped her waist. Angela raised her thigh, colliding, with exquisite contact, Rhiannon's aroused centre.

"Oh," Angela managed, her voice slightly muffled by Rhiannon's mouth.

Rhiannon broke their intimate connection and glanced down at Angela, her actions creating a greater degree of erotic pressure with Angela's thigh.

"Is that...did I?" Angela flexed her thigh, the remainder of her words dying on her lips.

Rhiannon slowly undulated against Angela. "Just for you."

Angela's eyes welled with tears.

Rhiannon reached down, her fingers lightly wiping the moisture from Angela's eyes. "Only for you."

Chapter Eleven

RHIANNON AWOKE TO the not unpleasant pressure of Angela's head on her chest, their limbs entangled. She draped her arm over Angela's bare back and lowered her head back to the pillow. Staring around the room bathed in the dappled morning light, she couldn't help but be amazed things had progressed so quickly between them. All the same, she was quietly pleased. The brazenness of Angela's kiss yesterday at the beach had taken her by surprise. Yet it paled into insignificance at Angela's ardour last night. Her tenderness and yet her passion, Rhiannon struggled to capture the moment with words and wasn't sure she wanted to try.

She tilted her head toward Angela as she lifted her head from Rhiannon's chest. "Good morning sleepyhead."

Angela reached up and rubbed the corner of her eye. "Morning. How long have you been awake?"

"I only just woke up." Rhiannon kissed the top of Angela's head. "Are you okay?"

Angela returned her head to its previous position in the hollow between Rhiannon's collarbone and breast. "I'm more than okay. I don't think I mentioned this to you but," she moved her hand across Rhiannon's ribs, "I haven't had many lovers in my life. Even then, *none* of them came close to how you made me feel last night."

Rhiannon brought her other arm around Angela's body and squeezed her. "I'm glad and I hope it's just one of many nights for us." She shifted, a gurgle in her stomach foreshadowing her other needs.

"What's that sound?"

Rhiannon shifted. "Sorry, it's my belly letting me know it's hungry. After all, the last big meal we had was the picnic yesterday."

Angela rubbed Rhiannon's stomach. "And the remains of most of those petit fours at one in the morning haven't done much to sustain me either."

"Poor baby. Too much activity."

Angela made to tickle Rhiannon.

"Hey! Don't start anything you can't finish, especially if you want breakfast anytime soon." She checked the clock. "Maybe I should have said brunch. Breakfast finished downstairs over half an hour ago."

Angela rolled over and studied the clock, which read ten fifteen. She shot out of bed. "Oh my God! Lachie!"

Angela ran out of the bedroom and into the lounge and back into the bedroom. "My clothes. Where are my clothes?"

Rhiannon lay in bed, arms behind her head, content to watch Angela's antics while she ran naked around the suite. "They're where you left them last night," she replied failing to suppress the laughter in her voice. The look of panic on Angela's face halted her teasing. She leapt out of bed and softly grabbed Angela's hand. "Hey slow down. What's wrong?"

Angela closed her eyes and breathed deeply. She returned her gaze to Rhiannon. "I'm picking up Lachie today; remember?"

"Of course, I do."

Angela's eyes scanned the room. "We're going to be late."

Rhiannon reached up and, with a featherlight touch, turned Angela's face to her own. "It's okay. Didn't you mention we were due at your mothers at two o'clock?"

Angela nodded.

"We're not going by stagecoach or walking, are we?"

Angela scowled. "You know we're not."

Rhiannon pulled Angela into her arms. "In which case honey, it's only just gone ten fifteen. Seriously, we've plenty of time to have breakfast and get back to your place for you to change. I promise you won't be late. And if you're worried, you can always ring your mum and set the time back. I'm sure she won't mind."

Angela released a shuddering breath and she returned Rhiannon's hug. "I apologise. I don't know what got into me. Besides, Mum's used to me not being on time. I'll call her when we leave my place."

"That's settled. And if you're still looking for them, your clothes are in the bathroom, where we hung them last night."

"They're fine for the moment." Angela disengaged herself and walked to the bathroom. "I need to wash my face and, you know."

Rhiannon smiled. "I understand. While you do that I'll see if I can find a menu."

Rhiannon padded into the lounge. She picked up the remnants of a small cake and popped it in her mouth and rummaged through the desk drawer in search of a menu. She pouted. "Not there." She closed the drawer and moved to the sideboard cupboard housing alcohol and condiments. Resting in a felt-lined recess was the room service menu. She flicked through the contents, searching for a list of items available between now and dinner. "What do you want for brunch?" she called over her shoulder and nearly dropped the menu at the feel of Angela's hand on her waist. She turned.

Angela pulled the menu from Rhiannon's grip and placed it on the top of sideboard cupboard. She reached down and grabbed Rhiannon's hand. "You," she replied, pulling Rhiannon back to the bedroom.

"STOP IT." ANGELA swatted Rhiannon's thigh as they made their way along the motorway to her mother's home. "It's not nice to make light of another person's misfortune."

"It wasn't me who dragged me back into the bedroom and caused us to lose track of time. Mind you, I have to say it was a *great* way to forget what time it was. Still, you should have seen the look on your face when you looked at the clock for the second time. I wish I had a camera handy. Ow!" Rhiannon dodged yet another blow from the driver's seat. "This passenger seat needs a safety rating!"

"Be quiet, or you can sit in the back on the journey home."

"We could have taken my sportscar. I've no doubt Lachie would have been impressed."

Angela spared a glance at Rhiannon and returned her focus to the road. "It's not much more than a two-seater. At least everyone has a seat in my SUV. And besides, where would I have sat?"

Rhiannon smirked. "You could have sat in my lap."

Angela shook her head. "You are incorrigible, you know that don't you?" She negotiated her way around the slow-moving truck occupying the left-hand lane. "I remember years ago, when we used to go on holidays to the Blue Mountains, the drive seemed to take us forever. But I think when you're a kid, you're far too focussed on getting there than taking time to look at the scenery."

"More about the destination than the journey and missing everything in between," Rhiannon said.

"That about sums it up."

"I know, I was much the same way. But then I had an epiphany in my senior geology class which made me realise the journey is just as valuable."

"How so?"

"The class was on a field trip to the Blue Mountains to study the geology of the Sydney Basin. We stopped at Glenbrook for lunch, which also gave us a chance to look at an exposed element of the Lapstone monocline. The bus had barely stopped and everyone, except Miss Pepper and I, made a beeline for a bakery right next to where we pulled up. As for us two, we were nose to nose with the closest exposed rock we could find. The folding of the rock was truly amazing. Especially when you consider the pressure it must have been under to achieve such a change. It was the part of the journey the rest of the group missed."

Angela eyes caught the sign signalling the Glenbrook turnoff. "I suspect you'd be hard pressed to see the monocline now. The road doesn't even go via Glenbrook and Lapstone anymore."

Rhiannon sighed. "While I appreciate how streamlined highways are these days, we miss very many opportunities to see the interesting parts of the country and its geology."

"I never knew you were so interested in the subject. My curriculum was so music-centric it left me little space for much else when it came to my senior classes. I was forced to take biology." Angela made a face. "I don't think I could ever look a frog in the eye again after all the dissecting we did on those poor things."

Rhiannon chuckled. "I completely understand. There was a good reason I didn't take biology. The idea of cutting into even dead animals turns me off my food. Speaking of which, thank heavens there was food at your place before we started up here or I'd have expired by now."

She patted Rhiannon's leg. "There, there." Returning her hand to the wheel, she glanced furtively at Rhiannon and bit her lip. "How…um…do you feel about meeting my mother?"

Rhiannon shrugged. "I don't know. I don't think I have any grave reservations about the idea, despite the fact in the past I haven't met too many of my partners' families."

"I'm surprised. Why didn't you? Didn't you want to?"

"No, nothing like that. I think it had more to do with the people I met and where I met them. Most of my ex-partners, and don't get me wrong there haven't been too many, were in transient careers, like myself. Often their families were in other parts of the world."

Angela fell silent while she mulled on Rhiannon's answer. In reality, both of their careers were less than geographically stable. When she was touring, she was often away for months at a time. As for Rhiannon, she had only mentioned the other night the twelve-month stint in Sydney was the longest contract she'd had in a while. What would happen when they were both forced to go in opposite directions?

Rhiannon reached across and tapped Angela's knee. "You're doing it again, aren't you?"

The innate ability for Rhiannon to sense her disquiet surprised her. "What do you mean?"

Rhiannon's hand came to rest on her thigh. "If I'm not mistaken, you're searching for the mother of all forks to eat that elephant."

"You have to admit we both have pretty transitory careers. I can't begin to remember how many different nannies and tutors Lachie's had, not to mention the number of different places we've lived in. I know one thing's for sure and that's I'm getting a little tired of it all." She shifted gears to accommodate the sudden incline. "You mentioned your current tenure was twelve months."

Rhiannon nodded.

"Where are you off to after you've finished there?"

"I don't know. I haven't given it a lot of thought. Ideally, I'd like nothing more than to settle somewhere and write for the rest of my life and I'm about in a position where that's achievable." Rhiannon snorted. "In actuality, I'm probably already there. I suppose I'm merely ensuring the presence of a fifth and completely unnecessary financial security net."

Rhiannon turned to Angela. "What about you? Setting aside the recital the other night, I know you haven't performed publicly for a little while now. With a talent like yours it would be wrong to not again share it with the rest of the world."

Angela acknowledged the compliment and observation. "I don't think a week goes by with my manager or me fielding some offer or another. I've certainly kept up my playing and could easily fit back into that world. It's just, until recently I haven't felt much like doing so. I'd lost my desire to play at the level necessary on tour, night in and night out. And without that they might as well install a pianola on stage."

Rhiannon smiled. "Hey, don't knock the old pianola! My Grandma used to have one of those. We spent many a Christmas around the old thing, pumping the pedals for all it was worth, delighting in hearing the mechanical music pouring forth." Rhiannon sniffed smugly. "It was about as close as I ever got to musical greatness."

"I don't think it quite works that way in a symphony orchestra." Angela snickered. "I can picture it though. Ladies and Gentlemen, this evening we're proud to announce the return of concert pianist Angela Drayton and her rendition of 'Beethoven's Fifth,' performed on her friend's grandmother's pianola. Take it away Angela!" Angela snorted at the mental image of her in concert attire, legs pumping furiously away to the tinny sounds of a classical masterpiece. "Somehow I don't think it would catch on."

"Not to mention I don't think my grandmother's pianola would have stood the stress."

"I expect not. Now my interest in performing has begun to return, I suppose I have some decisions to make." She reached over and entwined Rhiannon's hand with her own. "I have you to be thankful for, regarding my finding my passion again. It's been an extremely long time since I played like I did when you came over last Sunday."

"You floored me. To me, you and the instrument were symbiotic, an extension of each other. It was breathtaking to behold. Then on Tuesday, at the Conservatorium," Rhiannon shook her head, "I found it hard to contain the emotions you evoked in me. I suppose the only thing we can do is see where your playing and my work take us." Rhiannon's final words drifted off.

Angela glimpsed at Rhiannon, in time to see the concerned look on her face as she turned to the window. She squeezed Rhiannon's hand causing her to look in Angela's direction. "*Now* who's got their elephant fork out?" She glanced quickly at Rhiannon's face and returned her focus to the road.

Rhiannon humphed. "You're right. I'm also too focussed on the destination than the journey again. I think this might be a case of physician, or businesswoman, heal thyself."

They shared a laugh as they continued their travels.

RHIANNON COULD DO little more than gawk, open mouthed, when the SUV negotiated the dirt driveway to the rear of Maureen's home. The backyard, interspersed with native trees and shrubs, ended in a knee-high cut sandstone block wall which literally abutted against the surrounding Jamison Valley escarpment.

Angela turned off the engine and nudged her. "Come on, I expect Mum heard the car pull up." She opened the door and got out.

Rhiannon alighted and joined her. "It's incredible," she said, gazing at the view. "I don't know why but it reminds me of a thirties art deco movie scene."

Angela tugged her shirt into place. "There'll be plenty of time later to have a look around." The back-screen door opened. Angela turned and walked toward her mother's welcoming arms.

Rhiannon silently witnessed the greeting. Mrs. Drayton was undoubtedly an older version of her daughter. She was dressed similarly to Angela, in light blue jeans and a crisp white grandfather shirt. What must once have been honey blonde hair was regally peppered with white. Her smile and freckled face seemed to hint at a mischievous streak which belied her years. While there was a frailty unwillingly thrust upon her with the onset of age, she obviously still possessed a regal yet gentle strength, not unlike Angela.

Breaking the hug Mrs. Drayton looked across at Rhiannon. She walked to her and held out her hand.

"Welcome to Fern Gully, Rhiannon. I remember seeing you on the television the other day at the recital with Angela. It must have been wonderful to catch up with her at the reunion last Saturday."

Rhiannon took her hand, surprised at the deceptive strength contained there. "Thank you, Mrs. Drayton. It was. I must say you have a great garden. And the view is simply stunning."

Mrs. Drayton waved dismissively. "Please call me Maureen. Mrs. Drayton only serves to remind me how old I am. As for my garden, my husband Jack and I spent many a wonderful afternoon in this backyard. In fact, when he passed away, we held his ceremony down there." Maureen motioned to a far corner bordering the escarpment. "By the wall. We scattered his ashes in the winds of the valley below."

"I'm so sorry, I didn't mean to dredge up unpleasant memories." She sought out Angela to help her out of what she perceived to be a sticky situation.

Without thinking, Angela rubbed her forearm. Rhiannon's hasty glance was sufficient to catch Maureen's cryptic look at Angela's hand on her arm. Rhiannon moved slightly away, breaking the contact.

"No offense taken my dear. I certainly do miss him. But with his cancer it was for the best he moved on. Not to worry. I still believe he's around here now and then. Besides, I have every expectation we'll meet again."

The assuredness of Maureen's words took her by surprise. "You believe there's more to merely the end when life is over and done with?"

Maureen laughed. "Don't look shocked. It's not only you young ones who can have such new age ideas. Jack and I believed we were merely on a journey, one which will see us continue to reacquaint ourselves over our ensuing lifetimes. But enough of such talk. Your son is over at the Saunders, frying his brain with those computer games." Maureen nudged Angela in the direction of the house next door. "How about you go and retrieve Lachie, while Rhiannon and I go inside and put the finishing touches to our late lunch?"

Angela glanced at Maureen and Rhiannon. "I won't be long."

Rhiannon wasn't sure if Angela's words were less about time and more about reassuring her. The soft touch on her arm caused her to shift her focus from a departing Angela and back to Maureen.

"Why don't we go inside?"

Rhiannon swallowed nervously and followed Maureen up the back stairs and into a country kitchen.

Maureen gestured to the breakfast island. "Please have a seat." Rather than continue to prepare lunch, she took a seat opposite Rhiannon, Maureen's amber eyes piercing hers. "Now how about you tell me just exactly what's going on between you and my daughter?"

Rhiannon felt the colour drain from her face. Before she could make the mistake of looking at the back door in vain hope of Angela's quick return, she caught herself, instead allowing years of mediation experience to take over. "I'm not quite sure what you mean."

Maureen crossed her arms and leant back in her chair, her head slightly tilted. "I may be old but I'm certainly not blind. I admit I thought the actions I saw on the television the other day were those of an eager entrepreneur trying to gain my daughter's favour. But I see it wasn't the case at all. If that wasn't enough, your body language bespeaks an attentiveness toward my daughter which spells more than merely friendship. Please don't give me the coy answer of you don't know what I mean. Besides, have either of you looked in the mirror lately?"

Rhiannon closed her eyes then returned Maureen's intent stare. "My apologies. Despite what I do for a living, artifice is not my strong suit. But I do believe this is a discussion you should first have with your daughter. I can tell you though, she wasn't comfortable with the conversation she had with you the other day."

Maureen nodded. "I sensed she was being a little evasive. But at the time I couldn't quite understand why."

"I'm sorry if she came across that way. This situation is a little new to her and I expect she's more than a bit worried about how those who love her will react. Could I ask you to speak with her before we go too much further?"

Maureen scrutinised her face. "Is what's happening between you and Angela no more than a situation to you?"

"It's much more," Rhiannon replied vehemently. "To me at least." The screen door opened, and a blond headed boy made his way to the breakfast bar.

Lachie's attention alternated between his grandmother and Rhiannon. "What's much more and who are you?" he asked precociously.

Rhiannon tried vainly to find somewhere to hide as Angela walked into the kitchen, her hand coming to rest on her son's shoulder. "Rhiannon, you'll have to forgive Lachie. He sometimes forgets his manners. Where did you leave them this morning hmm?" She ruffled his hair, resulting in a series of giggles from him.

"Under the table, I think. Let me get them." Lachie crawled along the floor and made a pretence of searching under a series of chairs. He stopped and cupped air in his hands and made a great exhibition of shoving something into his pocket. The trio barely managed to contain their mirth as he straightened himself, tucked in his shirt and made his way back to Rhiannon.

He extended his small hand, his blue eyes solemnly looking up at Rhiannon. "I don't think we've been properly introduced. Hello, I'm Lachlan Drayton. Welcome to my grandma's place."

At that, the three could no longer contain themselves, and instead broke into gales of laughter, joined by Lachie.

Rhiannon was first to recover, and she took his proffered hand. "I'm Rhiannon, and it's a pleasure to meet you Lachlan. Or would you prefer I call you Lachie?"

"You can call me Lachie. I usually only get called Lachlan when I'm in trouble."

"Thank you, Lachie. Your mother has told me a lot about you."

He disengaged his hand from Rhiannon's and hopped up onto one of the chairs surrounding the breakfast island. "Are you and Mum friends?" He reached for an apple.

"Yes, we are," Angela replied. "A long time before you were born, we used to go to school together." She recovered the apple from her son's outstretched hand, returning it to the fruit bowl. "However, if you want to live to see lunch, best you go and wash up."

Lachie reluctantly got down from his stool and stood beside Rhiannon. He reached out and guilelessly squeezed her forearm. "You look strong. Do you play sport? Mum tries to kick the soccer ball around with me but she's not too good at it."

Rhiannon muffled a guffaw at Angela's shocked look. "You know she's good at other stuff, like piano playing and being a mum."

"But that's not soccer."

"I tell you what, do you have a soccer ball here?"

Lachie nodded.

"In which case, how about you wash up and after lunch we'll go and kick the ball around a bit. I hope there's a park around here though. If the ball goes over your grandmother's fence, I'm sure not climbing down a cliff to retrieve it."

"There's one down the street. I can't wait!" The boy sped off in the direction of what must have been the bathroom while Rhiannon helped Angela and Maureen finalise lunch preparations.

OVER THE COURSE of lunch, Angela didn't miss the look of preoccupation on Rhiannon's face. While she engaged in inconsequential mealtime conversation, it was clear her mind was elsewhere. Despite this, the presence of her mother and Lachie made it difficult to pursue the matter any further. This coupled with the sideways looks she infrequently received from her mum, made Angela wonder what the two of them had discussed during the short time she'd spent collecting Lachie.

The final dish was barely dried and put away and Lachie, eager to run off some of his energy, dragged Rhiannon down the hallway and out the front door.

"Be gentle on her," was all Angela could manage as the door slammed closed. She and Maureen made their way into the tranquillity of the back garden.

Maureen took a seat in the shade of a eucalyptus tree and motioned for Angela to join her. "Rhiannon seems a nice person."

"She is. It was lucky we met at the reunion. We'd been good friends at school. It was great to catch up with her again." Angela glanced away, painfully aware of what the mere mention of Rhiannon's name did to her face. She composed herself and returned her focus to Maureen.

Maureen searched Angela's face. "Is that all you are now, good friends?"

Searching for the words to make her mother understand how

she felt, Angela preoccupied herself with the brown leaves covering the seat. She raised her face to her mother's waiting features. "Would it bother you if I said we were more than merely good friends?"

Maureen stilled Angela's busy hands, clasping them in her own. "Given how you've been acting recently, I have to say I thought there was a bit more to the two of you than what you were letting on. And it doesn't bother me in the least. I'm very aware of the opinions some people of my age have on such relationships. But I'm not one of them. Besides, it's been such a long time since I've seen you this full of life, not since Patrick. And Rhiannon seems to have brought that out in you."

Angela breathed a sigh of relief. "When did you know?"

"It was a couple of things. I had an initial inkling when I picked up Lachie the other day." Maureen chuckled. "In all my years I've never known you to take any great amount of time in choosing an outfit. If Lachie's description of your room that morning is anything to go by, then I suspect you took a great deal of effort with what you wore to lunch with Rhiannon."

Angela exhaled and gazed out across the garden. "I did. And you're right. I've never done that, even with Patrick." She studied her mother. "What was the other thing?"

"I understand why, due to your touring commitments, you didn't bring Patrick to meet your father and me until after your wedding in Germany. That said, this is the first time you've actually brought someone home who you've begun a relationship with. All the same, I must say I'm surprised at the suddenness of it all. You've barely known each other for more than a week."

"We've only just caught up with each other again. But I think I've known there was something between us ever since the last year at school."

"You mentioned she used to listen to you rehearse of a morning, didn't she?"

"Yes. It was nice to have her sit and listen and be able to talk afterward. I think it helped us to become friends." Angela rubbed her face, her eyes distant. "But on our second last day during muck up preparations I fell, and she caught me. I don't think I'd ever felt so comfortable in all my life."

Maureen creased her forehead. "Did anything happen back then, between the two of you?"

"No. But I think we both knew there'd been a subtle shift in our friendship. And it was a change I wasn't willing to accept or put a name to. But Mum, on the evening of the reunion when I felt her presence in the rehearsal hall, it was as if those memories and feelings were as fresh as if it were only yesterday. It reminded me of you and Dad when you used to have those conversations. You could go for days without discussing something and yet pick up exactly from where you left off. It's how it feels for me with Rhiannon."

Angela stood and put her hands in her back pockets. She walked the short distance to the back wall and gazed at the valley in front of her. Its escarpments and lush green undulations reached the horizon. They reminded her of the Grand Canyon, albeit not so deep and covered in trees. She returned her gaze to where her mum patiently sat. "But I'd be lying if I said the idea doesn't scare me. I've never been in a relationship with another woman. Before Rhiannon, I'd never given it much thought. But with her it feels right. I loved Patrick, but the emotions I felt for him were so very different to what there is between Rhiannon and me. I can honestly say I've never felt this way before with anyone else."

Maureen stood and walked to Angela's side. "It sounds like you've still got a lot of talking to do between the two of you."

"We have. Besides, I haven't any idea how Lachie, or indeed my friends, will react to these new developments in my life."

Maureen sat down on the wall and patted a spot beside her. "My dear, you're a long time dead to be worrying about the opinions of your friends. If they want to react negatively to you and Rhiannon then that's up to them, and there's not much you can do to stop them."

Angela sat down on the cool stone. "I know Mum, but what *if* they're none too happy with the idea of the two of us?"

"I can tell you all the reasons why their perspectives shouldn't matter." She put her arm around Angela and drew her closer. "But at the end of the day it's how you feel which counts. As for your son, that's a little different. Do you know how Rhiannon feels about children?"

"We've not spoken about it at any great length. But she's said she hasn't got any intention of creating friction between Lachie and me. She's made it clear she'll willingly step back if Lachie struggles to come to grips with our relationship."

Maureen smiled. "That's very honourable of her. And if that's the case, you're indeed lucky she's as thoughtful as she is. That said, I don't expect your decision will be met by all quarters with open arms." She pulled Angela into a hug. "But be assured, you'll always get support from me regardless of what happens.

You're my daughter and I love you for who you are, not what your friends or the world perceives you to be."

Angela's eyes welled. "Oh Mum," she managed as she rested her head on her mother's shoulder and began to cry softly.

RHIANNON CHASED A giggling Lachie around the corner of the house, dribbling the ball as he went.

"Mum, Grandma, you should have seen it!" He ran headlong into Angela's arms. "Rhiannon knows how to play soccer and she knows heaps of tricks. She can dribble the ball and balance it on her knee. She even headed the ball for a whole minute! I counted."

Rhiannon watched Angela wipe her eyes, her face strangely composed. Had the discussion with her mother not gone to plan? She couldn't quite tell. She moved forward furtively searching Angela's face for any hint of disquiet.

Lachie released his grip and grabbed Angela's hand. "Come on Mum! I've got to finish packing. I'll tell you inside what Rhiannon said about soccer."

Angela stumbled as her son pulled her across the lawn. She smiled wanly at Rhiannon as she passed her. "I expect she told you plenty of things." Angela reached up and pulled open the back-screen door. "But did she tell you she represented Australia in soccer?"

The two made their way into the house, effectively muting Lachie's reply.

Before she could follow, Maureen grabbed her hand. Turning, she looked down into Maureen's smiling eyes.

"Angela and I have spoken, and I guess this is welcome. Thank you for bringing happiness back into my daughter's life. She's been far too long without it. All I ask is you be patient. I know she's still coming to grips with what's happening between the two of you."

Rhiannon felt the tension she'd had since her initial discussion with Maureen at last leave her body. "Trust me when I say I'll try my best to be patient. I've waited twenty years to find her again, and I want us to try and build on what we have now. But, in the end if she decides it's not what she truly wants, then I at least hope we can still be friends."

"I have to say I'm very touched by your nobility, especially in this day and age. But where does that leave you?"

Rhiannon shrugged. "Who knows? But it's something I'm

willing to take one step at a time."

RHIANNON GRINNED AS Lachie, from the back seat of the SUV, continued his blow by blow replay of their soccer game.

"And then Mum, Rhiannon put the ball on the corner marker and kicked it." He smacked his hands together in glee. "Right into the goal! She's a good soccer player, for a girl."

Rhiannon turned to better see Lachie. "I'll have you know the Australian women's soccer team is currently higher ranked than the Australian men."

Lachie grinned cheekily. "I know. I was just joking. I wished we could have stayed longer. I want to learn how you hit the ball so hard."

"It's all practice, Lachie." Rhiannon shifted in her seat, subtly aware of the presence of more than a few sore long unused muscles, courtesy of their game. "I've no doubt my lack of practice will catch up with me tonight."

"But you're very good. I bet you could teach Mum a thing or two."

Rhiannon eased back into her seat and looked at Angela. "I'm sure I could." She grinned at the blush adorning Angela's face.

"Can we play when we get home? There's a park not far from where Mum and me live."

Rhiannon scanned the orange hued landscape. "I think it might be a bit too dark when we get to your place. But I tell you what. I'm not working tomorrow. If it's okay with your mum, we could always have a picnic in the park. After lunch we can kick the soccer ball around. What do you say?"

Lachie kicked lightly the back of the driver seat. "Can we Mum? Please?"

Angela glimpsed in the rear vision mirror and Rhiannon turned, barely masking her laughter at Lachie's beseeching face. Angela quickly peeked at Rhiannon and returned her focus to the road. "I didn't know you had tomorrow off."

"It was a thank you present from the CEO of Gardely and Balen, for the presentation I gave on Saturday morning." Rhiannon nudged Angela's knee. "Are you up for a picnic and soccer practice?"

"I've got to do my rehearsals in the morning and get some of the washing done. But we should be fine for the afternoon."

Lachie's cheering halted any further conversation.

"Okay buster, enough," Rhiannon said. "Do you want me to

meet you two at your place?"

"What a great idea," came the gleeful voice from the back.

Angela shook her head at his antics. "Ditto for me."

"Given you'll be busy with morning chores, I'll get the hotel to make up a basket for the three of us."

"Let me give you some money to go toward the cost," Angela replied. "At this rate we'll be eating you out of house and home."

"If you feel you must then okay. But I think I can afford to spring for a picnic basket."

"Okay but it's my treat next time." Angela reached across and patted her leg, before quickly returning her hand to the steering wheel.

Rhiannon cast a cursory glance to the back seat, relieved Lachie had missed the interaction between them.

THE DRIVE HOME wore on and the sounds from the back gradually decreased as Lachie recharged his batteries with much-needed sleep. Rather than wake him on returning to Angela's place, Rhiannon effortlessly lifted the child and carried the sleeping bundle into the house.

Angela pointed down the hallway ninety degrees to the main entranceway. "Three doors down, on the right," she whispered, following Rhiannon, Lachie's bag in her hand.

Rhiannon carefully lay Lachie down, while Angela busied herself with getting him ready for bed.

"I'll get him into his bedclothes."

"Does he need a snack before he goes to sleep?"

Angela pulled off Lachie's shoes and socks and placed them by the wardrobe. "He had enough to eat when we stopped to refuel. He'll be fine until the morning. And if he's not, trust me, he'll be the first to let me know. Have you got time for a coffee?"

Rhiannon nodded.

"Can you put the kettle on and make us both one? The cups are on the bench and the coffee's in the cupboard to the right of the fridge. I'll finish in here and be with you in a minute."

Rhiannon headed to the kitchen and prepared the coffee. She carried the two cups into the lounge, took a seat and waited for Angela.

Angela wiped her hands down the sides of her jeans and sat beside Rhiannon. She reached forward, grabbed her coffee, and drank, her eyes momentarily closing. "Mmm. I needed that. It's a long drive to do up and back in one day."

Rhiannon placed her mug on the table. "I could have driven you both home."

Angela put her mug next to Rhiannon's and half turned to face Rhiannon. "I know. I suppose I'm just a little tired."

"You *were* up a little late last night."

Angela dipped her head and made a non-committal noise.

Sensing slight embarrassment on Angela's behalf, Rhiannon charted the conversation to safer waters. "I very much enjoyed today. How did the talk with your mother go?"

"Mum never ceases to amaze me. It seemed she'd already sensed there was more to us than what I was letting on." Angela rolled her eyes. "And I should have known she was more interested in ensuring I was happy than whether you were man, woman or Martian for that matter." She furtively glanced to the hallway and entwined Rhiannon's fingers in her own. "Things seemed to go well between you and Lachie. He's usually not so talkative around new people. Certainly not someone who's over six foot tall. I think he likes you."

"I like him too. He's a good kid. As for the soccer though, I suspect he's not too different than other boys his age. He'd fall for anyone who'd go outside and kick a ball with him."

"I'm glad it was you he could do that with." Angela stroked Rhiannon's hand with her thumb.

Rhiannon lifted their hands to her face and softly brushed her lips against Angela's fingers as she drew her close.

Their faces were mere centimetres apart. Angela moistened her lips and moved closer to their inevitable destination.

"Mum!"

Angela leapt off the couch, anxiously looking in the direction of Lachie's entreaty. "I need to see what he wants."

Rhiannon rose, carefully avoiding contact between them. "That's fine. I best be on my way. I'll see you two tomorrow for the picnic, if it's still okay I mean."

"Of course, it is. It's just—" Lachie called for her again. "Well—"

Rhiannon held up a hand. "Seriously, it's okay." She smiled reassuringly. "You go and see what he wants, and I'll show myself out. I'll see you tomorrow."

Rhiannon closed the front door and walked down the steps to her car. It was clear to her Angela's mother had no issue with the blossoming relationship between her and Angela. But what would happen if the same couldn't be said for Lachie?

Chapter Twelve

IF IT HADN'T been for her promise to Lachie, Rhiannon would have taken a rain check on the whole idea of a picnic and soccer in the park. The cumulative effect of jet lag, which she was still getting over, and a fault in the hotel's air conditioning, had turned her night from one of relative comfort to a sleepless and humid one. Adding to Rhiannon's lack of sleep and frayed nerves was the couple in the next room, who did nothing but argue well into the wee hours over the lack of air conditioning. Despite the hotel's profuse apologies and the promise of free accommodation for the evening, Rhiannon left The Gables, her mood still on a razors edge.

She shifted the picnic basket from one hand to the other as she strode up the hill to Angela's house. Why didn't she ring Angela and see if she could spend the night at her place, rather than stay in a bloody sticky hotel suite? She snorted derisively and quickly dismissed the idea. Given how Angela reacted last night when they were about to kiss and Lachie had called for her, it was unlikely she'd be willing to have Lachie and her in the same house anytime soon.

Finally entering the yard of Angela's home, she stretched her neck from one side to the other, trying to ease the tension brought on by her foul mood. Her hand had barely made it to the doorbell when the door opened hurriedly.

"Rhiannon! Mum, it's Rhiannon!" Lachie shouted down the corridor toward the kitchen.

Angela rounded the corner, the smile on her face faltering. She frowned slightly, obviously picking up on Rhiannon's mood.

"I guessed as much. As I'm sure, have half the neighbourhood." She motioned Rhiannon into the hall. "Come on into the kitchen. Do you want a cup of coffee while we wait for Lachie to make his bed?"

"Mum! It's school holidays! Can't I leave it unmade just this once? I'm only going to hop into it later on tonight. It seems a waste to make it."

Rhiannon struggled to hide a smile while Lachie pleaded with his mother, using all his boyish charm to try and effect a positive outcome on his behalf. It was clear his focus was on the park and soccer, rather than an unmade bed.

Angela ruffled Lachie's hair. "It might be school holidays, but it doesn't make any difference. Besides, it's not the first time you've left it unmade. As for the fact you're only going to sleep in it tonight, that doesn't cut the mustard either buster." Giving his backside a mock slap, she steered him in the direction of his room. "The sooner you get it done, the sooner we can be on our way."

Lachie's shoulders slumped and he shuffled down the hall.

Rhiannon took a seat at the breakfast bar and Angela pulled two cups from the cupboard, placing them on the top of the bench, near where Rhiannon sat.

"Everything all right?" Angela queried casually while she poured coffee into each of the mugs.

Rhiannon added milk and sugar to her cup and tried to tamp down some of her weary grouchiness. "A bad night's sleep that's all. The air conditioning broke down and the couple next door fought like cats and dogs about it for most of the night." She took a sip of her coffee. "The joys of hotel living I suppose."

"Are you certain you still want to go on a picnic? I'm sure Lachie would understand if you didn't feel up to it."

"I'm fine. My grumpiness isn't sufficient reason to ruin his day. Besides, it gives me a chance to be with you." She reached for Angela's hand only to see it whipped away from its resting place on the breakfast island. "What's wrong?"

"We just have to be careful." Angela cast her eye toward the hallway. "I don't know when Lachie's going to come through the door and I don't want him to catch us—you know—holding hands, if you get what I mean."

Rhiannon clenched her jaw, her lips thinned, her temper barely in check. "I understand. However, can't friends hold hands? I think it's a perfectly innocent gesture, one which I'm sure a child would have very little problem with." She halted at the wounded look on Angela's face. Rhiannon closed her eyes and rubbed the side of her neck. "I'm sorry. I'm a little out of sorts today. I understand what you mean, it's a little difficult I suppose."

"What's difficult?" Lachie asked, returning from his task.

Angela placed her mug on the bench and folded her arms. "Never you mind. Have you made your bed? I hope you haven't merely pulled up the sheets like you normally do. I think I'll go and check."

ANGELA LEFT THE kitchen not only to ensure Lachie had

made his bed but to also get her own feelings in check. She opened the door to Lachie's room and pursed her lips. "Just as I suspected," she uttered. While the doona covered the bed, the length of sheet she could see trailing on the ground was evidence he'd done little more than pull up the doona and replace his pillow.

She pulled back the sheets and duvet and proceeded to make it properly. She worked, her mind replaying her recent actions in the kitchen. Why was she afraid of Lachie seeing them holding hands? It was, as Rhiannon insisted, something friends would do. Despite this, she knew that would never be the case with Rhiannon. Her mere touch was enough to cause a visceral reaction in her. And it was a response Angela was sure she couldn't readily conceal from Lachie's or her friends' enquiring eyes.

Her mother's reaction to her declaration of her feelings for Rhiannon relieved her. And yet it seemed whenever she was away from her, Angela's fears at what their friendship meant for the rest of her life came creeping back in. She couldn't help but wonder how Lachie might react to what was going on between them, not to mention how her friends would respond to her new lifestyle.

"Crap," Angela muttered, picking up the clothes Lachie had discarded on the floor before throwing them into his laundry basket.

RHIANNON GAVE LACHIE a hand as he climbed into the chair opposite her. "She's a perfectionist sometimes. Everything has to be done just right."

Rhiannon shuffled Lachie's chair to align it with the breakfast island, in turn affording him a greater degree of balance. "Would it help if I told you she was like that when she went to school? Always perfection. And she was less than impressed if things didn't turn out that way."

"Mum as a schoolgirl, yuk." Lachie giggled. "But she's my mum and I like her a lot."

Rhiannon leaned across the distance between them and pulled Lachie to her. "For the record," she whispered. "I like her a lot too."

Angela's clearing throat caused Rhiannon to break the hug.

"Now your bed *is* made and your room clean. We better be on our way."

RHIANNON AND ANGELA'S walk to the park was a short one, filled by Lachie regaling them with stories of his soccer skill. He held Angela's hand while they crossed the street. But as soon as he was safely on the other side, he threw the ball a short distance in front of him and made to follow it.

Angela reached out and grabbed the back of his jersey. "Hang on you. If you head off after the ball, you'll never stop for lunch."

"Only a quick kick and I'll come back. I promise."

Angela released his grip and turned him to her. "What about your guest? What if Rhiannon wants to eat before she kicks the ball around with you?"

Lachie stubbed the grass with his toe and looked up at Rhiannon. "I suppose someone big like you needs food."

Rhiannon arched her brow. "I'm not sure how to take that comment but I'll assume you're referring to my height. Lunch first would be nice, and then we can start our game. I can see I'm going to need all the energy I can muster to be able to beat you."

THEIR MEAL WAS a selection of sandwiches, accompanied by fruit and a small cake. Lachie had barely managed his last slice of dessert and he was up and off, kicking the ball in front of him.

Rhiannon watched Lachie dribble the length of the oval. "He certainly is full of energy."

Angela picked up his discarded plate and stacked it with the other two. "He is indeed. And he does love his soccer. So much so I think he'd sleep with his soccer jersey on if he thought he could get away with it." She reached across the blanket to the basket beside Rhiannon.

Rhiannon picked up the basket. "Let me help."

"I can manage. How about you go and show Lachie some more of your skills." She reached out and snagged the basket from Rhiannon, their fingers grazing in the process. "I know you have many," Angela finished, a knowing smile on her face.

Rhiannon rose and looked down on Angela. "Thanks. I just might have to show you some more of those skills later on."

Rhiannon jogged across the park, in Lachie's direction. She was relieved the uncomfortable moment she and Angela had shared earlier in the kitchen had passed as had, for the better part, her own sour mood.

FOR THE NEXT thirty minutes Rhiannon put Lachie through a series of rudimentary practice drills. They ran up and down the field, feinting left and right with the ball, kicking it halfway down the field and chasing after it. She was surprised how quickly he picked up her instruction on how to continually bounce the ball on his knee. She was impressed that at his age he could manage three in succession.

Lachie trapped the ball just in front of Rhiannon. "You're a good teacher. I couldn't do the balancing thing and now look at me. Can we have a game now?"

Rhiannon made to move the ball out from where it was at Lachie's feet. "It's a bit difficult with only the two of us." She motioned over her shoulder. "Do you think we could get your mum interested in a game?"

She watched Lachie run across and grab a protesting Angela's hand.

"As Lachie's already told you, I'm not too good at soccer," Angela said, hands on hips.

Rhiannon passed the ball to her and watched Angela halt the ball's progress. "You're not too bad. How about a little game of two on one? You and Lachie against me?"

Angela sighed. "Why do I feel this is going to end up with Lachie and me being merely cannon fodder against your superior soccer prowess?"

Not waiting any longer, Lachie kicked the ball and ran away from where Rhiannon and Angela stood. "Come on Mum," he called over his shoulder.

Shaking her head, Angela jogged his way.

Lachie and Angela spent the next ten minutes kicking the ball to each other, while busily trying to avoid Rhiannon's capable boot. It was a task they were managing admirably until a misguided kick from Lachie sent Angela scampering toward the elusive ball.

Rhiannon closed in on Angela, all the while cackling gleefully as she did so. In what was a desperate, last-ditch attempt to rob her of her objective, Angela picked up the ball and began running as fast as her legs would carry her. Initially separated by a reasonable distance, it took Rhiannon little time to catch her and bring the protesting woman gently to the ground.

"Let go of the ball!" Rhiannon laughed, trying vainly to rest it from Angela's vice-like grip.

"It's mine! If I let it go, I'll never get it back!" Angela fought to hang onto the round mass which was rapidly slipping from her grasp. "And I don't want to have to chase *you* all around this park."

"If that's your final answer then you leave me no choice." Rhiannon proceeded to tickle Angela her into submission. It wasn't long before the ball dislodged itself and a giggling Lachie kicked it farther down field to near the goal posts.

"That'll teach you." Despite Angela's squealing protestations, Rhiannon continued her merciless assault on her sensitive spots. So preoccupied were the two, they failed to notice they weren't alone.

"Angela Drayton," an elderly voice called. "Is that you?"

Rhiannon watched Angela's face, as she seemed to search to put the voice to a name. Angela's eyes widened in shock and she all but launched Rhiannon into orbit in an attempt to escape the compromising position they'd been in.

She jumped up, quickly pulling down her T-shirt which had ridden up to her midriff courtesy of Rhiannon's attack. "Mrs. Frank, fancy meeting you here." Angela pulled tufts of grass from her hair. "How are you?"

Regaining her own footing, after being unceremoniously thrown from her previous position, Rhiannon watched, bemused, while Angela attempted to explain exactly what she'd been doing and who she'd been doing it with. She bent down and dusted her knees while she prepared herself for the obligatory introductions which would necessarily follow.

"Who is this with you Angela? I don't think we've met."

"Oh, she's just a friend."

Rhiannon's hand froze at Angela's words. She couldn't quite rightly put her finger on why Angela's explanation grated her like it did. What she did know was to stay and try and engage in civil conversation wouldn't be possible, given how she suddenly felt. With deliberate, precise movements, she brought herself to full height and nodded at Mrs. Frank.

"I'll leave you two to catch up with each other. In the meantime, this *friend* will keep your son occupied."

Rhiannon stalked off to where Lachie dribbled the ball, all the while endeavouring to mask her frustration at the turn in events.

Lachie kicked the ball to Rhiannon. "That's Mrs. Frank. I think she knows my grandma. She's a bit of a busy body. Mum calls her an extension of the local news service."

Rhiannon passed the ball back to Lachie, her emotions at odds with each other. It was bad enough to be known as just a friend. But given Lachie's subsequent description, they'd also managed to run into the local gossip. Returning yet another pass, Lachie covered his mouth, attempting to conceal a yawn.

"You're looking a little tired young man, and you've about worn me out also." She bent down and picked up the ball. "Come on sport, lets grab the picnic basket and your mum and head back to your place."

Lachie yawned again and walked over to where Rhiannon stood. He thrust his small hand into her larger one and they headed for the picnic setting. "I'm playing soccer on Sunday. I mean it's not a competition or anything. Mum says I'm not old enough for that. But our coach splits us into teams, like the real thing. Do you think you can come and watch me?"

Rhiannon mulled on his request, unsure of what the week held in store for her. As far as Rhiannon was concerned, Angela's mixed messages were also making it hard to discern just what things would be like between the two of them by then.

She looked down at Lachie, her face a shadow of doubt.

"Mum will be there. You two could talk when you're not watching me."

She placed her arm around his small shoulders. "I think that can be arranged. How about you go and rescue your mum and I'll finish packing this mess up."

"LACHIE NOT TOO far ahead please," Angela said as she returned to silently walking beside Rhiannon. Aside from a cursory goodbye to Mrs. Frank and the infrequent monosyllabic response to Lachie's ramblings, the walk home was hushed. Despite the silence, Angela's mind was a blur as she tried to rationalise the implications of Mrs. Frank finding her like she did. She covertly glanced at Rhiannon's face. Her features were stony, her jaw clenched.

Angela opened the front door and motioned a quiet Rhiannon toward the kitchen while she took the football from Lachie. "Why don't you go and get out of those dirty clothes?"

"Can I take my ball with me?"

"You can't sweetie. I'll put it in the kitchen for now. And don't leave your clothes on the floor," Angela called to Lachie's retreating figure. "Put them in the basket where dirty clothes belong."

Angela closed the front door and walked into the kitchen. She scrutinised Rhiannon's sullen features. "What's going on? You've hardly said two words since we left the park."

"I could ask you the same thing Angela, but not about me." Rhiannon motioned between the two of them. "About us. What's going on between the two of us? It seems every time you need to explain me to someone the best you can manage is 'she's just a friend,'" Rhiannon said harshly. "You did it the night when I met Phillipa. It was how you said you initially described me to your mum, and you did it again today. You make it sound like I'm no more than an afterthought."

"I don't know. When I heard Mrs. Frank's voice I panicked." Angela pressed her lips together. "Telling her anything is tantamount to seeing it reported in the press minutes after the event. She's the local gossip and more than capable of putting her own twist on a situation."

"What is there for her to gossip about or misconstrue?" Rhiannon demanded. She inhaled deeply, as if to contain her emotions. "I mean, can't two people of the same age and sex have some innocent fun with each other?" she asked, this time more softly. "Why is it everyone seems to be finding something sordid with the idea of the two of us?"

Angela stepped back, struck by Rhiannon's words and tone. "Is that what you think I'm doing, finding something sordid?"

"I don't know, you tell me."

Angela's fingers gripped the benchtop in an attempt to control her ire. She glared at Rhiannon. "Maybe you're right and maybe you're not, who knows? But for the moment I think it would be best if you gave me some time to work it out for myself. Maybe then we can take things from there."

Rhiannon roughly ran her fingers through her hair, head bowed, eyes clenched in frustration. "If that's the case, best I leave before we add any more negative fuel to this fire."

Angela made to follow her. Rhiannon held up her hand.

"Don't worry, this *friend* can find her way out."

Angela listened to Rhiannon's footfall, the clicking of the front door lock signalling her final, angry departure. She collapsed into the closest chair she could find. Head in hands, she attempted to reconcile how the argument had started and why both of them had allowed it to escalate to such a stage. The padding of small feet announced Lachie's presence.

"Mum, where's Rhiannon?"

Angela looked up at Lachie's expectant face. "She had to go back to the hotel. She's got some things she needs to finish before work tomorrow," she deflected. She pulled a freshly clothed

Lachie on to her lap.

Lachie hugged Angela. "Mum."

"Hmm." Angela wiped a smudge of dirt from the back of Lachie's neck.

"I like Rhiannon. A real lot."

Angela's breathing hitched as Lachie snuggled deeper into her embrace. "So, do I honey. So do I."

Chapter Thirteen

THE BOTTLE OF wine Rhiannon consumed in anger on returning to her hotel, coupled with a lack of sleep from the previous evening, resulted in her sleeping through her alarm. Given the amount of wine and the unlikelihood she would secure a car space at work this late in the morning, she instead elected to call a taxi. Now she found herself trapped in the quagmire of Sydney's peak hour traffic. If there was anything positive about the inconvenience she was in, it was it gave her time to again review the previous day's events and the ensuing argument between her and Angela.

She couldn't help but silently curse her lack of control. After all, she was the one who had suggested they take things one step at a time. And in the reasoned light of day, it was patently obvious rushing Angela would only result in their relationship not progressing much further. She pulled her phone from her suit pocket, opened it, and scrolled to Angela's number. It was clear they needed to talk but given the hour maybe it was still a little early to call. Angela would no doubt be busy with Lachie. She closed the cell cover and put it back in her pocket, making a mental note to ring Angela once she'd reached the office. Maybe it would be okay by Angela if she came over after work and then she could properly apologise for her surly behaviour.

She had barely poured her first coffee when Trish, the executive assistant the company had graciously provided her, poked her head around the door. "Rhiannon, the CEO was looking to speak with you if you have a moment."

She placed her cup on the table and rose, reaching for the phone as she did. "I'll head up there now. Any idea what he wanted to speak with me about?"

"He didn't say. He simply asked you make your way to his office the minute you got in."

"It must be about the presentation on Saturday." Rhiannon pulled the presentation papers out of her briefcase and weaved around her desk. "I shouldn't be long."

Rhiannon headed for the elevators and paused. Her truculent mood last night and her subsequent actions meant she'd failed to go on her morning run. "I think the stairs might be the better option," she muttered.

Walking up the five flights, she replayed the presentation on Saturday. Thomas had seemed quite happy with the briefing. I wonder what he's after, she thought. She opened the stair door to the corporate level and walked through.

She entered the lobby to where Susan, Thomas' executive assistant sat. "Hi Susan, I believe Thomas wanted to see me."

"He does Ms. Sharp." She motioned to the waiting area. "If you'll take a seat I'll see if he's available."

Rhiannon settled into a waiting chair, at a sudden loss over Susan's formality. Last week when she'd first met Susan, they'd both agreed they were more comfortable with first names, and this had pleased Rhiannon. In which case, why all of a sudden was she reverting back to her surname? An unsettling feeling began to fill Rhiannon's gut.

She glimpsed up at Susan's quick return and tried to read anything in her features. She found nothing. "Mr. Gardely will see you now."

Now it's Mr. Gardely, not Thomas, she thought. What the hell was going on? She schooled her features and walked to where Susan stood, by the CEO's ajar door.

"Ms. Sharp." Thomas motioned to the small conference table in his office. "Take a seat."

She sat down. Thomas rose from his position behind his desk, picking up a newspaper as he went. He halted short of Rhiannon and stood beside her, forcing her to crane her neck to look at him.

He pointedly placed the newspaper down in front of her and opened it to a flagged section. "I was wondering if you could explain this?"

Rhiannon glanced at what was the Sunday social section of one of New South Wales' oldest newspapers. Staring back at her were a series of standard black and white newspaper photo-graphs, taken at the function she and Angela had attended the previous Tuesday.

She examined the photos, a myriad of thoughts rushing through her mind. When she'd first arrived, she'd cast a hurried glance over the company's equity and diversity policy. She was almost certain what Thomas was asking had nothing to do with her personal association with Angela. Thankfully, the photos in front of her bespoke nothing more than a platonic friendship between them.

Perplexed, she looked at Thomas, who was patiently waiting for an answer. "I can honestly say I'm not sure what it is you want me to explain. An old school friend of mine had a recital at the Conservatorium on Tuesday night and she invited me to attend. Surely there can't be any problem with that."

Thomas examined Rhiannon's face, as if seeking any hint of duplicity on her behalf. Rhiannon was relieved to see him finally relax a little and take a seat opposite her.

"After your explanation, no, there isn't a problem. However, you'll recall the discussion we had regarding disclosure when you were contracted to us."

Rhiannon nodded, still completely oblivious to his line of discourse.

"Those clauses are binding. Any breach may result in legal action."

Mystified, Rhiannon studied the photos then the man opposite her. "I haven't an iota of an idea of what you're talking about. Firstly, I've been very careful in not knowingly or unknowingly being exposed to any information or projects of this company, outside the remit of my contract. Consequently, when I'm not working one on one with your company's executives, most of my time is spent with your HR department."

As she fought to tamp down the anger threatening to surface, Rhiannon's steely eyes bored into Thomas'. Without looking, she pointedly closed the newspaper and pushed it across the table to him. "Secondly, in *all* my years my integrity has never been questioned." She left the implication of her last response hanging in the air between them.

Thomas Gardely took the newspaper and folded it. "No one is questioning your integrity. It's just...well...you need to be aware of these interest groups. Sometimes they have an uncanny way of gleaning information from you without you even knowing it's happening."

"And I've already told you, I don't know what you're talking about. As far as I was concerned, I was attending the recital of a friend, certainly no more than that. Is there something else I should be aware of?"

Rhiannon watched the CEO as he seemed to weigh up his next words.

Thomas shook his head. "I don't think there is. But it would be remiss of me if I had not reminded you of the clauses within your contract." Thomas rose, signalling an end to the discussion. "However, I'm certain you've got better things to do than sit here with me." He ushered Rhiannon to the door. "By the way, your presentation on Saturday was quite impressive. I don't doubt you'll have some resistance on your hands. I expect it's nothing you can't handle though." He opened the door.

"If that's the case, this company won't be terribly dissimilar to a number I've worked with over the years. Speaking of which, I best get back to it."

Leaving Thomas, she walked down the stairs, still confused over what had just happened. There was clearly something on his mind beyond that of merely photos in a newspaper. But what was it? Maybe Angela knew more. She grasped the rail and closed her eyes as a curse softly escaped her lips. She needed to call Angela now more than ever, to see if they could sort out not only this mystery, but more importantly the falling out between them.

Rhiannon closed the door to her office and dropped her brief on the desk. Taking a seat, she pulled her mobile out her jacket and dialed Angela's number. The rings droned on before defaulting to the message service and the sound of Angela's voice. Listening to her melodious tones, she again wondered how she'd ever managed to get into an argument with someone she cared so very deeply for. Despite the convenience, she was not about to leave an apology on something as impersonal as an answering service. Maybe she could drop by her house that evening. Reconciled, she hung up and refocused her efforts to the day ahead, the gentle features of one said pianist never far from her mind.

ANGELA DELAYED HER departure as long as she could before leaving home for the Save the Con meeting, she'd impetuously said she'd go to yesterday. Phillipa had rung barely thirty minutes after her disagreement with Rhiannon, at a time when her thoughts and emotions were still all over the place. And to make matters worse, Phillipa sensed Angela's disquiet and refused to let the issue go. It was only after she'd agreed to attend the damn meeting, and using the excuse of Lachie calling her, that she managed to escape any further inquisition. Leaving her son under the watchful eye of her next-door neighbour, she reluctantly made her way to Phillipa's house for what promised to be another long and drawn out affair.

She parked her car behind a silver sportscar, not too dissimilar to Rhiannon's. Turning off the engine, she closed her eyes and centred herself, much like she would prior to a performance. Of course, nothing of that magnitude was awaiting her. But the exercise served to push her annoyance of not hearing from Rhiannon today to the recesses of her mind, rather than the forefront where it currently resided. Satisfied her mask was in place, she stepped out of the car and headed to the meeting.

Phillipa opened the door and motioned Angela through to the family room. "Well ladies, look who I found on the doorstep. If it isn't our social butterfly."

Angela turned and looked quizzically at Phillipa. "You've lost me there." She sat down in a chair and made herself comfortable, waiting for further clarification.

Phillipa theatrically flopped her body into the chair diagonally opposite Angela. Her immaculately manicured hand flicked her coloured locks away from her face. "I don't know how many times I've tried to call you this past week and all I've got is your damned message service."

Angela shrugged. "You know I'm not joined at the hip with my mobile like you are. I often leave it somewhere and completely forget about it," she dissembled. "Besides, I don't recall any messages. Maybe there's something wrong with my phone."

"You know I hate to leave a message on those damned things. My assumption is if you don't answer it's clear you're not there." Phillipa crossed her legs. "Speaking of which, where have you been? Other than last night, I haven't had any luck at all in reaching you since the recital."

Angela was at a loss. Despite the friendship they'd shared over the years and the fact the rest of the group were all friends, she was reticent to share with them more than rudimentary details about her private life. "I'm sure you exaggerate. I haven't been out much at all. I had dinner with some old friends during the week and went to the beach on Saturday before picking up Lachie from my mother's house on Sunday. Any other time I was most likely in my backyard doing some well needed gardening."

Phillipa smiled cryptically. "Was it gardening you were doing at ten o'clock on Saturday night?"

Schooling her features, Angela coolly took her bag from her lap and placed it on the floor beside her chair. "You know very well that ten o'clock is past my bedtime. I was obviously in bed asleep and didn't hear the phone." It wasn't too far from the truth. She *had* been in bed — Rhiannon's hotel bed — and wasn't likely to hear her phone, given she'd left it at home.

Sara Williamson, another member of the Save the Con committee nudged Phillipa. "For heaven's sake Phillipa, leave the poor woman alone! Just because she refuses to be set up with any of your male friends doesn't mean she can't have a life of her own." She clapped her hands in a businesslike manner. "How about we get down to business? There's a lot to cover this morning and we best get underway."

Phillipa scowled. "At least be civilised. We should first start with some morning tea and then we can cover the strategies we need to discuss."

Phillipa rose from her seat and motioned at two of the four women. "Janine, you and Sara can help me in the kitchen. Frances, you keep Angela company and make sure she doesn't up and leave, like she's done on many previous occasions." The three made their way across the sweeping hall and in the general direction of the kitchen.

Thankful for the respite, Angela relaxed back in her chair.

Frances turned and faced her. "She can be a little full-on sometimes. However, I expect her heart's in the right place."

"We've been friends for years," Angela replied. "But she can only be taken in small doses." The two shared a laugh while she observed Frances Ainsley. Frances was a school friend of Phillipa's who had in the past year returned from a working sojourn in England. Dressed in grey flannel slacks and a teal silk blouse, it would be easy to mistake her for no more than a Sydney socialite with too much time on her hands. Her refined, slightly tanned features and stylishly short brown hair made her seem deceptively casual, yet still quite in keeping with the social circles Phillipa frequented. Despite her looks, Angela was aware Frances was a barrister of some repute and had offered her time to do pro bono legal work for the Save the Con.

"I saw your recital the other night on the late news. You certainly haven't lost any of your fervour when you play, have you? When you first started the recital...Angela, what's the matter?"

Angela failed to hide her disquiet. "Was it also on the late news? At this rate it's a wonder it wasn't reported in the newspapers."

Frances tilted her head, eyebrow hiked, a knowing smile on her face.

Angela rolled her eyes. "Don't tell me."

Frances nodded.

"I don't believe it! With all the problems there are in the world you'd think the media could find something better to write on than a small social gathering."

Frances laughed. "I understand your frustration. But it's who you are, and the public do love you. By the way, who was with you? She cut quite a striking presence."

Angela caught herself before she could utter the phrase which seemed to have gotten her into so much trouble over the past few days. It was clear Rhiannon was not just a friend. She was much more. Now if she could only get past how others may react.

Angela scrutinised Frances' expectant features. "She's a very good friend from my school days. We caught up at a school reunion we attended over a week ago. She's new in town, having recently returned from working in the States. I asked her if she wanted to come along."

Frances leant back in her chair. She pensively tapped her top lip with her finger. "You don't know if she's seeing anyone do you?"

If she had been perched on the edge of her seat, Angela had no doubt she'd have found herself on the floor right now. The implication of Frances' words was apparent. What wasn't immediately obvious to Angela was how best to answer her. There was no conceivable way Frances could be aware of what was going on between her and Rhiannon. What Angela wasn't certain of was whether, after yesterday, Rhiannon was seeing her or not.

"I'm not sure but I expect she may be. Why do you ask?"

"If she wasn't involved with anyone I wouldn't mind if you knew where I could get in touch with her."

Angela stared goggle-eyed at Frances.

"What's the matter? Are you all right?"

"Are you interested?" Angela struggled to frame a coherent sentence. "I mean do you want to ask her...I mean..." She quickly looked over her shoulder before returning her gaze to Frances. "Are you gay," she asked, *sotto voce*.

Frances smirked mischievously. "I wasn't going to ask her out to compare musical interests if that's what you mean. Does it concern you, that I'm gay?"

Angela shook her head. "You surprised me that's all. I suppose I wasn't expecting to meet someone like you in Phillipa's circle of friends. And I mean...well...you don't look gay," Angela blurted, her thoughts all over the place.

"Of course." She made a point of smoothing her fringe. "The pink triangle on my forehead is cunningly hidden with some fairly heavy concealer. What *were* you expecting a lesbian to look like?"

Angela nervously ran her finger up and down the leather seam on her chair, her eyes avoiding Frances. "I apologise. I didn't mean to be rude."

Frances shrugged. "No harm no foul. But does your school friend look gay to you? Not all women are social stereotypes. In fact, we come from all walks of life, like people who are straight. And some of us hold fairly high paid and respectable positions."

Frances' words stunned her. How had Frances pinpointed Rhiannon so readily when she had consciously or unconsciously been blind to Rhiannon's sexuality during school and, initially, most recently. "How do you know she's gay?"

"It's the triangle. Under certain lights it's quite obvious," Frances teased.

Angela hoped her dour look was sufficient notice Frances had milked the allusion as far as she could.

"I don't know, she mightn't be. I may have read the situation incorrectly. However, in the overview they had on the late news she seemed impervious to the attentions of a couple of the males in her group and continually had eyes for only the women, in particular you if I recall correctly."

Angela was helpless to stop the blush caused through Frances' words.

Frances raised her brows and blinked. "I see. I didn't mean to butt in. I just wasn't aware of how things were."

Angela bowed her head, her hands clenched. "Neither am I and in fact I'm still not sure." She looked at Frances. "This is all very new to me and...well," she sighed. "I'm finding it a little difficult to come to grips with."

Frances took her hand. "I know what you mean. It's difficult, especially with family and friends. Remember though, regardless of how new this may seem right now, for those who don't accept you, ask yourself were they honestly true friends to begin with?" She reached into her handbag and pulled out a card.

Angela took it from her. She quickly skimmed the information it contained and placed it in her own bag.

"Give me a call if you want to talk." Frances lightly tapped her arm. "I have to say though I do envy you. She's a very beautiful woman."

The sound of footfalls in the hallway brought a halt to any further conversation between them, and morning tea was set up for the gathering.

RATHER THAN LAUNCH into strategies over morning tea the chat remained trivial and more centred on social gossip. Phillipa regaled the group with the latest who had been seen with whom, along with the current state of play between a long feuding couple and their respective lovers.

Angela listened politely but took little active participation in the discourse. Sipping her tea, she mulled over Frances' words. While they certainly weren't close friends, Frances had accepted her hesitant admission as if it were an everyday event. Despite this, Angela couldn't help but wonder whether her closer friends would be so unconcerned, if they knew about her and Rhiannon. Engrossed in her own thoughts, she'd completely disregarded the continual conversation in the room. A nudge from Frances brought her back to the present. She cast her eyes around the group of expectant faces. "Sorry, did someone say something?"

"You *are* away with the birds this morning," Janine said. "I asked how your friend enjoyed the recital the other night. She was quite charming by all accounts. Who is she and what does she do again?"

Angela cast a sideways glance at Frances, her face a picture of bland curiosity, in no way betraying the conversation they'd recently shared. She returned her gaze to the group.

"Her name is Rhiannon Sharp and we used to go to school together. I met her at the school reunion Saturday, a week ago, after not seeing her for twenty years. Phillipa decided she might need some..." Angela formed her index fingers into quotation marks, "'fresh blood' for her cause, so she asked me to invite her along. As for her work, I understand she's consulting at the moment."

Janine poured herself another cup of coffee. "Where's she doing that?"

"She hasn't mentioned it much." Angela searched her memories for the name of the company Rhiannon had told her during their discussion the other day. "If I recall correctly, it's got two names." She clicked her fingers. "That's it. Gardely and Balen."

A sudden silence descended on the room. Phillipa carefully placed her plate on the table beside her. She looked over the group before returning to Angela. "You're joking, aren't you?"

The look of shock on the faces of her friends unsettled Angela and a strange sense of unease began to settle in the pit of her stomach. "I'm not. Phillipa what's wrong?"

Phillipa leant forward in her chair and keenly scrutinised her. "Has she asked you anything strange lately? Maybe about your work with the Save the Con committee?"

"No."

"Are you sure it was you who invited her to the recital the other night and not the other way around?" Phillipa demanded.

"She didn't ask to be invited. If you recall it was *you* who asked me to attend and suggested I bring Rhiannon along, *not* the other way around." Despite her attempt to remain calm, she could feel her temper rising. She glared pointedly at the group. "Now would someone care to tell me what's going on?"

"Gardely and Balen are one of the primary firms who are financially and physically involved in vigorously driving disgracefully modern building changes to the Conservatorium," Frances said quietly, her features suddenly cold, as if carved in stone. "Of all the companies we've dealt with they are by far the most ruthless in underhandedly achieving success by any means. Even by personal means if they have to. It seems you may have been taken advantage of."

"You've got to be joking," Angela scoffed. "Can you hear how silly that sounds?" She sought the other faces around her, desperately seeking support from just one other person in her defence of Rhiannon. She found none.

"I told you, Rhiannon is an old school friend. She'd never do anything like you're suggesting. My God you all sound like you've stepped right out of a B Grade spy movie."

"That's not the case," Frances said resignedly. "There are documented instances of private firms, including this one, using old acquaintances to abuse a friendship to gain inside information on a project or tender. Usually the people are very close to the individual they target, taking advantage of the situation without the person actually knowing. Are you sure this isn't the case with you?"

The double meaning behind Frances' words wasn't lost on Angela. Despite this, there was no conceivable way she could believe Rhiannon would intentionally deceive her. Rhiannon's actions had been nothing other than honourable. During their whole time together, she'd never asked anything in great detail about the Conservatorium. But had Angela missed something in her concerted attempts to resurrect their friendship? As she mulled on the idea, she couldn't help but remember Rhiannon's eagerness to attend the Tuesday night gathering. Was this because she wanted to hear her play again? Or was it something else? Had she capitalised on Angela's situation to suit her own professional means?

It had been twenty years since she'd last seen her. What *did* she know of Rhiannon's life outside of what little she'd told her? How could she have been so stupid!

Outwardly battling to maintain a brave facade, the pain of possible deception insidiously seeped into her very being. Angela snatched her bag and simultaneously rose from her seat, innately aware of how close she was to losing control. "I've got to go and collect Lachie." She straightened her slacks and calmly addressed the group. "I don't know what the case is with Rhiannon. However, I can tell you I haven't betrayed any confidences regarding what we discuss at these meetings. Please leave this to me. I'll get to the bottom of it." She showed herself out and ran to her car.

She barely made it to the privacy of her SUV before silent tears began to fall. Had she been so gullible? Was Rhiannon after insider information rather than her heart? She furiously dashed the tears from her face and turned on the ignition.

She drove through the streets of Balmoral, replaying their interactions together. As she did, she became increasingly incensed by Rhiannon's possible deception. A car cut in front of her and she slammed her hand on the car horn. The lack of any response from the driver in front of her only served to incite her anger even more. By the time she reached home and retrieved Lachie from the next-door neighbour it was all she could do not to call Rhiannon and give her a piece of her mind.

She ushered Lachie through the front door and forcefully closed it. Angela tossed the car keys on the hallway table, only to see them skid off the smooth surface and hit the floor. Lachie's soft touch halted Angela's attempt to pick them up.

"Are you all right, Mum? Did someone say something to you at your meeting which wasn't nice?"

Angela glanced at the worried look on Lachie's face and pulled him into a hug. "I'm fine, love. It's been a difficult morning, that's all." She gave him a rub on his back and released him.

"Do you want to kick the ball around? You liked it when we played with Rhiannon yesterday. Maybe that would help."

Angela turned from Lachie, attempting to hide her hurt at the mention of Rhiannon's name as she picked up her keys. "Maybe a bit later but not now." She straightened and placed the keys on the table. "Do you want some lunch?"

"Mrs. Brooke gave me some before you arrived."

"If that's the case, do you want to play in your room or help me outside with the garden?" Angela asked. She headed toward the back door of the house, already sensing what Lachie's response would be.

"Um, I think there's something I need to do in my room." He skipped down the hall. "See you later, Mum," he called over his shoulder.

Angela closed the back door and walked down the stairs to

the garden shed. She wasn't the most capable of gardeners. But at the moment she had to do something, anything, to bleed off some of the anger pulsing through her every being. She snatched a pair of pruning shears and stalked to the back of the garden and a jasmine vine she decided was desperately in need of pruning.

Chapter Fourteen

RHIANNON ENTERED HER hotel suite, kicked off her shoes and relished in the feel of the plush carpet beneath her toes. She dropped her briefcase on the lounge, walked into her bedroom and collapsed facedown and spreadeagled on the bed. In the silence of her surrounds she finally released the deep-throated growl she'd barely contained for the better part of her day.

The mini-inquisition heralding Rhiannon's start to Tuesday merely served as a portent for what was to come. Sideways glances and conversations halted mid-sentence when she walked into a room were the essence of her morning. If that wasn't enough, a particularly belligerent company vice president occupied her afternoon. On arriving at his office for a pre-arranged presentation, she diplomatically ignored his somewhat puerile attempt to ensure she knew he was aware of her recital attendance and subsequent meeting with the CEO, courtesy of a newspaper laid open on the relevant page on his coffee table.

Rather than rise to the bait she continued with her briefing. But despite the many ways she tried to explain the benefit of mentoring and motivating his staff, he refused to budge. She used every mediation trick in the book while all the while he sat, arms folded, legs crossed, occasionally glancing at the offending newspaper. Against all of Rhiannon's experience and better judgement, she finally found herself having to tersely remind the VP of his CEO's position regarding her role with the company. Sadly, it was only this thinly veiled threat which resulted in him at last reluctantly listening to what she had to say.

She rolled over and raised her arms above her head, her shoulders popping with the effort. Exhausted, she flopped her arms out to each side. "I want nothing more right now than to get out of these clothes, shower and order up some food. Preferably with a glass or two of wine." She slapped the side of the bed with both hands. "But I need to clear the air with Angela. And I'm not doing that over the bloody phone." Rhiannon rolled to the edge of the bed, sat up and swung her legs over the side and onto the floor. "First things first. I need a shower."

She stripped off her blouse, putting it on the padded bench at the foot of her bed. She was patently aware that on more than one occasion her stubborn pride and leaving issues unresolved had sounded the death knell to what few intimate relationships she'd had. But the feelings those relationships evoked in her paled against what she felt for Angela. Discarding the rest of her clothes, she headed for the shower.

IT WAS EARLY evening by the time Rhiannon arrived at Angela's. She had used the intervening period from when she'd gotten back to the hotel to rehearse what she might say to her. Walking up the steps, she could only hope Angela would forgive her for her thoughtless and harsh outburst the previous day.

She rang the doorbell and stepped back. The sound of running footfall stopped on the other side of the door, quickly followed by a fumbling of locks.

Backlit through the opened door was Lachie, a tea towel in his hand. "Mum, it's Rhiannon." He pulled her inside. "We've just finished dinner. Have you had any?"

As she began to frame a response, Angela walked into the hallway, a stony look on her face. It was clear to her that, from the look Angela was giving her, coupled with her body language, she was still angry from yesterday's confrontation. Suddenly, acknowledging she hadn't eaten since lunch didn't seem such a good idea.

"I'm fine mate." She ruffled his hair. "Did you enjoy your dinner?"

"Yep. Mum made jaffles." He licked his lips. "And salad." Lachie scrunched up his face.

"Salad's good for you. It makes you grow up healthy and strong." Rhiannon surreptitiously cast her eyes to Angela's silent form. "I was hoping your mum and me would be able to talk adult stuff for a little bit. Is that okay with you?"

Lachie pushed the front door closed. "Do I get out of the rest of the drying up?"

Angela took the tea towel from his hands, her eyes softening. "Yes, you do. Do you want to watch some television in the lounge?"

"There's only adult stuff on now. Can I go to my room and play with my toys?"

"Of course, you can. Just don't make too much of a mess down there." She motioned him on his way and looked at Rhiannon. She silently headed into the lounge.

Rhiannon followed, still searching for a way to begin her apology. "Angela, about yesterday. I think we need...I mean I need to explain myself and my actions."

Angela bunched up the tea towel and roughly threw it on one of the lounge chairs. Wheeling, she glowered disdainfully at her. "I expect you do," she said, the iciness in her voice unmistakable. "In fact, I've got a few questions of my own, if you would be so kind."

Rhiannon was at a loss at Angela's clipped tones. Gone was the warm, reserved friend she'd reconnected with a little over a week ago. In her place was a taciturn woman, standing her ground and coldly keeping her distance.

Despite the hackles rising on the back of her neck at Angela's words, Rhiannon forced herself to remain calm. "I'd be more than happy to tell you anything you want to ask."

Rhiannon's apparent calmness only seemed to add further fuel to Angela's disquiet. She paced the room before coming to halt, directly within Rhiannon's personal space. "What is it you want from me?" she demanded.

Surprised at the vehemence of Angela's tone, Rhiannon stepped back. "What do you mean? I thought I'd made myself quite clear. What's going on here Angela?"

"That's what I'd like to know! Why didn't you tell me who Gardely and Balen were? Why didn't you mention they're heavily involved in a project relating to horrendous architectural changes to the Con? Was your visit to the Con the other night nothing more than a covert reconnaissance?"

Rhiannon held up her hand, her frustration building. "Hang on a minute. I haven't got a clue what you're talking about. I didn't tell you about Gardely and Balen because I didn't think it would remotely interest you. As for them having anything to do with the Conservatorium, this is the first I've heard of it. However, it does answer the question why the CEO fronted me today. I've already told you I wasn't aware of every project they're involved in and I don't need to be to do my job there." She paused at the scepticism mirrored in Angela's face.

"As for some sort of reconnaissance, are you crazy? Of course, that wasn't the idea! The only reason I attended the recital at all was to hear you play. Why would I have gone otherwise?" Rhiannon said loudly. She bit her lip, her eyes steely. "I've very little in common with those other people who attended the reception," she finished, her voice barely controlled.

At Angela's look of disbelief Rhiannon turned away and exhaled deeply. She scanned her surrounds and reviewed the actual meaning behind Angela's words. Her conclusion left her cold. She turned and again faced Angela. "Are you suggesting the only reason I began a friendship with you was to pump you for information?" she asked, voice again raised.

"I don't know. Was it?" Angela challenged, arms akimbo.

Rhiannon strode across the room, halting just short of her. "I don't know what's happened to you between now and yesterday. But obviously something has. I came over here to ask for forgiveness for my behaviour. I had no right to place unrealistic expectations on you, especially after saying I wouldn't. For those actions all I can say is I'm only human. My want to take what we have beyond a strong friendship caused more than a little frustration on my behalf and clouded my judgment. For that I apologise."

Rhiannon endeavoured to rein in her growing temper but the snowball effect of her day and Angela's inquisition was a bridge too far. "That said," she pointed at Angela, "*your* actions today are ludicrous to say the least. I started off my day with a grilling by the CEO of Gardely and Balen regarding a possible clash of interests. And I told him what I'll tell you now. Such suggestions bring into call my integrity and that's something I won't tolerate! If you think for *one* minute the reason why, after receiving notification of the twenty-year reunion, I resigned from a rewarding overseas position, got a lesser skills requisite and paying job in Australia and attended the only reunion I've attended in twenty years was to find you and pump you for insider information then you're sorely mistaken! I came back because for years I've wondered if I did the right thing. Why didn't I go after you that day? Did you feel the same way I did? Was there anything between us worth pursuing? Now I can't help but wonder if I entirely misread the situation. Obviously, this is all too hard for you."

So obsessed was she with her argument with Angela, Rhiannon failed to notice the sudden presence of a spectator in the doorway. "Rhiannon, what are you and Mum shouting about?" Lachie's attention alternated between them, his face a study of anxiety.

As Rhiannon silently cursed herself for allowing her emotions to get the better of her, Angela moved to Lachie's side and knelt down. "It's only a little disagreement." She pulled him to her and encased him in a hug. "Rhiannon and I have both had a long day and are tired." She cast a cursory glance over her shoulder at her. "In fact, I think she was leaving so she can go home and have a rest," she finished, her words brooking no disagreement.

Lachie disengaged himself out of Angela's embrace and

walked over to where Rhiannon stood. Placing his hand in hers he studied her as she lowered to her haunches to be on equal footing with him. "Just because you and Mum are yelling at each other, does that mean you won't be at the soccer on Sunday?"

Rhiannon looked over the boy's head at Angela's inscrutable features. "I don't know matey. I'm pretty busy at work at the moment, not to mention there are a lot of obstacles in my way." Feeling the boy's shoulders slump she pulled him into a hug. "But, if I can possibly make it, I'll be there. Don't you worry about that." She released him and tickled his belly. "How about you go back to what you were doing, and I better get going."

Before she could rise, Lachie pulled her into his own hug, rewarding her with a kiss on a cheek.

"I like you a lot," he whispered into her ear. He took off at a jog down the hall to his room.

Rhiannon furiously dashed her eyes, removing the tears created by his calming words. She stood and faced Angela, her calm façade now back in place.

"Despite how you obviously now feel about the two of us, my feelings for you remain the same. I would never willingly deceive or hurt you. I care too deeply for you to ever let whatever I do for a living cloud my judgment. Regardless of what happens between us in the future, you'll always remain at the forefront of my thoughts." She barely got out her last few words, her emotions raw from Angela's accusations. She moved past Angela and to the front door, knowing if she stayed any longer, she'd most certainly break down. And that was something she could do in the privacy of her hotel suite, rather than embarrass herself where it was clear she was no longer welcome. She opened the door and walked through it, not bothering to see if anyone followed her.

ANGELA LOCKED THE door behind Rhiannon and rested her head against the cool wood. What had she done? Unless Rhiannon was the world's most accomplished liar, it was now clear to her Rhiannon's friendship had never been a front for industrial espionage. Had she given Rhiannon a modicum of the trust she deserved then she would have seen that all along.

She turned around and slumped against the door. Why was she ready to listen to her friends and their ridiculous theories? And how was she ever going to be able to explain that to Rhiannon after what she'd said and done to her just now?

Scrubbing away the tears running down her face, she pushed

off the door. Cursing at her own stupidity, she stalked into the lounge and snatched the tea towel from where she'd wildly tossed it only moments ago. She shoved it back in its place in the kitchen, not caring to straighten it, as she normally, meticulously did. For the first time in her life she was suffused with the irrational desire to hit something...anything. She stared at her hands, her livelihood.

"Damn it," she cursed almost inaudibly, her fingers clawed into fists. Unlike the greater majority of humanity, striking something wasn't an option open to her.

Trying to conceal her tear-stained cheeks, Angela dashed water on her face. She wiped her hands on a towel and walked down the hall, stopping short of Lachie's door. Smiling hollowly, she lightly tapped on the post. "Are you okay in here?"

Lachie connected a piece of plastic he was manipulating to another similar brick and held it up to her. "I'm building a soccer stadium." He inspected the floor for another correct connecting piece. "This could take a while though."

She took the stadium from him and turned it over in her hands, her mind filled with the game the three of them had shared the previous day. It was such a perfect day. How had everything managed to go downhill so quickly? She handed it back to Lachie. "It's lovely honey. I'll be in the piano room if you need me."

Lachie took the bricks from her. "No worries, Mum." Without further thought, he returned to his construction.

Angela left the door to the piano room slightly ajar, her mind in an endless loop of yesterday and today's arguments between her and Rhiannon. She sat down and played, for the first time in her life deliberately disregarding the requirement to warm up. She didn't care. She needed to give life to the pain of her anger, in sinew and sound.

The first piece, by Liszt, while deceptively frivolous in its tone, was manic in its composition. She executed the Grand Galop at a frenetic pace, matching its tempo — her fingers traversing the keys at a dizzying speed.

Angela felt some of her anger leave her, only to be replaced with a growing sense of frustration over how she'd acted with someone who had only ever wanted to give her as much as Angela was willing to allow. She bowed her head, visualised the notes and again became an extension of the grand piano.

She executed the third movement of Beethoven's Sonata Fourteen *presto agitato*, the pace desperately unrestrained. She played, her eyes closed tightly, her fingers fleeing over the instrument, at times simultaneously striking the keys in synchronicity with the notes of the composition.

Exhausted, she bowed her head, her hands rubbing her burning forearms. The music had dulled her anger, but it couldn't assuage the pain she felt. She baulked at the soft hand on her thigh.

"Mum, what's wrong? Why are you upset?"

Startled by Lachie's appearance, Angela fought to gain control of her emotions. "I'm not." She reached out and smoothed his hair. "Mum just needed a little rehearsal time."

Lachie stepped away from her, disbelief written on his face. "You were too upset," he demanded, hands on hips. "You always play the galloping song and Moonlight part three when you're not happy."

Lachie's indignant stance and description of the works of two of the world's most accomplished composers lightened Angela's spirits, if only a little. She rose from the piano stool and settled in the lounge chair. She held out her hands. "Come here."

She settled Lachie on her lap. "When have you heard me play like that?"

Lachie looked into Angela's eyes. "You used to play it a lot around the anniversary of Dad dying. I could hear it through the walls sometimes. You always seemed very quiet after you played it though. I thought it must have been his favourite."

Lachie's innocent words were sufficient to cause Angela to again tear up. She wiped her face and gave him a hug. "It wasn't his favourite. But it did help me through some tough times. Sometimes when things seemed to be closing in on me, I'd play it to clear my mind. Besides, I never realised these walls weren't so soundproof." She kissed the top of his head and Lachie snuggled deeper into her embrace. "Do you miss not having a dad?"

Lachie eased himself out of the embrace. "Some days I do and it's not real nice. It's usually when I want to do things outside and there isn't anyone around to kick a ball or play cricket with."

"Hey! I'm here. I can do that," Angela replied in mock indignation.

"Let's face it Mum, you're not too good with outdoor stuff," he said with naïve condescension. "You can't even bowl a ball in a straight line, let alone kick one. Rhiannon can though. It's why she's so much fun. Not to mention she doesn't treat me like I'm some sort of dill. Not that you do either," he added quickly. "But it's nice to have someone else not treat you like a baby."

Angela's stomach clenched at the mention of Rhiannon. "She's good at that isn't she?"

"She sure is! She told me she once used to do a whole lot of state sports. For someone old like she is, she sure is fit." He paused, as if in thought. "Why were you and Rhiannon arguing this afternoon?"

Despite Lachie's young years it was obvious to Angela he wouldn't be satisfied with a trite response—to give him one would merely offend. "Sometimes adults say things to each other which are hurtful and dumb. Yesterday Rhiannon said some things I wasn't too happy with and today I hurt her with what I said," she said carefully. "Unfortunately, I don't know whether she's talking to me right now or if she's ever going to talk to me again."

Lachie seemed to weigh up Angela's reply. "Why don't you kiss and make up?"

Angela's eyes widened at the innocence of the statement. She searched Lachie's expectant face. "Normally two women or two men wouldn't kiss and make up that way."

Lachie frowned. "Why not? You and Grandma do it all the time."

"But she's my mum and mothers and daughters are allowed to do that. Just like mums and sons do."

Lachie shook his head vigorously. "Yeah but at school Ms. Haley and Ms. Wiles do it all the time."

It seemed her day was full of surprises. "You mean they argue a lot," Angela asked, careful not to misconstrue Lachie's words.

"No Mum! They kiss a lot. Or at least they do when they think no one's around. I saw them kiss about four weeks ago. And on the last day of school break when Ms. Wiles tripped and hurt herself and was crying, Ms. Haley hugged her and kissed her." Lachie tilted his head, a quizzical look on his features. "Why shouldn't men kiss men and women kiss women? I mean if you like each other, what's wrong with it?"

Angela couldn't help but wish it was all so simple. Or was it? Lachie certainly seemed to think so, and this greatly relieved her. If only the fracture between her and Rhiannon could be resolved by merely kissing and making up.

Angela chuckled ruefully. "I suppose you're right." She lifted Lachie out of her lap, and they made their way out the rehearsal room and onto the lit back deck. There Angela tried unsuccessfully to emulate Rhiannon's abilities with a soccer ball, all the while her mind wondering whether things would ever be the same again between her and Rhiannon.

Chapter Fifteen

RHIANNON EXITED THE elevator and stalked to Trish. She placed the handful of briefing papers on her desk. "You might as well shred those," she said pointing disgustedly at the pile.

"What happened?" Trish pulled the bundle across the table. "Was there something wrong with the content?"

"Oh, the content was fine. But I think they didn't appreciate the messenger. Ever since the discussion with the CEO about me attending the recital, I've been given the cold shoulder by almost everyone." Rhiannon dipped her head at Trish. "Present company excepted of course."

"But I thought you cleared that up with Mr. Gardely." Trish grabbed the first briefing pack and began to remove the papers from the folder they were in.

"I did. But obviously the message didn't filter down to everyone, especially the executives I'm supposed to be dealing with."

"What are you going to do?" Trish dropped the loose-leaf papers in the shredding box beside her desk.

Rhiannon sighed deeply. "I think I'm going to have to do something I've never done in my entire career. But I want to think about it first."

"Would a coffee help?" Trish grinned impishly. "With a chaser perhaps?"

"Thanks for the offer, on both counts. But I've had enough alcohol this week to last me a month." Rhiannon held up her water. "This will do me fine." She walked to her office. "I'm free if anyone needs to see me. But I severely doubt you'll be beating them away with a stick." Rhiannon saluted Trish with her bottle and walked into her office, closing the door behind her.

She sat down in her chair and rotated it to face the expansive view of an overcast Sydney. Shades of grey reflected off the multitude of office blocks in this part of town. Her eyes tracked to the harbour, visible between the buildings. It too was a tired grey, which was just how she felt.

She'd gotten little sleep over the past couple of days, her thoughts constantly preoccupied with how things between her and Angela had gone pear shaped so quickly. It wounded her deeply that Angela would think the rekindling of their friendship was nothing more than a ruse on her behalf. Yet despite the wound Angela's words had caused, Rhiannon still cared deeply for her.

She tore away the protective plastic covering the lid of the water bottle and brought her thoughts back to her present situation. She held the cool bottle against her forehead, in a vain attempt to ease a building headache. "What the hell am I doing here?" she muttered to the empty room.

It was clear she wasn't getting her message across. It was hard enough before her meeting with the CEO about the recital. Now it was damned near impossible. From the snatches of hallway and kitchen area conversations she'd heard, it sounded a lot like whatever the company was involved with regarding the Conservatorium wasn't going to plan. And from the ongoing snide remarks made by some of the executives about her recital attendance, she couldn't help but wonder if in some way they were laying the blame for their lack of progress at her feet, which was patently ridiculous.

She eased her head against the back of the chair and blew out a tired breath. There were a few in the organisation who she was reaching with her message, but they were far outweighed by the many. As much as it pained her, she couldn't see any other option open to her. For the first time in her life she was going to have to walk away. Sure, she'd experienced her fair degree of difficult companies and shitty negotiations. But she'd never been in a position where her presence was seemingly perceived to be the impediment to progress.

She'd have given anything to speak with Angela about what was happening. But it wasn't an option open to her anymore. They'd said things, hurtful things which couldn't be unsaid, and for which she was profoundly sorry. She massaged the back of her neck, attempting to release the tension contained within.

Given the continued calls Rhiannon received from the company she last worked for in the United States, she was certain they'd welcome her back with open arms. All the same, she wasn't sure she wanted to do any of this anymore. What she was absolutely sure of was the need to get away from Sydney. The pain of being close and yet so far from Angela was too much to bear.

She swivelled her chair back to her desk and picked up her phone. Scrolling through her contacts menu, she halted at Luke Daniel, the Co-CEO of Peak Personnel Solutions. Her finger hovered only briefly before she pressed the button to call him.

"Hey Rhiannon," Luke said. "To what do I owe this pleasure?"

She pursed her lips, trying to find the words to explain to him her predicament. "I don't think it's going to be much of a pleasure once I tell you what I'm calling about."

"Hang on a sec."

Rhiannon listened to Luke excuse the people in his office so he could solely focus his conversation on her.

"Okay, what's going on?"

Rhiannon took the next few minutes to avail Luke of what had happened in the past few days, including the frosty reception she was now receiving from the majority of the senior staff.

"Not good, not good at all," Luke said. "Where does that leave you?"

Rhiannon ran her fingers through her hair. "I feel it only leaves me one choice." She closed her eyes, her head bowed. "I think it would be best for all concerned if I stepped back from the project and gave someone else a go at working with them."

There was a prolonged silence from the other end of the connection then Luke again spoke. "Rhiannon, we've known each other for years."

"Yes, we have."

"In all that time I've *never* known you to walk away from anything," Luke replied.

Rhiannon rested her elbow on the desk, her forehead cupped in her hand. "I never have, but I've also never been in a position with a company where I'm seen as the problem. While there's absolutely nothing between me and their current work with the Conservatorium, there are obviously people here who think I'm part of why things aren't going to plan with that proposal."

"I believe you. Is there any way you think you could work through this?"

"There's always a way Luke, but at what cost? Notwithstanding such an approach is bound to take a hell of a lot more time, effort, and expense to both companies, there's also a price to me. And this whole project has already cost me a friendship which was very dear to me."

Luke cleared his throat. "I'm sorry to hear about your friendship."

"So am I," Rhiannon said softly. "I just don't think I'm in the right space to value-add and make a difference here anymore."

"I know how good you are at what you do. If there's so much obstruction to what you're doing there, is there any merit in us continuing an association with Gardely and Balen?"

"The easy answer would be no. But, asides from the contractual obligation to deliver the first tranche of work, there *are* people here I was able to reach, who I think my message genuinely empowered. It would be a shame to see those groups suffer if we broke contract. Who knows, those few might just be the revolution from within the company needs to drive the necessary change." Rhiannon paused and took a sip of water.

"I have a comprehensive database of my work, including what I was due to deliver next week. I'm sure this could be seamlessly transferred to another consultant."

"Hang on a minute. Let me check the computer to see who might be available," Luke said.

Rhiannon listened to Luke place his mobile on the table, obviously to free both his hands. At the same time, Rhiannon used one hand to scan her file tree, placing her most recent presentation against the executive team she'd been working with that afternoon. The shuffled sound of a cell being picked up interrupted her progress.

"Martin Stewart is available. He's been working a project in New Zealand and will return to work next week."

"I've heard of Martin. He's extremely skilled in what we're doing here and I'm sure they'll work with him. At least he can see you through the first tranche and then you can, without fault to you, re-evaluate any further engagement from there."

"That's a good idea. In fact, if Martin hadn't been tied up in New Zealand he'd have competed for your position, along with you. How do you want to play it from here? Do you want me to call the CEO?"

Rhiannon leant back in her chair. "I'll do it. It's the least I can do for leaving you in the lurch like this." She checked the messaging service on her computer and confirmed Thomas was available. She quickly typed a message to him. "Mr. Gardely is still here. Assuming Martin's agreeable, I'll have the pack ready for him by tomorrow afternoon, and I can discuss it with him early next week." A bleep on her screen heralded a positive response from Thomas regarding a meeting.

"When are you suggesting you finish up?"

Rhiannon quickly typed an acknowledgement to Thomas. "There was nothing planned with the executive group here until next Wednesday morning. When I started, they told me that on the last Friday of the month the company finishes early. I assume from there they head off to their respective decompression sessions. With that in mind I'll finish up here mid tomorrow afternoon."

"Fine by me. Are you interested in any further work? I'd be

more than keen to have you remain a member of my team."

Rhiannon rolled her pen across her desk, mulling Luke's words. The eagerness and sincerity in his tone confirmed his suggestion was more than merely a conversation filler. "I do appreciate the offer. But I think I need to take a break away from all of this. It's been about fifteen years since I've had time out. Now seems the right time."

"I certainly don't want to lose you Rhiannon, but I understand. If you ever want to work in this space again you know I'll always be very keen to have you back."

Rhiannon's eyes welled unexpectedly. "Thanks Luke, that means a lot to me. I can't say I'll be in touch. But if I come back, you'll be my first call. Say hi to Joel for me," Rhiannon said, with reference to Luke's husband.

"I will. Bye."

She pulled the mobile away from her ear and stood. Straightening her jacket, she made her way to her final meeting with Thomas Gardely.

IT HADN'T BEEN hard to tell the CEO of her decision and impending replacement. He had at least the decency to appear abashed when she told him. Thomas had even gone so far as to accept partial blame, explaining how he lost his temper during the executive meeting on Monday, when initially shown the newspaper article.

Surprisingly, it had been harder for her to explain her decision to Trish. Rhiannon was touched by the initial despair mirrored on Trish's face, one which was quickly replaced by anger. Rhiannon reassured her there would be a replacement early next week. All the same, Trish's assertion the company wouldn't know how good they had it with Rhiannon, even if it bit them on the left testicle, still rang in her ears as she shut down her laptop for the day.

Sliding her laptop into her briefcase, her mobile rang. The caller ID was Carol Bowen, her property manager. She had managed Rhiannon's portfolio for a number of years.

"Hi Carol. How are you?" she said, nursing the mobile between her ear and shoulder. "What's up?" She zipped shut the compartment which held her laptop.

"I'm fine thanks. I've got great news. Your house in Durack Street will be ready for you as early as this weekend."

Rhiannon cringed. She'd completely forgotten Carol was currently dealing with Isabella's home. "Thanks for moving this quickly. But now I can't help but feel I've caused you a great deal of effort, all for naught."

"What do you mean?"

Rhiannon sat down and lay the briefcase on her desk. "I don't think I'll be needing it after all. My contract wasn't as long as what we thought it was going to be. I've got to tie up a few loose ends and then I'll be good to move on, most likely not in Sydney though."

"Where will you go?"

"I think I'll head down to Arcadia for a while," Rhiannon replied, referring to her family's home in the New South Wales Southern Highlands.

"Do you want me to put Durack Street back on the rental market?" Carol asked.

Rhiannon appreciated the ready source of income renting Isabella's property gave her. But retaining it still tied her to Sydney, when all she really wanted was a clean break. "Can you manage the sale of it for me?"

"Of course. Did you have a reserve in mind for the house?"

"I didn't, and I'm not entirely familiar with the Sydney market either. You've managed my portfolio long enough and I know you're familiar with the local area." Rhiannon picked up her stress ball and squeezed it absentmindedly. "I think it would be easier all round if you handled the sale for me, if that's okay by you that is."

"No worries. I've never bothered to tell you this because I never thought you wanted to sell the property. I've had a couple of clients who have regularly expressed an interest in your house," Carol replied.

Rhiannon rolled the stress ball under her palm on the desk. "That sounds promising."

"Here's hoping it is. I'll give them both a call and see if they're still interested. If it works out, then it will save you a lot of money on advertising and the inconvenience of multiple showings. Mind you, being the only remaining Federation Style home in that street with those views, I doubt it will be on the market long either way."

"Thanks Carol, I do trust your judgement on this one. I'll wait to hear from you." Rhiannon ended the conversation and placed the phone in her inside jacket pocket.

RHIANNON HANDED HER keys to the valet and walked through the doors of the hotel. She glanced across to the elevators, where a large group of people stood. From the looks of their attire and luggage they were most likely tourists — family perhaps, who had recently arrived. She observed the casual interaction between members of the group, envious of the closeness they shared with each other. It was a closeness Rhiannon would never have, not anymore. Her eyes tracked the foyer, coming to rest on the entrance to the bar. Changing course, she walked in that direction.

She placed her briefcase beside her and took a seat at the bar. The man who had served her last time she was there held up a bottle of whisky.

"Two fingers please. Neat."

"Yes, Ms. Sharp." He retrieved a heavy crystal low ball. "Water on the side again?"

"Thank you."

The barman placed the drink, water, and dropper in front of her. "Do you want me to open a tab?"

"No thanks. I'm not sure I'll be here too long," she replied.

"I'll put it on your room."

As Rhiannon made to answer, she felt a presence slide into the seat beside her.

"I'll get that. Can you get me the same please?"

Rhiannon slightly turned her seat to the woman beside her. "Thank you, but you don't need to."

"It's my pleasure." She held out her hand. "I'm Gillian Eyre. I think I've seen you around the hotel. Are you a guest?"

Rhiannon nodded and she took Gillian's hand. "Rhiannon Sharp. I'm assuming you are also?"

Her grip was firm, yet intimate, her fingers caressing Rhiannon's when she finally released her grip. "Yes, I am," she replied, a knowing smile mirrored in her deep brown eyes.

Rhiannon didn't miss the obvious double meaning of Gillian's words. As Gillian went to speak, the barman placed her drink in front of her.

While Gillian busied herself with the tab, Rhiannon unobtrusively viewed the woman beside her. The gods must be laughing up a storm. Gillian was just about the epitome of what she normally found physically attractive in a woman. Dressed in a white polo shirt, her broad shoulders and tanned, lightly muscled arms bore testimony to an active lifestyle. Her stonewashed blue button up jeans complemented her tan iconic Australian leather ankle boots. Gillian's stylishly clipped brown hair, angular face and swimmers build vaguely reminded Rhiannon of one of the sisters who regularly competed for Australia in swimming.

Rhiannon masked her appraisal by sipping her drink. As the barman moved away, Gillian returned her full attention to her.

"I think I've seen you in the gym a couple of times," Gillian said.

"You might have. I work out regularly, wherever I am."

Gillian's eyes raked her body, making no effort to hide her interest. "That's obvious, even from a distance." She toyed with the gold labrys pendant on the chain around her neck. "And now, being this close only confirms the fact."

Rhiannon was no stranger to the direct approach. Hell, in her younger years it was one she'd used herself. All the same, she didn't welcome it now, regardless of the beauty sitting beside her. She placed her whisky down. "Look, I don't mean to sound ungrateful. But I'm just thankful for the drink, nothing more."

Gillian's middle finger circled the wooden grain of the bar top, intermittently lingering proximate to where Rhiannon's hand rested. "It could be more if you want." Her eyes tracked the barman as he walked across to clear one of the tables in the bar. Gillian returned her gaze to Rhiannon. "You're an extremely striking woman."

"You flatter me," Rhiannon replied, the warmth of her whisky beginning to settle in her being.

Gillian reached out and stroked lightly Rhiannon's fingers where they gripped the glass. "And one who, given the chance, I'd like to get to know better. But don't worry. I'm not after a life-long commitment."

Rhiannon looked down at Gillian's fingers and felt the sensual tug of craving. She swallowed convulsively. Suddenly her mind's eye filled with another vision, of Angela, her eyes hooded in desire, back arched. Rhiannon slowly moved her hand away. "Gillian, I don't mean—"

The ringing of Rhiannon's phone put a temporary halt to any further comment. She reached into her jacket pocket and retrieved her mobile. It was Elly. She pressed the receive button. "Hi Elly, can you give me a second?"

Rhiannon engaged the mute button on the cell. "I need to take this," she said. "You're very attractive. But now is not a very great time for me."

"That's what they all say," Gillian replied with mock good grace. She took a coaster, wrote her suite number down on it and slid it across to Rhiannon. "I'll be here for at least another week." She slid out of her chair and grabbed her drink. "Should you change your mind."

Rhiannon put the coaster in her pocket as Gillian moved away. She disengaged the mute button on the mobile. "Are you still there Elly?"

"I am, where are you?"

"I'm in the hotel." Rhiannon's eyes tracked Gillian's departure. "At the bar."

"Wow, it must have been a pretty shitty day," Elly replied.

"You could say that, and thanks for the call. It was very timely." Rhiannon picked up her whisky and took a small drink of the heady, warm contents.

"What do you mean? What's going on?"

"Let's just say I think one of the hotel's guests was after more than a drink."

Elly's laughter filtered down the line. "Was she good looking?"

Rhiannon glanced at the mirror on the back wall of the bar, in time to see Gillian make herself comfortable next to another woman. "Very."

"It sounds like it's feast or famine with you at the moment. Anyway, enough of your love life. What are you doing this weekend? Do you and Angela want to catch up again?"

Rhiannon closed her eyes and pinched the bridge of her nose. Her recent argument with Angela again thrust itself to the forefront of her mind. Aside from the soccer on Sunday, she really hadn't any idea what Angela was doing. She hadn't heard from her since Tuesday. But then again, after everything which had happened, she had no right to expect to hear from her either.

"Earth to Rhiannon, are you there?" Elly asked, the concern evident in her tone.

Rhiannon slumped back against the bar chair. "I'm not sure what Angela's doing on the weekend."

"I'm assuming something's gone pear shaped between the two of you. Do you want to talk about it?"

"I do. But not this way, over the phone." she turned her whisky glass on the coaster it rested on. "It's a little complicated."

"Do you want to come over and talk this weekend? Jen is taking Olivia down to see her grandparents in Bundanoon on Friday."

"I thought you'd go with her."

"Like you, it's a long story which needs privacy and alcohol to explain. I can feel a Friday night session coming on. Have you got anything planned?"

"Do you want to come for a drive? I'm heading down to Glenquarry on Friday afternoon, to fix up some things." Rhiannon paused at the barman who held up the bottle of scotch. She politely waved him away.

"That's where your house is, isn't it?"

"Yes, and if all goes to plan, it'll soon be my future abode. It's about forty minutes north-north-east of Bundanoon."

"You're leaving Sydney? What about Angela? What about your job?" Elly queried.

Rhiannon rubbed the side of her forehead. "Not now Elly. I promise to explain everything on Friday. It'll be nice to have someone to talk to about this."

"Are you there for the whole weekend?" Elly asked.

Rhiannon studied her whisky. Staying the weekend would allow her to get everything ready for her imminent return to her family home. But what about Lachie? He's such a great kid. And she'd all but promised him she'd be at the soccer on Sunday. Despite her discord with his mother, was it right for him to suffer?

"Just the one night. I need to be back on Saturday night. I've got a prior commitment on late Sunday morning."

"It suits my plans to a tee. Jen was returning to Sydney on Saturday afternoon. She can swing by and pick me up from your place."

Rhiannon opened up her contacts on the phone and texted the address. "I've sent you the address for you to pass on to Jen. Do you want me to pick you up on Friday? I was looking at getting away mid-afternoon if possible."

"Thanks, the address just came through. If I remember correctly, the other night when you were over for dinner you mentioned you were staying at The Gables."

"That's right."

"Jen has an appointment close to where you're staying. I can get her to drop me off and I'll wait for you in the foyer."

"That works." Rhiannon rose from her bar seat. "Give me a call when you arrive. I'm looking forward to catching up with you again."

"Will do and me too. See you then." Elly ended the connection.

Rhiannon drained the small remainder of her drink and

picked up her briefcase. She cast a quick glance in Gillian's direction, satisfied she was more than preoccupied with yet another potential conquest. She nodded her thanks to the barman and walked to the elevators.

Chapter Sixteen

"ARE YOU SURE you're going to be okay?" Angela carried Lachie's backpack to the waiting car in her driveway. "What have you got in here by the way? You're only going overnight, not forever." She waved to the woman waiting by the car. "Hi Louise. Thanks for picking up Lachie."

To mark Lachie's last weekday of freedom, as he so aptly put it, and before he again started school the following Monday, Angela had agreed to a sleepover at the Sydney Zoo. Thankfully, his best friend's mum, Louise, had agreed to chaperone the two boys. Angela was silently grateful. While camping may have a resounding appeal to Lachie, it was something she'd never had even a remote interest in.

"Hi Angela. It's no problem picking up Lachie." Louise opened the trunk of her car.

"Are you sure you're up to this?" Angela put Lachie's backpack in the space next to two other packs.

Louise smiled crookedly. "I can't say. But do you want to do it?"

"I suppose I could cope with being in the zoo for the better part of the day." Angela watched Lachie crawl into the back seat, next to his friend Brett. "It's the camping which does nothing for me," she whispered.

Angela walked around to where Lachie sat. She reached through the open window and pulled on the seatbelt. "Put this on please. You're not going anywhere until you do."

"Oh Mum," Lachie protested as he fixed the belt in place.

Angela shared a nod with Louise as she got into the car. "You behave for Mrs. Brooke. And I don't want to hear you've been up all night either." She put her fingers to her lips and touched Lachie's cheek with them. "I love you. Have a great time."

Lachie blushed. "Love you, too, Mum," he muttered.

Angela stepped back and waved as the car backed down the driveway. She returned to the house, wondering how much longer Lachie would allow her such public displays of affection with him. It was clear the time wouldn't be too far in the not too distant future. She walked through the now quiet house and to her office, aware she had yet to print Lachie's school schedule for the next two weeks.

Waiting for the computer come to life, her eyes scanned her surrounds, coming to rest on a grainy photograph on her bookshelf. The photo was old, some twenty years. It was the sole picture she had of Rhiannon. Unbeknownst to her, Angela had snapped it during a June softball game of Rhiannon's. She was on first base, her body in full extension, diving sideways to catch a ball. Her mouth was slightly ajar, her face a portrait of joy, the caught ball in the meat of her glove.

At the time Angela didn't truly process why she'd taken the picture. She just did. Now, it was clear her attraction for Rhiannon stretched much further back than merely the moment in the study.

She rested her elbows on the desk and steepled her hands. Closing her eyes, she rubbed her eyebrows with her thumbs. She hadn't spoken with Rhiannon since Tuesday which, given the argument between them, was not surprising. Yet despite it only being slightly over two days, the chasm it left in Angela made it feel more like they hadn't spoken in years. She raised her head when the computer warbled the first few bars of a Mozart piece, signalling she had mail.

She clicked open her mailbox. "Bloody junk mail. How in the hell do they get my email address?" Phillipa had told her it had something to do with biscuits, or was it cookies? All Angela knew was it was the bane of her existence, wading through unending swathes of advertising rubbish.

Deleting yet another message, her eyes came to rest on one which clearly wasn't merely electronic detritus. It was from the Armitage Symphony Orchestra in Philadelphia. The orchestra was world renowned, composed of artists who were all handpicked by the rich benefactor who funded the orchestra. No amount of money or talent could buy a musician's way into the prestigious group without them first being invited.

The subject heading gave nothing away, merely indicating the email was for her. Angela hovered the cursor over the subject title and clicked. She began to read the email and her eyes widened. The orchestra was seeking her to be the classical soloist for their very limited and exclusive six-week season, due to commence in three months' time.

She was astounded. To perform with the Armitage was momentous in itself. But to have this happen after her long sabbatical was almost unheard of. She scanned the rest of the email, noting they would need a response from her within the next couple of weeks. She sat forward and typed a hasty note thanking them for their email, advising she would respond within the required time.

She hit send and cupped her face in her palm. Sharing the great news with Rhiannon was the first thing which entered her mind. Angela checked the idea, dejectedly realising it was no longer an option open to her.

She left the office and wandered down the hall to the kitchen. After pouring herself a glass of juice, she took a seat at the breakfast bar and called her mum on the landline. She sipped her drink while she waited for her mum to pick up.

"Angela? Why are you calling me on your house phone and not the mobile?"

Angela scrunched her eyes and stretched her neck, attempting to release the tension there. "I seem to have misplaced it."

"*Again*," Maureen asked, her exasperation evident. "Did you lose it while you were out? Or is it in the house?"

Angela looked around the kitchen, as if her actions would miraculously result in her mobile appearing. "It's in here somewhere. Lachie's away at the camping thing I mentioned to you last weekend. I'll have a good look for it while I clean today."

"Make sure you call me on it when you find it. How is everything? Are you calling about anything in particular or just for a natter?"

"I got an email today from the Armitage Symphony Orchestra. They're an invitation only group of artists."

"Can I assume by the excitement in your voice they've asked you to play with them?"

"They have, for a set season in the United States. I need to let them know my decision within the fortnight."

"That's great news sweetie. Have you told Rhiannon yet? What did she say?"

Angela's excitement spontaneously disappeared, leaving her deflated. "I haven't told her. We haven't spoken in a couple of days," she replied, her voice devoid of emotion.

"Are you okay? Has something happened between you two?"

"Mum, I think I've made a mess of just about everything between us. The Monday after we left your place, we had a picnic with Lachie, here in the local park. Rhiannon tackled me and we were rolling around on the ground when Mrs. Frank found us. I kind of over-reacted when she saw us together."

"I can only imagine. I'm sure that woman's life is truly bereft of any purpose whatsoever, and her only joy is gossiping about others. I swear she's not happy unless others are miserable. Given you were with Lachie, I'm assuming you were only mucking around," Maureen queried.

"It's all we were doing." Angela ran her fingers through her hair. "But knowing Mrs. Frank like I do, I panicked. I don't know why. I'm a grown woman for heaven's sake. You'd think her opinion wouldn't count."

"Did she speak to you?"

"She did. I introduced Rhiannon as just a friend, which Rhiannon took umbrage to. It immediately put a damper on the picnic. We argued when we got back to the house." Angela's fingers trailed down the condensation on the side of her glass.

"That doesn't sound too bad. I mean I expect you hurt her feelings. But surely you can apologise."

"I could, if that's all there was. On Tuesday I had a meeting with the Save the Con team. I mentioned who Rhiannon was working for and Phillipa told me in no uncertain terms they were one of the heartless companies bidding to dramatically change the conservatorium. If that wasn't bad enough, one of the team strongly suggested Rhiannon had only reconnected with me because she was pumping me for information about the Save the Con group."

"Let me guess, you believed them."

"Yes," Angela said, fighting to control the tears which threatened to fall.

Maureen sighed. "And you broached the matter with Rhiannon, in a less than rational fashion."

"I just about accused her of industrial espionage and orchestrating unethical means to gain information about the Save the Con. How could I have been so stupid?" Angela managed, half hysterical, half sobbing. "She didn't even know about the group and yet I was willing to find fault in her rather than in the rationale of others. I don't think I could have handled the conversation any worse if I tried. We argued, she left in anger and I haven't heard from her since."

"Are you sure you're not merely trying to find excuses to pull back from what you have with Rhiannon?"

"No Mum, it's not it at all. I think I'm only now fully realising just how much she means to me."

"Then, my dear, what is it you really want? Do you want to play again, do you want Rhiannon, or do you want both?"

Angela's eyes searched the room, as if in doing so she would find the answer to her mother's enquiry. "Years ago, when we were schoolgirls, Rhiannon challenged me on my choice of a career over friends. I'd said I'd happily look for friends once I'd achieved my goals." Angela snorted regretfully. "She reminded me to not hold people at arm's length for too long because when I lowered my arm they may no longer be there. Mum, I know playing with the Armitage is the chance of a lifetime. Understandably, Lachie will come with me overseas. But I can't help but feel the experience would be pretty hollow if I couldn't share it with another adult, a friend. I'd dearly love to share it with Rhiannon, but equally so she's now committed to the job she's in and not likely to leave it on the whim of someone who very recently challenged her integrity. Oh crap, I've made such a mess of everything. I don't know which way is up at the moment."

The soft laughter of her mother filled her ear. "Life is full of choices and decisions, and you have quite a few to make. And I'd say one of the first ones is to decide whether to talk matters out with Rhiannon and see where things go from there."

"But—"

"There aren't any buts about it, Angela. Don't make choices on Rhiannon's behalf. Something tells me she'd be none too happy with that idea. At least speak with her."

Angela shoulders slumped. "I'll try. I just don't know how successful I'm going to be."

"Either way, let me know how you go. I better be going. I'm due at my book club meeting."

Angela finished the call. She rinsed her now empty glass and placed it on the sink to drain. She glanced through the window over her sink and watched two female Eastern Rosellas land on her feeder outside and help themselves to its contents. Could it be so easy? That she had to talk with Rhiannon went without saying. But after what had passed between them, would Rhiannon even be willing to listen?

ANGELA PUT AWAY her now clean plate from what had been her late, tasteless lunch. Over the past few days she'd felt very little like eating. If it hadn't been for the need to prepare meals for Lachie, she doubted she'd have bothered at all. She hung the tea towel on the rack just as her doorbell rang. She wasn't expecting any visitors today. Straightening her blouse, she walked through the hall, released the bolts, and opened the door to a less than impressed Phillipa.

"Where have you been?" Phillipa demanded. She brushed past Angela and walked into the lounge.

Angela closed the door and silently followed her.

"I've not seen you since you took off from our meeting on Tuesday, as if the devil were on your heels."

"My apologies." Angela sat down, motioning for Phillipa to join her. "I didn't mean to leave in such a rush."

Phillipa sat and smoothed her skirt. She scanned the area around her and tilted her head. "Where's young Lachie?"

"He's at an overnight camp at the zoo, with a friend of his and the boy's mother." Angela settled back into the sofa and folded her arms, in anticipation of what she expected would be yet another grilling from Phillipa about not being in touch.

Phillipa scrunched her nose. "Ugh, bugs and smells. But I expect he'll enjoy it. After all, it's what little boys do seem to enjoy. I tried to call you on Tuesday night, to see if everything was okay but your mobile went to message bank. And you know I won't leave a message on those damned things."

"I've misplaced my mobile. It's somewhere in the house," Angela replied, somewhat sheepishly.

"Again! I don't know why you don't keep it in a pocket or something. This is the third time this year, isn't it?"

"Yes," Angela replied.

A look of disappointment crossed Phillipa's face and Angela kicked herself. It was obvious Phillipa wasn't solely here to berate her. Despite wanting nothing more than to have the afternoon to herself to try and sort out how best to approach Rhiannon, it was clear Phillipa had something she wanted desperately to share.

She unfolded her arms and slightly turned to Phillipa. "What brings you over this side of town?"

Phillipa's eyes lit up. "I've got the most wonderful news. Early this morning I got a call from my real estate agent, about a house I've coveted for years."

Angela raised her brow. "You've fancied quite a few if I remember correctly. Which one are you talking about?"

Phillipa rubbed her hands together gleefully. "It's the one in Balmoral."

A sickly, unsettling feeling began to take root in Angela's stomach. "Where in Balmoral?"

"It's in Durack Street."

Her heart beating a rapid tattoo, Angela fought to control her breathing. She nodded silently, urging Phillipa to continue.

"It's a real beauty. It's the last—"

"Federation Queen Anne in the street," she said, her voice

dying away.

"Yes." Phillipa slightly turned her head and frowned. "But how did you know?"

The colour drained from Angela's face as the unceasing roiling in her stomach threatened to erupt. She abruptly stood. "I think I'm going to be sick." She pressed her hand to her mouth and bolted to the guest bathroom in the hall. Slamming the door shut, she only just made it to the toilet before losing the greater majority of her lunch.

Impervious to Phillipa's repeated banging on the door, she continued to retch, her stomach constricting at every attempt.

"Angela, are you okay? Listen, I'm coming in."

"Wait," Angela managed. She spat the remains of her lunch into the bowl. Reaching across, she grabbed a piece of toilet paper and wiped her mouth. Supporting herself against the hand towel rail, she stood and flushed the bile and paper down the toilet. She barely made it to the basin before the door slightly opened and Phillipa's worried face appeared.

"Are you ill? Do you want me to take you to the doctor?"

Angela rinsed her mouth and spat the remnants into the basin. She turned on the tap, flushing the last of her midday meal down the sink. "I don't need to see a doctor." She reached up and grabbed the mouthwash from the cabinet mirror.

"Then tell me what's wrong," Phillipa demanded. "Your reaction on Tuesday, your mood today." She motioned to the toilet. "And now this. Something's going on with you." She walked forward and lightly touched Angela's arm. "Let me help you."

Angela bowed her head, her grip tightening on the mouthwash. Given what had just happened, there was clearly no way she would get Phillipa out of the house without an explanation. "Let me rinse my mouth and I'll meet you in the lounge."

"Are you sure?"

"Yes, give me a minute."

Phillipa cautiously backed out of the bathroom, softly closing the door behind her. Angela unscrewed the mouthwash lid and took some of its contents into her mouth. She swilled the liquid, wondering how she would explain her reaction. It was crystal clear to her what had evoked the response. And it was something she was too tired to run away from anymore. She spat the liquid out, rinsed her mouth with water and joined Phillipa in the lounge.

Phillipa placed a glass of water on a coaster on the coffee table and sat down. "I thought you might need this."

Angela sat and took a small sip, conscious of not creating a repeat of what had just happened. "Thank you."

"How did you know about the house in Durack Street? I don't think I've ever specifically mentioned it to you before."

Angela placed the glass down and sighed loudly. She leant back on the lounge and tilted her face to the ceiling. "I know about it because it's where Rhiannon was planning to stay for the next twelve months." She leant forward and studied her hands. "If she's selling the house it means she's evidently not staying in Sydney."

Phillipa reached out and lightly gripped her hand. "Angela, what's going on?" she insisted, her voice barely above a whisper. "I've known you for a long time. But I don't think I've ever seen you react the way you did the other day, when it was suggested there was more to Rhiannon's friendship with you than just getting back in touch with an old school friend."

Angela pursed her lips. "You were wrong. I should have realised that at the time."

Phillipa held up her other hand. "Okay. I know that now even if I didn't at the meeting. Come to think of it, I don't know why I suggested it in the first place. But your reaction now, when I mentioned the Durack Street sale. I've never seen you physically ill like you were just then. Is it Rhiannon?"

Angela nodded wordlessly.

"She's more than just an old school friend, isn't she?"

Angela looked at their clasped hands. She was unsure of how Phillipa would react to her next words, but she had to say them. It was no longer enough for her to suggest in words or actions Rhiannon was merely a friend. "So much more."

Phillipa smiled warmly. "I thought so. The first night when I saw the two of you together at the Con, as she helped you out of the car. The look on both your faces, when Rhiannon placed your wrap over your shoulders. It was such a private moment between you two. I felt like I was intruding on something quite personal."

Angela cast her mind back to the incident, in retrospect certain Rhiannon had wanted to kiss her. "I didn't realise you saw anything."

"I did, and I was very curious to try and find out where Rhiannon fitted in your life. I dropped subtle hints while I was showing her around." Phillipa shook her head as she chuckled ruefully. "But she was very good at being obtuse in all of her replies."

"At the time we'd only begun to explore how we felt about

each other." Angela toyed with her thumb. "I suspect she was being evasive because she was trying to protect me from the true nature of our friendship being exposed before I was ready."

"I think I was little relieved she did. Despite probing Rhiannon, I wasn't sure I wanted to know either."

Angela released the grip on Phillipa's hand and shifted away from her on the sofa. "Why? Did you think Rhiannon was leading me astray? Because if that's the case, I can tell you I was a more than willing participant the first night when she visited here." She pointed to her chest, her eyes afire. "This is who I am now Phillipa."

"That's not what I meant," Phillipa insisted. "I think I was jealous Rhiannon was sharing something with you. I've been your friend for all these years, and I thought you'd found someone else you'd prefer to be with. Maybe it's why I reacted the way I did at the Save the Con meeting." Phillipa reached across and again grasped Angela's hand. "But I can tell you without a shadow of doubt, I could not care less if you're a lesbian. I can't speak for others but you're still my friend and I love you dearly. I just wish you'd told me sooner."

Angela's shoulders slumped in relief. "Thank you. I think I didn't tell you sooner because I was afraid of how you and the rest of my friends would react."

"Bugger your friends if they can't love you for who you are." Phillipa lightly tapped Angela's leg. "Are you sure Rhiannon selling the house means she's not staying in Sydney? Don't you think you should call her and ask her yourself?"

"I can't," Angela muttered. "Her number is on my mobile."

"And," Phillipa said, the word drawn out, "would it be the mobile you can't find in the house?"

Angela nodded.

"I assume she's staying here in a hotel. You must know which one it is."

Angela blushed. "I most certainly do."

Phillipa smirked. "That sounds like a story for another day, one which I'm dying to know. If you know her hotel, why don't you call the front desk?"

Reluctance quickly replaced Angela's newfound relief. "I can't."

"Why can't you?"

Angela rubbed her forehead. "What if she won't take the call? I don't think I could handle that level of rejection."

Phillipa skirted closer to Angela and again took her hand.

"You're genuinely that serious about her?"

"Serious as I've ever been. And I think Rhiannon is…was, as well."

"Are you sure? I don't mean to belittle what you're saying. But you haven't known her too long."

"That's not the case at all," Angela said vehemently. "I've known her for twenty years. But I'm only now beginning to realise how I feel, and how I really felt about her all those years ago."

"Look, I know you're not a nun. You haven't had many, but I *know* you've had male relationships since I've known you. And what about Patrick?"

Angela eyes tracked across the room to her wedding photo, remembering the one man, other than her father, who meant so much to her. "I felt very strongly for Patrick. He was very dear to me. But I don't think I'd have married him if it wasn't for Lachie, who I love with all my heart." She looked at her hands, then Phillipa.

"But that's a mother's love. As for something shared between two adults there's been nothing substantive to fill the void. I feel like I've been on an emotional treadmill for the better part of the last twenty years, moving but not going anywhere. With Rhiannon's return, for the first time it's like I can finally step off. Just a look from her completes me, like no one has ever done before."

"If you feel that way then you've got to call her," Phillipa insisted.

"You must have been speaking with my mother. She said much the same thing."

"Do you want me to wait with you while you make the call?"

Despite Phillipa's offer, this was one call she wanted to make in private. While hopeful, given their last words were uttered in anger, she hadn't any clear idea of how Rhiannon might react. She stood and Phillipa joined her.

"I think I'd prefer to call the hotel alone. But thank you for your understanding. I do appreciate it."

Phillipa leant down and picked up her bag. She pulled Angela into a hug. "It's what friends are for. Please let me know how it all turns out." They walked to the door. "Maybe when this is all sorted you and Rhiannon could come over for dinner."

Angela's eyes watered. "Thanks. I'm sure she'd appreciate that."

After closing the front door Angela walked into the kitchen. She fired up her tablet, searching for an entry for The Gables. Within seconds the search engine had given her exactly what she needed. She took a seat at the breakfast island and pulled the phone to her. She lifted the handset, took a shaky breath, and entered the number.

"Good afternoon, you've reached The Gables, this is Megan speaking. How may I help you?"

"Hello, my name is Angela Drayton." She quickly peeked at the clock on the wall. It was mid-afternoon, still too early for Rhiannon to have finished work. "I was wondering if I could leave a message for one of your guests."

"Certainly, Ms. Drayton. Can I have the guest's name?"

"It's Rhiannon Sharp."

"You're in luck Ms. Drayton. Ms. Sharp's just out front, helping another lady into the passenger side of her car. Do you want me to get her for you?"

Angela's heart plummeted, the smile on her face forgotten. "No," she barely managed to utter. "I don't want to disturb her. I'll try another time." She hung up, not caring to hear the farewell platitudes of the voice on the other end of the line.

Angela staggered down the hall, her mind devoid of rational thought. She shuffled like an automaton into her rehearsal room, slumped onto her piano stool and did the sole remaining thing she was still capable of doing. Lifting the piano lid, she began to play the first thing which came to mind. It was the first movement of Beethoven's "Piano Sonata Fourteen."

She sat hunched, like a wounded animal trying in vain to conceal its pain, all the while her fingers moving slowly yet deliberately over the instrument. Angela's tears spilled uncontrollably onto the keys; her surrounds filled with the distinct, mournful notes of profound loss.

Chapter Seventeen

RHIANNON WAS RELIEVED to finish work shortly after lunch on Friday. Truth be told, there was little for her to do. She completed the pack for Martin and emailed it to Luke, advising him she'd be in town next week to discuss the project with her successor. She left her building pass with Trish and was home by early afternoon.

The day before, shortly after speaking with Elly, she'd rung Barb and Georgia, the managers of her family home, to let them know she'd be down on Friday night. Georgia assured her that while they were away at a function Friday afternoon and evening, she'd ensure the house was ready for her.

Elly's timely arrival at the hotel all but ensured they'd gotten across the harbour and out of the city proper before the Friday afternoon exodus of Sydney traffic began in earnest.

To get around the last of the Spring snow traffic heading to the New South Wales ski fields, Rhiannon bypassed the greater part of the Hume Highway, electing to travel the backroads to her home. During their trip, Rhiannon deliberately kept the conversation between her and Elly light, preferring to discuss what had happened between her and Angela when she didn't have to keep a focus on crazy Friday afternoon drivers.

Elly glanced out at the green paddocks flashing by her window. "This is beautiful. It's hard to believe this much bush is just about on our doorstep."

Rhiannon slowly negotiated around a tractor which had eased onto the verge, allowing her to safely pass. "It's about an hour and forty minutes out from the other side of Sydney. The trick is getting across the bridge outside of peak hour, or not travelling during that time at all. From where we are now, we're about twenty-five minutes from home."

"It seems so far away from everything. It's lovely."

Rhiannon checked the mirror and gave a wave to the man on the tractor she passed. "The distance can be deceptive. The largest town proximate to where we're going is Bowral. It's about fifteen minutes away. We could have headed through there. But the traffic can be a little hectic at this time of day."

Elly glimpsed at Rhiannon. "From what you've mentioned during the reunion and dinner, you're overseas more often than not."

Rhiannon nodded.

"Who looks after house when you're away?"

"It's managed by Barb and Georgia. They live on the property all year around except when they head off on holidays of course. I don't know if I ever mentioned to you or not, but my father was a vet and specialised in treating horses. He bought the property and established his practice there before I was born. This allowed him a reasonable amount of space to treat larger animals, while at the same time giving them somewhere to recuperate."

Elly smiled. "What a great way to grow up. You must have loved it."

"It was special." Rhiannon grimaced. "Except when he'd talk procedures at the dinner table. Georgia was a vet nurse who worked for Dad from when he first opened the practice. Not long after Mum and Dad moved here, they built a new house on the property which, when all was said and done, proved to be fortuitous."

"How so?"

"One morning Georgia came into work, her face a mass of bruises. My dad had previously seen such injuries but never so bad." Rhiannon's lips thinned at the memory. "Georgia always used the excuse of her own clumsiness when Dad or Mum had previously asked about her cuts and bruises. But that morning her face couldn't hide she was clearly the victim of domestic violence."

Elly reached across and reassuringly patted Rhiannon's thigh. "It must have been awful. What did your dad do?"

"To cut a long story short, that beating was the last straw. Georgia left her husband and Dad offered her the old house to live in. She accepted, and in their will, they gifted the house to Georgia in perpetuity. The only caveat was she manage the other house and the grounds until I came of age."

"Oh my God, for your parents to do such a thing for someone else. They were obviously very special people. I'd have loved to meet them."

Rhiannon swallowed, fighting to get her emotions in check. Even after all these years she still struggled to conceal the pain she felt over their loss. "They would have loved to meet you too."

"Was Barb part of the reason for Georgia leaving her husband?" Elly queried.

"No. Georgia and Barb met at a greys' growing old disgracefully dance in Moss Vale." Rhiannon indicated and turned onto the road leading to her home. "They clicked and things went from there. When I came of age, I negotiated a business arrangement regarding their ongoing management of Arcadia which they were more than willing to happily accept."

"What happens if you move back here? Will they stay?"

"This will always be their home, for as long as they want it to be and regardless of where I am. And besides, there's plenty of space for all of us."

Elly took in the lush green pastures and rolling hills lining either side of the winding road. "Arcadia, as in Greek antiquity?"

"One and the same. My father chose the name. He was a sucker for the Greek classics."

"I must say he was right on the mark. I couldn't think of a more delightful place to live and work."

Rhiannon chuckled. "He used to call it his and Mums own little piece of Utopia, hence the name Arcadia." Rhiannon slowed the car and turned into a dirt road driveway. "Here we are. If you give me a moment, I'll get the keys from the lock box and open the gate."

Rhiannon alighted from the car and walked to the cleverly concealed box, where Barb and Georgia had left the keys to the gate and house. Retrieving the keys, she unlocked the gate and swung it to its full length. At the sound of a horn she raised her head, in time to see a truck drive slowly past her entrance. Rhiannon returned the wave of the person within and hopped back into the car.

Elly looked behind the driver's seat at the truck which had stopped farther down the road. "They're a friendly bunch around here."

"Yes, they are. I'm not sure who it was though."

Rhiannon drove through the entrance. She closed the gate but left it unlocked and made her way back to the car.

After a short drive, she pulled the car to a halt in an empty parking space to the side of her house. "Here we are." She popped the boot and got out. Elly joined her.

"Holy crap Rhiannon. This isn't so much a property as an estate. How many acres do you have?"

Rhiannon gazed at the green undulating hills dominating the Arcadia landscape. They seemed to roll on forever, finally meeting the heavy wooded forest in the distance, heralding the beginning of Kangaroo Valley. "We've got about thirty-two hectares, or eighty acres in the old measurements." She pointed to the distance. "And it abuts Crown land which means we can never be built in."

The sound of a truck coming down the driveway halted Elly's reply. Rhiannon turned. It was the same truck she had waved at earlier. It came to a halt and a short woman alighted, her head covered in a tan, wide brimmed hat. By Rhiannon's estimation she was roughly the same age as Elly.

"Hi," the woman said. "You must be Rhiannon Sharp. Barb mentioned you were coming out today. I'm Joanne Monkland, your next-door neighbour."

Rhiannon didn't miss Joanne's blatant appreciation of her. "Hi Joanne."

"Joey will be fine. It's what everybody calls me."

"Hi Joey." Rhiannon motioned across to where Elly stood. "This is an old friend of mine, Elaine Matheson."

Joey exchanged a shake with Elly, which wasn't nearly as prolonged as the one she'd shared with Rhiannon.

"What can I do for you?" Rhiannon asked.

"I don't want to take up too much of your time. But I was wondering whether you'd be interested in agisting some of your property. I have a small herd of Belted Galloways and they're a hungry bunch. Given the recent lack of rain I'm running a bit low on feed and looking for options."

Rhiannon cast her eyes across her paddocks before returning her gaze to Joey. "I've got no issue at all. But I'm only here for tonight for this visit. Would you be able to send me an email with what you're proposing, and we can discuss it from there?" She reached into her wallet and pulled out a card. "Here's my email address."

Joey took the card, scanned it, and put it in her shirt pocket. "Thanks. That'll be a real help." She shoved her hands in her front pockets. "I better let you get back to it. Maybe when you're next down you can come over and see the cattle," she said before walking back to her truck.

Rhiannon waved as the truck headed back down the driveway. At Elly's barely concealed snort she turned.

"That's a variation on come up and see my etchings, if I've ever heard one." She snorted. "You *are* a magnet for lesbians, aren't you?"

"Huh?"

Elly walked around to the back of the car and pulled her overnight bag from the trunk. "First the woman in the bar and now farmer Joey."

Scowling, Rhiannon pulled her bag out and closed the trunk. "Yeah magnet all right. Sadly, I repel the only one I truly want."

Elly threw an arm around Rhiannon's shoulder and they walked inside.

OVER DINNER RHIANNON gave Elly the abridged version of events regarding what had happened between her and Angela in the past week. She assured Elly she'd tried to call Angela on the Wednesday morning following their argument, only to have Angela's mobile go unanswered.

Over dessert, Elly shared with Rhiannon the reason she hadn't accompanied Jen and Olivia for a visit to Jen's parents. It seemed, despite all the years they'd been together in a loving and stable relationship, Jen's parents were still less than completely accepting of what Elly and Jen had.

"Do you ever go down with Jen when she visits her parents?" Rhiannon closed the door of the dishwasher and turned it on.

"I don't." Elly leant against the kitchen island and took a sip of her wine. "Olivia is a very intuitive child. During the few times we've met them in Sydney, Olivia has picked up on the friction between us and was very affected by it. It's something Jen and I would rather avoid, and so it's easier if I step back during these visits."

Rhiannon picked up the bottle and her glass and motioned Elly to follow her. "Still I expect it can't be all that easy for any of you." She walked through the living area and into a glass-encased hallway leading to the home's indoor swimming pool. "I thought we might chat in here. It's always been a favourite place of mine."

Rhiannon put the bottle down and turned on the lights, exposing glass-enclosed surroundings which reflected the dark of the surrounding night. She reduced the lights to their lowest level and toyed with another switch. Celtic music filled the space, the soft instrumental sound creating a calm, intimate setting. She turned the volume down till it was barely noticeable in the background.

"My God this is gorgeous." Elly walked across to the pool, knelt, and felt the water. "This is warm enough to swim in."

"I should have mentioned that you could have bought your cossies. It's an all year-round pool. The heated floor also helps to keep it warm. And during summer we can open the side glass panels, to catch the breezes. I used to come here a lot when I was a girl, and still do anytime I visit." Rhiannon juggled the bottle, her glass and a small remote. She motioned to the lounges to the right of the pool. "Take a seat and I'll show you my favourite part of this room."

Elly placed her glass on the small table separating two grey fabric lounge chairs. She adjusted the seat setting so she was semi reclining.

Rhiannon placed her glass and bottle next to Elly's and sat on the recliner beside her. "Look up at the roof." She scanned the remote she held and pressed the green button. What had previously been opaque was now clear glass.

Elly looked up then across at Rhiannon, a look of surprise on her face. "How the blazes did you do that?"

Rhiannon grinned. "It's a smart glass which can transform from opaque to clear with the press of a button." She placed the remote beside her and raised her eyes to the wealth of stars, seamlessly revealed through the glass above their heads. "Don't ask me how it happens, but I do love it."

Elly reached across and took Rhiannon's hand. "Thank you for sharing it with me."

Although she was more than aware of Elly's relationship with Jen, Rhiannon was painfully mindful of the contact she now shared with Elly. Despite a desire to stroke her hand, her own self-discipline wouldn't allow her to act on it. She gazed across at Elly. "Does Jen know about me and you and..." She released Elly's hand and reached for her glass. "Back then?"

Elly shifted her gaze from the stars above, to Rhiannon. "She does." She studied Rhiannon's face. "I told her before you and Angela visited." Elly rolled onto her side, to face Rhiannon. "Even if I hadn't, she still picked up on the undercurrents between us over dinner. She told me as much when you both left."

Rhiannon sat up quickly and faced Elly, her eyes wide. "I didn't know. I'm sorry, I wasn't aware I was consciously doing anything." She dragged her fingers through her hair. "I mean I was there with Angela, for Christ's sake."

Elly reached across and cupped Rhiannon's thigh. "Hey, don't worry about it. I think there'll always be something between us. It's just..." Elly shrugged. "*There*. But relationships are a lot about trust, and Jen trusts me. If I thought for a moment something might have happened between the two of us tonight, I wouldn't have come."

"I would never —"

"I know. You're far too honourable to even consider such a

thing. And besides, your heart is already somewhere else."

Rhiannon searched the room, her eyes finally coming to rest on Elly. "Is it?"

"You *know* it is," Elly replied quietly.

Rhiannon exhaled deeply. She massaged the side of her scalp with one hand, desperately attempting to ease the tension created through Elly's words and her feelings about Angela. "If it is, then my heart's all by itself." She poked roughly at her chest. "The rest of me is *here*."

Elly sat up and steadied Rhiannon's hands with her own. "Do you love her?"

Rhiannon looked down at their hands. "Have you ever felt like every bit of air you have in your lungs has been expelled and yet you're more alive than you've ever been? And the feeling in your gut is like a roller coaster which, having reached its apex, is careering to a bottom you can't see, and you couldn't care less? And in this maelstrom of emotions, you look at her, and the noise around you fades away, and you're enveloped in a cocoon of serenity and warmth which fills your every being." Rhiannon sought Elly's eyes. "That night at the reunion, when I saw Angela again, *that's* how I felt. If that's not love, then I'll willingly accept it as a poor substitute."

Elly's face creased with a small smile. "I have two bits of advice for you, Rhiannon. The first is to give up what you're doing now and concentrate on writing. Your words just then — you have a profound skill which you need to share." She reached across and turned Rhiannon's face to hers. "Secondly, when the moment is right tell Angela what you just told me. What you've described *is* love, it's not a poor second. And she has every right to know how you feel."

A lone tear trickled down Rhiannon's cheek. "I promise I will." Her thoughts went to Lachie's soccer match on Sunday. It was the best and earliest opportunity she had to speak with Angela. "I only hope she listens."

Chapter Eighteen

ANGELA AGAIN SCANNED the oval before looking down at her son.

Lachie stubbed the grass with his soccer boot. "She's not coming," he said disconsolately, refusing to meet Angela's gaze.

She knelt and smoothed down the front of his soccer jersey. "Remember, Rhiannon did say she was a little busy. However, she'd try to make it if she could. Maybe her work held her up."

Lachie looked anywhere but at her, clearly not caring terribly much for rational words.

She pulled him into a hug, so he couldn't see the disappointment mirrored in her own eyes. She rubbed his back comfortingly, at the same time wondering who would do the same for her.

"I'm sure she'll be here if she possibly can. But in the meantime, you've got a game to play. You don't want Rhiannon to arrive and find you sulking on the sidelines, do you?" He shook his head against her chest. "That's the way. How about you go out there and have some fun? She'll be here soon enough." For a myriad of reasons, she could only hope saying those words would make them true.

Lachie disengaged himself from her arms. He gave her a sloppy kiss and trotted out onto the field to join the rest of his team. She straightened up, only then becoming aware of the cursory sideways look given to her by who she assumed was a father of one of the other children.

"Your boy needs to toughen up and learn to roll with the punches. Get his father to whip him into shape. If he wants to be any good in life and soccer, he's got to grow up and take the good with the bad."

Angela turned and faced the arrogant man beside her. She reigned in her temper, searching for a way to diplomatically respond to the parent's callous unsolicited advice. "Thank you for your suggestion. However, my son doesn't have a father. He died some years ago. And as for toughening up, this is a game of junior soccer, not the national competition."

Before the man could reply, the whistle blew and he occupied himself repeatedly shouting instructions from the sideline to a somewhat embarrassed boy on the field, who Angela figured was his son. Disgusted and annoyed any parent would treat a child in such a manner, Angela returned her focus to the game and Lachie.

She stifled a laugh at the antics on the field. Fanned out in an arrowhead formation, behind the lead boy who was too busy dribbling the ball to look where he was going, were the players of the two teams. The frantic pace at which the little bodies, fully kitted out in their soccer garb, chased their elusive prize was priceless. It reminded her of the musical piece, "Flight of the Bumblebee." She studiously blocked out the insensitive cries from the rude man beside and allowed herself to be carried away with the contest.

RHIANNON WALKED ACROSS the field to the match already underway. She was relieved last Monday, while they were playing soccer, Lachie had mentioned he'd be playing on this same field and at what time. Given she hadn't been able to reach Angela since Tuesday, she doubted she'd have been able to work out where his game was.

She took up a place on the sideline opposite to where the families of the children stood. In deference to Angela's response on Monday, when she was found with Rhiannon at this same field by Mrs. Frank, she felt it best to stay on this side. There would be sufficient time to hopefully approach Angela once the soccer finished.

She watched the ball kicked a little too hard by the lead boy land well clear of the soccer field and behind a hedge dividing the field they were on from the next. Rhiannon jogged after the ball and kicked it around the bushes to Lachie.

The ball continued to roll past Lachie, and he launched himself headlong into her legs. "Rhiannon you came!"

Rhiannon knelt down and pulled Lachie into a hug. "Of course I did champ. I'm sorry I wasn't here at the start. Have I missed anything?"

"We just started. Mum's here." He pointed. "She's on the other side of the field."

Shielding her eyes from the sun, she saw Angela's lithe figure, her body language clearly indicating she wasn't all too happy with something.

Is it me, or is something else bothering her, she thought.

She raised her hand and waved, which Angela cursorily acknowledged in return. Given she was clearly uncomfortable about something, Rhiannon elected to stay where she was.

At the sound of the whistle, she pulled her gaze away from Angela and back to Lachie. "Hey look, they're playing again. You better get back out there. They might need you."

Lachie grinned and released Rhiannon's hand. He ran, his gait somewhat impeded by his soccer boots and the grass, to where the game was now back in full swing.

ANGELA WAS HEARTENED Rhiannon had kept her promise to Lachie. Given she made no attempt to join her, Angela couldn't help but regretfully conclude she was here for Lachie alone. A cheer from the crowd caused her to return her focus to the children on the field.

Rhiannon's appearance seemed to be the salve Lachie needed to lift his mood. Whereas previously he hadn't chased the ball like he normally did, now he was playing to the best of his limited abilities. This infrequently saw him tangle with other boys, often resulting in them inevitably falling to the ground.

"Your son should be more careful." Again, the arrogant tones of the man beside her interrupted Angela's thoughts. "Soccer's a game of finesse, not something thugs play."

"I seriously don't think he meant to trip the other boy," she offered, her tone conciliatory. "He's a bit excited, nothing more."

Muttering an answer under his breath the man returned his focus to the game. "For God's sake Nigel, trap the ball! Don't let the midget get it!"

Angela clicked her tongue in disgust. "Come on Lachie!" She cheered when he made a mini break away from the hoard following him.

Lachie dribbled the ball toward the goal mouth, his attention completely focussed on the ground at his feet. So intent was he, he failed to see the child who, in an attempt to halt Lachie's progress, had taken a position in front of him. As the full weight of his little body met the static object, both boys fell to the ground, a tangle of arms and limbs.

The daunting figure of the man who had been nothing but derogatory to his own son, not to mention rude to Angela, abruptly occupied her personal space. "That fucking brat of yours did that deliberately!"

Shocked, Angela stepped back. "Oh, for heaven's sake. Lachie was focussed on the ball, not the child standing still in front of him."

Refusing to let the issue die the man closed on her again. "He did it deliberately. He's nothing more than a dumb thug and doesn't deserve to be on the team!"

As parents distanced themselves from the argument, Angela held up her hands, trying to placate the continually advancing man. "I can assure you it was an innocent mistake."

THE ANGRY VOICE of the man towering over Angela filtered across the field to where Rhiannon stood. She watched, stunned as the obvious father of the fallen child berated Angela. Snatches of Angela's conciliatory tones drifted across the field as the children in the middle stared, the game forgotten, at the scene between the two parents. Rhiannon was about to slowly make her way around the pitch when she saw Angela raise her hands, only to see one grasped forcefully by the man in front of her.

She could never quite recall how long it took her to reach Angela's side. But as Lachie told the story later it was as if she had flown across the field to his mother's rescue.

"Do you have *any* idea whose hand you're holding right now?" Rhiannon's voice dripped with barely controlled aggression as she whispered in the belligerent parent's ear.

The man turned his head, retaining the grip on Angela's hand. "Who the *hell* are you and what the hell do I care whose hand I'm holding!"

Words died on his lips as Rhiannon's thumb applied pressure to a sensitive point along his jaw. "Let me tell you why you should. She's a concert pianist and her hands are her life." He winced as Rhiannon increased the force of her thumb. "So, unless you want to end your poor excuse of an existence, I suggest you let her go." Rhiannon's menace rolled off her in waves, her voice barely audible to the audience observing the confrontation.

He released Angela's hand and jerked his head, effectively releasing the pressure of Rhiannon's thumb. He stepped back and rubbed his chin, disgustedly looking Rhiannon up and down. "And who's this?" he sneered, attempting to regain some shred of false machismo.

He turned his gaze to Angela. "Is this your big dyke girlfriend coming to the rescue? I can see now why your boy's bloody hopeless on the field. With a dyke for a mother what more could he hope for? Now I know the real reason why he doesn't have a father."

Rhiannon took in Angela's shocked, silent features and the

confused look on Lachie's face as he now stood beside his mother. There was no doubt in her mind he'd heard the man's insult.

Realising Angela was at a loss for words and innately understanding if Angela and Lachie were to continue to be welcome within the group of children and their parents, Rhiannon took charge. "I'd expect something as narrow minded from someone like you. That's not the case at all. Angela and I are just friends."

HEARING THOSE WORDS uttered by Rhiannon was the catalyst for Angela. Until then she hadn't truly comprehended the inadequacy of such a phrase in expressing what existed and she hoped *would* exist between them.

Disregarding the curious looks from the parents observing the unfolding drama, Angela moved to Rhiannon's side. Unsure of how Rhiannon would react, but for the first time in her life throwing caution to the wind, she placed a possessive arm around Rhiannon's waist. "That's not true. She's more than just my friend." She smiled as she took in Rhiannon's startled face. "It's only a shame it's taken me this long to wake up to that."

Angela returned her stare to the poor excuse of a parent in front of her. "As for you and your small mind, why don't you go and take a look at yourself? As a parent you set a poor example for your son. And as a man," her eyes disdainfully travelled the length of his body, "if you're all the male species has to offer, I'm happy right where I am."

"Bravo," one parent called, and broken clapping interspersed between the rest of the gathering. Beaten and embarrassed, the man grabbed his reluctant son by the arm and made a beeline for what could only be his car.

Rhiannon gazed down into Angela's eyes, her arm encircling Angela's waist.

"Excuse me ladies."

Angela looked at the umpire/coach of the Mini-Mites soccer team. "Hi Taylor. I didn't mean to react the way I did. But he was way over the top."

"It's me who needs to apologise. I should have dealt with the situation much sooner than this. Mr. Keeling has been a problem parent for quite some time now. Unfortunately, if I ask him to leave it's not only him who's punished. It's his son also. Thank you for what you said. Maybe this might force him to learn some manners before he returns."

Taylor paused and bit his lip, his gaze alternating between

her and Rhiannon. "I hope this won't turn the two of you off coming back to watch the Mini-Mites play?"

Surprised yet pleased by Taylor's obvious acceptance, Angela glanced at Rhiannon, who nodded. "We'll be back and when we do hopefully Lachie will have a few more skills to his repertoire." Although only a simple thing, Angela couldn't help but smile at her use of "we" when referring to her and Rhiannon.

Taylor turned to the larger group and clapped his hands. "I think that will just about do us for this morning's game." The loud moans of the children temporarily interrupted his words, and he held up his hand. "I know it wasn't a long game. But I promise we'll play extra time next Sunday."

Still not caring to have their morning's fun cut short, kids trudged reluctantly to their respective parents.

Taylor grabbed the kit bag and headed to his car with one of the other parents, leaving only the two of them and Lachie standing by the field. Angela struggled to find something to say, only to be gazumped by her son.

"What are you doing now Rhiannon? Do you want to come back to our place?"

Rhiannon smiled at Lachie and returned her gaze to Angela. "Isn't it polite to ask your mum first before you invite friends over?"

"Can we Mum, please?" The sorrowful, pleading look was too much for Angela and she broke into laughter at Lachie's antics.

"Of course. In fact, if your 'friend' wants to, how about we have a movie afternoon and night in the lounge room?" Lachie enthusiastically jumped at the idea. "Of course, if you're going to go to the movies and having an indoor picnic you need to get cleaned up first." Angela pulled a small sod of dirt from the near Lachie's ear. "I swear you've got half of the soccer field behind here."

Not waiting, Lachie made a beeline for the family car, stopping only long enough to take off his shoes while he waited for Angela to follow.

Grateful for the modicum of privacy, Angela turned to Rhiannon. "You don't mind, do you? I really want to speak with you and, if at all possible, explain my actions over the past few days. But if you can't make it—" Angela got no further, her words silenced by Rhiannon's soft fingers on her lips.

"I'd love to. I think we've both got a little talking to do. But for now," Rhiannon looked to where Lachie stood, eagerly hopping from one foot to the other, "if you don't make your way to your car, I'm afraid Lachie might just run home. My car is on the other side of the park. Why don't I pick up some snacks and finger food and meet you at your place?"

"Can you also pick up a roast chicken? I've some fresh rolls at home, so we can at least make something a healthy option to go with the finger food." Angela reached into her purse. "Let me give you some money."

Rhiannon jogged backward, away from Angela. "It's fine. I can cover the cost. I'll meet you in about thirty minutes." She pirouetted and continued to jog to her car, a distinct spring in her step.

ANGELA OPENED THE door to the house, juggling a soccer ball in one hand and junk mail in the other. "Now young man, if we're to get ready for our picnic and movies you better get those clothes off while I run you a bath."

Lachie scampered down the hall, bouncing off the walls as he attempted to pull the soccer jersey over his head. Angela placed the mail on the hallway table and followed him, rolling the ball into his bedroom before continuing to the bathroom. She turned on the water and tested its temperature. Satisfied, she put the plug in the bath.

While the bath filled, she pulled Lachie's toys from the cupboard, along with a sandalwood bath gel which was a favourite of his. She dropped a face washer into the bath and waited his arrival.

Lachie finally ran into the bathroom and came to a halt, hugging Angela in the process. "I'm ready!"

Angela disengaged his arms and turned him around, barely containing her mirth. The dividing line between skin covered by soccer gear and that which wasn't was patently clear, with his exposed skin liberally coated in dirt and grass. She checked the water, re-confirming it wasn't too hot. "In you go," she said, searching the bathroom cupboard for the shampoo.

Lachie grabbed the face washer and, after generously coating it with bath gel, launched an attack on his legs to get them clean. "That man wasn't very nice today, was he?"

Angela pushed the faucet spout out of the way of Lachie's industrious cleaning efforts and sat on the edge of the bath. "No sweetie he wasn't. In fact, he was very rude." She watched as Lachie managed to get almost as much water on the floor as there was in the tub.

Lachie swirled the washer in the water, watching the suds form a mini whirlpool. "Mum, why did he call you and Rhiannon a dyke? What does it mean?"

Angela took the flannel out of Lachie's hands. She applied a little gel onto the cloth then turned him around and began to wash his back. She struggled to arrive at an appropriate response, all the while thinking how very much easier things would have been if Rhiannon were here to help her explain.

"A dyke is a word sometimes used to describe two women who like women instead of men." Lachie looked over his shoulder, his face quizzical. "You remember earlier this year how I told you about boyfriends and girlfriends?" Lachie nodded. "It's similar except you have two girlfriends. Am I making any sense?"

"I think so." He grew silent, as he seemed to consider her words. He turned in the bath to face Angela. "Is that what you and Rhiannon are? You know, girlfriends I mean?"

The inquisitive, serious look on her son's face brooked no room for a less than a candid answer. "Would it bother you if we were?" Angela held her breath as Lachie innocently pondered her query, unaware of the multiple ramifications of his response.

He shrugged his shoulders non-committaly. "Not really. I think Rhiannon's great and she can kick a ball much better than you." Lachie giggled and he dodged the soft bath toy thrown at him. "When you and she are together, except for the other day, you're happy and you don't wander around the house like you've lost something. Is Rhiannon going to stay, I mean for a long time? Not only for this afternoon and evening?"

"I don't know son. Would you mind if she did?"

Lachie flicked at the toys bobbing along the surface of the bath. "No, that way she'd be here whenever she wanted to play soccer with me."

Angela smothered a relieved laugh at Lachie's childlike interpretation of Rhiannon's role in his life.

"But Mum what happens if you go overseas to play in the orchestra you told me about? Will she come along?"

The reality of the situation sobered Angela's relief of Lachie's acceptance. She poured an amount of shampoo in her hand and began to lather Lachie's hair. "I don't know son. I expect we'll have to take it one step at a time."

It wasn't too long before Angela had washed and dried Lachie and was handing him his shirt when the doorbell rang. She barely managed to restrain a half-naked boy from tearing down the hall.

"Just a minute," she shouted, hoping Rhiannon had heard her. A muffled response confirmed she had.

Lachie pulled the shirt over his head and smoothed his hair. "I'm ready. Can I go answer the door now?"

"Have you finished your holiday homework? Don't you still need to write a story about your holidays?" She smothered a laugh at Lachie's crestfallen face.

"I can do it after the movies. It's only two paragraphs," he pleaded.

"You can't, little man." Angela pulled open Lachie's desk drawer and extracted a notepad and pencil.

Lachie's eyes lit up. "Can I tell them about how Rhiannon saved you today?"

Angela's eyes twinkled as she considered the response such a story might receive. "That's a very special story. Maybe you can write that for just Rhiannon and me. Why don't you write about your camping trip to the zoo instead?" She moved to the bedroom door. "You can read it to Rhiannon and me when you're finished."

Lachie climbed onto his chair, opened his notebook, and picked up his pencil, his focus already on the task at hand.

Angela walked down the hallway and opened the front door. She quickly reached out and grabbed the box Rhiannon was trying to precariously balance between her chest and chin. "Let me get that. You do realise it's only the three of us don't you?" she said as she headed to the kitchen.

RHIANNON KICKED THE door closed behind her and followed. "I did, but you can never have enough of char-grilled chicken and finger food." She hiked the multiple bags up onto the kitchen bench.

"And I suppose this is dessert?" Angela made to open the box she'd been carrying.

"I hope you like it. The patisserie next to the chicken shop was open and they had the loveliest strawberry tarts." Rhiannon glanced into the lounge. "Where's Lachie?"

"He's got a composition to write for school tomorrow." Angela picked up the box and placed it in the fridge. "He was supposed to do it yesterday afternoon but didn't get around to it."

An awkward silence fell while both seemed to search for

something to say.

"I tried to call you on Wednesday, after," Rhiannon said, inherently sensing Angela would glean what she was referring to.

"I lost my mobile in the house either late Tuesday evening or early Wednesday morning. I can't be sure. I only found it this morning."

"Where was it?"

"It was in the linen closet." Angela looked intently at Rhiannon. "I tried to call you through the front desk of the hotel, on Friday afternoon." She glanced away. "They said you were helping a woman into your car."

She walked to where Angela stood. Angela's eyes sought out any other part of her surrounds except Rhiannon. "Did you think I'd moved on?" she asked softly.

Angela momentarily closed her eyes then settled her gaze on Rhiannon. "If this past week has taught me anything about you, it's not to assume." She reached out and tentatively caressed Rhiannon's face. "I did that already, and consequently nearly lost you. I'm not willing to do it again. I only hoped you'd be at Lachie's soccer game today so I could at least speak with you. And as for who the woman was, you don't owe me any explanation."

She took Rhiannon's hand in her own. "I'm sorry for the way I've acted over the past few days. I certainly didn't mean to speak to you the way I did or to challenge your integrity. I think I allowed myself to get too tied up in the opinions of others, instead of listening to the ones which meant the most to me." She brought Rhiannon's hand to her lips and kissed her knuckles. "Can you forgive me? Do you still want us to be together?" she finished, uncertainty in her voice.

Rhiannon pulled Angela into her arms, her searing kiss leaving little room for doubt where she stood on the matter. She eased out of the embrace and found herself lost in the intensity of Angela's brilliant green eyes. "I think these past few days have been the worst I've been through in a long time. I too said some pretty horrible things the other day. Can *you* forgive *me*?"

Angela rested her head on Rhiannon's chest. "Of course, I can. I think we both said things we didn't mean. And as for my frame of mind since when you left on Tuesday, it hasn't been the best either. Poor Lachie has borne the brunt of my bad mood."

Rhiannon cupped Angela's hand and kissed her palm. "And just to set the record straight, it was Elly. She came with me for an overnight trip to Arcadia."

"What's Arcadia?" Lachie walked into the kitchen and climbed onto a kitchen stool, oblivious to the intimate contact Rhiannon shared with Angela.

Rhiannon made to slowly disengage from Angela's embrace, only to have Angela capture her hand with her own. "It's my home in the Southern Highlands, at a place called Glenquarry."

Lachie frowned. "But I thought you had a home here."

"She did," Angela interjected. "But she's selling it."

Rhiannon raised her brows. "I'm surprised. How do you know that? I only made up my mind to sell the property a few days ago. How did you find out so quickly?"

"It would seem Phillipa has had her eye on your aunt's house for quite a while. She got a call from her realtor on Thursday evening, asking if she was still interested."

Rhiannon nodded. "That makes sense. My property manager Carol mentioned she had a couple of clients who might want to get an early jump on the property. What a sliding doors moment though."

"But Mum said you live in a hotel," Lachie stated, halting any further conversation between her and Angela regarding her Sydney home. "Why can't you live there?"

"I don't need to anymore. The job I was doing wrapped up early." Rhiannon faltered at the shocked look on Angela's face. *It's okay. Later*, she mouthed over Lachie's head to Angela, hoping she'd get the message. Angela nodded, a relieved look on her face.

"Besides, I can't live in a hotel all my life." Rhiannon clapped her hands, effectively ending Lachie's line of questioning. "Didn't someone say something about movies and food?"

THE REMAINDER OF the afternoon and the early part of the evening was taken up with a picnic and movies which were more suited to a seven-year-old than Rhiannon and Angela. Despite this, neither seemed to matter. They were far too involved with each other, eagerly waiting the chance when they could continue the conversation they'd started earlier.

The hours lengthened and Lachie's energy waned, and it was soon obvious sleep wasn't too far away for him. Angela turned off the television and gently nudged Lachie's semi somnolent form. "Come on mister. I think it's your bedtime."

Lachie rubbed his eyes as he stood from the position he'd previously occupied between Angela and Rhiannon. He turned and hugged Angela and repeated the same action with Rhiannon.

Rhiannon hugged Lachie tightly, turned him around and patted him softly on the backside. "Off you go champ."

"No reading before you go to bed tonight. It's too late." Angela said as she stood. "I'll be down in a minute."

Lachie stopped at the door, as if he'd forgotten something. Turning, he looked at the two of them. "Are you going to have a sleepover?" he asked innocently, blissfully unaware of the double meaning behind his words.

Rhiannon was terribly glad she'd finished swallowing her mouthful of coffee, or it could have just as easily ended up all over the carpeted floor of Angela's lounge. Collecting herself she chose her words carefully. "I'd like to." She spared a glance at Angela. "But it's up to your mum. It's a bit like inviting people for picnics and movies you see. You have to ask first."

Lachie turned to Angela, wordlessly waiting her answer. Angela smiled at him and looked at Rhiannon.

Rhiannon held her breath. Despite the obvious progress they'd made during the evening, she was still unsure what Angela's response might be.

"I'd like that too, especially on a more permanent basis, if it's okay with you Rhiannon."

Rhiannon froze in place, her jaw agape. She closed her mouth and gulped. "Are you sure? You *do* realise what you're asking don't you?"

Lachie, who only moments ago had been tired, now leapt about the space. "What a great idea! We can have heaps of fun together! And I can have two mums instead of one." Lachie again hugged Angela. "Not everyone has two mums, do they?"

Angela returned the hug. "They don't. And yes, we will be able to have lots of fun."

While Rhiannon rolled the decidedly pleasant idea of being called mum around in her mind, Angela took her hand.

"And as for you, I'm *very* sure and I *do* realise what I'm asking. I know we've still got many things to work out. But I've had enough of us coming and going in each other's lives. And I certainly don't want to waste another twenty years waiting to see you again. I now know, if you feel the same, I want you to be a part of our life."

Before Rhiannon could answer, Lachie interjected. "Can we have a slumber party out here tonight, Mum?"

Angela laughed, her gaze locked on Rhiannon's. "That's *not* exactly what I had in mind. I know you brushed your teeth when you went to the bathroom earlier. So how about you head to your room and give me a yell when you're ready to be tucked in?"

Lachie skipped out of the lounge and down the hall, singing a nonsensical song as he went.

Angela tracked Lachie's progress then turned to Rhiannon. "Are you okay? I saw your look when he referred to you as another mum."

Rhiannon released a shaky breath. "I'm okay. Just surprised and very relieved at how accepting he is of us."

"So am I. But he's always been very open with others. You should have been here the other day when he asked me why we'd been fighting. When I gave him the very abridged version, his solution was we should kiss and make up. Just like his two female teachers do at school."

The sounds of Angela's son echoed down the corridor.

"I've got to go and tuck him in." Angela entwined Rhiannon's fingers in her own. "Do you want to help me?"

They headed down the corridor into Lachie's bedroom.

Angela chuckled lightly when Lachie failed to conceal a jaw breaking yawn. "By the looks of you, I expect you're relieved tomorrow is only a half day at school and that it doesn't start until midday." She bent down and tucked him in before kissing his forehead. Rhiannon mirrored her actions. Angela dimmed the light and backed out, leaving the door slightly ajar. Rhiannon followed.

"He doesn't have trouble sleeping. But he prefers not to have the door closed for some reason."

"I was much the same when I was his age. It doesn't seem to bother me so much now, though." Rhiannon walked toward the lounge, only to have her arm captured by her partner. Damn, she liked how it felt, to think of Angela in that way. Turning, she tilted her head in question.

Angela pulled her through the door of the master bedroom, turned on the light and dimmed it to a more intimate setting. She kicked off her shoes. "That's good to know. I'd hate to have Lachie stumble in on us during the night." She closed the door and drew Rhiannon in the direction of the bed.

Surprised by Angela's candour, Rhiannon struggled to regain control of the situation, something not made easy by Angela's industrious fingers, as they proceeded to unbutton her blouse. She peeked at the door as if expecting Lachie to burst through it at any moment. "Are you sure it's okay?"

Angela smiled while her fingers intently peeled the blouse

away from Rhiannon's shoulders. She leant forward, her lips grazing Rhiannon's flesh. "It will be fine. We'll need to be a little quiet though."

"Just like you were at the hotel," Rhiannon asked, all the while knowing that clearly hadn't been the case.

Angela lightly backhanded her stomach. "And whose fault was that?"

Rhiannon stroked the back of Angela's neck, while Angela busied herself with releasing the clasp of Rhiannon's bra and relegating it to where her shirt lay on the floor. "I didn't hear any complaints from you on the matter."

Angela's hands skimmed lazily across Rhiannon's body, coming to rest on her breasts. "You..."

Rhiannon's breathing hitched as Angela's thumbs grazed her now hard nipples.

"Certainly..." Angela slightly bent her body and flicked her tongue across Rhiannon's nipple.

"Didn't," she replied, backing Rhiannon toward the bed.

Rhiannon's knees connected with the bed and she collapsed onto it, pulling Angela with her. She reached down and pulled Angela's shirt from her pants. Not bothering with the buttons, she yanked it over her head and unceremoniously dropped it on the floor. Angela's bra shortly followed.

An intimate warmth spread within her as Angela's nipples made contact with her own. She insinuated her hands under the waistband of Angela's pants and began to slowly tug them down. "We'll just have to see how quiet you *can* be." She nuzzled the pulse point on Angela's neck, delighted by Angela's moaned response. "Won't we?"

Chapter Nineteen

RHIANNON WOKE, HER body spooning Angela's, her hand lightly cupping her partner's breast. She took a deep breath and relaxed into their embrace. This was a great way to start the day. And she was exceedingly hopeful it would be one of many to come.

"Good morning," Angela said, snuggling her bottom back into Rhiannon's groin. "How did you sleep?"

Rhiannon nuzzled Angela's hair. "You mean what little sleep I got."

Angela rolled to face her. She traced her jaw with her fingers. "It was quality sleep though. And as for lack of sleep," she arched her brow, "I'm certainly not complaining."

Rhiannon entangled her legs with Angela's. She snuggled closer, relishing the feel of Angela's silken curls against her thigh. She dusted a light kiss on the edge of Angela's mouth. "Neither am I," she finished, capturing Angela's lips in her own. Rhiannon's hand teased its way down Angela's waist. She cupped her backside, pulling closer into their embrace.

An insistent knocking on the door broke the moment.

"Mum, can I come in?"

Angela tore her lips from Rhiannon's. "Just a moment please." She grinned and disengaged herself from Rhiannon. "We're still waking up." She rolled to the side of the bed and stood. "Are you okay if he comes in?" she asked, in a voice meant for Rhiannon's ears alone.

"I'm fine. But I need to put something on."

"I think I've got a large shirt here somewhere." Angela crouched down and retrieved the trail of hers and Rhiannon's clothes and shoes from the floor. She tossed Rhiannon's underpants in her direction and placed the remainder of the clothes on the chair near the window.

Angela rummaged through her drawers and pulled out a well-worn shirt. "I sometimes use it as a sleeping shirt. It's big on me, so it should fit you."

Rhiannon gratefully took the shirt from Angela's outstretched hands. "Thanks. I'll just use your bathroom."

"And I'll put some sleepwear on and meet you back in the bed," she said quietly.

Rhiannon closed the bathroom door and attended to her immediate morning ablutions, along with a requisite, non-delegatable task. She washed her hands and splashed her face with water and attempted to bring her unruly raven locks into some semblance of order. She scowled. Her hair looked like a hoard of small creatures had taken up residence in it. No amount of brushing could tame the locks sticking out in opposing directions. Spying a hair band in a bowl on the bathroom sink, she picked it up and pulled her hair into a ponytail. Satisfied, she returned to the room and the bed where Angela sat, patiently waiting for her.

"Okay Lachie, you can come in now." Angela barely got the last word out of her mouth when the door flung open and a small body propelled itself across the space and onto the bed, landing between the two of them.

"Morning Mum, morning Rhiannon. Did you like the bed?"

Rhiannon spared a glance at Angela's pink features and returned her focus to Lachie. "It was very nice thank you. Did you sleep okay?"

"Yep. Do you want to play soccer now?"

"Maybe not now champ. It's a bit early in the morning don't you think?" Rhiannon attempted not to grin at the downcast look on Lachie's face. "Maybe we can kick the ball around when you get home from school."

Angela got out of bed and stood. "Instead of soccer, what about an omelette for breakfast?"

Lachie's face lit up. "Can we have ham and lots of cheese in it?"

Angela reached across and pulled down his bed shirt which had ridden up beyond Lachie's belly button. "We can. But while Rhiannon and I get it ready, do you think you can wash your face and comb your hair? You can have a bath after breakfast I think."

Lachie rolled off the bed and came around to Rhiannon's side. He took her hand in his own. "Now you've seen our house, do you think Mum and me can see yours?"

Rhiannon pulled a giggling Lachie to her and gave him a hug. "Of course, you can. We could all go down next Saturday and stay the night, if it's okay with your mum that is."

Angela walked around the bed to where Lachie lay, semi-reclined in Rhiannon's embrace. "That's a great idea." She patted Lachie's backside. "But for now, how about you get yourself cleaned up and we have some breakfast?"

Chapter Twenty

RHIANNON NEGOTIATED ANGELA'S SUV down Arcadia's driveway and past the kangaroo reclining in the dappled shade of a gum tree. She glanced in the rear vision mirror at the sound of Lachie's window coming down.

"Is he your pet?" Lachie asked, his head hung out the window.

"He isn't, but this is his home. We have quite a few 'roos around these parts. As well as wallabies and wombats, a platypus in the dam, and a menagerie of native birds which I'm sure you'll hear during the day."

"What's a menagemie?"

"It means lots of different native birds," Angela replied. "How about you get your head back inside the car? We'll be at Rhiannon's place in a moment and then you can have a good look around."

Rhiannon watched Angela eagerly scan the vista in front of her, innately understanding how she felt. Regardless of how long she was away from here, it always felt like a new experience for her whenever she returned. She pulled the car into a parking space and turned off the engine.

In the instant the car was quiet, Lachie was up and out of the vehicle. Rhiannon quickly disengaged her seat belt and got out. Angela did the same. Rhiannon strode around the car and carefully snagged Lachie's arm. "I know you want to go and meet the kangaroo. But you need to remember he's a wild animal. It's not the same as the petting zoo at Taronga."

"You mean I can't pat him?"

Rhiannon released his arm, assured he wasn't about to bolt to where the kangaroo lay. "I don't think it's a good idea. He mightn't want you to. Besides, he's sleeping at the moment. How would you feel if someone was patting you in the middle of the night?"

He sighed. "It would be strange and not nice. Can I watch him from here?"

"Sure." Rhiannon turned at Angela's light touch on her arm.

"This is beautiful. The grass is like a green, rolling carpet of hills." She pointed to her right. "Is that Kangaroo Valley over there?"

"Yes. It's about a twenty-minute drive from here," Rhiannon replied. She was extremely proud Angela liked the property. She could easily envisage the three of them spending weekends down here, out of the hustle and bustle of the city.

"Arcadia, utopia—it sums it up incredibly well." She walked with Rhiannon to the back of the SUV and Rhiannon pressed the liftgate release. "If I lived here, I'd never leave. What do you think Lachie?"

"It's great." He retrieved his soccer ball from the trunk and bounced it on the driveway. "I could kick my ball and never worry about it going into Mr. Robotham's yard."

Rhiannon pulled one of the bags out of the back of the vehicle. "I didn't want to leave either, when my parents died." She handed a small bag to Lachie and a larger one to Angela. "But given I was so young, I couldn't have stayed here by myself, which was something I didn't quite understand at the time."

Taking the bag, Angela looked over Rhiannon's shoulder and motioned with her head. "Who's that?"

Rhiannon turned. Walking around the pathway located on one side of the house and talking into her mobile was a grey-haired woman in faded jeans and orange shirt. A broad brimmed hat covered her head, shielding her face from the afternoon sun. "It's Barb. Remember, the women I told you about on the way here? Georgia must be still down at their house."

"Did they know you were bringing someone down today?" Angela asked.

"I only told them I was bringing someone special and her son. They didn't ask anything else, but I didn't expect they would."

Barb finished the call and put the phone in her back pocket. "Hello stranger. It's been a while since I saw you." She pulled Rhiannon into a hug. "We were sorry we missed you when you were down last weekend."

Rhiannon returned the hug and pecked Barb's cheek. "So was I. Was that Georgia you were speaking with?"

"It was Joey. I happened to mention you were here, and she said she might head over. It was nice of you to agree to allow her cattle to graze on the property." She cast her arm around the surrounding landscape. "Despite how green it looks, there hasn't been a lot of feed for the stock here this season." Barb turned and smiled at Angela. "Hello."

"Oh, where are my manners? This is my partner, Angela Drayton."

Barb took Angela's hands in both of hers. "It's a pleasure to meet you Angela. Georgia and I have some of your recordings. But we've never had the opportunity to actually see you live." She chuckled. "You wait till I tell Georgia who's staying with us." Her eyes sparkled. "She's gonna pee her pants." Barb looked down at Lachie. "And what's your name young man?"

Lachie put his ball and bag down, stepped forward and offered his hand to Barb, his face a study of seriousness. "I'm Lachlan Maxwell Drayton but you can call me Lachie."

Barb returned the shake. "It's a pleasure to meet you Lachie."

Lachie released his grip, picked up his soccer ball and began tossing it from one hand to the other. "It's nice to meet you, too. We're down here for a sleepover, like Rhiannon had at my place."

Barb spared a glance at Rhiannon and Angela, a slight grin on her features. "Is that so? I hope you enjoy it."

Lachie nodded eagerly. "I will. I love slumber parties. I have them all the time at home." He tossed the ball up in the air and caught it. "It's what we had last Sunday, Rhiannon, Mum and me. But I always get into trouble when me and my friends make so much noise at our slumber parties, like Mum and Rhiannon did."

Dumbstruck, Rhiannon blushed furiously. If only the ground would open up and swallow her right where she stood. She glimpsed between Angela and Barb, the same cheeky grin on both their faces.

Rhiannon cleared her throat, attempting to compose herself. "Do you and Georgia want to come up later for drinks?"

Barb patted Rhiannon's arm. "That would be lovely. I better be on my way though. I've got a cake in the oven and I don't want it to burn. I'll see you later." She gazed at Angela and Lachie. "It was nice to meet you both."

Angela moved to Rhiannon's side while Lachie, oblivious to his earlier comment, now dribbled the ball between his feet. "You should see the look on your face," she uttered. "It's priceless."

The tooting of a horn halted Rhiannon's reply, and she watched a truck head down the driveway. "It's Joey."

Angela frowned. "Who's Joey?"

"She's my next-door neighbour. We met last Friday when I was here. I suppose she's coming to say thanks about my agreement with her to agist her cattle on Arcadia." Rhiannon clasped Angela's hand and they walked to where Joey's truck had come to a halt.

Joey's face slightly altered when she took in Rhiannon and Angela's hands. She quickly regathered her composure and strode their way.

Joey took off her hat and smoothed her hair. "Thanks very much for letting me agist my cattle. It's a great relief to know I'm not relying on hay, especially when there are so many other properties around here who need it as much as I do."

Rhiannon acknowledged her thanks. Despite being out of Australia for so long, she was painfully aware the greater majority of New South Wales was in drought, with even Sydney, for the first time in eleven years, also the subject of water restrictions.

"What's agist mean?" Lachie asked.

Angela placed her hand on Lachie's shoulder and shook it gently. "Where are your manners? Don't you think you should introduce yourself?"

"Sorry Mum." He held out his hand and repeated the introduction he'd given to Barb only moments ago.

"Nice to meet you Lachie. Agist is when someone, in this case Rhiannon, allows someone else," she pointed to her chest, "in this instance me, to graze their cattle on their property for an agreed price." She looked at Rhiannon, her brow raised in question. "A price which you seemed to have waived." Joey dipped her head respectfully. "That was very generous of you."

"Not a problem. Besides, you were the one who had to put in a gate down in the lower paddock, between our properties. And I'm sure that wasn't cheap." Rhiannon placed her hand in the small of Angela's back and motioned her forward. "You've met Lachie. This is my partner Angela—"

Joey quickly wiped her hand on her trousers and held it out. "Drayton." She carefully took Angela's hand. "I love your music. I saw you when you last played at the Opera House in Sydney."

Angela returned the shake, her eyes slightly narrowed in reminiscence. "That was a while ago."

"A few years now. But you were fantastic. And the way they broadcast you playing onto the big screen. What a stroke of genius. Seeing your fingers dance across the keys, I was getting cramps just watching you." She held up her hands and wiggled her short fingers, three of which were slightly bent. "They're nothing like my farmer's hands. I bet you take good care of yours."

"I do, but I still manage to injure them every once in a while, working in the garden or cutting up vegetables. I am careful though." Angela studied her fingers. "They are my livelihood. I'd be lost without them."

Rhiannon moved closer to Angela's side, as Lachie tapped

Joey's trouser leg, attempting to get her attention. "So would I," Rhiannon whispered softy.

Angela whipped her head around to Rhiannon's face.

"Priceless," Rhiannon mouthed at Angela's astonished, red face.

Angela smothered a smile. "Behave," she mouthed in return.

Rhiannon caught the grin on Joey's face when she knelt down to face Lachie. It was clear her comment to Angela hadn't been said softly enough to not be picked up by Joey.

"Yes, mate," Joey said.

"What sort of cows do you have?"

"They're called Belted Galloways. They're a breed which originated years ago in Scotland." Joey eased herself off her knee and stood. "And it's a good thing they're used to the cold, because it can get mighty cold here."

Lachie's eyes scanned his surroundings, expecting one to materialise for his viewing. "What colour are they?"

"They can be black, red, or a greyish brown. What makes them special..." Joey grabbed Lachie's waist and gave it a shake.

Lachie giggled and pulled himself out of Joey's grasp.

"Is they all have a white belt which runs around their middle. I'm about to bring them down into Rhiannon's lower paddock."

"Can I see?" Lachie turned to Angela. "Can I, Mum? I promise I'll behave."

Angela looked at Joey. "Is it okay with you? I wouldn't want him getting in the way of your work."

Joey shook her head. "It isn't any trouble at all, so long as you don't mind him being gone for an hour or so. I've got to do one final check of the surrounding fence, to make sure there haven't been any new breaks caused by burrowing wombats since I checked earlier in the week. Once I've done that, I'll move them in and get them settled."

Angela rubbed Lachie's back. "You can go. But listen to everything Joey says. And don't bother the cattle or get too close to them."

Rhiannon put her arm around Angela's waist. "Don't worry, the cattle won't let him anywhere near them. If you're not doing anything this evening Barb and Georgia are joining us for drinks. Do you want to come over?"

"That would be great. When were you looking at?"

Rhiannon checked her watch to gauge the current time. "Probably about seven, if it suits."

"That's fine. It'll give me time to finish up my chores and

have a shower. Besides, the last thing you want is someone in close quarters, smelling like they've spent the day mucking it with cattle." Joey motioned to Lachie. "Come on buster. We better be moving some cows."

The truck pulled away and Angela lightly punched Rhiannon's arm. "I can't believe you said what you did."

"What," Rhiannon said innocently. She dodged another blow from Angela. "You mean about your fingers?"

Angela pursed her lips, hands on hips, eyes demanding. Despite her best efforts to look affronted, laughter filtered from her lips and she dropped her arms. "Of course."

Rhiannon shrugged. "Well I *would* be lost without them, on so many levels. To start with, have you any idea how hard it was to watch you play when I visited that first night?"

She lifted one of Angela's hands and toyed with her fingers. "Your strength and your passion. It was all I could do to stop myself from not ravishing you on the spot."

Angela quirked her brow. "It would have made for an interesting evening."

Rhiannon kissed Angela's fingers. "I'm sure it would have." She walked to the back of the SUV and picked up Lachie's bag and her own. She carefully kicked Lachie's now-discarded soccer ball to a shaded spot near the front door.

Angela picked up the other bag. "Was what Joey said about wombats true?"

Rhiannon swiped the motion sensor which closed the SUV's liftgate. "It is. It's an occupational hazard around here. They tend to burrow where they want to, with little regard for fences. I mean they obviously don't mean to. They were here a long time before we were. But they can make a mess out of even the hardiest of fences."

Rhiannon paused at her front door, unlocked it, and ushered Angela through. "If you go down the hall and through the door on your left, it leads to our room."

She followed Angela into a space with windows dominating two of the four walls. Rhiannon placed her overnight bag on the bed and pressed a button on the bedside table. The curtains directly opposite the bed parted, affording an uninterrupted view of the lush valley beyond.

"Oh, Rhiannon." Angela walked to the window. "Why would you ever want to get out of bed?"

Pleased, she halted behind Angela and encircled her waist with her arms. "You wouldn't." She kissed the top of Angela's head. "And I've got even *less* incentive to do so now. Speaking of which, if you grab Lachie's bag and follow me, I'll show you where he'll be sleeping. Given his earlier comment, his accommodations are thankfully at the other end of the house."

Angela followed Rhiannon through a living room simply decorated with clean lines. Throw rugs were tastefully scattered around, with leather furniture which looked sufficiently comfortable to swallow its occupants. A large fireplace dominated one wall, its fire already ablaze.

Rhiannon opened another door. "I think I'll put Lachie in here. It'll give him the best opportunity to see the kangaroos grazing of a morning." Rhiannon opened the curtain and pointed to a copse over a fence and to her left. "On most mornings and afternoon, they feed there and then head off to other parts of the property."

Angela put the bag down. "He's going to love this."

Rhiannon walked out the door and toward the kitchen. "Do you want a coffee?"

"Thanks, but I think a cold drink will suffice." She gazed at the picture window over the sink. "God, even the washing up woman has a view."

Rhiannon chuckled. "That they do." She pulled a glass from a cupboard and opened the fridge. "There's not a lot in here. Will water be okay for the moment? We'll do a quick trip into town later, to pick up supplies for this evening."

Angela nodded, still somewhat preoccupied with the view at the kitchen window. "Your old girlfriends must have loved visiting here."

Rhiannon filled the glass and offered it to Angela. "Setting Elly's visit aside, and not that there have been too many, I've never bought a partner or a potential partner out here, or anyone else for that matter. This," she cast her hand around the space, "is my sanctuary. It's very, very dear to me. And a long time ago I decided I wanted to wait until I could share it with someone who meant just as much to me."

Angela moved into Rhiannon's arms and rested her head against her chest. "Oh honey. How is it you can make me feel so special with merely words?"

Rhiannon returned the hug. "It's easy when I feel about you the way I do." There were words, right on the tip of her tongue that she was longing to say to Angela. But was it the right time? Not yet, she thought. "Barb and Joey seemed to know who you were."

"They seem like nice people." Angela moved out of their embrace and took a sip of water.

"Were you okay that they knew you?" Rhiannon studied the bench and returned her face to Angela's. "I mean, you weren't too comfortable with..." she tilted her head, "you know."

"I'm fine. I only hope all of my friends are as accepting of our relationship as yours clearly are."

A kernel of worry began to form in Rhiannon's stomach. "Are you concerned they mightn't be?"

Angela placed the glass on the bench and took Rhiannon's hand in her own. "Maybe last week but certainly not now." She rubbed her thumb across Rhiannon's hand. "This is part of who I am and it's something I'm now very comfortable with. If they can't accept that, they can either remain silent on the topic or go and find another friend. Speaking of friends, Joey seemed quite interested in you," Angela said, a cheeky grin on her face.

Rhiannon threw her head back and snorted. "Elly said much the same thing when we were down last Friday." She pulled Angela into her arms and kissed her soundly. Slightly breaking their embrace, she tenderly stroked Angela's face. "But it doesn't matter. My heart's already taken."

"So is mine. But, for a long time I think it's really only ever belonged to one person." Angela's palm came to rest on Rhiannon's chest. "And that's you."

A sense of wonder and absolute completeness filled Rhiannon and she could not hold her feelings in any longer. "I love you," she whispered as she searched Angela's face. "I was hoping to make the setting more romantic than the kitchen, but I couldn't wait."

Angela's fingers touched Rhiannon's lips, her eyes shimmering. "Oh baby, I love you too. And I couldn't care less where you told me. I'm just glad you did." She reached up and lightly kissed Rhiannon's lips. "And I look forward to telling you that for a long time to come, in any location we find ourselves in."

Rhiannon enveloped Angela in her arms, content to stand and just listen to the world around them. The last two weeks had certainly been a rollercoaster of emotional highs and lows. And yet in her wildest dreams she couldn't have imagined they'd at last arrive at where they both were now.

She released Angela and took her hand. "I've got one final room to show you."

"What's through there?" Angela asked as they passed a glass hallway.

"It's the indoor pool and it's fully heated."

"Now I understand why you told Lachie to pack his swimmers."

"Yep, and it's a good depth. He should be okay to play in the shallow end so long as we're with him." Rhiannon opened another door and pulled Angela through it.

The large room was sparsely furnished. To the right of the entrance was a sound system which while old, would clearly have been state of the art in its day. Almost centrally positioned was a carved, light wood sheet music stand, bereft of any music. Near the stand and against the wall was a desk, its left top corner filled with a pile of musical scores. The only other furniture filling the space was a contemporary leather chaise lounge, its modern curves affording its occupant a comfortable respite from everyday living.

Rhiannon pulled back a solitary curtain, revealing a small bubbling stream running outside the window. "This picture window is the only triple glazed one in the house." She turned to Angela. "It helped to maintain an integrity of sound for my mother, when she rehearsed in here."

Angela trailed her fingers along the chaise lounge as she took in her surrounds. "It's beautiful. I can only imagine the inspiration she must have gotten, creating in a place as lovely and peaceful as this."

"She'd spend hours in here. But for all the time she would spend in here, she was always so refreshed when she finally came out. It was as if it exhausted and recharged her in equal measure." Rhiannon ran her fingers through her hair, forcing her thoughts to the present. "But I believe it's about time this space was used for its primary purpose again. Just let me know what piano would suit you. I'll happily purchase it for you and then have it delivered and tuned. The space won't be as soundproof as your place in Sydney. But we can always have it adapted to suit your needs. That way, when we visit, you'll always have somewhere to rehearse."

Angela walked to where Rhiannon stood. "Why?"

Rhiannon frowned. She was sure Angela liked Arcadia. In which case, what exactly was she saying? "I don't understand. Don't you want to rehearse when we visit?"

"Yes, I do, but visiting implies a lack of permanency and that wasn't what I had in mind." She paused and scanned her surroundings. "Living here was."

Rhiannon's brows hiked up almost to her hairline. "I'd love

for you, me and Lachie to live here. But what about his school-ing?"

"During our journey down here today, you mentioned the school you went to when you lived here and how much you loved it. Is its educational standing still highly regarded?"

"Yes, given the most recently published school rankings I received because I'm a Reibey alumni. But won't Lachie be sad to leave his friends?"

"Why don't we ask him? I suspect the decision to live here is as much his as it is ours. If he wants to stay in Sydney, then of course we will." She hooked Rhiannon's arm in her own. "But he's always been good at making friends, either at school or on the sports field. Besides, there's nothing stopping him from going to Sydney for the weekend either."

"Or inviting his friends down here," Rhiannon added. "There's certainly plenty of space." She turned and faced Angela. "But what about your profession?"

Angela shrugged. "In this day and age, I'm only a call or email away from anyone who might need to contact me. And Syd-ney is less than two hours away if I need to go up there for any-thing." Angela closed her eyes, a pained expression on her face. She looked at Rhiannon. "I'm sorry. I didn't think of your work. Do you need to be in Sydney?"

"I don't. In fact, I've decided to write full time. I might even put some effort into writing my first novel." Rhiannon shook her head. "I sincerely doubt I'll be working a nine to five job ever again. But enough about me. What about your friends in Sydney? Aren't you going to miss them? And what about when you start touring again? Lachie mentioned to me over breakfast you'd received an offer from an orchestra. How are we going to man-age?"

Angela gazed at Rhiannon, love and a hint of mischief reflected in her eyes. "You know, a very smart woman once told me difficulties can sometimes seem as insurmountable as eating an elephant." Angela's hands skimmed lazily across Rhiannon's body, coming to rest on her breasts.

Her breathing hitched as Angela's thumbs grazed her nipples through her shirt. "She had a solution which, until now, I didn't fully comprehend or appreciate."

She leant forward and nipped Rhiannon's neck. "Take just one bite at a time." She flicked her tongue across Rhiannon's ear-lobe. "One little bite at a time."

Epilogue

Five years later

Rhiannon walked onto the back terrace of Arcadia and placed two cups of coffee on the outdoor table where Angela sat waiting for her. She pulled a newspaper from under her tucked arm and sat down, placing the paper on the table between them.

"Is Lachie up?" Angela tasted her coffee and pulled the sugar to her. "I didn't see him this morning for breakfast."

Rhiannon pulled apart a croissant and reached for the raspberry jam. "He was up early this morning and having breakfast when I went out to the kitchen to get a glass of water. Apparently, he got a call from Joey, letting him know one of the Belted Galloways was due to give birth in the lower paddock." She scooped a dob of jam from the jar and placed it on her plate. "He said he was heading out as soon as he finished eating."

Angela measured a half teaspoon of sugar and placed it in her mug. "I wonder if your father would be proud."

Rhiannon popped the jam laden piece of croissant in her mouth and looked at Angela, her eyes questioning.

"After all, he was a vet. It sounds like Lachie also aspires to possibly follow in his footsteps."

Rhiannon swallowed and grinned crookedly. "Let's wait and see how he reacts to a cow giving birth. It isn't the fastest, nor is it the most glamourous of things."

Angela stirred her cup and placed the spoon on the side of her plate. "At least if he does choose that path, Reibey has an established and very well regarded extra-curricular animal husbandry program."

Rhiannon wiped her jam-stained hands on her serviette. "I've got to admit, even now I'm still surprised how effortlessly he initially adapted to his new school. I thought he'd miss his friends a lot more than he did."

"How could he?" Angela scoffed. "They're down here just about every other weekend."

"I suppose they are." Rhiannon reached over and picked up the newspaper. "There's an article in here about your performance last Friday."

Angela scowled. "You know I still don't care for those stories."

"Too bad." Rhiannon made a grand pretence of shaking out the paper. "I'm going to read it to you anyway. Or at least the good bits." She picked up her reading glasses and put them on.

"On Saturday, a large group of fortunate Sydneysiders were privy to a command performance by some of Australia's most noted classical artists. The concert, titled Classically Proud, was a cornerstone event for the Sydney Gay and Lesbian Mardi Gras festival. Held at the Sydney Opera House, the concert featured a number of Australia's accomplished performers. By far the evening's crowning glory was the recital by world-renowned concert pianist Angela Drayton-Sharp." Rhiannon peeked over the edge of the paper at Angela and waggled her eyebrows. "Recently returned from her second season as classical soloist with the Armitage Orchestra, Ms. Drayton-Sharp was accompanied by her wife, author Rhiannon Drayton-Sharp and their son. Her recital covered a selection of music from the great classical composers, finishing with a work titled 'Just for Her,' written by Angela for her wife, with all three movements played for the first time to a live audience."

"Well they wouldn't be a *dead* audience, would they?" Angela reached across and snagged the newspaper from Rhiannon's hands. "I think that's enough," she said, laughter filling her voice.

"I'd just about finished anyway. It was a great evening though. I think Joey, Elly, Jen, Barb and Georgia really enjoyed themselves." Rhiannon grasped Angela's hand. "And thank you for getting Barb and Georgia backstage. I don't think it's something they'll soon forget."

Still hanging onto her hand, Rhiannon rose and moved to where Angela sat. She took the cup from her hand, placed it on the table and pulled Angela into her arms. "God, I love you."

"I love you too, if possible, a little bit more every day." Angela's lips met her own, her tongue lightly brushing Rhiannon's, seeking entrance. As their kissed deepened, the loud bellowing of a cow shattered the intimate moment.

Angela chuckled and she rested her forehead against Rhiannon's. "How long did you say the birth might be?"

Rhiannon took Angela's hand and pulled her toward the door of their home. "Long enough love," she said, her eyes twinkling, her brow arched invitingly. "Long enough."

About the Author

Born and living in Australia, Helen resides in one of the lovely leafy suburbs of Canberra. After over 33 years in the Australian Regular Army, she is now retired, and happily spends her days as house spouse to her wife, Kate and their two kittens. When she isn't engaged in her favourite hobby of cooking (and the eating which necessarily follows), she spends her time travelling, reading, writing, and finally paying sufficient focus on completing her family history. Helen has always had a love of writing and poetry, completing her first body of work—a piece of poetry, at 15. Once an active sportswoman, she is now an avid spectator rather than participant. For any questions or comments, Helen can be reached at hmac65@hotmail.com .

MORE REGAL CREST PUBLICATIONS

Brenda Adcock	Soiled Dove	978-1-935053-35-4
Brenda Adcock	The Sea Hawk	978-1-935053-10-1
Brenda Adcock	The Other Mrs. Champion	978-1-935053-46-0
Brenda Adcock	Picking Up the Pieces	978-1-61929-120-1
Brenda Adcock	The Game of Denial	978-1-61929-130-0
Brenda Adcock	In the Midnight Hour	978-1-61929-188-1
Brenda Adcock	Untouchable	978-1-61929-210-9
Brenda Adcock	The Heart of the Mountain	978-1-61929-330-4
Brenda Adcock	Gift of the Redeemer	978-1-61929-360-1
Brenda Adcock	Unresolved Conflicts	978-1-61929-374-8
Brenda Adcock	One Step At A Time	978-1-61929-408-0
K. Aten	The Fletcher	978-1-61929-356-4
K. Aten	Rules of the Road	978-1-61919-366-3
K. Aten	The Archer	978-1-61929-370-0
K. Aten	Waking the Dreamer	978-1-61929-382-3
K. Aten	The Sagittarius	978-1-61929-386-1
K. Aten	Running From Forever: Book One in the Blood Resonance Series	978-1-61929-398-4
K. Aten	The Sovereign of Psiere: Book One In the Mystery of the Makers series	978-1-61929-412-7
K. Aten	Burn It Down	978-1-61929-418-9
K. Aten	Embracing Forever: Book Two in the Blood Resonance Series	978-1-61929-424-0
K Aten	Children of the Stars	978-1-61929-432-5
Georgia Beers	Thy Neighbor's Wife	1-932300-15-5
Georgia Beers	Turning the Page	978-1-932300-71-0
Lynnette Beers	Just Beyond the Shining River	978-1-61929-352-6
Lynnette Beers	Saving Sam	978-1-61929-410-3
Tonie Chacon	Struck! A Titanic Love Story	978-1-61929-226-0
Sky Croft	Amazonia	978-1-61929-067-9
Sky Croft	Amazonia: An Impossible Choice	978-1-61929-179-9
Sky Croft	Mountain Rescue: The Ascent	978-1-61929-099-0
Sky Croft	Mountain Rescue: On the Edge	978-1-61929-205-5
Mildred Gail Digby	Phoenix	978-1-61929-394-6
Mildred Gail Digby	Perfect Match: Book One	978-1-61929-414-4
Mildred Gail Digby	Perfect Match: Book Two	978-1-61929-416-5
Mildred Gail Digby	Stay	978-1-61929-422-6
Mildred Gail Digby	Uncovered	978-1-61929-430-1
Cronin and Foster	Blue Collar Lesbian Erotica	978-1-935053-01-9
Cronin and Foster	Women in Uniform	978-1-935053-31-6
Cronin and Foster	Women in Sports	978-1-61929-278-9
Emily L Quint Freeman	Failure To Appear: Resistance, Identity and Loss	978-1-61929-426-4
Melissa Good	Eye of the Storm	1-932300-13-9
Melissa Good	Hurricane Watch	978-1-935053-00-2
Melissa Good	Moving Target	978-1-61929-150-8

Melissa Good	Red Sky At Morning	978-1-932300-80-2
Melissa Good	Storm Surge: Book One	978-1-935053-28-6
Melissa Good	Storm Surge: Book Two	978-1-935053-39-2
Melissa Good	Stormy Waters	978-1-61929-082-2
Melissa Good	Thicker Than Water	1-932300-24-4
Melissa Good	Terrors of the High Seas	1-932300-45-7
Melissa Good	Tropical Storm	978-1-932300-60-4
Melissa Good	Tropical Convergence	978-1-935053-18-7
Melissa Good	Winds of Change Book One	978-1-61929-194-2
Melissa Good	Winds of Change Book Two	978-1-61929-232-1
Melissa Good	Southern Stars	978-1-61929-348-9
Danielle Grainger	Wrecking Bernadette: Book One in the Bernadette Series	978-1-61929-428-8
K. E. Lane	And, Playing the Role of Herself	978-1-932300-72-7
Kate McLachlan	Christmas Crush	978-1-61929-195-9
Kate McLachlan	Hearts, Dead and Alive	978-1-61929-017-4
Kate McLachlan	Murder and the Hurdy Gurdy Girl	978-1-61929-125-6
Kate McLachlan	Rescue At Inspiration Point	978-1-61929-005-1
Kate McLachlan	Return Of An Impetuous Pilot	978-1-61929-152-2
Kate McLachlan	Rip Van Dyke	978-1-935053-29-3
Kate McLachlan	Ten Little Lesbians	978-1-61929-236-9
Kate McLachlan	Alias Mrs. Jones	978-1-61929-282-6
Hope Milam	Welcome Home, Bailey	978-1-61929-438-7
Lynne Norris	One Promise	978-1-932300-92-5
Lynne Norris	Sanctuary	978-1-61929-248-2
Lynne Norris	The Light of Day	978-1-61929-338-0
Schramm and Dunne	Love Is In the Air	978-1-61929-362-8
Rae Theodore	Leaving Normal: Adventures in Gender	978-1-61929-320-5
Rae Theodore	My Mother Says Drums Are for Boys: True Stories for Gender Rebels	978-1-61929-378-6
Barbara Valletto	Pulse Points	978-1-61929-254-3
Barbara Valletto	Everlong	978-1-61929-266-6
Barbara Valletto	Limbo	978-1-61929-358-8
Barbara Valletto	Diver Blues	978-1-61929-384-7
Lisa Young	Out and Proud	978-1-61929-392-2

Be sure to check out our other imprints,
Blue Beacon Books, Mystic Books, Quest Books,
Silver Dragon Books, Troubadour Books,
and Young Adult Books.

VISIT US ONLINE AT
www.regalcrest.biz

At the Regal Crest Website You'll Find

~   The latest news about forthcoming titles and
    new releases

~   Our complete backlist of titles

~   Information about your favorite authors

Regal Crest print titles are available from all
progressive booksellers including numerous sources
online. Our distributors are Bella Distribution and
Ingram.

www.ingramcontent.com/pod-product-compliance
Lightning Source LLC
Chambersburg PA
CBHW070452030726
47503CB00004B/1012